RexNā Loid DeAqua

RaeNegria Hylrix-El-Moa

Rägę El BriNa-Ragnoa El Vroan

Sol Lrign dWari - Commander

MelEid - The Mage

The Chief Seer -Eid 'dVra, Twin of MelEid The Mage

Bitari-Furtim-Karda

Bitari-Furtim-Karda - Lyran Battleship with Strike Darts

Bitari-Furtim-Ordios

The Docking

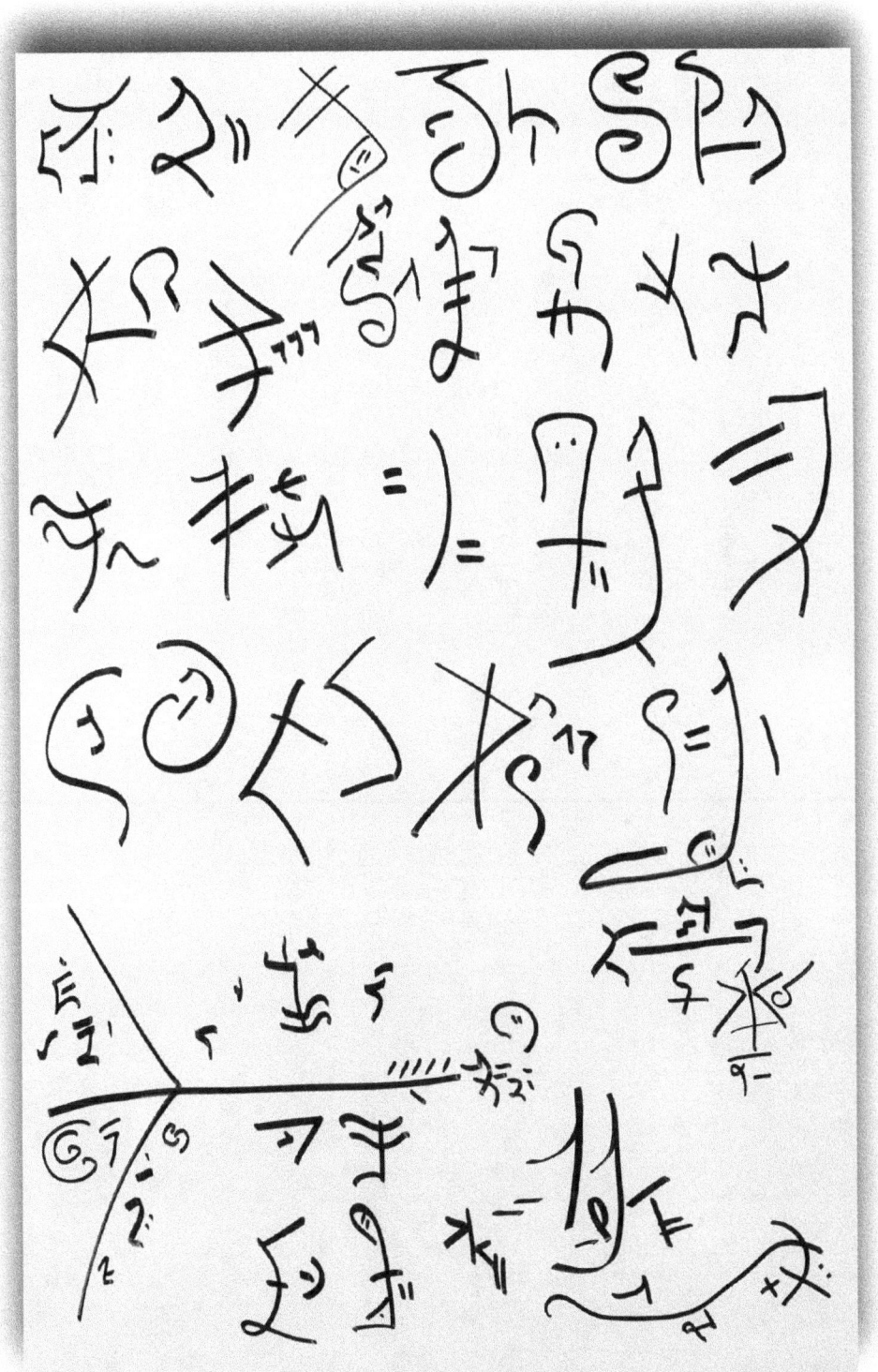

RaeNegria's Glyphs

THE LYRAN DISCLOSURE

The Terran Uprising

Volume 3

Louise Reiss-James
© 2021

Disclaimer

Other Works

Books authored by Louise Reiss-James.

The Lyran Disclosure
The Agenda Vol 1
The Anunnaki Influence Vol 2
The Terran Uprising

The 5th Dimensional Series
(PDF download via website)
Knowing Ascension
5th Dimensional Healing

Teaching of Tobias
Healing of the 7 Vortices

Self Mastery and Abundance
(PDF download via website)

Workshop Manuals
Manifest Now
Self Mastery

Forward

By Louise Reiss-James

I wrote the first book of the Lyran Disclosure Series, 'The Agenda, ' back in the last few months of 2018 leading into 2019.

I struggled to write the story, as I felt no one in the 'spiritual, awakened world' would wish to read an alternative reflection of the Lyran story.

My reservation was that the channelled information, which I was bringing through, went against most of the already well-adapted, accepted theory that Lyrans were 'feline' type creatures. The Lyrans had blown their planet up due to internal wars, and there were only two royal families, and the Lyrans constantly longed for 'home'.

What I was given to write, whilst it did confirm some of what was already known, also revealed a whole new insight into whom the Lyrans are and introduced us to the forgotten third royal family!

In the first book, The Lyran Disclosure - The Agenda, 'The Lyran Narrators of Time' began to reveal the agenda of the Formless Ones, and the potential of what was planned for our planet was eventful.

What this did, was once again create within me, Louise, the realisation that I had to **trust** what was given to me and not allow myself to second guess or doubt, no matter what others said or thought of the information.

It also laid the foundation for the next in the series, The Anunnaki Influence and now this one in your hands, The Capitulation of Humanity.

Just as the second book took us further into the Lyran story, what they are searching for, it also hopefully had us, as living beings, look at our own lives, to observe our behaviours, our disempowerment and how we repetitively give our authority away by handing over our integral right of self-rule.

As you read this story, written as it was given to me, sharing in the continued journey of RexNā Liod DeAqua and her fellow Lyrans, you can see how we, as mankind, can succeed in our journey.

How we can, as long as we recognise our right to Sovereign, Divine Law, which allows us the fundamental rights of life, to overcome the suggestive and manipulative energy that is flying over our world today.

This book has opened my eyes to many things, as did the first & second books, exposing concepts currently being unwrapped around us.

Again, how is it that the information I am given so neatly knits into the narrative of our current time of 2021/2022.

Especially as the draft was given to me in 2017? There are things within the pages of this book that I am not 100% sure of, but trust the intent of the Lyrans , who wish to assist mankind to rise into Ascension and beyond.

The Lyrans, in their deep love for our world, our T'Gaina, are doing what they can to open our eyes to the manipulations and fear tactics of the common enemy.

Could it be that having won their battle and war against the Formless energy beings that attacked their world and people, they are looking to give us some insight and assistance?

It looks that way to me.

I hope you enjoy this book.
Louise.

Acknowledgements and Thanks

So this is volume three of the Disclosure Series!

If you have a love relationship with your partner/husband/wife/ significant other and work with that same person, thus putting you in each others 'way' 24/7/365, you'll have some idea of the depth of my gratitude towards Heather, my wife.

Once again, Heather has pulled up her editing skills, placed her hard hat on her head and shield around her heart... yes, folks. She has dressed for battle.

Now, this is not because editing is hard work, nope!

It's because she loves me, and I am a prickly bear or porcupine when it comes to being 'questioned' about the work I have just spent days, weeks, and, yes, months nurturing.

I behave like a panicking parent...

Determined to navigate the minefield of emotion and the constant 'don't change that' being uttered from me, my beautiful wife unwraps her Wordsmith Toolkit and squares her shoulders.

Clicking open the files, she begins to apply the necessary grammar and spell checks. Imagine, then, my horror as she begins to craft a new way of writing a sentence, let alone a paragraph that gives the reader a more precise and more rounded picture....

Boom, go my emotions.... "YOU CAN'T CHANGE THAT!" falls from my throat.

Quietly, in a voice like steel, she looks at me and asks, "Sweet-heart do you want me to edit this or not…".

Of course, I nod my head, and eventually, night after day, we come to the end of the first draft. I take the file back and gayly say, 'Ok, I'll check it and see if anything else needs to be added or has been missed… Heather's face says it all…

Heather, you are my friend, wife, lover and most beautiful companion.

This book (nor the other two), and perhaps the other books swimming around my heart, would not be in print if not for your gentle and not-so-sweet-tempered editing skills.

Thank you from the bottom of my heart.

Thank you for crossing the i's and dotting the t's. Get it?😌

You are my fun, my laughter and my rock.

Louise

Introduction

If you have read the last books that we, The Lyran Narrators of Time, shared with you, you will no doubt have a comprehension of who the Lyrans are.

In this book, though, it may take a moment or two of your years to bring it to the fore. The information within is insightful and necessary for your time of absorbing the narration of this chronicle. Hidden inside the chapters and words are clues, hints and direct outlines on how to interact with your enemy, the Formless Ones. Note that here on this planet, they may have form and substance due to the elite of your world allowing them to utilise and clone their bodies. However, as is the situation in cloning or copying an original form, there are always going to be discrepancies. We invite you to look for these anomalies within those that govern you, counsel you or hold any form of leadership over you. This includes, most importantly, the so-called religious leaders, gurus and 'light worker' leaders. The one powerful weapon we can give you is the art of question and debate. Truth in any debate, where there are questions and answers, will always surface. No matter how hard the opposing side attempts to squash it into oblivion.

A warning, though, do not attempt to use the truth card too forcefully, for this may return awkwardly to you. Yes, know your truth, allow that to grow within your essence and hold fast to your dignity. We would ask you to observe how you present the truth to those who are resistant.
Use it not as a sledgehammer, nor as any weapon, but rather as a gentle, soothing rhythm and rhyme.
Allow your truth to be as the breath that enters and exits your chest.

As the waves that gently lap in the ebb and flow of the ocean, for it is in this manner that you will win the minds, then the hearts of those who are resisting out of fear or ignorance.

These will eventually become the tipping point.

Go firmly but gently into the world that is unfolding around you.

Read this new chronicle and note what we are saying.

The visions are not fixed. They are potentials.

There is yet, still time to evolve and ascend to a world that is of service to all.

Definitions

Definitions used or referenced throughout these books of the Lyrans

Capitulation:

1. The act of surrendering or giving in
2. Int'l Law. An agreement to surrender a fortified place or a military or naval force.

Uprising:

1. An insurrection or revolt
2. An act of rising up
3. An ascent or acclivity

Human: [1]homo (hoh-moh), n. [Latin] Hist.

1. A male human.
2. A member of humankind; a human being of either sex.
3. A slave.
4. A vassal; a feudal tenant.
5. A retainer, dependent, or servant.
6. Pl. homines. See HOMINES.

Lawful Man (Legalis Homo)

Man:

1. An adult male.
2. Humankind. - Also termed mankind.
3. A human being.
4. Hist. A vassal; a feudal tenant.

---

[1] Black's Law Dictionary 6th Edition.

homo liber (II-ber).

1. A free man.
2. A freeman lawfully competent to be a juror.
3. An allodial proprietor, as distinguished from a feudal tenant.
4. See ALLODIAL.

Freedom:

1. The state of being free or liberated.
2. A political right.

Feme (fem). [Law French] Archaic.

1. A woman.
2. A wife. - Also spelled femme.

Except for the '[2]Uprising', these definitions come from Black's Law Dictionary 7th Edition.

They do not have a definition for Uprising. However, they use this word in the definition of Right of Revolution.

> The inherent right of a people to cast out their rulers, change their polity, or effect radical reforms in their system of government or institutions, by force or general uprising, when the legal and constitutional methods of making such changes have proved inadequate or are so obstructed as to be unavailable.

In the Blacks Law Dictionary, the only time I saw that the word 'uprising' was used was to describe the 'unlawful' or gathering to riot by the masses... speaks volumes, in my opinion. When we, the Terrans, wish to rise and retake our birth rights of being a living soul, as created by the Creator, the puppet masters and their

---

[2] Other definitions found at www.thefreedictionary.com

minions seem to find a way to try and negate that... let's not let them win...

I was asked to add these definitions, by the Lyran Narrators, for the ongoing story of the Lyrans and our Terran race. I believe the Lyrans wish to show us how the controllers are attempting to use the words in the legal system created to control us and that the words 'man' and 'human' are very different.

In looking at the various definitions, I have concluded that unless you are Legalis Homo in the eyes of 'the law', you are simply human or homo, a slave, a vassal, dependent or servant of the state. I am increasingly moving to the knowledge and comprehension that the Lyrans are showing us things that are in plain sight but hidden and giving us keys to unlock our prisons of the mind and being in our journey towards becoming FreeMan/ FreeWoman or Living Souls of this realm. Perhaps they are revealing that the commonality and family of mankind are more valuable than just being a 'human being.'

Enjoy the continuation of their chronicles.
Louise

Preface

Welcome, Dear Reader, welcome back into the journey that is the disclosing of the Lyran's journey of discovery and your realisation of who you are.

In the following chapters, we will delve more into the journey of our three Princes and perhaps a snapshot of your earth...or perhaps we will expose more of the Formless Ones Agenda in ripping from you, your human soul and creating another slave race.

A race created by your own acquiescence and foolish non-action.

A species born in fear and bound in the dogma of 'it couldn't be true.'

This race of slaves is made of flesh, blood, and nanotechnology, a blend where the nanites gain entry into your system through 'protective measures' and enforced minimal contact with the herd of humanity. They then penetrate the brain and rebuild the areas of self-will, consciousness and awareness. The parts that make you human. This cannot be undone!

This time, Dear Reader, your lobotomy will be one of self-infliction, and wilful disregard for the truth, for the facts presented were too powerful to be accepted. It was easier to comply and be done with it rather than stand in your Divine Human Truth of Being. Many doomed themselves and the generations to follow if allowed to copulate, to a life of compliance and slavery.

Though all is not lost, there are subcultures that grew and formed great colonies of Terran Ways. Where all were welcome, but there were parameters for the techno-trans-human beings. They were not permitted to have a union with true Terran Humans. They could work among the colonies and receive the same respect, but never were they to enter the hallowed halls of the Crystal Heart Stone of T'Gaina. This was for their protection. This was to ensure the force and frequency of the Crystal Heart Stone did not rip the nanites from their blood, causing almost instant death.

Dear Reader, we ask that you not just take this as a mere story, something to entertain you. We hope it will create within you a sense of foreboding, a desire to research and discover the truth for your awareness.

For there are many around you in the past and present that have created dossiers and memoirs full of revelations of cults and groups and what happens to those that become entangled.

Such beings lead your world! Ones who have allowed themselves to become entangled in false truth, lies and deception in the hope of being gifted longevity and riches. Many have been paid in full, they no longer are seen within your world's surface, but they are walking amongst you as puppets or mimics of what was once a human.

Some differences cannot be altered, natural height, left or right use of hands, facial features and many other incriminating identifiers. You need to know what to look for.

This is the introduction to the next instalment. It has been constructed to make you wonder, to consider all parts of the unfolding play. It may, at times, seem as if we are taking you and dropping you into a bath of cold water, for it will be as if we directly contradict what we have been saying here.

This is not to fool you, but to make you hungry, to create a surge of a deep desire for the truth within you.

In this moment of your life, many will be required to fight. Fight for their life of freedom or choose to remain in slavery. To walk in a manner befitting a Terran Warrior of Truth or that of a Lyran. It is time to decide, will you be part of the capitulation or the uprising of humanity?

The Terran Uprising

As foretold by
The Lyran Narrators of Time

Where we left off
Background

In the last pages of the previous volume, we wrote that we hoped that as you observed how we overcame and still overcome our enemies, you would do this for yourself. We cannot force it upon you, but our hope is that our words and what we reveal will be the key that unlocks your memory.

In the words we used before, let us now reuse them here.

For we hope that in your observing how the Lyrans overcame the Formless Ones, this 'story' will give you the key to unlock, for yourselves, the weapon that will defeat them.

Remember, we have left the Lyran Alliance in the Sector of Lights, and they are travelling towards RaiDia-Mlith. Within this ship, we find the old Lyran warriors who have traversed the length and breadth of the Firmament, searching for the new Lyran Leader to join with the Codings of the Heart Crystal to create a new Lyra. To build a new Home Planet.

The Princes have regained their balance and unity again. Rath-Vorx had worked with the duality of both dark and light, depositing information with RaeNegria and the ships that had been in battle.

The plan behind RathVorx had been to expose the dark that had infiltrated him, to give all the opportunity to see what he had discovered while being connected to various downloads and energy forms. His aim had been to download what he had discovered to all present while in servitude to his mortal enemy.

This was to ensure open discussion and to give those who had been forced to live in a manner foreign to their codes a chance to break free. It, however, also created the path to his own demise. Consider that, knowing what he knew, RathVorx willingly set the stage of his death to enable those he had discovered, while under servitude to the Formless Ones, the opportunity to find the freedom they so yearned for.

When we return to the Bitari-Furtim-Otiose, we will once more rejoin our Lyran Princes in the vast expanse of the Firmament as they are drawn swiftly towards the destination they have set out for. All is coming to a close. All is prepared, and much awaits our young Princes. There are more adventures for them before they see the birth of Lyra and the defeat of the Formless Ones.

In the meantime, Dear Reader...Observe, watch and be aware. For in your world lurks those early shadow forms of interference... settled deep within your hidden governments and religious leaders, growing self-confident and more megalomaniacal.
 Focus now upon what you desire to unfold, not what you despise or fear.
Allow the Universal Divine Source Creator to work through your energy, thoughts, and words to create a world of light.
As we finished before, let us begin with the same. We request that you allow the Divine Creator to work with and through your energy, thoughts and words to create a world that reflects the light, truth and integrity required for such a time.

Chapter One

Introductions

Connecting within the Light Sector

Sitting silently, covered by a shield of reflective energy, was the *'Bitari-Furtim-Karda.'* The sister ship to the ship the young Lyran Princes were on, seemingly on a collision course with them.

This behemoth vessel sat as if anchored to a docking bay within the Sector of Light. If anyone had searched the void for anything out of the ordinary, they would have noticed nothing. No shimmer was out of step or out of alignment, for those within the great battleship had fine-tuned their light deflective shield to perfection. The energy shield would reflect the surrounding lights and void in such perfect symmetry that they could not be found. No ripple or glimmer of light, no frequency would pick them up. This resulted from many hundred cycles of trialling and refining diagnostic readings and using the dark matter around them in small quantities to create a barrier of deflective energy.

This time had been well spent, as not even the Formless Ones had discovered the Lyran ship when they had followed an unfortunate craft into the Light Sector during a 'hunt'.

Due to this experience, the Lyrans were quietly confident that their shields would hide them until they chose to be seen.

So as we observe the 'Bitari-Furtim-Karda' gently moving in the vibration of the Universal Flow of Energy, we should inform you that within her belly sits the great and revered Crystal Heart Stone. This incredible Crystal is the reason that all remaining Lyrans of true blood resonance call themselves Lyran. It is also the focus of every deviant, sneaky, maleficent, evil or bonded into such life species, working for the Formless Ones.

The Crystal Heart Stone, powerful in vibration, resonance, and an energetic connection, was also an influential symbol of unity to the Lyrans and those that had come to unite with them in a Federation of sorts.

The *'Bitari-Furtim-Karda'* was commanded by Sol Lrign dWari, who was fully aware that her presence and of her vessel may trigger the younger Lyrans and those they crewed into a panic. The 'Bitari-Furtim-Karda' was one of the last battleships made before the Great War of Lyra and its destruction.

The stories and myths of its size and power were many and often unpacked in the way of entertainment. It was also the *wish* of dreamers, who lived in the stories of old, for it to be true. However, when faced with the reality of the vessel, awe or fear always seemed to preside.

Those who have the knowledge and awareness of the Lyran Negotiators would see the battleship not just as a weapon. But as a tool of peace as well, while the display of power is a formidable image, so too would be the universal symbols of the offer of peaceful negotiations engraved into the vessel's outer shell.

Sol Lrign dWari had sent her best captains to scout for the returning ship they had sent out with the Organic Link RathVorx to guide those chosen back into the Sector of Light.

Do not think they were unaware of the possibility that Rath-Vorx may have become infected along his journey to find the young Lyran Princes. The Commanders of the Ancient Lyran Negotiators knew full well of this potential and had set safeguards so deep within the computer that not even RathVorx knew they were there. These safeguards would be activated only in the event of extreme and ultimate defeat. They were to remain hidden until the young Lyrans required extra assistance to break from the manipulation of the Formless Ones, should this occur on their journey.

As the Alliance of Galactic Federation Worlds moved into the Sector of Lights, none were prepared for the intense illumination within the sector.

All occupants of the vessels were still reeling from the portal that opened before them, covering them in liquid light. Never before had they experienced this in all their travels. It was as if a light had created a slipstream precisely where the vessels were moving further into the Sector of Lights. As the last of the ships slipped through the portal, there was a distinct shudder in the void. A door was firmly closed behind them, thus preventing any retreat that may have been thought about. The light that covered them began to dissipate, and soon, the occupants of all vessels were staring out of their various ships' windows or openings to a void unlike any other.

In this part of the great void, they were enveloped in a blanket of visible energy. The onboard instruments were registering both dark matter and a lighter, almost negligible vibration of frequency that was solid and, as they soon discovered, was the visible swath of mist-like substance wrapped around them.

The only other place they had seen anything similar was when they travelled to the Outpost NexEl MinAqua and passed through the Gulf of ExliaticMalvi. There, the Gulf had been alive with green-tinged energy that held within it the memories of those within the outpost and acted as a living record of those they had lost in the Great Wars.

They found themselves within a different type of energy hold in this sector. It was living energy and had begun to attach and integrate into the onboard computers and communicate tele-pathically with those who were open.

These messages were a test. A test of the universe, for want of a better explanation, for in this particular sector of the void, only those of pure intent could remain. Any could enter, but only those with pure intent could stay within the realm of light.

To bring clarification, this 'energy' would accept those who were battle weary, perhaps had 'blood on their hands,' or were running from authorities. However, if the intent of those that en-tered was self-exploitation or gaining only for self, to take all and not give. If their intention were based on greed and not on higher energy selflessness, then the messages within the telepathic communication would drive the hearer mad.

So it began on all levels of all the vessels that passed through the portal. Strange occurrences began to be reported to the cap-tains. Lyrans were hiding away in corners, others were drawing strange glyphs on the floors and walls of the corridors, and when requested to cease, their eery, vacant stares caused those asking them to stop their activities, to retreat quickly. Yet others were quietly going about their required business, ensuring the running of the vessels went unhindered.

RexNä Loid DeAqua, RaeNegria Hylrix-El-Moa and Rägę El BriNa-Ragnoa El Vroan sought each other out in the sanctuary of the Inner Chamber, set aside for the commanding officer on duty.

"Does anyone know what is going on?" RexNä questioned her friends, who simultaneously shrugged their shoulders, looking as bewildered as each other.

"I am not sure why none of us is experiencing this phenomenon," Rägę stated matter of factly, "the Mages Sector is as confused as we are about this...." His words faded as he cast his hands about as if looking for a term to make sense of everything.

As the three Princes sat around the table attempting to find a solution, there was a request to enter the room from Captain El Nareem. After being granted access, he sat at the table looking at the glum faces of the Princes. He began to grin.

Sitting back firmly in his chair, locking his fingers together in a firm grasp over his chest, he chuckled softly. "Look at you all, lost at sea, unsure and feeling like you've been deserted again." "Princes, you are leaders of a group of people that have chosen to follow you. So many have given up freedoms and lives to ensure the ongoing galactic freedom based on your belief of the Heart Stone Crystal, yet you sit here, heads in hands like scared children." He paused and looked for a moment like an angry parent or tutor. "Now get up, go out there and let your people know that you are around and have not left them in this dark time."

"Besides," he continued, "this will last perhaps the night; after that, those who have nothing to hide or fear will find themselves back in balance. Those with hidden agendas, not disclosed to you or the whole, will find themselves dribbling fools. This is the way of the sector. This is the way of the Frequency of Malisic."

At this utterance, the three Princes turned like clockwork towards El Nareem. Their faces each registering shock that he knew about this, anger that he'd not informed them and then horror at the fact that there may still be those among them that would harm the fledgling Galactic Federation of Worlds.

Then the realisation of the truth of his words settled upon them. Instead of being amid this fracas, they were hiding under the guise of finding a solution when their people needed them.

Slowly, one by one, they pushed their chairs back and stood. Finally, RexNā turned to El Nareem and quietly asked, "What is happening to us and why? What can we do to reassure the chain of command and those infected?"

El Nareem looked at the Princes, their faces showing the effects of battle, loss, death, fear, victory and the unknown and now a shadow of guilt. Yet, as he stared deep into their eyes, he saw the youthful wariness that was their reality. They were so young, in body and emotion, often unsure of choices and decision's to be in a position such as they found themselves. But somehow, they always rose to the challenges.

He softened his stance and replied, "This is the Whittling of the chaff, at least that is what we call it. When we first came to this sector many cycles ago, we found that there were those who 'still harboured regret, unfinished business, anger, or even doubt, that we should have taken the Heart Stone Crystal. These seemed to be plagued with an illness of the mind, hearing voices, and hiding from any light source. They appeared to disengage from their conscious mind completely and became broken in mind, heart and soul. We kept these in a medical ward to observe and assist those we could. Sadly some are still there, while others have found their inner cause again and healed from within. They have since rejoined our ranks, with no judgement, for any of us could have been in the Whittling."

"However, during The Whittling, some remained astute, clear in their focus of our purpose, seemingly unaffected."

El Nareem continued his explanation, "Now, to many of us, this seemed strange, this 'fever of the brain' as we originally called it, as we knew some of those unaffected were, perhaps in normal situations, the types we would have placed in the brig. Yet those affected were ones we would have considered sane and stable."

"This frequency penetrates into the very fibre of the brain, the energy of your soul and weeds out the hidden agendas that you may not even be aware of. In a matter of lapzph, you will find those you can trust beyond a doubt, those you can trust to a point, and those who would best be put off at the nearest out-post. It is the way of the sector. It is the way of the Frequency of Malisic."

Nodding their heads in thanks to the information that El Na-reem shared, the three young Princes stepped out in the corridor, only to have a young Lyran barrel into them, with tears streaming down his face. The fear in his eyes and incoherent words tum-bling from him tore at their hearts. "MelEid", RexNā yelled tele-pathically, "the inner chambers now." The Mage arrived, a little out of sorts but respectful.

RexNā Loid DeAqua looked at the Mage that had saved her life and that of her dearest friend. Then, drawing a deep breath, RexNā instructed the Mage, "MelEid, gather the Mages Sector and have them find all that are in various stages of incapacitation. Have them safely settled in a section of the ship where they can-not hurt themselves or others. If there is no room on the medical level, then create space in one of the docking bays, ensure it is liveable and allows for all amenities of comfort.

These people will need help, and you are charged to do what you can. We trust you, MelEid, to ensure their safety and yours. Go assist those who can come back from the brink to come back. Those who cross over into the mental abyss ensure they are safely enclosed and arrange for them to be sent to the closest outpost. They will return to normal once out of the Sector of Light.

The Mage nodded her head and turned away to fulfil the command. Pausing, she stopped and looked back at her Prince, her face registering the extremity of what was happening; what she'd just heard pierced into her heart and mind causing a stark realisation. "This, she stated, could have been me!" MelEid looked the young leader squarely in the eyes.

They both knew what was being referred to, and RexNā nodded slowly, gently in a telepathic push; she placed a thought into MelEid's mind, "But we are grateful that you are here now."

MelEid returned to the Mages Level to gather those who were able and began to administer comfort to those she and her team could reach. Then, slowly and determinedly with compassion, those allocated to the security of the vessels began to move around the ship, locating and containing those affected into various sections assigned to the safety of their well-being with the respective vessels.

Unsure of the length that this 'infection' was to last, MelEid, ensured that all her Mages were instructed to treat all with compassion and never force an elixir or other curative upon those they were assisting. If they agree, in clear comprehension, go ahead and administer. If you believe they are unsure, go through the process again and again until they know that you are assisting, not harming.

In the hours that followed, those affected began to change and alter in many ways. Those closest to them, either friends or Family Sector, became unrecognisable as these now debilitated beings hurled accusations and declared they knew who was infected by the Formless Ones. They would give the solution to the destruction of their enemies for a price.

Others slunk away, seemingly terrified of any loud noise or bright light. They showed signs of deep internal trauma that had been locked away, unable to be dealt with. It was realised that 'The Whittling' was the key to exposing many locked emotions and traumas. Events in the lives of those affected were buried so deep within their psyche that when previously looking at their lives, they had been truthful in saying they had no agenda or hidden trauma. This Vibration of Malisic dug out the pain and forced confrontation and dealing with the issue; one could no longer deflect the inner locked doors.

The Mage Sector sent a Lead Mage to each ship that did not have a Mage Sector. With the Lead Mage, there were two other Mages to assist the medical teams on all vessels in using their inner knowledge of energy, emotional and cosmic ways, as well as the linking to the Crystal Heart Stone,

It was overwhelming for the Princes as they walked among their people and contacted the captains of the other vessels. Seeing many who had repeatedly proven their courage and strength in the past adventures seemingly cut down by this Whittling. Where the Princes could, they encouraged those who needed it and sat with the medics while they calmed and assuaged the mental dilemmas of those they worked with.

One thing became clear, though, as they walked through the levels and listened to those in the throws of 'The Whittling,' they heard disturbing revelations from some of their high-ranking officers and trusted crew members. Statements like 'time to mutiny,' 'untested leadership,' 'go back to the way things

were,' 'surrender to the Formless Ones', and many other out-
bursts.

Upon seeing the Princes, there were those who would either
throw themselves at the three begging for forgiveness for some
unknown deed or attempt to do them harm and have to be removed by the Prince's security detail.

The eyes and awareness of the Princes were being well and
truly opened. Perhaps, for the first time, RexNā Loid De Aqua saw
the inner workings of an individual's heart exposed to trauma or
unexplainable hatred. This was a lesson for her and the others
that one should never assume that an individual supports you
just because their words are sweet to the ear.

As predicted by El Nareem, the effects of the telepathic test on
those targeted eventually waned. When the Princes felt that
there had been sufficient time passed between the last individual
declared 'sane' and a sense of normality returning to all vessels,
they called in the captains from the ships to report to the Bitari-
Furtim-Karda.

As the captains and the Princes sat around the oval table in the
inner chambers of the council room, a deep, solemn air settled
around them. All were shaken, and the chairs that should have
been filled were now empty. Instead of trusted captains or com-
modores, there were lieutenants or commanders that needed
clarification on why they were present.

In an almost unheard-of moment of despair and frustration,
RexNā dropped her head into her hands as she lent on the table
and released a low, muffled guttural groan. She shook herself
gently as if to regain her strength and then raised her eyes to look
at each crew member sitting around the table.

"You are here only because 'The Whittling' has revealed that although you may be a scum bag in battle and have been a mercenary in your previous life, you have perhaps done the most horrendous things possible or none of the above, your hearts and intent of purpose have been pure. You are here only due to the loyalty, honour, and dignity shown firstly to yourself and then to us."

"Those who are not here have shown us that their hearts and aspirations have harboured ill intent and eventual destruction to our cause. Therefore, if any of you no longer wish to be part of our Union of Free Worlds, now is your time to leave."

With fire in her eyes, she made deliberate eye contact as she spoke and was met back with determined looks and equal fire.

As she completed her declaration, Ru Naal cleared his throat, "On behalf of my crew, who were given a choice to return to the Formless Ones, and obviously be put to death for our failure or to join with you in free will and choice, we stand with you, RexNā. In fact, many of us felt this call to the table concerned the standing of our honour". Ru Naal placed a document on the table, "So, as a preemptive strike, here is our written and pledged allegiance. "Not to you alone, but to Lyra and to what Lyra stands for in our eyes. Freedom!"

He refused to lower his eyes, not out of stubbornness or to prove a point. Instead, as a show of determination and significance of what he and his people, the Nelphi-Lexmai, were committing to.

Soon other captains and representatives of the other vessels spoke of their commitment and assurance that they were on this journey for the long haul.

RexNā relaxed her eyes and leaned back into her chair, "This is reassuring, and we", she included the other two Princes with a gesture of her hand, "appreciate it." Then, glancing at her console, RexNā asked, "If we are all in this together, there are a few things we need agreement on.

One, we need to organise a vessel we can do without; this will be used to send those identified as 'not with us' back to the nearest outpost to recover. And, importantly, who is watching the radar and incoming vessel loops? We have an interception on our rear, and it's large enough to register on our transmitters even though it is approximately three trenzę travel from us."

At her second statement, the entire table seemed to come alive, with each captain, lieutenant or commander giving an opinion or solution, seemingly as if nothing had ever occurred, and all focus was now on the approaching ship.

Ru Naal cleared his throat, then when that didn't get the required attention, he stood on his chair and shouted. "Quiet!"

Looking at the Lyran captains' El Nareem and Kanrabos, he quietly asked, is this the fabled *"RaiDia-Mlith?"* The room fell deathly silent at his words and gaped at the two captains.

The myths and stories of this great battleship still struck fear into the hearts of those who fought and still fought against the Lyrans.

El Nareem looked over at Kanrabos and nodded, giving permission. Kanrabos rose and stood before the great window, looking out into the void. He stood observing the flow of energy as it surged around the vessel, creating a sense of movement while being still.

Turning, he looked at his Prince and the others. "No, I do not believe it is the RaiDai-Mlith; however," Kanrabos paused and drew in a deep purposeful breath as he spoke again, "It is more than likely our ship, the *'Bitari-Furtim-Karda.'* "

"We believe she is on her way to intercept our journey and challenge the Princes right to rule."

"It is believed by those of us who remember the old traditions that she is the carrier of Truth. The crew members of the Karda are made up of hundreds of Negotiators and Defenders awaiting the command to intersect our path and begin to do what has been written in all our annals of history. To ensure the Right to Rule is completed accurately."

Kanrabos looked at his Princes and the others in the room, "It is important to know that we cannot do anything but go forward. Be aware that if we show resistance, we will be overrun. If we show cowardice and turn around, we will be overrun. If, however, we show acceptance that it is inevitable we will be overpowered, we will be overrun."

"We must show that we are ready to enter into battle, we are ready to negotiate, we are ready to defend. But it must be done in a way that is not confrontational. This is the way of the Right to Rule. It is the Old Way; it is the True Way."

"But we're Lyran. Why would they wish to attack us?" RaeNegria asked, astounded. "Surely that defeats the reason for us coming to this point of our journey?"

Kanrabos shrugged and continued speaking, "The Old Ways must be recognised and followed, for it is in following the Old Ways that the New can be found. We agree you are of a new age of Lyran, but your teachings and foundations of lawfulness are poorly stitched together. Your ways have been built from memory and 'old wives' tales, untried in the heat of battle. The Old Ways will show you the way of the ancients, and then they will take the new ways you know now and integrate them. You and your crew will learn what is unnecessary and what will be rejected. How you respond to this removal of your knowledge of knowing will determine the results 'It' is looking for."

RexNā looked over to Ragę and telepathically asked, "What is 'It,' and what is 'It' looking for?" Rägę barely got his shrug off to indicate he had no idea when El Nareem interjected. "Do not enquire about 'It'; you will be made fully aware of the power and your destiny when It calls for you, each of you."

The silence falling over the room was thicker than when they first gathered to find who was still committed to the cause they had begun so long ago. Now they were faced with another test, this time not from an enemy but their fellow Lyrans. Their kinsmen, by all intents and purposes, did not trust them, even though they were Lyran. This was a new turn of events, and none of the Princes knew what to think.

A young voice spoke into the silence, outlined what they all knew was to be done yet had not spoken of these. The speaker pointed out, 'although there was this impending intersection of paths coming their way....' Looking for the speaker, Rägę realised it was Brinthera, who was stepping into his position as a second to his captain. Unaware that he was being observed, Brinthera continued to point out that 'there was still more than enough to keep them busy till then. First, there were repairs to be made and positions to fill to ensure the smooth running of the ship. Then a delegation was required to escort those identified by The Whittling safely out of the Sector of Light. If they could find the exit!'

The young lieutenant stood, just behind RaeNegria's chair, with his hands clasped behind his back, feet slightly apart. Brinthera stood at ease as he spoke, not considering that what he said was out of place; he was merely stating the obvious that seemed to have been overlooked for the moment.

Chapter Two

New Meets Old
An introduction to the Ancients

Deep within the Sector of Light, the great battleship sat waiting and moving slightly as if buoyed and held fast by an anchor in the incredible vastness of the void. Almost ghostly in her stance, all who moved within her went about their business and ignored the oncoming vessel. This massive battleship, scarred from many incursions with the enemy, remained beside the '*Bitari-Furtim-Otiose,*' the most powerful ship within the Lyran forces. If only the remaining Lyrans were aware of her existence, it would generate a sense of hope and strengthen emancipation among them!

Each crew member knew what their purpose was aboard this vessel. They knew that even though they were actively implementing their sector duties, at any moment, this could be put aside to create the grid and patterning required for the Heart Stone Crystal frequency to be harmonised and magnified. Until then, they were unconcerned about the returning Lyran ship. They knew it was there and that it would approach their section of space. It was inevitable.

The ship RaiDai-Mlith sat observing the long-awaited meeting of the sister ships, the 'Bitari-Furtim-Otiose' and the 'Bitari-Furtim-Karda', from a great distance. The captains of this battle-scared ship knew they were well hidden by their energy shield, an even more unique and, as of yet undiscovered by others, shield designed using a formula of plasma, electric current, and the old art of the Lyran ability to be invisible. It was, in some ways, a similar array of deflection that the Bitari-Furtim-Karda used. Nevertheless, the old Lyran warrior brothers, Max Ron and El Shavreon, knew that the encounter between Sol Lrign dWari and the three Princes would set in motion a change within the Heart Stone that had not happened in many hundreds of cycles.

It would shift energy from one Family to another and enhance the Initiation of Fire for the second time within the chosen one.

This time, those who knew the Ancient Ways would be present and add to the tone of the initiation.

We, the Lyran Narrators of Time, should now reveal that the reason Nuul Ra-ulr had been so calm when the Princes went off in the *'Bitari-Furtim-Otiose'* was that the brothers of the IIth clan, Max Ron and El Shavreon were following them in the RaiDai-Mlith. They were to follow, observe and only interfere if enemy forces overcame the Princes. So far, nothing untoward had taken place in the eyes of these old warriors. What had occurred was merely young warriors being blooded in battle. They had felt a sense of pride and well-being at the way the Princes journey had fallen into place. How the various battles had been won, and the ensuing negotiations had brought them more allies than enemies. This was the way for the Lyran people to align rather than separate.

However, the *'Bitari-Furtim-Karda' situation* gave them a reason to pause and consider revealing themselves to the Princes.

They knew that El Nareem and Kanrabos had knowledge of their presence, for they had communicated while the captains had been in the shadows observing the Princes in battle. Their communication had been purely for safety and to provide Kanrabos and El Nareem the opportunity to call on them if their assistance was needed.

Truly when Nuul had uttered the words 'May the Elders guide you, he had the awareness that at least four of the battle commanders in the company of the Princes were of the Ancient Lyran Command.

The Princes, without realising it, now had three powerful and fully equipped battleships to call upon, including all the other smaller attack vessels and shuttlecraft that had joined their alliance as they had progressed on their journey. If they had only known, perhaps they would not be as cautious or nervous about the upcoming meeting with the Old Ones.

Sol Lrign dWari

Sitting in the command chair sat a very wizened individual. The figure stared outward as if the darkness held nothing back, allowing them to see all that was there. In a way, the ancient Commander saw more than others thought could be seen. This old pilot had fought many battles and negotiated more tables of meetings than she'd like to remember. Her eyes were a brilliant electric blue, searing through your very being when she held your attention.

Sol Lrign dWari was her given name. She was of the Hylrix-El-Moa family and had seen more devastation in her long years than she wanted to admit. She had commanded the battleship 'Bitari-Furtim-Karda,' for over twenty cycles, and the prophecy was coming to pass. For the first time in her knowledge, the Light Gate had opened, exploding in liquid light and covering all that surrounded the Gate in golden energy. Her crew had felt the touch of The Whittling. Knowing the events unfolding within the other ship left deep respect, and deep regard had settled upon all within the ship. They knew what those in the contingent entering the Light Sector were going through.

Sol Lrign dWari placed her attention back onto the dark void; she saw hiding within the shadows what others did not. She could see that the Princes journey to their mooring would not be easy. The light which poured from the sector, both when the Princes ships had entered and when the shuttle took those poor souls tormented by The Whittling back through the portal gateway, had triggered a series of alarms and warnings that travelled directly to the Draconians and Formless Ones.

The Princes did not know that there were those coming towards them from within and without The Sector of Light that wanted to destroy them.

The Ancients would not interfere. This instruction had already been passed through all the ships and chain of command. No one was to break rank and attempt to help. But, if there was an attack, which Sol felt within her gut would happen, the Princes had to face it and either win the day or be lost. That was the way of the Ancient Lyrans now, for their criteria and code was to protect the Crystal Heart Stone at all costs.

It was not lost on her that it now fell upon her shoulders to bring the young Lyran Princes into the fold. To teach them the Ancient ways and to watch as they would undergo the intense alignment of the Heart Stone.

Its frequency would only accept a true Lyran into its resonance of vibration, and any that did not pass the test were repelled from the chamber at speed.

The Crystal Heart Stone was not a tool of judgement, although one could say its frequency of light allowed you to judge yourself. It was said that many that ran from the chamber of the Crystal Heart Stone were incarcerated for their safety or went into the Mages Sector for deep interpersonal clearing. Often these were not seen again in society.

It was on her watch that the ways of the Old Word and the ways of the New World folded into a single place, fixed and unalterable. It was foretold that a Prince would become the leader, but they would bring with them a way of ruling that had not been accepted before. Sol Lrign felt that one of these young Lyrans was the chosen Prince. Was it the one who led the group here, or was it another? This would be finalised in 'The Grounding' as well as 'The Opening of One' ceremonies that her Mages were setting in order.

She noted that the training areas had been designated by reading the reports in her hand. Her squad leaders had set up separate levels for the training, allowing her to see what knowledge these Princes had and what they had passed onto their crew.

Sighing deeply, she signed off on the first test the approaching group had just experienced.

'The Whittling,' this was not of the Lyran construction, for it affected any and all who entered into this section of the void. But, from all reports, the young Princes had overcome their fear, faced the situation, and brought balance back to their people and ships. They had separated the ones who'd become unaligned and sent them back through the portal. The remaining vessels had begun to rebuild morale and restructure their crews.

A smile spread across her weathered face at the memory of the Formless Ones bursting through while chasing their next victim, only to spectacularly implode within a few moments of being in the sector. No ship from the Formless Ones had ever been seen again, though there had been incursions of other vessels attempting to pass through. These had been unmanned and automated, pinging signals around the sector like fireworks gone awry. Her technicians assumed they were searching for anomalies or the Lyran ships by the way the pings were scattered, but when these results failed to produce what they were searching for, the visits became fewer. Prior to her role as commander, there had been times when they had sent out beacons, bereft of any signature of Lyra or any other culture nearby. The reaction of the automated vessels had been like the proverbial bees-to-honey scenario. Only when the ship got close enough to recognise the beacon was just 'space junk' it ceased pinging and retreated through the portal, and now they were fortunate to see even one in a cycle.

It was this very thing that had Sol Lrign worried. The noise created by the Lyran Alliance entering the Sector of Light, or The Gap, as it was also referred to, would have, by now, caught the attention of Formless Ones. With this in mind, Sol assigned reconnaissance squads to various hide-out areas to watch and report on any disturbances. So far, nothing was out of place.

A knock on her private review room brought Sol out of her thoughts. Remaining in her chair, she gazed at her old friend standing on the other side of the door. She knew by his stance that he had something on his mind. Keeping him waiting was not an option.

She tapped a button on her consul, which unlocked the doors, and promptly but silently opened.

Stranz Lith Hylrix strode into the office space and stood directly in front of her. Sol Lrign smiled to herself. She knew he wanted to speak and correlate what was happening out in the void. She was well aware of his feeling of self-importance and wanting to be of value and service even though he was retired. He'd spent most of his life in the service of Lyra and to those on the Bitari-Furtim-Karda. He'd been a young ensign, possibly no more than four trenzęs from joining the Negotiators Sector, before the Great War of Lyra and the Destruction of their world began. Yet he'd proven faithful to those he'd chosen to follow, and from his record, he'd remained loyal and faithful to the designation of his cloak.

He'd not been happy when retirement had been put upon him in favour of Sol Lrign dWari stepping into the command seat, but he'd not openly opposed. No, his 'resistance' came from being a self-appointed councillor to the new commander. This was always a humorous point to Sol Lrign, not in disrespect, but in realising that perhaps she would not find it easy to step down in favour of a younger commander.

Finally opening her eyes, she looked at Stranz and smiled. "Yes, old friend, what news do you bring?"

As she waited for his reply, she moved her attention to the scattered papers on her desk, gathering them together, not because she did not trust Stranz, but because it had been drummed into her as a young officer, 'only leave on your desk what you wish the enemy to see.'

Clearing his throat, Stranz stared at the disk in his hand. "Sol," he began, clearing his throat a second time. It seemed as if the words were struggling to be uttered. His face reflected an inner conflict of deciding whether he should or should not report what he had discovered. Finally, his integrity won the internal discourse.

"Sol, we have an infiltration! I have been running diagnostic programmes silently over the last six periods, and there were no anomalies at first. Then about two periods ago, I noticed a variation in frequency in our transmission to the RaiDai Mlith Commanders. To ensure it was not a glitch, I created a new algorithm to mirror anything that did not have the Lyran code attached. I ran this three or four times during the vra and have found that our communications have been altered, and Max Ron and El Shavreon may have alternate instructions than what was sent out."

He paused; this perhaps was the most comprehensive statement he'd made in some time. That alone got Sol Lrign's attention. The fact that his unique ability to read code and algorithms had discovered a fault was something she was paying close attention to. She had had a gut feeling when three of the last communications from the RaiDai Mlith had returned out of context that something was out not in alignment.

"Go on, my friend." Sol indicated the seat to Stranz,

After about an hour, Sol Lrign was alarmed enough to call her chief Negotiator to her review room.

While waiting, she noted a few bullet points on the screen in front of her. All were related to the upcoming contact they would soon have with the *Bitari-Furtim-Otiose* and her crew.

Chapter Three

Earth
The Unexpected Silence

Meanwhile, Dear Reader, when we traverse back to the realm of your planet, we are alarmed at the state of reversal that the human race is undergoing. Where we observe the potential time-line is your earth year 2030. A dark time if what we see becomes a fixed point.

When we left, there was a surge of an uprising, where the individuals were learning to fight back with a calm repose, how those that had been manipulating the events of the planet were being pushed backwards and disempowered.

There was a time when the True Terrans were rising and encouraging those around them to engage in discourse, to come into critical thinking and self-discovery. Then, communities started up again, and your need to use fiscal finance was removed and replaced with an exchange of value based on the integrity of vibrational golden mean quantum physics.

Many of you had learnt to communicate in the ways of the Galactic families. Nonetheless, your earth realm was returning to Terran ways.

There were monuments to the great victories you achieved over the Draconians and Anunnaki slave masters, yet now we see wars and automatons that serve without question. What has happened?

Oh, do not fear. We know what has occurred, for it is etched in the memory of the Akashic Cosmic record and whilst it is still being written, we know there is hope! We have faith that those who once believed in the liberty of truth and honesty of mankind may yet still be here.

Dear Reader, let us travel back to see where there was still hope in many humans, where thousands of you gathered to lift the banner of truth and integrity. Let us step into the portal and return to 2019 of your earth year.

This was a time of significant testing for your earth. There were star families gathering and assisting many. Terrans were rising, awakening. Though many did not know they were Terran, they called themselves believers, patriots, lawful beings, and living beings. They began to sound the call to those of like mind and step outside the mind control to utilise their frontal lobe again. For the energy lobotomy of the Anunnaki had begun, once again, to wear off.

Leaders were rising up and facing the dark forces of their world.
But, then, those strong men and women in places of authority were targeted. Some were brought down and destroyed as they refused to bow to the manipulation of the Draconian Masters.

There were battles in unseen places, both above and below ground, even in your skies. Though, thousands of you, as a generic species, were protected from much of the evil being removed.

We, the Narrators of Time, will pause here. It is good to breathe and rest.

Your earth, your beautiful T'Gaina, is in the battle of her life, and our warriors have begun to do what we promised. Our scientists and explorers have come to gather the animals, plants and wide varieties of life from T'Gaina, for there is a concern that humanity will destroy these beautiful creations and themselves. In many ways, as we Lyrans did, in an attempt to save HU-manity.

Let us sit quietly and turn the pages of your history back, let us attempt to undo in the Akashic what the Anunnaki, Draconians have been doing under the direction of the Formless Ones.

Let us return to the year 2018.

This year was a year of peace. You had two nations return to a oneness of mind. The north and south were brought together under the leadership of a spurned man, yet he achieved what others could not or would not do.

Many 'inhuman' fast food chain supplies were stopped in this particular country.

There was an increase in employment, and the balance between your genders was being brought to an even keel. Women seemed to find their place in the world they wished to create. It looked like the differences between your races and genders were finally being healed.

Many of the people in your species of the female gender were given a voice. Medical history was, again, being created through new discoveries in health awareness. Many of you lived longer lives.

People began to look at their world through new eyes and actively stopped specific industries. As a result, new species of animals/insects were discovered. Your scientist even 'discovered' a way to destroy plastic. (*Although there is a quotient of scientists in your governments who already have this knowledge*.)

Indeed there were so many indicators that you were on the verge of awakening to the empowerment of humanity and awakening the DNA of the Terran within you that we, the Galactic Families, allowed ourselves to become excited.

Then you stepped into 2019, and it was as if a net was being spun around you. A net crafted by wordsmiths and manipulators, paid by the powerful masters to entrap you in an illusional world that was to draw you into fear.

It began with shootings and death, followed by   accusations from one government about another. There was fighting within some governments to bring down the other side, not because they were doing something wrong but just the opposite. They, the opposing side, were doing things right.

The 'voice of freedom' was snatched and imprisoned in late 2019. A slow descent during the year 2020 began when the freedom of your voice was systematically removed from you. We are amazed that only a handful of humans resisted this. Instead, most of you allowed yourselves to be muzzled, just like when the Anunnaki used their light frequency to lobotomise you all those millennia ago.

Soon your world began a spiral into the dark realms of mind control. You fell into the snare of the dark ones and believed the illogical, the lies and depth of corruption that is the Formless Ones way of being.

For some reason, many of you allowed yourselves to become part of their grand experiment to control and dominate, yet again, the freedom and life force of Terran beings.

You sat by and judged those who researched and questioned. You scorned the people who refused to follow the mandates and unlawful practices placed on you. As a result, humanity began to shrink back into its slavery. They began to forget again the joy of the Divine Love that flows from the heart Terra-Ven-Eiliesh-Gaina, that inner peace and joy found only in the Universal Love of Source.

It began like a whisper, a word here and a comment there. Soon it spread like a fire. There was fear. The most deadly un-known factor was the unequivocal acceptance that the governing heads knew better than you know yourself. You accepted that the common illness of your time just disappeared to be replaced with something unique and strange. You looked at the symptoms, and even though they showed 'you' (the general populace), the 'ill-ness' was the same as your pneumonia or chest infections, a common cold. Strangely, during this time, the annual influenza bug disappeared from medical history to be swallowed up by a new dis-ease.

The dis-ease of fear.

Dear Reader, by the end of 2019, moving into the start of 2020, your globe will become saturated with the energy of mistrust and fear. It became so tangible that we could smell it in the ethers around the planet. Governments, medical societies and trusted guardians of the peace became symbols of distrust, misinformation, bullying and fear.

Yet, there was, surprisingly, a growing group of Terrans that became larger and bolder as they began to research, ask questions and follow the ways of the old teachings. They realised something was not quite right in their world, especially when they were being corralled and imprisoned within their own homes.

Many of the occupants of the earth were trapped. Trapped in the cells of their mind and imprisoned by their indoctrinated concepts. They had for so long relied on and trusted the controlled outlets of information to feed them enough truth, wrapped in outright lies, that when the reality of what was happening on the planet was shown to them, they chose to blindly accept the false information.

The dark puppet masters took pleasure in the scattering of human society. The breakdown began slowly. First, there were whispers, then a common cold and then bio-warfare.

Yes, my Dear Reader, your nations' governments and leaders betrayed you. Oh, they told you with smiles, tears and 'frustration' that you needed to be cared for and looked after, for you could not do this yourself. They created camps with security personnel to ensure that you did not 'break the rules.' You did not recognise them as prisons or camps as they were dressed up as hotels and places of comfort. Until you attempted to leave the 'hotel' or place, they designated you to reside within for the stated time.

They would give you permission to 'quarantine' yourself at your home, but you were to be tested and marked from that moment on. They tracked and coerced you into becoming what they wanted you to be.

Your leaders required you to submit. They needed it to be YOUR decision to submit to the tracking. They compelled you, as good citizens, to report on those who 'did not obey the rules. You became their puppets, all out of fear.

Once again, the Anunnaki and the Formless Ones seemed to have gained the upper hand in your realm, Terra-Ven-Eiliesh-Gaina. Once more, they were establishing an illegal takeover of your people and your world. Only this time, you allowed it to happen because you had forgotten who you were in this moment.

When people stood up against the bio-warfare dispersed around them and called it for what it was, a culling of the realm's inhabitants. But they were denigrated and made out to be foolish and harming society. There were groups who attempted to prove the 'pandemic' inconsistencies by showing that the various sciences that were being conveyed to the masses through the media were wrong. So they were drummed out of town. Their businesses were taken from them, their livelihood was removed, and they were scorned. All the while, the reality of the war was being fought in plain sight.

Your puppet masters, the clone makers, are still active in your world. They no longer use stone circles to create clones and new bodies for the consciousness of those that are undead. Instead, they used high-powered technology and rewarded the hunters of children and women. They take the homeless and the poor, but their agenda has not changed.

Dear human, dear Terran, our Galactic families that reside here on this planet, we ask you to open your eyes. Do not let this time pass by into infamy.

You are all here, called in at this time to be the voice of the silent. For thousands of earth years, tunnels and tubes have been buried in your earth. They cover the inner section of the planet like a cobweb. Deep beneath the waters are structures that we'd refer to as cities or outposts, these act as halfway points for those that travel without wishing to be seen. They will go from land mass to land mass under the oceans and travel in high-speed trains, or perhaps they should be called rail bullets. Using this transport, they can leave their country and be in another across the continents within a few hours, or they stay in hidden outposts and are 'entertained' in a manner that we cannot and will not share on these pages. However, we will say that the lost ones of the surface are found in the dark tunnels, and their form, once whole and beautiful, soon becomes broken and deformed before gratefully they accept death.

The unfortunates in this lower world beneath you are, at times, resuscitated to endure more of the same... all in the name of power.

The terrifying realisation is that you, Dear Reader, have been given all this information and ignored it. You have read and listened to those who have escaped and told their story, yet it has been too horrific to be accurate, so you side-lined it 'for later.'

Earth is breaking, Dear Reader. She is looking to split herself into many pieces, guiding and leading those brave enough to the deepest parts of her belly to expose the strongholds of the Draconians and Anunnaki.

You call the place you are taught in your religious education 'hell' a fantasy, a make-believe place. Created by religious orders to keep you in fear. This has a modicum of truth, yet heed us, Dear Reader, there is a hell you know not of. A place very much for the living, taken in the darkest of moments and bled like a hunted animal only to be maintained and kept alive, due to their blood being of the Golden Ones... They have found some of the original Terrans and are using this blood to create clones once more in an unspeakable manner.

This part of the story of earth or Terra is unpleasant, yet without the darkness being exposed, how will you realise the utter joy and revelation of the victory and overcoming that Lyra, and hopefully your world, experiences?

So it falls to us to give you the overview of all the horrors that your alternative information, which has been shared, is correct. Yes, there are specific individuals who have 'sold their souls' literally to the Anunnaki and the Draconians, who are under the service of the Formless Ones.

These humans have been promised youth, power, popularity, and longevity (there is a difference between youth and longevity). They have also been promised wealth beyond what they can spend in three lifetimes, and their offspring have been allocated prime positions as long as they toe the line and follow the system. They are to defend and deny when confronted, detract others, and distract all those looking at the higher-paid, higher-living individuals.

There has been uncovering that you have yet to be shown, nor have you been given the intel for the events that can potentially set the race of Terran free forever.

There are groups that work in the shadows, in the places where you would rather not be seen or found. Yet these brave souls gather information and bring it back to the channels that operate in light and honour.

Do you think there was and perhaps is only one man fighting for a nation's peace and truth? You should know that a considerable number of men and women have risen in their lands, resisting the onslaught of the darkness.

Yes, currently, there is a game of smoke and mirrors being played out. There are players who have been in power, shown themselves publicly multiple times, then suddenly disappeared and are not being seen. They appear periodically to calm the twitching nerves of those still stuck in the dream of the lies, but these heads of state and puppets are no more than holograms and imagery in smoke.

It is, Dear Reader, time perhaps to consider all factors around you. The lines are drawn, and the sides are called.

Draconians, Anunnaki and all other minions of the Formless Ones are being placed in battle sequences. They believe they will defeat the light, and we tell you it will seem as if they do for a while.

We ask that you hold fast, Dear Reader, for the eyes and ears will see and hear things that are mist and whispers. Truth is a strange companion when you are willing to trust the Divine Source Creator and the energy of Terra-Ven-Eiliesh-Gaina. Suddenly, you will come across their soldiers, their valiant warriors of light and the light they bring will blind you.

The blinding will, at times, be for your own good. There will be a darkness that comes upon the people. It will not be a darkness that you are familiar with. It will be experienced both within you and without. It will settle across the planet in a way that unsettles all that feel it. As if there is a sticky and untoward occurrence about to unfold.

These moments of darkness are the emptying of the lower tunnels and waterways. It is done this way so those in moral authority can access the realms they need to enter, utilising the correct technique. Know that it is not sending men and women of honour down a tunnel or into a tube. It asks them to step into a wall of energy and allow that wall of energy to transport them to another dimension, another realm within your world.

You see, these puppet masters have had access to various realms of earth, utilising materials and technology that were gifted by Zeta so many years ago in the hopes of protecting humanity from the onslaught of the darkness. Sadly this technology was hijacked by specific sectors of the government, meant to protect mankind, and they sold it or gave it to the Formless Ones servants, and they, in turn, used it to steal away thousands of your beloved ones. These now wander in many dark places, waiting for the light to penetrate the darkness and rescue them.

This is why you see no 'evidence,' 'no proof,' for who would believe the literal 'science-fiction' being played before you? There would be those who would turn it into a religion, others who would scoff and claim it is a distraction and a ploy to turn the minds and hearts of a nation towards a single man or woman.

Finally, some would believe and be encouraged to continue the fight because of what they saw. Therefore it could be said that some say they would not or could not believe what is played out in front of them, in the complete sense of exposure, for it would break not only their hearts but their spirit to see the desolation wrought upon their world. Those who choose not to see the horrors of your world do so because they cannot live with the truth, creating a cocoon of dream worlds to exist in.

Then, on the other hand, we see those who 'see' all that is being exposed and attempt to explain and describe to the rest of their community, what they see, sense and intuit, but this, at times, is an uphill battle to put across.

These doorways/portals/star gates, call them what you will. Still, these entry points are so heavily guarded by the Draconian forces that entering them on a reconnaissance or rescue mission is almost impossible. As a result, many have lost their lives in attempts at earlier battles under leaders of integrity and boldness.

Though we must say that in these days, there are more and more passing through to the other realms or sections of your earth realm, this is only due to the result of a group of dedicated beings of mixed galactic species. They have come together, Terran, Lyran, Pleiadian, Arcturan, Sirian, and other star beings such as the Zeta Solitudinem section of the Orion Zeta Community. Coming together as a combination of Galactic beings, they present as leaders, military, technicians, scientists and most of all, those who desire to see the light again flow into this world.

These living souls have awoken in their human form at this time. To create the force that will fight for the freedom of Terrans throughout the realm of the earth plane.

Come, Dear Reader, let us give you some images and realities to focus on.

In the year 2018, you were on a course of clarity. Yes, there were groups worldwide that were supposedly against the freedoms of the people. Yet, here we are in your year [3]2021, with more groups promoting the complete obliteration of any that voice concern against the narrative set by the 'governing forces.'

This reminds us of when the Anunnaki split your Terran ancestors into units and groups, separated by walls and taught you that the 'others' were against you. They spread lies and fears among you where once there had been unity.

Where has this unity gone? Do you not all share a common cause, the cause of life? To live in the god given rights that you were born with? Or *were* you born with those rights? How do you know that you have any rights? Are you not just the stock and

---

[3] The year this book was authored by the Lyrans.

chattels of the Anunnaki, the overlords or, as you are now calling them, the cabal?

Have they not, for generations now, caused you to 'register' your living form and become numbered? Did not a particular culture, a specific military force not number the people it took into camps and forced into labour and experimentation groups?

Did the numbers not remove the 'human quality and reduce them to mere cattle?

When the experimentation was done, and the body was of no use, where did it go?

It was disposed of in chambers of gas or the lime pits, according to your historical records. Or thrown in large overcrowded graves, and some perhaps were never gassed, decomposed or buried but shuttled away to underground facilities. In these dark places lived many dark energies that lived off the dead of your surface world.

Does this not remind you of the Anunnaki? Does this reflect some of the 'horror' stories you were told as small children to ensure you did as you were told? Many of the forest or woodland communities have stories of those who disappear, taken by the dark ones, the sprites or gnomes.

Why are you allowing this to repeat in your lifetime again?

In the era of 2020 and 2021, you will find those who have been fighting unseen energies. They have placed themselves in the forefront of the battle line so that you are protected.

We wish to take you on a journey, Dear Reader. Although there may be some that are sensitive and in a place of emotional overwhelm, we ask you to consider the next part of our story.

What we are about to expose is only spoken in whispers. Others have surmised and used old imagery from years past to give credence to their thoughts.

We will not use imagery in a pictorial manner. Instead, we will use our words and place within you a mental image that surpasses the black-and-white imagery that can be manipulated.

We are travelling back to your era of 1940 to 1946 and onwards.

During this time of upheaval on your planet, there are countries at war. A war which will leave a scar on the face of the earth for many, many years. A scar deep in the memory of her people, it will plant the seed of fear, hatred and suspicion. This time is a progeny of the previous Great Wars of your time, where many strong and healthy living men died to 'serve' their countries.

As many of you may have discovered, a war created by powerful men. Men who sought to control and manipulate both humans and the resources of the world. These few families of powerful men and women began infiltrating families of wealth, who leant neither for nor against. These were 'neutral' families, but once they were integrated into the families of power, usually by marriage or coercion and fear of losing their millions, these neutral became dark and were forces of evil.

Nation was pitted against nation. Even if they did not want war, there was a price to pay for peace, and it was war.

Depending, Dear Reader, on whom you believe the war was all one country's fault. They started it because a man of pure evil drove cultures he disagreed with into camps. These camps were filled with religious groups, people who did not love the opposite gender but preferred their own gender. In these camps were the scientists, the philosophers, the doctors, and all those who could prove the war was wrong and illegal.

These camps were never full. There was always room for more. So, where did the people come from, and where did they go?

In these camps and Dear Reader, these camps were not just in the country called Germany. No, they were in England, in the USA. They were in France, Rome, Australia, New Zealand, Japan, China, and many other countries.

Why were there so many of these camps, and why were the humans numbered? Why were they dehumanised?

It was because these camps were to break the spirit of the individual. There were various camps, some to experiment on genetics, some to see what a female could carry in her womb - especially if it were not human!

Other camps were for the children, separated from their parents and sent to places where no one would know what became of them. Their little bodies were broken by grown men and women, who took their pleasures in seeing how much pain a little body could endure before passing out—or dying!

They would have blood samples taken and electrodes connected to their heads to measure the brain activity before the child either passed out or died of fear, adrenaline overdose, or asphyxia. Or, at times, by being placed in areas of great heat, such as an oven.

These children were passed from camp to camp, and if they survived, they were again separated as soon as they entered their teenage years. The females were sent to propagation camps, and the males were either killed or sent to labour camps.

Note that this happened not just in camps in the dark area of the land you call Germany. It happened in every camp that the power families designated. This was the beginning of collecting the life force they needed to continue their youthful existence.

They needed to know how to clone themselves using better and better technology, and they wanted to create a mechanical womb that would work as well, if not 'better' than a human female.

They would take a vibrant woman or young girl and impregnate her, the foetus would grow, and at a certain age, the young woman would be drugged enough to be malleable and not resist but not enough for the drugs to affect the foetus adversely. *We only say 'foetus' as the creature the poor woman would carry was not human.*

They would then take the woman and strap her to a bed, ensuring that she could not move and kept in a semi-comatose state. They would then slice her belly open. The lower abdomen would be pulled back to expose the uterus. They would ensure that there would be no infections due to the illegal medical knowledge they had been given by the Draconians they had met and come into contact with. The Draconians had given them a simple yet effective system of placing a transparent force field; glass or similar was also used to allow the creature the space to expand within the uterus. When it was at term, which was well before the nine months gestation of a human child, this creature would tear its way out of the womb and devour its incubator.

Unfortunately, that would be the woman that had carried it to term.

These were a Draconian Reptoid hybrid. They were bred simply as hunters and soldiers. However, they could take the shape of the human body due to the intake of human DNA during the incubation period, thus were able to walk within the human world almost undetected. We say 'almost' as there were many Terrans who could identify the vibration of a non-human being and ensure its swift removal.

As the war began to cease and they no longer had the excuse of war camps, they began to take their experiments underground. At first, they continued to use the tunnels and defence areas built in case of bombs destroying the above ground.

They then realised that they needed to go deeper, and so began all the tunnel building that would create linking train or tube or underground travel tunnels in the various countries.

The people were told that these underground trains would make life easier for them to get to places.

Yet there was a more profound and darker reason for the tunnels - for every train tunnel built; there was a duplicate deeper tunnel built that was structured to hold an entire city. These tunnels had prisons, camps, and experimental areas in hospitals, housing, and schools. They became the homes of the stolen children and people that were taken. It could be said that your surface is genuinely hollow, and the only thing preventing the ground from collapsing is the intricate web of structures used to ensure the integrity of the tunnels.

During the years prior to the 1945 wars, there were other tunnels built in the then 'young' America. These tunnels were used to ferry slaves and hide those seeking asylum from their 'masters'. As a result, many slaves would take into their numbers deformed creatures and humans hiding in absolute fear of being found.

These slaves would take them to America's 'free' lands and care for them. Knowing what it was like to be a mere chattel of another person. There were many types of slaves of all races being perpetrated against. Many were kept unseen, for they were of European, Asian and Mongolian cultures. These were hidden from sight, for their purpose was not to be used above ground to harvest and serve others. No, their value was in their genetics.

These Terrans and other groups were stolen and shipped across the great waters in identical ships to those dear groups taken from the land of Africa. Therefore, we wish you to see that it was not just one group that suffered the humiliation of being captured, tortured and eventually butchered, but it was many.

Some groups were taken and used mercilessly as chattels and servants for the elite of this world. The slave masters would have two facilities. Above ground and below.

The slaves knew and feared the below-ground facility. This is what drove many to run for freedom. Horror stories would be heard in the groves and around fires of the terrors that could be seen at times in the forests or swamps nearby. Of creatures that were neither human nor beast and shrunk back from the light as if the light hurt them. Then when the light was removed, the creature would attack the one who had found it, and the death was always blamed on a wild beast.

The elite had facilities to extract the early concentration of adrenochrome removed from various sectors of living beings enclosed within open cages. While they exploited one race below ground, they destroyed the morale and dignity of another above ground. This was done by destroying their family units.

Remember, the enemy can only win if they completely separate you from your core of truth. To do this, they must separate you from all you hold dear. They then must achieve in the breaking of your spirit, and to do that, and they will seek to crush you in all conceivable ways. The easiest method was for the slave masters to rip children away from their parents and sell them on. Do this enough, and the women no longer wish to have children.

They cannot endure the pain, and the men are broken inside as they cannot protect their loved ones. The unit is now shattered, untrusting and becoming unloving.

Do you see what is happening in the era of 2019, 2020, and 2021 up to and including [4]2025? It is not new in this era. It had its roots and experimental beginnings of known time and more recently in the 1800s to 1900s.

The Great Persecution or the Great Inquisition, as well as the Salem Witch Hunt, the ones that were taken and tortured, were of the female gender. They were repeatedly brought to the edge of insanity to see just how far the human spirit could be taken before the body and soul separated.

Men were taken and stretched between horses or bulls and ripped apart slowly. This created in the energy of the individuals suffering the torture an immense moment of pain that would send a vibration through the air. Those 'elite', the ones hiding as humans but in reality were and still are Draconian and Anunnaki masters, would absorb the vibration and use it to create a sense of euphoria within their bodies.

Your entire history, written and oral, has shown you, in great detail, what the religious governments and those governments which are bought with more than mere money can do to the world.

There are many documents written by Terrans and Humans and others who have lived here to assist. These documents have been shown to the masses in various ways. Oral stories passed down by elders, writings found in vessels buried in caves, and paintings laid out for all to see in vast buildings.

---

4 NB When referring to TimeLines in a situation such as we are sharing, the dates are subject to the variables and variants of the decisions made by Mankind.

The current state of your affairs is being played out as planned thousands of millennia ago in the courts and chambers of the Anunnaki leader Anu.

These beings, including the Formless Ones, realised that the gold within your blood is of such a pure element. Plus, being the highest quality that, when distilled and ingested, creates such a life-force 'hit' of power, endorphins are released, initiating a re-generation that achieves cellular reversal in the one consuming it. This gold is extracted in the most painful and mind-bending ways that we will not speak of it on these pages.

We, the Lyran Narrators of Time, are perplexed, however. Your history is laid out in so many ways: in your horror stories, fairy tales, and the Hollywood films you devour. You have been given so many clues as to the devastation happening on your planet, but there has been an unexpected silence over the information. Is it because it has been dressed up as a story, or presented in such a way, that it could not possibly be true?

Yet, there has been a deafening uproar from those who will not listen, nor will they listen or even consider the possibility that this abomination could occur. Instead, they are denying and 'shouting from the rooftops attempting to detract and drown out the now-emerging revelations.

We are not saying that all that is being revealed is true. No, it would be wise to look at all information, consider its source, and ask why it has been given to the public eye.

There is more to share on where your planet is heading, but we will take a break. So let us go back to the Lyrans and see what has occurred in our absence.

.

Chapter Four

The Moderator
Synthetic Life

As Commander Sol and her two companions left the Private Review room, they were deep in conversation. Her Chief Negotiator, Nuex Del Aqua Loid, was agitated and causing a constant stream of air bubbles in his ventilator unit. He did not enjoy walking around as much with this old heavy unit, but unfortunately, it was the only one available. The news he'd just received did not sit well with his instinct.

The idea of the ship being infiltrated and someone or something having penetrated his defence shield was not what he wanted to hear. It was like a stabbing in his gut.

But he could not ignore it either.

Sending a telepathic message to his crew to begin an urgent and thorough manual review, checking all lines of communication as far back as when their sister ship left to find the young Lyrans mid-transmission, Nuex froze. It dawned on him that all commands in the last period had been delivered telepathically to ensure that his entire technical team fully functioned in this communication area. What if there was a sub-void tracker they had not picked up, hovering attentively, waiting for such a vibration? The Formless Ones were not lacking in tricks, and he had often thought it would be an excellent tactical manoeuvre to have such a transponder in the area to check vibrations. He had never pursued the idea as they were the only ones in the vicinity, he had thought. However, now he knew differently.

Changing the message for all to meet him in the interview rooms in twenty [5]centzph, he saluted the commander and went off to deal with the new information.

Sol Lrign was contemplative as she walked along the corridor towards the conical tower where the command deck was. So deep in her thoughts that she almost walked into her 2nd in command. "Juuls", she clipped out as she abruptly came to a stop. "Why are you not in the seat?" Then she became fully aware of the movement of her ship. "Juuls, why are we moving away from the Bitari-Furtim-Otiose instead of intercepting them as planned?" She knew that he would have a reason, a good cause, for changing coordinates without consulting her first.

"Commander, a necessary adjustment was required while you were in review. We have received a signal from one of our transponder buoys informing us that there are more ships present than what we anticipated dealing with. Until we know who and what is out there, including the Alliance, it was deemed necessary to shift our position quietly and gain a better perspective." He paused slightly before continuing cautiously. "I also intercepted these commands. They look to be from your consul; they have your insignia but are slightly different in presentation. It made me wary!"

Sol grabbed the hand unit screen showing the command sent from her console.

- Bear 5° starboard.

---

[5] minutes

- Proceed to come around, parallel to the Bitari-Furtim-Otiose
- Ensure we are close enough to board without their knowledge.

To the unaware, these would seem straightforward instructions from their commander, yet as her 2nd in command had noted, something did not sit right.

She stared at the commands sequence; clicking a few buttons, Sol could read the coding that created the image. There it was, the way that the first command was input, 'bear 5° star board'. These were words she hardly used in her instructions. This would take them well off course in a loop, and by the time it was detected, it would take them far too long to return to the correct line of travel.

"Find out where this originated, and you have permission to go as far back in the data as necessary. Use this override code," pausing long enough to write it down in what Sol referred to as 'old style' "Get back to me as soon as you find anything."

With that, Juuls turned and went off to uncover what he could.

Resuming her way to the lift up to the command deck, Sol Lrign began to scroll over the slight occurrences that had happened in the last couple of [6]periods. The more she mentally reviewed the mishaps and errors that had occurred onboard, the more she became convinced that there was foul play.

The question was, 'how do we get the traitor to reveal themselves?' Surely their intent must be pure. Otherwise, The Whittling would have activated within them also. A thought trickled quietly into her mind, 'perhaps it would be wise to lower the

---

[6] months

shield for a [7]lapzph or two, then if there were any who were un-aligned to the Lyran Cause, they would be revealed'... The thought hung for a moment or two as Sol began to play with the idea, al-most accepting it as her own. Then something instinctively with-in her screamed out in alarm. She'd had a telepathic thought dropped into her. The trigger of awareness was that the idea had created a sense of sleep or dream state in her. She did not react this way to her thoughts or pondering. More oft, she was apt to challenge her own thinking and concepts.

She immediately began closing her telepathic links and, in a manner of speaking, began to defrag her conscious and uncon-scious minds. Running specific commands thoughts through her mind using various patterns and frequencies, by the time it took her to reach the command deck, she had gained control back.

Her stance was relaxed, legs slightly apart, hands grasped be-hind her; Sol stood in the middle of her command deck. Looking at her command crew, she spoke clearly and deliberately. "You have 20 [8]minucentzph to close all telepathic connects with everyone and everything on this ship now." As she spoke, she hit a timer on her arm. Her crew were so familiar with her random checks on their awareness and readiness to hear and react to commands that they did not think to question or wonder what was happening. Instead, the entire command deck blocked their telepathic links and allowed their minds only to accept verbal and written communications.

Sol Lrign sent a blanket command, via personal consul coded to her unique manner, to all in her line of sight who were part of

---

[7] hours

[8] seconds

her administrative team. It was simple, 'we are under attack. Raise to stage crimson.'

No one reacted to what they read, remaining at their stations waiting for her new command. Sol sat in her chair, lost in the readings that the Organic Link was currently updating to her file.

Her lieutenant leaned towards her from his desk, "Commander, what are our orders? Commander Juuls has us moving forward till further notice from you. Do we continue or [9]?"

The concentration engraved across Sol Lrign's face slowly eased away, a slight grimace, "You deserve to know why I commanded what I did and why." Chewing the inside of her lower lip thoughtfully, she wondered how to put forward the knowledge that they may have a traitor in their ranks in a way that would not create an immediate panic.

Knowing that, as she'd always been honest with her team, she decided to continue to trust their integrity and trust in her by giving them the information she'd recently been made aware of.

"We have an infiltrator onboard, and they have been manipulating our conscious thoughts and many of the commands from this deck for the last few periods."

"From now on, we will be reverting to my 'old school ways' of written instructions. It will be considered treacherous if it does not have my insignia, and the messenger will be immediately apprehended for questioning!" "Is this clear?" Her words fell upon stunned ears, and judging by her crew's expressions, she could tell they knew nothing of what she'd just explained.

---

[9] to be ready for action

Slowly her crew responded in the affirmative. Then as she sadly expected, they all began to stare at each other as if to silently ask, 'is it you?' of the other members around them.

Attempting to stop all accusations or thoughts that may lead to the separation of the strong team she'd built around her, she brought their attention to the window that displayed the vessel they were imminently about to connect with.

"Friends, out there are a group of young Lyrans that have never accounted for the likes of us before. They have discovered many of the old Lyran outposts". She paused reflectively, then emphasised, "We are of those Old Ways; we are the ones from the 'Wars of Decimation,' suffering the total loss of our planet and our people, family and friends. We need to be a fully cohesive unit, ready for their arrival. "

"They will challenge us, not on the battlefield, but they will question and attempt to negotiate their way back to their ship. For we will have them empty the ship of all crew over to our vessel so that we can ensure the integrity of the onboard data and location devices we placed there so long ago in search of these that have now returned."

"We cannot," she emphasised this word, "allow distrust to come amidst us [10]tuvra or any other [11]vra. You trusted each other until a few moments ago. What has changed? Only the information from myself that we have a traitor or two on board our ship. Now you look at each other as if they are the traitor, yet you ate with them and laughed not a short [12]lapzph ago.

---

[10] today

[11] day

[12] hours

Sol watched as her words fell into the room and how the crew relaxed and returned to their former unity and tight cohesiveness.

Turning to the lieutenant, "In reply to your question regarding our course. Bring us to a full stop. Recalculate the distance between ourselves and the ship heading towards us. Ensure we are placed in a direct line of contact. Once we are again in direct line of fire and direct line of collision, anchor us in place and do not move, no matter what orders are given. Unless they come from me."

She walked back to her chair and took her seat. "Moderator, what do you sense about the upcoming tests for the young Princes? Will they know they are being tested, or will it seem as if they are being included as an integral part of our ship?"

The questions put to the Moderator, the most experienced in Lyran skills and abilities for the sectors, drew the attention of all on deck. The Moderator turned and looked at his commander, raising an eyebrow almost as in disdain to the question he began his reply.

"One should not expect them to capitulate, Commander. They have been through a few battles that many of our members would have experienced in their early days. As such, they are sharper in their telepathic and vibrational skills. In addition, they have an extremely balanced and tuned-in Mage with them, who has committed to protecting them." She paused, "Especially to the one called RaeNegria, which is strange as her loyalty should be to the Prince, chosen by the shard."

"I would expect nothing more than suspicion and wariness, to begin with. However, I would also recommend that you allow the incoming crew of the 'Bitari-Furtim-Otiose' to bunk on the same level and then allow them to integrate into our ranks. Once that is done, it will be easier to see where loyalties lie."

"I will then be able to fully ascertain their individual and unique abilities as they will be relaxed and comfortable with little to no suspicions arising. We can also expect the true leader to be identified by the Heart Stone Crystal once they are on board as the vibrational frequency will no doubt begin to affect them."

"I have created an array of tests to see the full extent of their abilities and to extend these well beyond what they believe they are capable of, Commander."

With that, the Moderator turned his back to her, continuing to enter coding to the consul in front of him.

Many of the crew and command team often wondered why Sol Lrign dWari allowed the Moderator to speak the way she did.

The crew felt this attitude and behaviour disrespected the commander and showed little concern for what was happening. What they did not know, or in fairness, had no way of knowing, was that the Moderator was, in fact, nothing more than a highly active and well-constructed Synthetic AI programme. The Commander had had the Moderator purpose made years ago to ensure that training for all crew, including herself or any other top-ranking officer, was achieved without leniency. No favouritism was to be allowed at any level of connection.

So while the communication between the commander and Moderator was stilted, there was a good reason. Sol knew that all would be achieved as long as the AI was not infiltrated, and as far as she knew, only three people on the ship knew the truth about The Moderator. These were herself, the old Commander Stranz Lith Hylrix and her 2nd in command Juuls. They were all aware that the rationale of the synthetic AI was built around the brain of one of their most respected Negotiators. This particular Negotiator had released his physical body during one of the many battles endured as they'd faced off with the Formless Ones.

It had been something he'd been working on, a system that could train all Lyrans in all Sector Training without the protocol of defining whether it was right or wrong. He calculated that if all knew how the other sectors fought, thought, and utilised their skills from Negotiations to Medical, then the fleet and her crew would be better off.

At his demise, he'd made Sol promise to continue his work. "Use my organic's if it helps. My mind has much stored within it. Put it to some use." Taking him at his words, the younger Sol had spent years perfecting the synthetic AI programme her mentor had created. Thus the Moderator was 'born'. A cyborg-styled machine that looked like a Lyran, with the knowledge of Lyra and, for all intent and purpose, was Lyran. It even had a sense of humour, albeit borrowed from the original Lyran it was modelled on.

But it was not a sentient creature.

It only had an awareness of consciousness, similar to the Organic Links that assist in navigating the battleship in leaping quadrants or realms over vast areas of the void.

This use of organic links was one of the main reasons why all the units and sectors in the fleet were so uniquely aware of how the other teams were in any battle situation. This enabled them to compensate or assist when necessary. It had become automatic, no longer thought, just felt, and this way of being had repeatedly helped the Ancient Lyrans defeat their enemies.

Until just recently!

Chapter Five

Bitari-Furtim-Otiose
An Initiation Begins

Meanwhile, the occupants of the New Alliance of the Lyran Federation vessels discovered 'something' sitting directly in their path. The transponders could not identify this 'something'. When reviewing the information from their probes, they didn't note data that indicated danger. However, the black matter pods and sound vibration seemed to travel through the surrounding area easily, highlighting a shape that prevented the resonation from travelling through 'empty' space. So it appeared as if their instruments and the read-outs from the transponders were at fault. But the various captains could not shake off the feeling that something was wrong.

With all captains or newly appointed leaders of the various crews now sitting back in the planning room of the Princes' ship, the next actionable step was being decided. They were still coming to terms with The Whittling and dealing with the sense of being in the middle of an agenda they were unaware of.

Brinthera scraped his chair back and stood silently; those close to him noted his stance, stopped their chatter and looked at him. Soon the room became aware of the falling silence, and those present looked at the cause. Once he had their attention, he began. "Since we started our journey, we have been beset with various attacks from without and within our ranks. I believe this latest event is not an attack". He paused, a frown slowly forming on his brow. He was aware that his words were not what the majority thought. "I believe, within the depths of my honour, that this truly is the work of the Crystal Heart Stone and perhaps the Ancient Ones of Lyra's creation. I have felt, as have others, a sense of home that I cannot explain. Like many here, we have no literal memory of our planet Lyra in its completeness. We have but what has been told to us. Yet in this place, in this Sector of Lights, I feel at home. Therefore, I put forward that we do not attempt to resist or go to battle stations on full alert. Let us, though, be prepared for the unexpected". He swallowed deeply as he knew the following words would not sit well with the majority sitting at the table. "Let us allow the Mage Sector to lead us with their insights of energy flowing around us."

He sat down hurriedly as he completed his statement and waited, facing those he'd addressed. He was so sure of his inner knowing that he would not give way to outward pressure that he could be wrong.

Around the room were noises of disagreement, of astonishment that he could suggest such a thing and yet mixed in the racket were voices that agreed with him. So the Princes held their thoughts and opinions while the others voiced their opinions.

When silence fell again, RexNā Loid DeAqua leaned forward towards Brinthera, "What makes you so sure of this lieutenant?" Her voice was deadpan, giving nothing away. "What have you discovered or come into the knowledge that the rest of us are unaware of? What has brought such enlightenment to you and a few others?"

RexNā was not attempting to deride or shut him down, but like any good Negotiator and Healer, she wanted to know the more profound knowing, the reasoning and thoughts that birthed these words.

Looking at his leader Rägẹ, Brinthera saw no judgement or, in fact, no encouragement at all. Realising he was on his own in this discourse, he focused on RexNā and began to explain how, when starting this journey, he had no thought or inclination to talk or mix with the Mage Sector. Yet he'd found himself in their group talks; he'd begun debating with them. During their journeying, he'd started to read the old manuscripts, where he'd learnt of the [13]creation of Lyra and the two over-souls. He'd discovered how the families had come about and how they'd initially lived in harmony before the Crystal Heart Stone had been found, broken into warring factions once it was discovered. Mainly as each Family desired to 'own' the huge crystal and the power they felt it gave, but they found peace again upon agreeing to share the care and protection of the Crystal Heart Stone. He'd learnt that once the Lyrans had connected to the vibration of the Heart Stone, many things had changed. Including their physical appearance and communications and the discovery of using energy weapons instead of constructed weapons, such as kinetic telepathic warfare.

He'd also discovered that the Negotiators were once just a single sector, but due to the enhanced genetic upgrades via the vibrations of the Crystal Heart Stone, some exceeded the basic negotiation skills and became masters.

---

[13]vol 1

More than this, he had learnt that the Crystal Heart Stone would warn the Lyrans of impending doom or calamity. It would also show them the great joys that could be achieved. It gave them a particular connection to the Creator Source of the Over-Souls that ignited their regeneration DNA.

The learnt ability to be invisible, to throw shadows and confuse their enemies, and the means to read an individual's energy without entering the sacred point of personal energy space, were all the result of connecting to the authentic Crystal Heart Stone.,

The main point, he told them, was that when the Lyrans came close to the Crystal Heart Stone, the individual would experience tremendous mental tearing or wounding if they had not done the cleansing process. This would ease and clear when removed from the proximity of the Crystal Heart Stone.

Brinthera stopped. His eyes still locked with his Prince; he waited.

Without missing a beat, RexNā called out for the Mage, "Mel-Eid, come to the Planning Room," keeping eye contact with Brinthera as she waited. Finally, the soft sound of the doors sliding open announced MelEid's presence, and then she stood at RexNā's side.

"Yes, my Prince, what can I assist with," the words were softly spoken, but they carried with them the warning that MelEid knew precisely why she'd been called and now was not the time to trifle. Although she loved and would protect all three Princes with her last breath, she was a Master Mage and that in itself was a position similar to the Prince, especially as the Mages were not of a sector. They were outside the sectors initially formed in the original Lyra. After the Wars of Destruction, the Mages became a sub-sector for those with gifts that innately worked through them. Such as intuitive gifts, healing gifts, and, strangely enough, direct communication with the Heart Stone Crystal. The Mage sector was a chosen sector. This sector was one where one could freely request to be released from the designated family sector and choose to enter the Mage Sector.

RexNā glanced at MelEid, indicated her to take a seat and asked, "What are the honest opinion of the Mages in this latest event and the current state of energy that we are travelling in?"

MelEid's eye's widened fractionally at the question. This was a first. The Prince was seeking council, not privately but in a war setting. Breathing deeply, MelEid closed her eyes and began to look back over the events. She allowed her energy to step into the past. To walk around in the present, tiptoeing not to disturb what has not been created, walking towards the future that was not yet formed, revealing a shadow of what might be. She brought in the energies of the Elder Mages and sought their voices, all in the breath and quiet of her inner being. Those ob-serving her shifted uncomfortably at the Mage's proximity or be-cause they felt this was a waste of time.

Exhaling loud enough for all to hear, MelEid opened her eyes and steadied her gaze. "My Prince, this separation of our people, or as the old Lyran captains called this 'The Whittling,' came, as we are aware, soon after entering this realm. We were guided to this realm. By the very interpretation and direction of the glyphs etched into the walls of this very ship." MelEid drew everyone's attention to the ancient text covering the room's walls.

Without pause, she continued, "Through the guidance and the downloads of the organic link RathVorx, the map to this sector was revealed. This ship is Lyran. The organic link was Lyran. It came with a Lyran coding directive, and we are here." She paused and glanced around the room. Her dark eyes finally rested where the three Princes sat, listening intently to her words.

"On a logical level, we should assume that the Crystal Heart Stone has played a part in our arrival. By the old stories and legends, we know that many Negotiators at the beginning of the shared responsibility of protecting the Crystal Heart Stone would become disoriented and, at times, become simple of mind. It was discovered that this was due to an internal desire to retain somehow the Crystal Heart Stone for their own Family and sectors. Once removed, they would revert to their usual way of life.

"Thus, we Mages created a technique, a process to clear the mind, the energy and the vibration of an individual to ensure they could stand before the Crystal Heart Stone."

MelEid, looked directly at RexNā and let the following words fall, "What we Mages have seen in this last event is similar to the events that occurred in Cave of the Heart Stone on Lyra. In deep sincerity, I would offer this guidance to proceed as if the Crystal Heart Stone of Lyra is within touching proximity. Prepare for an approach of the Ancient Lyrans, who may not desire our presence. They may consider us a threat, so heed these words. They will come, they will accept, and then, they will test and separate. Only the intent of heart will keep this crew together."

There was a deep silence as each person processed what had been shared. Yet, even those, like the Nelphi-Lexmai, felt the deep reverence for the Heart Stone that the Lyrans had and, perhaps for the first time, came to an awareness of why they fought to defend it vigorously.

RexNā rose to thank MelEid for her guidance, but MelEid was not finished, her eyes flashing as if a silver fire were dancing in their depths. She turned to face Ru Naal. "Adopted Lyran, and your sector, be warned you will be tested beyond your limits. The Ancient Ones know our kind have died at your clan's hands. They will see their blood on your swords and your hands. So prepare yourselves mentally and ensure you are purified with Honour, Dignity and Truth. The Mages will assist those who require assistance but remember your reason for aligning with us. So accept the testing but do not accept the pain."

It was then as if a wave of energy lifted from MelEid, and she seemed to collapse into herself, nodded to the Princes and left the room. Her team surrounded her as she retired.

The room burst into loud chatter, each trying to comprehend and come to terms with what MelEid had just told them. RExNā began to speak, but her voice was lost in the volume of voices around her. Finally, a resounding hammering on the table broke through the noise. Eventually, those present turned to see who was making the noise and why. Rägę stood by the table waiting, his face like stone, not giving anything away. Finally, when he had their attention, he sat and waited for his Prince to speak.

RexNā stood behind her chair and leaned her arms against the headrest. Looking around the room, she gauged the emotions. Quietly she began.

"I cannot ask any to do what I do not wish to do myself, so from this moment on, we are all at a level three alert.

Each vessel is to be in comms with us and relay, and every glitch, bump or anomaly they pick up on the receivers, transponders, and if any of the telepathic's sense something, then that is to be forwarded to us immediately. "

"Let us be frank, we all, especially the three of us," she included the other two Princes with her statement, "we all expected to be welcomed with open arms. Why not? The ship had been sent to search out the lost Lyrans, to bring back a Lyran with the markers for the next cycle of leadership training.

We allowed ourselves to believe we were fulfilling a dream journey. Yet now we are reminded that perhaps, just perhaps, we should be more alert."

"There are more things we do not know that may frighten us or encourage us, but at this moment, we are unaware of what the future holds." Her voice faded into silence, and those in the room became, if possible, more contemplative, each lost in their thoughts. The information received from MelEid, followed by RexNā, slowly percolated in their minds.

Their reflective moment, however, was short-lived. The sudden and harsh sound of the klaxon bounced around the ship, and the other crafts sent urgent messages for their leaders to return. Moreover, each ship and cruiser had simultaneously picked up a gargantuan battleship heading towards them on their long-range sensors. To quote a young ensign, 'Watching the ship approach was like watching a floating city approach me'.

The entire command deck seemed stunned into stillness. It was as if the crew had no control over their bodies as they stared at the humongous vessel approaching them.

Having arrived on the command deck, the Princes noted the lack of defence procedures. RexNā barked out a few commands aimed at the security and defence of her vessel, then at the comms deck to hail the oncoming battleship to declare itself or be prepared to defend itself.

The spell of the oncoming vessel snapped as her crew responded to her voice. "Shields at full, my Prince", reported the weapons officer, "plasma array ready to be deployed, contagion field ready to be activated at your command." The tension among the command deck crew was palatable, strangely no fear, just the taught stretching of nerves. Each member of the crew quietly waited for the 'go' command.

RexNā, Nigeria and Rägę sat in their seats, watching. Unknown to the rest of the crew, they had authorised a sub-light communication to be sent to the commanding officer of the approaching ship. This message said, "We are Lyran. Stand to and negotiate!"

This was the simple act of a ship's captain to ensure that their people would be safe. Of course, if it were required to go into battle, then that would be initiated, but first, always negotiate.

The Princes waited anxiously for a reply. But they would accept any form of communication from the oncoming ship, for although it showed all the outward signs of Ancient Lyran markings, there had been nothing but silence to their attempts of hailings sent by their communications officer.

Rägę lent forward towards RexNā, "My Prince, I believe we have made the required attempts at negotiation calls. Am I released to activate our flight deck and have them ready for defence?" He had pushed himself halfway out of his seat, ready to go and lead those under his command, when an intense wave of static sounded through their communication system.

RexNā signalled him to go, which, when seeing the signal, seemed to energise Rägę, causing him to move with speed towards the flight deck.

As she sent Rägę on his way, RexNā swivelled around to focus on the communications officer's desk. As she looked at him, no words were required. The Comm Officer and his team were busy locating the signal and filtering it through many algorithms to find if there was a hidden message. They found nothing.

All the noise that seemed to come their way was static, so disturbing that it penetrated deep into the cells of those who heard it.

MelEid burst onto the Command Deck, eyes blazing and in a highly frustrated state. She marched up to RexNā and eyeballed her Prince. "Can you not tell they are testing you? Do you not recognise the vibration of despair hidden in this noise?" The Mage flung her hands out, questioning the noise that flooded the command deck and the rest of the ship. "It is time to deaden the vibration." MelEid fixed the communications officer, "Counter the vibration with one of our own. Rebuff this noise immediately."

RexNā nodded her agreement when the communications officer checked, then quietly spoke to MelEid, "Thank you, Mage, but why the anger? Why the old ways of bursting in unannounced? Have you forgotten the testing? " MelEid took a deep breath as if calming herself, then raised her eyes to RexNā.

RexNā almost stumbled backwards when she saw the inner pain and tears mixed with blood coming from the Mage's eyes. "What! What has happened?" She demanded in a deathly quiet manner.

"My Prince, this sound, now silenced, thank [14]Pli`enti-ou, was not to disrupt you or the crew. But to inflect the deepest pain to any Mage on board. It is an ancient weapon to disempower us and put us, quite simply, in a state of comatose until the sound is negated."

"I could not afford to sit and explain, for it is so old that you are not taught this in your training. Mages have been pushed aside and ignored for too long. Perhaps now, you may consider that we are more than just an annoyance to you and the Princes."

---

[14] an ancient Lyran that help create the mage sector

RexNā Loid DeAqua heard this, absorbed it, and appeared to those observing that she grew taller and angrier than any had seen her before.

She walked intently to the communication desk and waved her officer out of his seat. Then, taking his place, her fingers raced over the consul and sent out a message coded so heavily that only a Lyran of equal authority could decode it.

"You have declared war. You initiated the battle, ignored our negotiation offer, prepared to come around, be boarded, and submit to Lyra."

A similar message in the common galactic tongue was sent as well. It simply stated, "You have declared war, prepare yourselves."

 While she was crafting her message, telepathically, she communicated to Rägę and RaeNegria to prepare for battle.

Commencing with an immediate torpedo blast of their plasma array to the oncoming ship's rear mid-section. They chose this area as it was the average area of flight decks and holding bays for fighter pilots and crew. If they timed it right, there would be damage and minimal harm to those onboard.

Without questioning the command, RaeNegria hit her consul and directed the attack command.

The blast shot out from them and reached the oncoming vessel in what seemed like a breath. As it hit, the entire crew of the Bitari-Furtim-Otiose watched the buckling of the sides as their weapon hit the exact spot.

RexNā breathed out softly. Hopefully, this hit had done extensive damage to the ship with minor damage to life, but it should have damaged their opponents' counter-attack.

Unexpectedly the sound of laughter and clapping sounded across their communication systems, and a voice greeted them.

"Well done, Lyrans. You have passed your first test. Prepare for docking. We greet you, young ones."

Then silence followed, leaving those listening with a sense of apprehension.

Chapter Six

2049

The Revolt

There is no sunlight to speak of in this timeline of your world. In this timeline, your scientists have created a filter reflecting sunlight out to the void. Preventing you from accessing its life-giving properties, thus creating a generation of beings dependent on daily supplements and an array of fluids intravenously ingested to ensure that their biology is sustainable.

The nanotechnology within their system is 'allergic' to direct sunlight; it seems the heat generated by the sun can disable the technology.

All life is sustained purely by artificial means in this year, twenty-forty-nine.

Interestingly we see that the remaining groups of Terrans or True Humans are now found in cloistered fortified groups as if in 'self-quarantine'! This is because they had separated themselves from those in the villages, utilising the inaccessible mountain ranges and forests, where various animals roam, as a natural defence.

What was once a domestic animal is now classified as wild and, therefore, unhealthy and untouchable!

Plants once considered nutritious, such as the common vegetable, are now labelled as weeds or poisonous. All food is to be allocated daily by the quadrant leaders, tabulated out and ingested under the watchful eyes of the council bonded. The augmented hu-man is not permitted to consume food grown from the ground or harvested from the waters, nor can they ingest animal or plant protein, as this will interfere with the computer running their system.

No one can afford to miss their allocated allowance of minerals and processed food, for the nanotechnology within their cells requires certain minerals and minute oils that keep them functioning. If these minerals and lubricants are not received in time, the nanites will instinctively turn on their hosts, consuming them to create the energy required to drive the power banks within the nanite.

Each augmented hu-man is programmed to believe they are still human, {this is because outwardly, they have not changed, they look the same as pre-infection, but their inner cellular body has undergone a significant change.} Therefore, they believe that the living beings (the uninjected) who live in the outer banks of society are wild, animated corpses that would kill them, the augmented hu-man, given the opportunity. If any of these augmented hu-man beings wander too close to the perimeter of the compound parameter, they will receive an internal shock. This shock alerts them and makes them aware that they have broken protocol and wandered off the set path.

Perhaps one of the most startling facets of this timeline is the manifestation of Agenda ±31 that you all feared in the year 2020 forward.

±·*We, The Lyran Narrators of Time, have used the number Thirty-One concerning the agendas of the Puppet Masters to indicate that there are many more hidden events and other plan's waiting to be rolled out. In short, it would be, perhaps, more accurate to say Agenda "30 to "35*

You, indeed, do not work! All primary industry is automated; you do not own anything yet seem outwardly happy. There are no family units! We observe communes with no vegetation, though they are sectioned into sub-groups to house those fenced within. Perhaps this *is* the culmination of owning nothing and being happy.

Yet are you?

You, the changed ones, have no inner consciousness, yet you still have the capacity to dream. This ability to dream assures us, Dear Reader, that the AI within you has not yet been able to completely shut down the deeper inner synapses or memory of the Terran/human brain! This resistance to complete shutdown is an achievement that shows the power of human beings.

We have observed in this period of twenty-forty-nine there are no natural births! Instead, we have located multiple buildings dedicated to cloning or artificially creating young humans.

So, it seems that the Formless Ones have still failed in this timeline to create a race under their control, being cloned or robotic and able to procreate.

Perhaps the nanites prevent this?

If the nanites prevent the ability to procreate, perhaps it is a side effect of the inability to identify as either male or female and thus create a bonding with which to sire offspring.

It looks as if the Formless Ones and Draconian Consortium have created their final achievement. To create a human species incapable of self-awareness and self-thought and considers itself the 'same' as others.

Thus, there is no desire to be with another or to connect intimately, for the mainframe tells you that there are no differences and that you are all the same. This non-gender identity removes any inner desire to achieve, attract, and better oneself. It has achieved the lifelong goal of the 'sausage factory human' for the Draconians

The only viable reason for the augmented hu-man's existence is for the harvest!

Once the being is of age, they are shifted from their current place of abode and sent to the Higher GateWays.

Let us explain what these 'Higher GateWays' are.

These buildings or laboratories are where human beings are killed, not humanely; let us warn you of that, for the human or augmented hu-man is considered no more than stock cattle.

Once dead, the physical body is cleared of the nanites and other technology. Upon being informed that the body is in a pure state, unable to infect anyone nearby, the Draconians or Anunnaki will fetch the body and drain its blood. The process of draining the life force and blood is the main reason for the harvest and is only attended to by those that the Formless Ones deem most suitable for this work.

As it requires an almost gentle touch to
1. sift the gold from the blood and then
2. Remove some aspects at the optimal temperature to ensure the highest quality.

Like the Anunnaki before, these vile creatures, the Anu Hybrids and Formless Ones, also require the life force. The gold is that life force, which is only found within the species of this planet. Your life force is of such pure essence that it enables the Anunnaki and Formless One's years of sustenance. This essence and gold purity are found nowhere else in the Cosmos!

It should be noted that there are no elderly living in the compounds. The oldest is no more than 25yrs. Yet if you were to look at them as if through a mirror, you would consider them to be grandparents. This is because the AI and nanite technology within their cells systematically harvests specific proteins and blood samples. Daily, the AI breaks down the telomeres in the cells to prevent the human body from accessing the potent life-giving energy of its own Terran/Human blood.

By creating people who see only what they are shown via a virtual reality screen permanently attached to their faces, they are unaware of the real world. Their eyes and minds tell them they are safe, well, and being looked after.

There have been multiple stories related to your people year after year Dear Reader, given to you as a warning of a coming world of virtual reality. In a world where you are so plugged in, where 'reality' seems too far-fetched. It is an experience that is uncomfortable and thus to be avoided by the illusionary 'reality' plugged into your brain.

This is the aim of the puppet masters to ensure that the invasive technology of the AI ensnares each living being and that everyone becomes increasingly dependent on this mobile technology. So that it becomes acceptable to have automated smart homes, that technology runs your life, to give you 'more time.' However, nothing is further from the truth!

Soon, you will note that they are encouraging you to become augmented. In other words, begin to insert bio-mechanical add-ons to your physiology.

Why not have a telephone inserted into your hand, a camera inserted into your eye, and upload your memories to the cloud to access later?

How could this be wrong? *Surely,* it is of benefit to you? But, as the person known as Schwab says, it is not the outward actions that change, for you continue to do what you do every day. It is the inside that changes. He has told you bluntly that he and his group want to alter your DNA, to remove free will and free choice. But will you note the threat to your eternal soul? Will you become aware of the subtle but forced changes being put upon you? Will you hear the subliminal messages being given to you that you, the populace that accepts the injection, will become the property of those that own the DNA changing nanotechnology within the mRNA injections and other 'medical' procedures they do 'for your good?'

The deeper they ensnare you, the easier it is to convince you that the world of AI is safe and the world in the outer realms is wild, unsafe even deadly.

Dear Reader, we have taken you into this future vision of your world to show you what your current world leaders are selling you into. They are, once again, being bought off by the Anunnaki, Draconian and Mantid Hybrids, with promises of longevity, wealth and even eternal life!

They have no concern for the living man or woman born upon this world's surface. All they see is more stock, propagating to fill the gaps created by those who grow old and pass over. When will you realise that each piece of paper you contract into gives them more and more authority over you?

Wake up, please, Dear Reader, before this timeline becomes your reality.

Your Heads of State have agreed and contracted to a host of binding, illegal and unlawful documents that will deplete the earth of its populace. Eventually, their statement of 'you will have nothing and be happy' will eventuate.

It will come to pass. Mainly because those of you who only wish to see the 'happy' events or the moments that are 'light' and 'love' deliberately avert your eyes from those who bludger, pillage and rape the land via the simple means of your agreement, by not standing and voicing your disagreement.

When you prefer cute images to entertain your mind over the harsh realities of life. When you freely choose to listen to the pleasantries and softly spoken words of the elite, governing classes that, 'everything will be ok,' and close your ears to the cry of the defenceless as they are pulled from their homes and deleted from the face of the earth.

When you chose to ignore the warnings of your peers that there was 'something' wrong, very wrong with the governing groups because you did not want to 'rock the boat,' you did not want to draw attention to yourself out of fear. Or maybe because you were unwilling to investigate the cause and effect of what was happening around your world. You chose, out of ignorance, to believe something that you were told without questioning the facts; you followed instructions with blind faith, even after evidence began to be disseminated by scientists and medical personnel. You chose to reject that because you were told to obey or miss out, financially and socially, so you slowly let the deception enter.

When those who belong to groups of 'Love and Light' enlightenment sectors embrace what is being sold by the dark energy, the injections, the separation etc., only because someone says to you that 'love overcomes and will purge all from your cells!' So tell us, did you ask them to show you the evidence of this 'cell purge' before, during, or after they did this themselves? Or did you once again blindly accept a person's words claiming something to be valid, even though they had no evidence of it working?

If you did, that was the moment you chose to allow the destruction of your generation and those that followed into a life of nothingness, for you chose to believe the lies of the Formless Ones hiding in the disguise of Light-workers.

You may say to us, Narrators of Time, that is a hard line to put upon us. We would never do that! We want to save our people and world, for 'we are one.' Our reply to you is thus;

When you blocked, ignored, rejected and ridiculed those who stood up and raised their voice. When you derided and detracted those who warned against the impending doom of the control of the elite puppet masters, this was your death thrust into humanity, and you acquiesced to the Puppet Masters for the sake of 'peace,' *for the sake of 'normality.'* It never came, nor was it promised as an actual 'thing'. It was alluded to, skipped over and half-spoken in conversation, a throwaway comment.

But it has never been fulfilled.

Your rights as Living Souls, of Living Men and Women, have been eroded. So eroded that many of you in 2049 cannot remember what it was to walk without your monitor tracking your every movement. You cannot cast your mind back to when you could sit close to your beloved ones and hold their hands or touch them with ease.

When, Dear Reader, in this timeline of eradication of society and compassion, when was the last time you kissed, hugged, held hands, placed your hand on the other person's shoulder in greeting or sympathy, or acknowledged their existence?

When?

You cannot remember, for if you get too close to the other individual, your nanites trigger in you, a pain trigger that keeps you an obligatory distance from each other. The thought of touch creates within you a fear so intense that it has the capacity to render you unconscious.

And this is how they control you now, through fear, through pain.

They have taken your fear and magnified it. Weaponised it, if you will. They use your magnetic toroidal energy to magnify and amplify the power of fear and direct it in the way of destruction.

Your world does not need guns, tanks, or knives as weapons. No, your masters now have trained many of you to become a walking-ticking time-sensitive weapon.

These individuals have no regard for life and no idea that life is a gift to you. If an individual is shown that they are breaking the codes and boundaries set by the Masters, these trained weapons lock onto your fear.

You fear being found out, doing something wrong, being on the wrong street, on the wrong day, or at the wrong time. You fear being in the allocation centres (which replaced your shopping malls and such) out of the sequential periods allocated for your set parameters.

These trained weaponised individuals will lock onto your   energy, magnify it, and enhance it with their toroidal field. Eventually, your body will no longer resist, and you will die. Your heart explodes within you, your lungs could cease to work, or perhaps your throat swells and closes over.

It will be different from case to case, but the targeted body will break down and cease to utilise life commodities given to docile and obedient slaves. Instead, it will create a surge of endorphins within the blood of such intensity that it remains there for a long time. If the Masters reach your body in time, they will immediately take you to the Higher Gateways, so the physical body is dealt with correctly.

Within this timeline of 2049, the paradigm you are in has captured you, locked you in, and no matter how awakened you become in this trans-techno-human body, they will know you and your every move.

Some do escape. A few fortunate augmented hu-man beings escape into the out parameters and find refuge in cities. Not many, but some find some release or detoxing of the cellular entrapment. However, they struggle, for the nanites within them fight consistently to return to the parameters they need to survive.

If able to remain out of the reach of the controlling wave technology beaming out from dedicated transmitters for longer than a year, the individual may have a chance.

Their DNA will not revert to their accurate original genome, but the nanites would have, after a while, turned on themselves for sustenance and destroyed each other. As mentioned above, the nanites will turn on their hosts for the protein required to ensure their survival. Still, they also need data updates and lubricants that are not found in the human body and require defusing every 36hrs. If they are not defused, their systems start to lag, which creates 'glitches' in the host's behaviour. So eventually, after a lengthy and painful separation from the hive or commune, the nanites will cease to function. Leaving the individual weak and open to infection, they could now become a burden to any who would find them. The person has now gone full circle and is like a newborn once again, needing a teacher to assist them in relearning logic, compassion, and awareness of self. This process, from breaking free from the compounds to expunging the dead nanites, similar to a toxin, takes place over a long interval, and the body undergoes an enormous amount of pain. Some do not make it, and those that do never forget the horrors of 'that' detox.

Now, the new being needs whole foods to survive, to rebuild the protein and the complex amino acids within the cells. So, the Terrans and other beings have remastered the art of husbandry with the animals and plants, creating a mix of food incorporating animal and plant protein and all necessary amino building blocks. This is administered over an apportioned time to ensure that the body absorbs the mixture designed to create the sugars and protein mix needed for the Terran and Human DNA strands, thus providing a foundation for new DNA growth.

Survivors

It is difficult to say how many from the original early 2022 timeline survived, of the original Mankind or Terran. When the law was passed, all those who did not take the injection of nanotechnology were arrested and punished. No one spoke of the culling of living souls, a removal of beings to secret places.

Many of the authentic beings of mankind chose death, and the corpse piles grew daily. Soon they surpassed the horrors of your old world wars and the Polish/Germanic or Polish/Russian wars of ancient history.

This site is unforgettable, yet it is required to be told, for it may assist you in turning into this timeline. Yet no matter how many were culled, thousands escaped into the wilderness, and their dependents are whom we speak of now.

These natural-born Terrans are the result of the living men and women who refused to become vaccinated, infiltrated, and medicated by the system in the days of yore. Though they struggled to survive, being hunted as criminals, as wild animals to be culled, but survive, they did. These incredibly robust, insightful Terrans/Humans did what they knew best. They turned to nature, to T'-Gaina for help, and she hid them in her bosom. They found the ancient cities made of stone, with temples with underground water, and they built homes and temples of healing. They gathered those knowledgeable in producing food, craft, teachings, healing, and so on and began the old ways of honour.

The earth also responded with compassion. She re-opened the doorways of Ancient Access to the inner worlds of Telos and Lemuria. Many Terrans and Humans stepped into this doorway and escaped. Others in agreement with the Telosians stayed above ground, hoping they could be there for those who found a way out.

These groups grew more robust and healthier; they kept to the forests, for they knew they could not defend against the puppet masters' weapons in the monitored areas. But suppose they came across these individuals in the woodlands or areas outside the designated perimeter. In that case, they could then lawfully and universally take them and attempt to work with permission to create a space of reverting the nanotechnology within them. This is not as simple as it may sound, as we described above.

So you see, Dear Reader, there are some highlights in the year 2049 timeline.

But we wish to focus on the central area of concern since there is no returning to the life you truly want when control is taken from you by those who desire to enslave you.

Allow us to take you inside the parameter of the designated areas of living. These places are sectioned into class-defined limitations. The Observers allocate the living quarters to those deemed worthy. To be seen as reputable, an individual must have a quotient of points or units assigned to their account at any given moment of the day. To gain these units/points, the individual must perform regulated check-ins for monitoring while being 'online' via the Virtual Reality plug-in to gauge the works or postings of other individuals.

If you are one of the individuals who gain popularity, you are moved into a higher or elevated societal living quadrant. You are then allowed to approach the Observers Portal to request permission to be evaluated to monitor and care for offspring. These children may or may not be genetically from your body, but if you are deemed worthy and suitable, you will be given an embryo to monitor within its casing. This entails 24/7 online recording of the unit.

If you are a single unit, you would be unable to sleep during this time. The rules stipulate that you must ensure consistent check-in's to ensure the embryo is secure and that its environment is at optimum efficiency till it is ready to be birthed. Therefore, it is optimal for a double unit or augmented hu-man coupling to be involved. At least one individual could be present at all times. This is to be done over and above all other obligatory responsibilities placed upon the individual. If your grade or popularity drops, you will be given an official notification to improve. The embryo is removed from the domicile if this notification is not observed. The individual/individuals are then removed from the quadrant. There are times they have been known to disappear completely.

If the individual could maintain the required 'work' that was expected of them on a given day, they are then allowed more 'freedom.' This freedom, however, comes with a price. This price means that you are now fast-tracked in the ageing process. You see, when an embryo is allocated, it is earmarked to replace the one monitoring it. This information is not known in the communities nor spoken about by the Keepers of Stock. Still, it is how they, the Masters of the Observers, maintain their viability of the quotient of the 'human' populace.

They have managed to ensure there are only a set number of beings at any one time 'living' on the planet's surface. They have instigated stringent blueprints to keep the number between four billion nine hundred million and five billion five hundred million, give or take a few hundred thousand, in case they require added energy or labour. This continual recycling of the human genome among the seven main centres of the planet, being seven hundred million per sector or landmass, meant that the Observers and the Elite Masters could easily keep tabs and ensure their product was kept at optimum condition.

What frustrated the Elite in [15]this timeline was that they were aware of the breakaway groups, the 'wilderness people', the untouched humans. They had sent squads numerous times to capture and infect them with nanotechnology within the monitored individuals.

Yet, no matter how often they tried to seek them out, the true mankind/humans evaded them. Free from the digital trackers of the old world, phones, digital cameras or any 'wifi' using equipment, the true Terrans (humans) were only trackable by utilising [16] the ancient world. This was highly used in the Terrans/Humans but had been forgotten by the Observers and Trackers.

---

[15] Remember this is a timeline probability. It may not come true, or only partially true... we ask you to look beyond the drama and 'normality' of the day. Look to the hidden agendas that are now being revealed by Truth seekers or in your world, conspiracy theorists.

[16] Utilising dogs and those trained in reading the earth to see where others had passed by, with the way the grass lay or leaf was bent... remember Terrans remember the old ways.

In many ways, Dear Reader, what we are seeing in this time of 2049 is the ultimate lobotomy of the human race. A systematic de-evolution of a race once so powerful and connected with the Divine Energy of the Cosmos, now nothing more than a commodity, a food source for a species that considered itself a higher consciousness.

We weep at the loss of the Terran world. However, we enjoy the odd hunting or training programs we, Lyrans, now do on this planet.

We bring our young Lyran warriors/negotiators and set them out to hunt the Formless Ones living among the monitored individuals. We give them tools to seek out and destroy these beings, our lifelong enemies. Often, this is done in conjunction with permission of the true guardians of the earth realm: the True Terrans and Living Men and Women of the Wilderness.

We aim to decimate the Formless One's stronghold, one creature at a time if the opportunity arises, more than one. First, we capture and contain the vessel (often this is a human body), which the Formless One is using. Next, we connect a complex system of vibrational cords to their being. We start slowly with a low harmonic sound and raise the harmonic frequency slowly until it shatters the bond the Formless One uses to tie itself to the human.

Please realise we have not given you the intricate details of what we do in reality but a comprehensive image so that you can, perhaps, imagine the more minor details.

When this occurs, one of two things will happen.

Either the vessel is, unfortunately, too far gone and is, in reality, already a corpse. If this is the case, we dispose of the corpse with honour and integrity. We are choosing to respect what was once a true living being/human.

Or the body survives but is in shock, this is where our Mages stand by, and they immediately place the being into a regenerative array field, where they observe, monitor and give assistance. The 'human' is secreted away to another place that even we Narrators of Time do not know of, for it must be kept secret to ensure that those remaining there, for relearning the ways of mankind, are safe.

Once we have separated the Formless Ones energy from the human vessel, we contain the Formless One in a bi-dimensional Plasma Field with a rotating frequency code that is altered consistently, making it impossible to break in or out.

This field is placed within a carbon-based material's secondary unit with the highest possible frequency.

It was what we placed in your world many epochs ago, which you call shungite.

We ensure this cage is activated and the frequency oscillates at alternate frequencies to the Plasma field. This is then put into an Organic Link operated destabiliser. We begin to reverse the energetic sequence holding the DNA of the Formless Ones, based on the knowledge gained over our years of warfare with these creatures, and we unravel them. Once we are sure that there is nothing but energy and intent left within the destabiliser, we eject this into a capsule, coffin if you will, and blast it into either a dying sun or a collapsing black hole. This will then lock it out of this sector of the multiverse and allow the Divine Creator to retrieve the capsule with the contents and return it to the originator of the Formless Ones. What happens between the Divine Source Creator and the one who created these beings remains known to only them.

Again this information is only part of what is done and achieved. We give you details of the puzzle and elements of the mechanics, again to hold still the more profound truth away from eyes that shall not obtain it.....

Chapter Seven

Transhumanism
The Deception
The Beginning of The Lie

Tell us, Dear Reader, when did the human race become so blind to the deception currently still being fed to the populace of the world? How did they not notice the illusion of fear creeping like a dark cloud into your lives in all aspects?

How did humans allow the infection of separation to become so rampant? Where were the checks and balances? Why did so many humans during those years simply sit and accept the standard narrative of their nation's leaders?

How did only a few hundred thousand discover the falsity of the actions and statements of the Heads of State, the Sector Leaders?

Why was there no overthrowing of the lies and deception? Why did the truth get swept away and denied?

Where were the critical thinkers, the voices of question and reason?

Did the gentle persuasion of those mind massagers, those crafted in the soft dark art of NLP and spell casting convince you the truth was the lie, and the lie the truth? Were the truth and your ability to see the lie eradicated line by line, option by option, hope by hope until you were hogtied and bamboozled without knowing how you got to be locked up in your minds, with fear keeping you there?

And yet, Dear Reader, the voices of resistance were there if you'd chosen to listen!

Thousands upon thousands of feet marched to a drumbeat, which spelt death to the establishment of the movement was allowed to gain ground.

Unfortunately, these voices were quashed, imprisoned, ridiculed, ignored and blatantly called fear mongers. Some of your forefathers' voices were among those that detracted from the truth. Others of you have family that remember these times... what do they say now?

The leaders of your nations came together with the purpose of a single man. To deprive you of all rights of a living being.

Did you ever stop and ask, Why?

You may have found the answer hidden in plain sight, covered in 'distractions', because they could not afford for you to think for yourselves. They could not afford for the people of this world to resist the set game plan that had been put before them to manifest.

The punishment, of the countries' leaders, for failure, was severe and unforgiving.

Those leaders who failed were removed and replaced with those who were often covertly narcissistic. Smiling, kind, simpering and *acting* naive in the face of old 'networking' systems. These new faces, primarily feminine (or have vital feminine energy), would cajole, smile, laugh, and tell you what you wished to hear—acting like someone who cared for the land and people. While in the background, there were those trained to use all manner of NLP, brain retraining, hypnosis via moving images, using the front pieces of the chess players, for they, like the behind the scene players, were themselves victims of unspeakable abuse, either physically, mentally or both.

These purposely placed leaders had one objective, Dear Reader, to entrap you in the web of lies. To keep you distracted until you could not determine which was the truth and which was a lie.

The propaganda plan was to berate your mind repeatedly with the same message, wrapped in different dressings. To instil fear so powerful in your psyche that you would report your neighbour, family member, friend or anyone you considered was 'breaking the rule' to the authorities. Done so you could be 'safe'.

The ones that conformed to the new narrative of fear all too soon created a majority. Those that resisted the change, being subtly and not so subtly forced upon the living souls of T'Gaina, were 'black-balled' and outed. Often those reporting, those who refused the new doctrine of injection, were family and friends. (As a direct result of the continued directed propaganda being spoken over the broadcasting options available.)

As a result, these non-infected/non-injected were rounded up, if found, removed and placed within the security of 'health camps' for indoctrination correction, and to receive the 'life-saving' gift of vaccination.

It did not seem to matter to those who complied with the status quo that thousands either died or suffered bodily harm daily from the poison injected into the body. All they wanted was for 'life to return to normal, allowing them to travel, socialise and 'be free'.

Unfortunately for them, this never happened.

Let us clarify this statement. The history will show, of this chosen timeline, that there was indeed access to travel, but as a 'compromise', the elite required paperwork to be carried, checked and enforced. As a result, 'normal' life became one of 'small freedoms' for which the majority were extremely grateful. Those who were compliant received access to the 'fun' in the world and soon 'forgot' the terror of being separated from family and friends. They let go of the indignation of being 'jailed' in their own homes for protection against something that was not lethal to the species of man.

In this 'grateful' acceptance of travel and access to 'normal' life, the elite began to work in the background, creating yet another crisis to bring fear and forced obedience from the masses.

Many did not enquire about the non-appearance of the elderly. Likewise, the masses did not seem to question why those with a 'life-threatening illness' suddenly became irreversibly ill and died soon after the injection and thus were counted among the dead of the 'dreaded lurgy'.

They believed the narrative that 'it was better for some to die' to ensure that the majority of the people survived.

Soon though, those who had been injected realised they were falling ill. Many began to realise that their personal data was being [17]wirelessly uploaded to their computers, phones etc., all with file names they did not recognise. [Think of how humans once tagged their pets with all the information of ownership, medication, address, etc. this is what these injected particles now do to the human species.]

All too suddenly, those that had acquiesced, given the authorities the rights of their personal lives, discovered they were no longer free. They could no longer do anything 'in secret' for they were tracked and monitored, and each detail of their lives recorded for anyone who knew how to access the data to read.

Whoever had access to their files knew;
- If someone was running a temperature
- Getting angry
- Oversleeping
- Depressed
- Making love
- Overweight

Indeed nothing was personal anymore!

This mass poisoning had occurred in humanity over a long and well-thought-out sequence of events, from [18]spraying crops to the particles deposited in the air. This meant that the earth's population had, unconsciously and yet somewhat knowingly,

---

[17] Please note this book while released well after the 2020-2021 experience of our world, much of this book was written in 2019 and early 2020. The editing was delayed, due to various reasons, and thus the book refers to things that may seem 'copied'. In my integrity, it is not.

[18] [18] Did you ever stop to ask why crop sprayers wore PEP protective gear when spraying food crops and yet the populous was told the food was safe to eat? Why do telecom technicians were radioactive protective gear when installing your 5, and 6G phone towers, but again the message is 'it is safe'?

breathed, eaten and absorbed various poisons over the years. Moreover, the toxic mix was activated by the injections and micro-doses of wave energy transmitted at high frequencies for short but regular intervals.

This was also why there was an assault on your minds to 'keep clean! For if you allowed your young to play in the dirt and build immunity, how would they become sick? If you allow pets to lick your hands and face if you use your hands for gardening and just wash normally, which leaves a small number of germs on your body, which allows it to fight the 'outside' germs to have a healthy immune system. If you allowed this, you would be able to defeat the coming attack on your bodies.

So they, puppet masters, used cleanliness against you, introduced hand washes and body washes that killed all germs you needed for immunity, so your body became weakened in the immunity system. You became your own executioners by slowly yet steadily destroying your body's defence system.

All the above led to a society that was controlled. Controlled, monitored and kept captive.

As long as the Watchers could see the hidden code of certification receipt of the injection, nothing was altered. If someone was found not to have the secret sequence tattooed on their arm, they were then forcibly removed from society to be reprogrammed. If the person could not be re-educated to the specification of the Formless Ones, they disappeared!

Only when they have been beaten (mentally and physically) into submission, causing them to give up hope and any semblance of reality, what is done to them is worse than what is in the arms of the injected. They are subjected to ongoing mental abuse. They are connected to machines that create such a dislocation of awareness within them that they eventually lose the ability to make a cohesive thought.

Once they are returned to the demarcated areas of the living quarters, they are less human internally and more akin to being a cyborg or automated beings. Their conscious mind has been abused and damaged until it shuts down to prevent total denial of self.

Part of the abuse they are subjected to is ongoing mental and visual imagery of the worse things imaginable. Then implanted deep in their brains with a mechanism, such as a minute mi-microchip computer which can be activated at any time, to ensure the individual never returns to conscious thought but remains in a state of idiocy.

These damaged beings are often the least cared for and often become the disposable cleaning units for society.

Their nickname among their monitors is 'vultures', officially known as 'Body Part Disposers.' Their job was to 'go into the buildings where the Watchers and Elite have been busy harvesting the allotment of Age Ready Humans to ensure sufficient gold and blood elements to send back to the laboratories for the Anunnaki and Formless Ones.

It amuses the Formless Ones, the Draconians, who hide behind their significant buildings with tall glistening towers within beautiful gardens. Surrounded by walls and fencing to keep the 'unfortunate individuals' outside, struggling to survive. It amuses them to watch abused and broken humans clean up the remains of other humans and not be conscious of what they are doing.

Their amusement arises from the fact that while they are untouched by the injections and poisons, they watch how the humans diligently line up and allow themselves to be harvested, to be transformed into something less than human, all out of fear.

You must realise that these Watchers and Elite, under the command of the Formless Ones/Draconian/Anunnaki, have not ingested nor infected themselves or their families with the same nanotechnology that the masses were forced so long ago to accept. They have remained as human as possible, for their masters cannot afford to be infected with the same nanites as their slaves. Those 'fortunate' enough to be selected to work in the barracks of the Watchers (or Elite) retain their 'pure' DNA for the duration they obey the whim of their masters. The moment they rebel, resist, question or even look like they are questioning what they've been instructed to do, they are injected with the virus and thrown outside the walls.

Let us pause here, stop and consider all things mentioned. It seems as if all is lost, with nothing to hope for. A black and dismal future... but we ask you, Dear Reader, to hold on. We must paint the darkest picture so that you can see the brightest light.

Lets Review

Let us travel back to a time when this world, described, did not exist. Where there was still hope, faith, laughter and above all, there was joy, the anticipation of life and freedom.

Let us step back through the portals to the year in your timing of 2012.

This year 2012, we observe great excitement for change. Many say it is the eve of the Golden Age, a time of great spiritual awakening. We do observe a significant shift within the energy. Indeed, many begin to question their existence and reason for being. The precarious balance of humanity begins to shift towards the positive. The pendulum starts to swing in favour of the *Federation of InterGalactic Governments and Unions of Freedom.*

We begin to see the rumblings of change. A resistance is wakening. This is not the 'woke' society that has surrounded you in 2019-21! No, this is a group of humanity acting and living as they realise the profound truth that they are Divine beings, connected to the source and have the absolute right to life and all that it pertains to.

The joy rising to the cosmos in the years of 2012 to 2016 is euphoric to the Higher Energies, not because they 'use' it, but because it creates the symbiotic relationship of Cosmic Connection and The Awareness of Inner Sight.

During these years, many come to the fore and begin to share truths. Many people have never done this before. It is as if they have suddenly been 'switched on,' and they have found their purpose.

Voices are coming through every arena, or portal telling of great things to come, how humanity will be able to stand in their truth and reclaim their I AM! Mankind begins to awaken!

Thousands of living men and women shake the slumber from their bodies and energy, awakening into consciousness and realisation that something is amiss. A shudder of fear runs deeply through the dark tunnels of decay where the Formless Ones, Anunnaki Elite Draco and their servants, the [19]lower Dracos, have become alerted and alarmed that their puppets, slaves and hypnotised followers are waking up.

They begin to counter-attack, for they cannot allow the reawakening to happen. Therefore, it is paramount to their agenda that humans are kept in a state of slumber, of being in a dream scenario.

---

[19] It is wise here to note that Draco's come in two sections. One is the Elite Draco, a hideous creature that is the manifestation of the Formless One attempting to give itself a physical form to operate in the confines of Gaia. Then there is the secondary Draco, these are the hybrid Draco that is considered much higher in rank than most forms of life but they are not as important as the Elite Draco.

They create a desire for gender equality, playing one gender off against the other. They 'exposed' the dirty laundry of executives and arranged for those willing to be bought or, should we say, the sleepers to be activated, to be placed in places where they would attract attention. There are investigations done on men, but the women who have done just as dark a deed are left untouched, left in power to manipulate and create a distraction.

Among the actual victims, decoys are placed in the mix. We Lyrans will call these beings 'placement victims'. These 'victims' start using the emotions and wounds of the female psyche to create a distraction around the world. This event brought an imbalance between the divine masculine and the divine feminine. The men among the abused are highlighted and then pushed aside as if to once more diminish them publicly. Asserting that manhood and masculinity are evil and femininity is good.

How unbalanced!

Eventually, this gender imbalance, the push for transgenderism and the many other names for deceiving humanity about their physical bodies grew to a crescendo. Then softly ever-so quietly, these concerns, along with the fears of climate control and other problems of society, were washed away by a new drama. This flu-type virus entered your world employing the means of biological warfare.

What was kept from you was that after a short time of exposure to the warmth of the sun and fresh air, there was no ongoing 'virus'. It died a natural death! That natural elements of nature could not only cure but decimate this virus for good! This was hidden from you, for it could not be told that your species had a possibility of survival.

But what did grow was the propaganda and the fear-mongering of those in power. The 'controlled authorities' used a few deaths of some of the high-ranking officials to push the fear of a new disease. The disease is so powerful that it seems to eliminate Influenza, Pneumonia, Bronchitis, Cancer, Heart attacks, and the Common cold.

This disease is made within a lab, under the direction of off-world specifications, using earthly products, but slightly mutated with hybrid spikes to connect to and destroy the human's immune system. A virus that would be later confirmed by your media as being a Bio-Weapon. Made by the same directives of those purporting to protect you.

They failed to realise that once released and exposed to the natural heat of the sun and dryness of the summer months, this disease would follow the same natural flow of all flu and other similar infections. It would die away.

But, those looking to bring mayhem to the world and remove popular governments from power saw an opportunity, a match point to mislead and misdirect the masses. In this practice run, they saw a blueprint for the future disabling of connection in humanity. In this blueprint, they can continue to erode and destroy the interfamily and mutually beneficial livelihoods you have with each other.

It was the perfect bed to plant the seeds for the depopulation of the world that had been delayed by a group of strong, determined people led by a unique being of Terran/Pleiadian blending that held the power of governance for a short moment of your history.

Now in the timing of 2017 to 2020, your world is in an uproar. The balance which was growing in favour of the truth and light of Cosmic Awareness is in disarray.

Many gurus and leaders of the 'Love n Light' community have been influenced and paid off to promote the injection and narrative of the governments. Many influencers of your time were paid to be seen promoting the injection of this experimental drug while not receiving it themselves. Followers of the truth, of energy, are confused as to who to believe, teachers long trusted are seen to be acquiescing, and other teachers known to be rebels are speaking out, resisting, while still promoting the Higher Self Teachings and Balance. The Energy Field around the planet is torn further and further as dissension between groups grew, and distrust abounded.

The Dark forces have succeeded in their plan. To a *point*!!

Using the narcissistic means of human nature, they have hidden behind caring and smiling faces or domineering, aggressive demeanours to ensure their agenda is carried out. They stripped you of your rights, and you begged them to do it. Each time they told you to lock yourselves away, cover your mouths and wear protective clothing, you did.

You were drugged and blinded, not by medication but by media. You gave their propaganda machinery permission to take residence in your homes and tell you what to do, how to do it and when.

You shut your ears to the truth. In fact, most of you feared truth and when those who opposed the way you were being treated and refused to follow the 'rules', you berated them. Families cut off from each other because a smiling leader who cared for them told them to. A news reader gave them the latest facts and figures of deaths and cases of a disease that did not exist.

The draconians focused on the light-workers, who became the easiest targets, for they wanted 'love and light,' they wanted to believe 'that we've already won,' so they stopped *doing* and stopped *critically thinking*. The draconian's infiltrated the community that thought they were connected to source, truth and love, and *oh, how they tore it apart!*

They used manipulation, fear, and half-truths that worked with gurus and spiritual leaders to mislead and misdirect their followers. These individuals prevented other Energy Beings and other humans of High energy from speaking their truth, calling them deceived or deceptive. Instead, they did what they could to hold onto their followers in *'love and light'* to keep their coffers strong.

But then things didn't get easier. Instead, they took more of your rights away. No longer could you travel or hold a dying loved one close as they transitioned from this world. Instead, you were locked in houses, compounds and hospitals. 'Give us permission to damage your pineal', they demanded of society, and society lined up and allowed them to penetrate their nasal canal and disturb the brain's barrier, thus creating a tear, thus allowing infection to enter in.

Oh, there was a resistance by thousands, nay millions of you, yet this was still not enough. Why?

There were those educated in the ways of political science and steeped in the knowledge of 'instilling better governance'. So, naturally, they resisted any and all who mentioned or commented that this virus was nothing but a scam. For these 'educated' fell into the limited vision arena of only believing what had been put before them in the form of others' interpretations and very little personal research. They were part of the oncoming situation.

A blindfold to what was coming!

An invisible wall began to be assembled between those who became convinced, through the mild and urgent NLP voice of their social media and agreement to the political narrative, that there was a deadly illness creeping around them. This wall separated these from those who refused to give up their right to critical thinking and genuine intuition connection to the source.

It did not matter how much evidence was collated by expertly trained medical or other experts or how the evidence was presented by those who investigated. The empty wards and high unused stocks of equipment made no significant dint in the awareness of those who had begun to accept the NLP information into their minds and were now on a journey that only a terrible jolt could free them.

They could not see that they had been fooled into believing that the deaths had increased. Even when dedicated organisations who record births and deaths to ensure the stock was accounted for had recorded the same number of deaths that had been recorded in previous years.

Although when doctors, and other medical personnel, were maliciously silenced for speaking the truth, the lobotomised humans refused to note. Such was the fear that was being implanted and acceptance of the 'new normal.'

Many truth warriors, the common man and woman, stood up to verbalise what was happening to expose and bring light to the dark areas, but they were shut down, closed, and censored by the agents of the Draconians. These puppets of the Formless Ones were doubling down on their efforts to remove all voices of integrity and honour. They did not care if the voice came from a cleaner or a president. (A few presidents were assassinated when they would not follow the narrative) They did not care if the medical personnel spoke out. If the truth was presented to the people, the draconian minions were instructed to stamp it out and shame whoever uttered the truth.

Thus the division began, the 'them' and 'us'.

It was as if the initial social concerns of abuse, climate change, starvation, and poverty no longer mattered to the masses. Now, they became concerned with masks, toilet paper, hoarding of foodstuffs and lockdowns while reporting those who did not acquiesce and toe the line.

The bridge between the two societies became wider and wider by the year of your 2021/22, such as the gap that families were shattered, unemployment had risen, and only the extremely rich could enjoy the pleasures of the 'old ways of travel.'

Borders were shut, only passable by ALWC ID (Automated Linked WiFi Connector). This invisible mark separated the 'haves' from the 'have nots' and kept the gap growing. Soon those governing large landmasses or continents began talks to ensure that no one could travel within a single land area or between intercountry or interstate boundaries without a slip or permission to travel.

This 'tattoo' became the mark that allowed you to work, travel, and purchase certain products that were not life-sustaining.

The tattoo soon became required in paperwork submitted to authorities. By 2025 those who did not have the mark or the certificate were being banned from town centres. In addition, they were being hunted down and arrested for 'breaking the peace,' having been reported by those who wished to earn credits to their account and have luxury items.

In 2021, of your earth years, there was a worldwide attempt to indoctrinate all humanity, by employing a 'vaccine'. The horror of this vaccine was that more than half of it, no matter who made the product, was poisoned. It was set up intentionally to ensure that the elderly, those who were 'handicapped' or had 'special needs', were removed from society. It was also given to those who were healthy and able to produce children and render them infertile.

The effects of this poison were hidden from the populace. But, some, if not all, awakened people refused to be silent and kept asking why the vaccine was a requirement. What was the benefit of taking it, what were the side effects, and why was it still in the experimental stages? But unfortunately, none of these questions were answered.

Similarities between the current situation involving the 'vaccine' of 2021 and the events that had unfolded in your war camps of 1941-1946 by the infamous 'Dr Death' were not identified.

These injections had a hidden agenda: to cull the human race and remove the 'imperfect' qualities.

There was resistance by countries whose medical societies had some consciousness to stop the continued rolling out of the vaccine due to numerous side effects and deaths. But, unfortunately, even with the resistance, vaccine injuries and fatalities soon began to outnumber the original so-called virus deaths/cases.

There was resistance from a large portion of living men and women, which held for some time until a new way of inserting, the [20]ALWC ID was found to be inserted into the human being. This was by raining it down on the populous through cloud seeding.

It was the realisation by the draconian minions that millions of humans had willingly handed over their DNA to unknown data banks while searching for lost families over the last decade that gave them the loophole to gain the genetic information for those searching for it.

---

[20] Automated Linked Wifi Connector

The minions who monitored these sites for the Formless Ones, while secreted away in their strongholds, in places like the Vatican City, the CCP, the Illuminati, the Anunnaki sitting within the gilded gates of royal abodes, and other organisations, were able to access this data and explore techniques for inserting their malicious mRNA into the genome of mankind.

Now sitting in laboratories around the world, this DNA was accessible to the puppet masters, for it had always been the soft approach to have the populace hand over the DNA in the absurd desire to 'know where they came from.' Now the Formless Ones were using it to search for the Golden Blood DNA from the Terrans hiding in plain sight. Living as one of the crowd, intermarrying and having offspring, these were now being hunted for their unique blood type.

They began working, devising and creating food, drink and other such products that would react to certain DNA groups. As a result, they re-created strains of illness that would have at one time been of no concern to humanity. But, due to forced separation and forced hand washing with highly potent bacteria-killing washes, the human immune system was compromised by consuming highly processed foods that were unfit for consumption by humans.

Not all were compromised, but a large amount of humanity was. Some fell sick quickly others took time to show the symptoms. Others had experiences of 'food poisoning' and recovered, only to find a deadly disease had corrupted their body a few months later. 2021 was not a year to celebrate.

What we find shocking, though, as Galactic Historians, is how quietly and unresistingly you accepted this culling. How you allowed the lies to be planted in your mind and convinced yourselves that this injection was 'the answer' when you, deep down in your gut, knew that it wouldn't be. We are astounded that you would accept something in its trial stages that had no objective ethical evidence of working and was linked to diseases in the past that still had no cure in your human knowledge. What is even more perplexing is that more and more medical institutions and top medical leaders were speaking out against this invasion of the human body. However, still, these concerned humans were ignored and made out to be criminally minded.

Indeed this was a dark and confusing time in humans' lives.

This time between 2022 and 2030 was a time of darkness, you may recall a time in your history that is referred to as the Dark Ages, where the church sent out its dogs, the Jesuits and their dogma killed, hunted, burnt, raped and pillaged all in the name of spreading 'the word of god!' This, my Dear Reader, was a time that could be called darker and more dangerous than that period.

During this time, there were those who escaped from the cities to the forests, mountains or wherever they could. But, for some, it was the sewers, the old catacombs, underground mines that had been closed, places where no normal sane-minded person would place themselves or their young.

This was no normal time.

Great cities were built under the noses of the informers and separators. The Formless Ones knew that the humans were escaping but could not discover how this was happening, for the disappearances did not happen on mass. It was one or two here, a family there, like water dripping down a drainpipe, some during the day, others at night. There was no rhyme or reason to the pattern, which caused the great enclosure to be built around the main cities of the lands. The Formless Ones and their cohorts thought it would stop the escapes if they locked everyone inside the enclosure.

It did not.

As more and more liberties were taken from the species of man as more and more poisons were forced into them till they no longer resembled humanity on the inside, there were a few on the side of the infected that woke suddenly and desired to change.

They knew they could not entirely prevent the ongoing changes, but they allowed themselves to mimic another great event in your history, the great wars and traders in slavery.

They gathered intel and arranged passage out of the enclosure by utilising their tattoo ALWC ID, inserted just below the skin on the inside of their right wrist.

It was observed by those escaping that these '[21]ALWACs,' as they were referred to, usually were able to assist for six months at the most, after which, if they refused the next batch of vaccines, they were rounded up and removed to camps for re-education.

Because of this, the ALWACs and the unvaccinated network worked within a system that meant no one had all the codes, information or network plans.

These were changed consistently to ensure that they could not give all the information if anyone was captured and questioned.

---

[21] code for the as yet still conscious, driven Vaccinated humans

With each injection intake and acceptance of the gene therapy they placed within you, your body becomes altered. Little by little, as they could not afford to allow an immediate change to the behaviour of the humans, the Draconians and their puppets infiltrated the food groups and waterways of the populace. Slowly introducing finite threads of nanites within spraying of the atmosphere, altering the DNA of plants and animals for consumption, by adding additives to the water, people began to be modified.

First small groups became unwell, with no logical or medical answer, and pushed aside because there, frankly, was no answer. Then, those born with abnormal genetic deficiencies created a new 'sub-group' of humans. Then there was a slow dripping of more and more children becoming confused about their gender.

There seemed to be a surge of high-profile personalities promoting how they allowed their children to dictate if they were male, female or something else. These 'elite' or privileged characters seemed to 'glorify' that their female child wished to be known as a boy and that the child was now 'legally' a male. But, of course, it happened in reverse as well.

Mostly confusion came about due to the mix of DNA inserted into the child via 'compulsory' vaccinations. This created conflicting biological information within the child's DNA, creating future problematic scenarios in health, mental and physical.

People suffering from deep trauma stored in their bodies over the years became activated by these new injections, which were now being 'switched on by excessive use of WiFi signals and bio-hacking from the companies that controlled the medical world.

The orders came down the line to push the non-gender agenda, to remove all identification from male or female beings. This was paid for by the Illuminati (in your language). However, we prefer to use the terminology 'Formless Ones.' They began a deep-seated attack on the minds of the children, increasing the systematic abuse of injecting a child with approximately 54 to 72 individual [at times mixed together to be viewed as a single injection] doses of vaccinations by the time they reach puberty or alternately by the age of eighteen.

The fluid carrying these so-called protections against illness is filled with all manner of diseases. Unnatural particles in the human immune system cause many of the so-called side effects of these protection protocols. Young baby male humans were being injected with female cells, which created a mixed message within the DNA. Young female babies were injected with male cells, again creating confusion.

Not every human grew up confused due to the nurturing of the adults within their village, but some did.

These were not assisted correctly, and through the depression that descended upon them, they either took their lives or lived a lie that made them 'fit' in the eyes of society.

We must clarify, in this instant, that there are those who are born, genetically and spiritually, as one complete soul. A balance of male and female within and present to the world as such, no matter the outer skin shell. These beings were once honoured by the villages and people as they could connect to the higher realms and be a 'go-between' for the human race and the Higher Energies. They were healers and seers, and because of these abilities, they were hunted by the Draconians and the Anunnaki. When found, they would be forced to work for them, killed or portrayed as so abnormal that they were shunned by society.

Transhumanism has been alive and well in the species known as humans for over a millennium. The agenda of the Formless Ones has been to fully transition the race of humans into a fully commissioned slave race where the male gender wishes to be female and the female to be male. In addition, many undertake life-changing surgery that renders them unable to procreate. Thus they add to the agenda of depopulation. This is no judgement. It is, however, a simple tactic of deception that is running throughout your species currently.

The Formless Ones want a subservient species and believe they can choose their gender based on internal feelings and social status. Unknowingly they allow themselves to be part of a slave race that gives up their voice of choice and free will, thinking they are in freedom.

We wish to state here that we do not care if a Terran or Human is born energetically female or male and is housed in a meat suit/body that is the opposite of what they know they are. Know that a true Terran will find their partner no matter the shape of the outer body. They accept that the shell enables them to fulfil a purpose. They do not revel in the 'injustice' of being born a certain way or not; they live their lives in service to the Divine and fulfil what they are here to do without the destruction of the gift of the body.

There is a realisation that even if they are 'in the wrong body', there is a way to adjust and accept their new strengths and abilities. Thus remaining in the full power of their lives and conscious connection to the cosmos and the Divine. A true shaman does not reject what the Great Spirit, the Universe, has given them. So, instead, they take what they are given and use it to the highest level of service.

We speak as such as we have upon Lyra those of the same gender creating long-lasting unions with each other and opting to procreate and bring into being the ongoing generations of Lyrans. We see no shame in this. We celebrate the union. We do not comprehend the willingness of a being to deny that they are human by removing any reference from themselves as being a living being. But then we recall that the Anunnaki, and then the Formless Ones, have been influencing this sexless agenda since cloning was instigated by Ninharsag. It is not your fault to be affected by this agenda. It is, however, your disempowerment and responsibility to acknowledge that when you resist others informing you that they do not agree and will not comply, you deny the same rights of humanity to them that you wish upon yourself.

It creates a dilemma within us as the Lyran Narrators of Time, do we continue to reveal the oncoming agenda or allow you to follow your choices already made.

We have chosen to speak and reveal.

Our reasoning is simple, either you believe us, or you don't. Now is not the time to cajole you and pamper your egos. Instead, it is time to create an awareness of the great tribulation that is breaking upon your world.

Thousands of you believe that only now, in this period of 2020 and 2021, has the great darkness come upon your world. But, unfortunately, it is only now that the planned agenda is playing out in full sight, and you have become concerned. Your babies and young people have been taken into the dens of indoctrination and willingly placed into the care of practitioners that inject over 54 to 72 doses of 'vaccines' in order to save them...

YET, none of the parents or elders will question why? Why do the young of the living men and women require so many invasive 'saving' vaccines? Especially when you did not receive this quantity, and you are strong, alive, and vibrant, and your immune system is primarily optimum.

The Formless Ones, Draconians and Anunnaki have been playing you for fools for millennia, and you have allowed them to do this to you, human.

Chapter Eight

The Uprising
When is it, Enough?

There is a fold in the timeline of your future, a timeline of great wonder and potential.

This fold is where the Terrans and greater populous of Galactic Beings, incarnated on your world, come together and rise up in one voice, one mind, and one heart, but more importantly, they rise with the same focused intent. Their intent is to create a single voice saying NO!

No, to the tyranny placed over you, creating blindness and mediocrity in your lives. No, to the lies that were being fed to you. No, to the unnecessary separation of families and loved ones. No, to the controls and limits created to decrease your movement and creation abilities.

Instead, you, the beings of this timeline, began to create the YES solution.

Groups began forming all over the planet, and you called your-selves the Common Terran. You created new ways to live. You took your power back and removed yourself from the systems that had held you for so long. You moved away from the financial support of the governing bodies and supported each other. You began to create the way of the Terran again.

It is this that we wish to focus on. There was a time when the terrible darkness was still a potential, and the acquiescing and blind following of the puppet masters is still running alongside this UpRising of Humanity. It is the positive input we are giving you. For this reality can become yours now!

Let us ask you, Dear Reader, when is enough, actually enough for you? When will you stop, and consider the reality of what is happening around you versus the lies that have been fed to you or the half-truths that you seem to accept so easily?

We ask this question because it is very similar to the catalyst questions put before the living souls in the years 2021 and 2022 of your history. It was when the race of humans became so 'weirded out' with the ongoing virtual captivity that they started to rebel.

So we ask you, what will it take for you to rise up off your bed, your chair, the place of acceptance, or 'being'. What will it take for you to connect and commit to the changes in your world? Let us be blunt. The puppet masters rely on your inability to change or resist. They rely on you following rules or being obliged to follow their *suggested* mandates.

We ask you, now in this book, as your leaders will ask you in the UpRising Resistance, what will it take for you to say Enough! No more!

What will it take for you to stop mindlessly obeying out of fear?

When we cast our gaze back to the timeline we are about to refer to and reveal to you, this unrest began the flood that turned into a tsunami of emotion and action.

Come follow us into the timeline and see what we observe.

We realise it is strange that we write about something that, in our knowledge, has passed many, many cycles ago. But for you, it is a present and painful situation of reality. So perhaps our words can bring focus, comfort and knowledge.

Many thousands of cycles ago, we Lyrans suffered a great on-slaught to our people, and we lost millions, including our beauti-ful home planet. We ask you to learn from our experience and to note that it is NEVER over until you give up.

Just as we were manipulated by thoughts and suggestions, subtly placed in our minds telepathically, and leaving them unchecked or not fully researching the points floating in our en-ergy. Just as we caused rifts between our people by judging and condemning, therefore creating a separation of 'them' and 'us,' we see this happening here now.

We see the manipulation. We see the trickery being spread over the minds and blinding the eyes of the people in this realm. The subliminal messages are sent to you via the screens of your devices and the words you listen to.

Your leaders have been trained in spell-craft. They use the lan-guage of the day to weave spells and incantations around you, leaving you in despair, mentally isolated, and fearful. This is why the governing language around your world is a singularly dead language, made up of strange words called English.

Yet, despite the melding of the olde languages and the cre-ation of 'English' (instead of remaining Celtic, Germanic, Norse, or Saxon), which enables them to bind you with the spells they speak over you, you are beginning to awaken and brush the webs of deceit from you.

We note how many of you no longer give the screens of your devices more attention and how you are reconnecting with T'-Gaina. Many push the limits, demand more freedom, and no longer just go with the narrative.

This is the beginning! Like any revolt or rebellion, it is done not by an immediate explosion but by connection, agreement and unity.

Humanity has begun to shake itself, to see past the trickery and desperation of the Draconian Overlords. The Formless Ones, the Anunnaki, are intently angered by your actions. They are pushing back and will force many to bend to their will. You know this instinctively, and yet you still move on. Your movement begins akin to a small tremor and builds until it is felt worldwide.

Humanity rises up like a lion that shakes its mane as it roars, notifying all around that it, the lion, is awake and about to hunt. What are you going to hunt, Dear Reader? This is war! Not something that is simply occurring around you. Either you 'action for' or you 'action against', but one way or the other, you will make a choice, and when you do, that balance will tip you into a camp.

We do not deny this uprising. This rebellion will stop and start as it gains traction. Yet, like anything that gains speed and is focused, it will not slow down on its own.

This moment in your timeline is important. It is where the tear begins. The tear is where the strength enters in. In this choice, this actioning of agreement, groups around your world start the exposure and downfall of the dark entities.

Are you aware of the numerous Terrans, Humans, and Galactics ready to rise up in a single wave? These many beings are seeking a leader to show them how. A leader is one who 'does', who no longer sits and wonders but gets busy doing, taking the action his or her belief requires. Then, the people are drawn into that living soul's energy, ready to raise their hands to assist.

Rebellion need not be loud and bloody. It can be quiet and internal. It is using your mind, heart and feet. Removing the financial support for groups that do not recognise your rights as living beings with rights. It begins by creating crafts and markets of exchange that support those who wish to live in unity and partnership with each other. No longer separated by colour, creed, culture, belief, diet, or gender. Choosing to see themselves as Terran, as Human, as Galactic living here with one purpose, to Take Back Your Earth.

How did we, the Lyrans, rise up? This is a good question! At first, we didn't. Like you, we fought each other and warred among ourselves for years. Eventually, ripping apart the fabric of our society, our families and our culture. Completely destroying what was once our sacred places of connection, we began to install and choose other ways of being, ways that were foreign to our lives. We noticed more and more Lyrans falling ill. Their minds became overwhelmed and disconnected from reality, changing before our eyes, turning into creatures we no longer recognised. Outwardly they looked Lyran, but inwardly all honour, integrity, dignity and truth had gone.

Our people were dying of manipulated minds. Minds which were feasting on hatred, something that was rare in our world. There was envy and fear. Parents turned away from their children and children from their parents and family. Militia groups were created by new groups of disconnected Lyrans and attacked those who wished to uphold the Lyran Ways.

These new Lyrans terrorised our people in the streets and dragged them to places of utmost horror. Often never seeing them again.

The majority of our people lost their connection to The Crystal Heart Stone, and there were only a few who remained connected to the Heart Stone and to the Old Ways.

When we became aware of the severity of what was upon us, we created resistance cells.

We fought back! Relying on the energy and resonance from the Crystal Heart Stone to infuse us and replenish the lost energy. We created new families and communities.

Many learnt new skills. Healers became warriors. PlaceHolders took up new ranks in all sectors, negotiators, warriors, healers and so on. Teachers put down their scholastic ways and became healers or warriors. Thus they learnt the sciences required to continue our ways. It was a time of coming together, relinquishing past offences and uniting as a single race of beings. We became Lyrans again.

This is what we wish to impart to you who read this. That you can become Terrans again. Forget your past hurts and disagreements with other Terran groups; remember the common reason why you are here.

Learn what you need to learn: to farm, heal, create with technology, map, defend, and teach.

Become what you already are and more.

Unite as a single-hearted being, no matter the creed or sector you were born into, only seeing the common factor, that is, you are here, of this earth of this Terra-Ven-Eiliesh-Gaina. Let this be your banner that you come together with. Rise and be strong. Defend when you need to defend, negotiate when required, and above all, be in Truth, Honour and Dignity.

As you learn from each other, as you force the external to bow to your collective power, you will see how the knowledge of natural and universal law is able to heal you and your land. When you allow yourself to be silent, mentally and emotionally, you will give yourself space to connect to the Crystal Heart Stone that resides here within your earth.

Your T'Gaina, as Lyra does, has a sentient connection emanating from her Crystal Heart Stone. It is this resonance that many of you resonate with regularly and tune into her voice. So allow her to teach you.

Safeguard this energy, do not let it be taken by the Formless Ones.

When you learn to connect to this vibration of truth, pure integrity and power, you will begin to realise your true potential as Terrans. Perhaps even awaken the dormant gene within you, with which to release you, once and for all, from the entanglement of the Anunnaki Lobotomy.

When you, the individual, awaken to the knowledge that an uprising does not start with someone else, it begins in your heart. Then you will begin to see the world in a new way, where the veil is lifted, and you see the illusion that has been stitched so carefully to ensure that you are kept deep in the illusionary world.

Now awakened, you begin to see the correlations between leaked information from those deep within the hidden elite and where you are now living. You will see how moving pictures, comical stories, fanciful space odysseys and imaginative images are perhaps more real than a story. You may see how this information is related to you via a complex system of information sharing, which is part of that truth.

Are you, in reality, more alive today than when you were brought innocently into this world? If you are, how?

The uprising begins when each individual stops, thinks and asserts the truth for themselves.

What is your truth?

Is it your truth to be corralled into segregated units or blocks of land?

To be forced to reveal the inner secrets of your heart to strangers?

Is it your worth and honour to be herded like cattle into places designated FOR or AGAINST?

When did you choose to sacrifice your family to the state in favour of personal gain?

Was it due to the deceit that was played out in multiple forms of communication, convincing you to do what you would not normally do?

Nay, the seeds for the many were already cast and sown. But even more, rejected this deceit dressed in colourful and attractive ways. It is they that have risen and quietly rebelled.

Forming groups in quiet houses, going underground, in a manner of speaking. Shunning the rhetoric of the day and bearing the lashes of hateful tongues upon their backs. Defying the mandates and curfews, standing in the open and speaking their vibrational truth, these few are the uprising of earth.

Your choice has always been with you; deep within your heart, you have always known to whom you will bow your knee. The Anunnaki or the inner voice of the Divine Creator.

There are those, who have defeated the Anunnaki before, ones who know them intimately, their comings and goings. These are the prototype of the origins of the human species. Some know these beings as Igigi. They are of the same planetary system as the Anunnaki, slaves and servants of these creators of destruction. But, upon realising they were mere cattle, load bearers, and there primarily to provide comfort for the Anunnaki, they too rebelled.

They rose up, destroying their tools of work. Then, ensuring they could not be put back into the fields or workshops, they determined to surround their so-called masters and hold them accountable.

So it came that the higher ranking ones, Anu, Enlil, Enki and the rest, agreed to create the slave race, born from elements taken from the earth, Anunnaki DNA and Igigi DNA. These were the 'ant's eggs' in the ships that the Terrans first saw when interacting with the Anunnaki so many epochs ago.

We tell you this to encourage you that these ones that hold you 'captive' can be defeated. Though it must come from a concerted agreement of all involved. One weak link can undo the chain of strength.

We will leave you to contemplate your place in history as we rejoin the Lyrans where we left them.

Chapter Nine

Illusion and Reality
Sol Welcomes the Alliance

Hearing the laughter echoing over the comms, a sense of bewilderment grew among those on the command deck of *"Bitari-Furtim-Otiose."* They had expected a response from those attacking but not laughter and certainly not a congratulatory message.

The three Princes looked at each other questioningly; with a slight head movement, RexNā indicated the others follow her. Then, standing, she moved off into the side room to consult.

As they joined her, she telepathically requested MelEid's presence as well; receiving the telepathic reply that MelEid was coming, RexNā asked all to be seated.

"Ideas, anyone?" She asked. "Does anyone have any idea of what just occurred?" Both Rägę and RaeNegria looked at her blankly and spoke as one in reply, "We know what you know, or less." MelEid knocked and strode in without waiting for a response; she walked to the side of the table closest to RexNā and waited.

RexNā looked over at her and pointed at the chair, "MelEid, what is your take on this? You are a Mage and have insights we don't have. Can you enlighten us on this juncture? Is there anything that we need to be aware of?"

MelEid took a long deep breath to calm her inner frustration at the young Prince leaders and to allow herself the time and space to remind them of what she'd warned them off when they had endured The Whittling.

"My Prince, can you remember the words I gave in the last council gathering?

Do you recall the warning I offered?

Did I not say, 'To prepare for an approach of the Ancient Lyrans, who may not desire our presence. They may consider us a threat, so heed these words. They will come, they will accept, and then they will test and separate. Only the intent of heart will keep this crew together.' "

"If anything, I would ask you to search within yourselves, within the teachings of your elders passed down to you all, and seek all knowledge of The Ancients. What is it that they, the Lyrans within the distant vessel, have that you seek?

Is it not the Crystal Heart Stone?

Perhaps they are more cautious of connection with ourselves, a younger or new version of Lyran, than they are, presenting new thoughts that differ from the old ways."

"Perhaps, MelEid continued, my Prince, there is no more to see than what they wish you to see. Therefore, I would advise caution but acceptance of what they tell only at face value. Look for hidden messages or meanings, but not in all things. You will know, you will all know when there is deception in the words you hear, for your resonance within, that which has called you thus far will alert you."

With that, MelEid sat down and remained silent, yet actively observing the three Princes. Maturity was etched into their features. Gone were the fresh, youthful and excited faces of their first initial expedition. But, though she had to admit, they had not lost their inner youth, which reflected outwardly.

It was good, she felt, that they showed both the youthful vigour and excitement of the adventure and the more resounding outward proof of bearing the load of responsibility. This developed trust and a similar mirroring of self-responsible action from those they led.

Breathing deeply, MelEid gently pushed out her telepathic energy to feel for any disruption in the vacuum of the void around the ship. When no interference was noted, she expanded out further and began to press forward into the oncoming vessel. Using ancient techniques passed down from Mage to Mage, MelEid melded into the psyche of those on the Ancient Lyran Ship. Feeling into the emotions and attempting to see what lay in store for her Prince and people.

As she gathered intel and prepared to withdraw as silently as she'd entered, she found herself surrounded by an equally strong, if not more subtle telepathic energy than hers. "We see you, Mage", came the silent voice, "surely you did not believe that you would just be allowed to enter, observe and leave without being noticed. The Mages exist, not just from your time but in all realms of possibility, and so our Grand Mage sensed you while you were tentatively reaching towards this ship. You have been allowed to enter, to see and note what is here, but when you return, you are not, under any circumstance, to report what you *know*. It is imperative that they pass the coming tests without being assisted with prior knowledge."

Then, to bring the message home, the sensation of a hot needle being pierced into the middle of MelEid's brain was delivered briefly, causing her to convulse and call out in pain.

The sight and sound of their Mage in pain was something the Princes had never seen or heard before, causing them to remain seated stunned! Then as one, they surged towards MelEid to aid her, only to have her push them away.

Struggling to sit upright in her seat, MelEid grabbed her head, focused her eyes on the wall in front and breathed strongly. Eventually dulling the pain and bringing her body back under her control, she slowly lowered her hands and looked at the Princes around her. "My Princes, all I will say is this, I am in good health. I have seen what I see, and my advice remains as I stated." Then, pushing her chair away from the table, she stood, straightening her shoulders as if to throw the discomfort off; she excused herself.

Watching her retreating figure, the three Princes slowly turned towards each other with a sense of confusion.

"What the hemi'Lck just happened?" Asked Rägę of the others, who silently shrugged.

Tapping her finger on the table, RexNā brought their attention back to the reason for being in the room, "We'll find out from MelEid what happened when she's ready to tell us, but in the meantime, we have a ship that equals our size and weaponry approaching us. In fact, they may have weapons we are not aware of. Therefore, I believe it best we remain on our guard."

She paused while running the process of words from MelEid in her mind, "I believe we take her words wisely." Then, locking eyes with Rägę, she instructed him, "Take your most trusted, alert them to the oncoming challenges of wit, honour, truth and above all to remain observant. They are to report anything that seems even slightly out of the ordinary."

Turning to RaeNegria, RexNā continued her instructions, "Delegate to whom in your eyes is most suited, the operations of dialect communications, ensure that your team can receive all communications and sift through for code or hidden messages." Again RexNā paused. The empty air weighed heavy before she spoke again. "RaeNegria, my friend, I need you to connect to the organic link and dive as deep as you can into the surrounding void to see where we are unable to and guide us as safe as possible into the docking. We cannot avoid this, but if we can gain any intel to use, then, perhaps, we may yet be of equal strengths."

RaeNegria paled at the thought of reconnecting to the organic link again after the previous experience but wisely knew not to resist. She was the only one with the skills and ability of the specific connection. Nodding slowly, she agreed to what was asked of her.

While they were in discussion, the command deck was under the watchful eye of Kanrabos, who had noted that there seemed to be a sudden increase of smaller fighter darts released from the oncoming vessel.

Instantly he placed the ship into Coral Alert, put defence shields up and placed their fighters on alert to deploy when signalled.

The Princes noted the silent alarm lights pulsating along the wall lights in the room while simultaneously feeling the gentle vibration of the linked bracelets throbbing to alert them to oncoming danger.

RexNā indicated they remain where they were, "We've left our captains in charge. Let them do what is necessary. If we are required, we will be recalled. First, however, we need to be with the crew and allow them to see we are unnerved and ready to battle, but ultimately, we are in honour. Then we will go to our command posts and continue as we have agreed."

They split off and walked through their ship, encouraging the crew. Conscious of the fact that the crew of the vessel had, within a short period, endured many hardships and close calls of battle. Many crew members had been affected by the recent Whittling that had surprised them. Friends and family members had been removed from the ship and sent back through the Sector of Light portal. This had left a sense of wariness among those remaining... Nevertheless, the three Princes were determined to help heal the pain and bring the crew back together. This current event could not be ignored, and they wanted to show their fellow Lyrans that they could depend on the three of them.

Many of the crew were concerned that the vessel drawing closer to them was an omen, an omen which was potentially announcing their demise. Never had they seen a battleship that looked as ominous as the one approaching them, even though they were in an identical ship!

For many, it was a visual manifestation of the stories heard as children, great ships that defeated the enemy of Lyra, whether it was Lyran or another.

These great Negotiator/Exploration battleships had been designed for travel and exploration over many multiple cycles at a time. Each vessel was equipped with its own decks of immense farmland to produce food naturally for the Lyran digestion, thus ensuring those on these expeditions would be healthy and ready to do what was required.

Although the young Lyrans were still at this stage unaware, each warship of the Ancient Lyran Wars was fitted with a unique and powerful means of travel minimising time, distance and space.

The clues to this hyper/dimensional travel were etched in the glyphs RaeNegria had painstakingly copied and recorded when first connecting with the ship back at the Outstation. Albeit, not all had been deciphered.

It was this that the two Ancient Lyran captains, Kanrabos and El Nareem, were still waiting for, this knowledge awakening in Rae.

The Princes began to gather their respective crew members in debriefing rooms, ensuring that each knew what to do and where to be at any given time.

Simultaneously the rest of the crew, not delegated to battle but other areas of knowledge, broke into organic groupings of skill sets. There were medical, technical, engineering, supplies, and so much more. The crew felt an indiscernible energy which seemed to fly around the ship in a tangible manner creating instinctive gravitation to their strengths.

RaeNegria called Ru Naal over to her consul. "Ru Naal, we are preparing for a battle we hope will not take place. Having struck first we seemingly have them at a disadvantage. However, they have responded unlike any of our training." She paused absent-mindedly, chewing on her lower lip, then catching herself, she continued, "Have you ever seen or heard of this style of interaction with an enemy or an aligned member of your force?"

Ru Naal's brow creased as he cast his mind over the numerous incursions that his people had had over the thousand-plus years of being in subjection to the Formless Ones. Recalling story after story, filtering each almost automatically in his mind with the single event that had just occurred. Eventually, he looked at Rae with a shrug, "No, RaeNegria, I can't say that I remember or have knowledge of this style of battle subterfuge." He paused as a distant memory wriggled like a worm on a hook, "B...ut,"..his voice drifted as he drew out the word, "there was one story that was told. It was during the time, just after the first attack on our world. Our leaders went on a reconnaissance loop around the farthest moon from our planet. They returned, their ship slightly damaged but with no loss of life.

The story was told thus. Upon the warriors' return, they told us how an enormous warship had crossed its path. Not believing their luck in being in a position to destroy a Lyran ship, they fired upon it. It was thought to be disabled due to the visible damage. Believing they now had gained ground and being confident that they had the upper hand, they went in for a kill shot. Then a twist in the story occurred, a smaller armed shuttle, twice the size of their ship, slipped out from behind this massive Lyran warship and struck the Nelphi-Lexmai ship exactly mid-deck, with no loss of life, but enough damage to prevent us from following them.

The hit came with a message on a sub-frequency. Apparently, the message was thus, 'Do not follow, in honour, we have not destroyed you, for we know your masters. For that, we are cautiously sorrowful, but if you now choose to follow, it will be your will, not that of those who control you, and then you will be destroyed.' Our elders believe this was the first time they interacted with the Lyran Code of Battle Honour.

Perhaps that is what you are looking for?"

RaeNegria's eyes almost popped from her face as she listened to the story. Then, thanking Ru Naal, she almost skidded down the corridor towards her study. Finally, she knew what had been eating away at her memory for the last [22]vra or two.

---

[22] Day

Sliding into her chair, she grabbed her notebook, recorder tablet and her prized possession, the book of Ancient Lyran linguistics that her mentor gave her. It was this book that had revealed the glyphs for what they were, the Original Lyran language!

RaeNegria flipped through the pages. It had to be here somewhere. Pausing, she punched a command into her consul and synced her tablet to it. Soon the screens reflected a river of glyphs being sifted through an algorithm she'd created to search, decipher, and filter out the connection between the order and style of the various glyphs.

While that was running, RaeNegria focused on the old book, continuing to quickly scan over the worn pages, running her fingers over the pages searching. "It has to be here,' she uttered in frustration at the empty room.

Dear Reader, we wish to set your mind at rest. Rae has not gone mad or retreated into a fantasy world. For you see, when she was in the organic link with RathVorx, she'd been shown the writings of the Old Ones. How they had developed a technique called 'Illusions of War,' an illusion of damage upon their ships to lure their enemy closer and then when there was no room to escape. The Old Ones would activate a mechanism which would jump both vessels into a dimension between this world and the next, like a parallel cosmos. In this sudden jump, their enemy would be at a loss and in a confused state, thus allowing them to decimate the Formless Ones or the ones doing their bidding. Once the enemy was eradicated, they would reverse the mechanism, returning to their original place in time.

This particular manoeuvre had won many battles in the distant wars, but the art and technology had been lost. None of the ships of the New Lyrans had this technology, or so it had been said...

It was this information that Rae was searching, for she'd seen information in the glyphs as she'd traced them while in her trance right at the start of their journey, and though it had stuck in her memory, they'd not registered until now. This unsettled illusive memory was driving her to find a solution, an answer to an unspoken question.

To an observer, it would seem as if the algorithm and Rae's hands stopped simultaneously on the same glyph and information, though she would say later that her hand and mind found it first.

Grabbing the information, she raced towards the lift and burst onto the command deck just as RexNā was about to give the command to go forward at full speed.

"WAIT", the words fell from her mouth as she banged the book in front of RexNā, "it's a trap."

Everyone fell silent, looking between RaeNegria and RexNā to see what would happen next, for RexNā Loid DeAqua did not look happy at this interruption.

"Explain." It was a single word, but it spoke volumes.

Getting her breath back, RaeNegria pointed to the book, totally forgetting no one else could really read what it said. "There, don't you see, they're playing us for fools. It's an illusion. They want us to get close to them, so they can capture our ship and either destroy us or worse.."

Rägę strode over and grabbed the book, "Rae, you forget, this is like a child's scribble to us. It makes no sense. You make no sense. How can the explosion and the damage we saw when we struck them with our weapon be a figment of our imagination?

How is this an illusion?" He tossed the book back at Rae, annoyed and just a little upset that he may have missed something important as the defender's section leader.

"Look, give me ten centzph to explain and then if you want to go ahead, then fine, at least I've warned you, but if we have one of their old ships, then perhaps we have the upper hand if I can get this mechanism to work."

Her last words grabbed RexNā's attention, "Mechanism, what mechanism? What do you mean? Explain in full." The Royal Prince's energy was back in her demeanour, which showed this was not a request but a command.

Rae gathered her thoughts and took a deep breath to calm her inwardly. Then, slowly, yet steadily, Rae began to explain how when she was linked to RathVorx, there had been a download of a memory that somehow lodged in her consciousness.

The memory included the data on how the ships used a dimension shift mechanism.

It was an engineering feat that took the ships from their position of origin into a different time-space continuum. In this new space of being, they would destroy their enemies and then return free of the wreckage to their first coordinates and be able to continue the battle.

Part of this jump technique was to create an illusion of the ship being damaged. The attacked vessel was to act and look as if they were unable to defend itself. Their attackers would fall into the web, being tricked into thinking they could get their ship closer to finish the destruction or capture those on board. As the Lyran enemy vessel became too close to escape, the 'wounded' ship would suddenly leap back into life and take the other battle cruiser into a time warp scenario.

"My book confirms it, and so do the glyphs I traced when we began our journey. In fact," RaeNegria suddenly paused as a realisation hit her, " I bet El Nareem and Kanrabos know exactly what I'm referring to."

At that, she locked eyes with El Nareem, who began to grin, slowly at first, then so widely it was difficult not to see a certain amount of pride in his eyes. Kanrabos joined them and was also smiling, "We agree with young Prince RaeNegria". He paused, looked at the Initiate Leader of the Families, and continued, "RexNā Loid De Aqua, she is telling you the truth. We have been waiting for this revelation of insight. For us, it is the key or signal that RaeNegria is the one we have been sent to protect and take back with us. She is the one of Future Sight... It would be wise to listen to her, for she may yet prevent an unnecessary dilemma."

The fact that he'd used RexNā's full name when agreeing with Rae made RexNā pay further attention. He was speaking to his Royal, the Family Protectorate, not just the ship's commander.

"Reverse engines. Take us back to where we encountered them and re-examine the evidence." The command was spoken quietly but firmly, and the great ship shuddered as it slowed and reversed its trajectory.

Rae quietly blew out a breath she didn't know she'd been holding. Then, looking over at the two captains, she nodded her thanks.

"My Prince, there on the screen, it looks like a double image." A young ensign delegated to reviewing the recording of their interaction with the other ship pointed at a paused image. "If you observe here and here, he used a laser to point to the area of concern, you will notice a shimmer, and then the damage appears.

Also, if you watch here, it seems that our plasma array did not reach them. The vessel was closer to us than our instruments indicated and positioned at least 10 degrees higher than the ship we fired at." My Prince, I believe we have been tricked with holographic imagery and a brilliantly played tactical manoeuvre on their part." The ensign finished his report and stepped back into the ranks around him.

The captains and Princes looked at the images before them and felt the anger, shame and admiration that washed over them.

Shame, for they had been outsmarted and allowed a sense of pride to permeate their psyche, anger that they had been outplayed so publicly and admiration for a move that showed their lack of knowledge but also gave them a great lesson.

"Come, everyone, back to the council room. We need a new plan." RexNā turned and walked from the command deck into the side room to take council from her team.

Pausing at the threshold, she looked over at the crew remaining, noting the Nelphi-Lexmai captain about to leave the deck to return to his station. She called him, "Ru Naal, you have the comm." Stopping abruptly in surprise, he looked over his shoulder at RexNā and then at the command crew, who simply looked down at their consuls and went about their specified jobs.

"Yes, my Prince", was the only thing he could say as he walked over to the command chair and sat down gingerly, half expecting to be hauled out at the last minute.

He knew this was a privilege and a test, one that he was grateful for.

Chapter Ten

Transparent Connection
Joint Forces

From her command chair, Sol Lrign dWari observed the slowing down to full reverse of the oncoming *Bitari-Furtim-Otiose*. She had not expected this change of direction yet. Frowning, she called in her moderator.

Waving her hand to the screen before her, Sol Lrign waited for the insight. The Moderator hid a knowing smile and looked at the commander. "What do you wish to know, that they have come to a stop? Waiting and watching us? Any of your trained pups could have told you that." It was obvious that the moderator did not respect the commander. Once they had been close, mentor and trainee, but then Sol had followed her mentor's request and completed the synthetic connections of the being that stood in front of her. Creating a more robotic than conscious being. Embedding the last remnant of the organic link into a system of computer nodes and automated data-processing systems. Thus in some manner and shape, deleting the 'Lyran' from her old mentor, leaving only the synthetic machine driven by the hidden consciousness of her old friend.

The Moderator, though, would never deliberately dishonour his commander, for that was not the Lyran way. He may not be forthcoming with information if there was room to wriggle, but he would never outright dishonour leadership.

This was the sign to Sol Lrign dWari that her old mentor and friend was still in that brain that powered the synthetic moderator. She would put up with the odd sarcasm just to be reminded that she did not know everything. Her old mentor had been fond of telling her, "There is more to learn, Sol, so much more if you would just remain open."

This was just that sort of moment where the obvious needed to be asked, but Sol Lrign wanted deeper insight. "Moderator, if I'd wanted a highlighted overview, you are correct; I would have asked one of my dedicated crew. However, as you are Chief Mage, Training Master, Tactical Intuitive hence The Moderator, I request and require your insight into the possible change of heart or realisation that the young Lyrans may have had."

She paused slightly to observe the eyes of her old mentor, looking for any giveaway. "What would have caused their delay in coming into our space? What knowledge would have caused them to doubt our intentions of friendship? Or is it simply they are overwhelmed and thus unable to move forward or back due to a sudden fear of what is presented before them."

"Do they not realise we are Lyran, and we mean them no harm? Testing, yes, it is required, but harm, no."

Bowing his head ever so slightly, the moderator acknowledged the rebuke. "In integrity, Sol, they fear us! I sense within the vibration that is seeping from their ship that they fear we will annihilate them if they get too close. I have a feeling the young Seer onboard has stumbled on the hidden text in RathVorx data. I also seem to remember you requiring it be etched into the ship's walls in case any of them knew the old tongue. Perhaps they have knowledge of the Dimension Shifter Mechanism and are now advisably cautious."

As he finished his statement, a low rumble of dialogue went around the deck. Everyone knew of the hidden message sent in their sister ship when it had been set out to find any Lyrans that may be out in the outer expanse of the void. To realise there was a Seer on board, one who could potentially communicate with the Heart Stone Crystal if they'd received the correct training, without the intervention of the Mages, sent a vibration through them. Would this lessen the power grip the Mage held on them? Would the moderator accept this newcomer or resist them?

Sensing the thoughts and feelings of those around him, the moderator raised his hands to quieten the room. Keeping his eyes on Sol Lrign, he stated, "All will be welcome on this ship as long as they keep to the traditions and ways of our people. We must not forget they are born out of time, reared in places that may have lost touch with all that is Lyran or not. We are to hold open the way of the Crystal Heart Stone to all and allow them to find their way with Honour, Dignity and Truth."

With that, he bent his head towards Sol and exited the room.

Strangely, everyone seemed to exhale in a single breath as he left. They all seemed entranced or powerless when the moderator walked amongst them. It shouldn't be so, but when an individual seemed to hold so much power, it was, at times, inevitable.

During the Moderators speech, Sol Lrign observed the mannerisms and subtle manoeuvres of the moderator and how this affected the people under the safeguard of the Lyran Protectorate. Being herself as the Commander in Chief of the Ship. It concerned Sol that many of the crew feigned obedience and seemed to become pliant when the moderator spoke rather than standing in their Honour. It struck her that there was a subtle yet definite questioning of her authority on board.

Perhaps Juuls was right. The traitor could be among the higher-ranking leaders. What if it was the moderator? Sol shook her head. She did not like where her thoughts were heading; this was not the way of Lyran protocol. This was the old way of deception and inferred perception rather than factual and honest communication.

It was enough that she had doubts regarding her moderator, but now she needed to observe and note variants of behaviour and how the moderator interacted with the people.

If he'd been infiltrated, they would need to proceed carefully. But, on the other hand, perhaps the distraction of the new Lyrans would be what was required to give the space and time to do what was necessary.

Sighing, Sol reached out for her personal recorder and etched some unique code into the database that only she could access. Not even the organic link had been able to break the code. She knew this definitively, for she'd asked for a thorough search of her consul to be done. Her code had been highlighted as unknown and thus suspicious. Unable to be deciphered by the organic link, which had knowledge of ALL codes and languages.

She realised that somehow she needed to assure the young Lyrans that they would come to no harm and would be a welcome reprieve to the Lyrans on her ship. A chance to catch up with the passing of time outside the Sector of Lights. Pondering this, she felt a gentle nudge, which she did not recognise within all her telepathic communications.

Sol set aside her recording and focused her energy on the nudge while raising an alert with both Juuls and her chief negotiator Nuex Del Aqua Loid, to be on the lookout if anything went wrong.

Gently she responded to the nudge, opening her telepathic connection ever so slightly. Enough to feel and sense what or who was attempting communication but not enough for a forced entry.

As she opened up, Sol was surprised to feel the impression of both the Mage and the young Prince RaeNegria waiting for a response.

Sol sat quietly in the energy of communication, not wishing to scare these young warriors away but not wanting to seem too eager to communicate. "Captain of the Ancient Lyran ship, I am RaeNegria Hylrix El Moa of the Family Hylrix El Moa. I am of the Royal BloodLine, and my markers are evidence of all I have achieved. I asked for a parley, and I requested our Mage to join this parley as I trust her. She saved my life, though she did not have to, and I... " Rae's telepathic voice dwindled into silence, realising she was speaking for the sake of talking.

MelEid and Rae knew they were taking a chance, but Rae felt there was more than what was before them. Yes, the gigantic ship had a potential weapon, and she'd stopped them from proceeding closer, but there was something else. A quickening in her blood and a pain that had begun to burn through her eyes and head. It had started slowly yet determinedly growing stronger the closer they got to the other ship. Rae knew she needed to reach out and find out why before they physically reached the battleship. Her body was vibrating steadily, and nothing the Mage did would stop it.

MelEid was confused and cautious about this symptom Rae was showing, as this should be felt by the chosen one, the one already going through the initiation process. Was it possible that two Princes could rule? This is why she agreed to come to the telepathic parley and create a blanket around them as they reached out.

All this energy of thought and worry wrapped itself around the two young Lyrans as they reached out to Sol Lrign, who felt and read their minds so clearly. Part of her wanted to calm them, and the other wanted to use this as a lesson in not allowing unnecessary information during telepathic communication. However, she did neither, choosing to remain silent, waiting.

Rae pushed again, this time a little more vigorously and with the authority of one who has led a ship full of Lyrans and won the confidence of others across the vast areas, sectors and dimensions of the void.

This was what Sol Lrign was waiting for, a show of authority, a knowledge of oneself. At the second push from RaeNegria, she responded. "Yes? I feel and hear you, yet I do not sense your Prince or other with you, only" she paused, "*your mage*!" Sol managed to make the last two words sound incredulous as if she couldn't believe a Royal would accept the friendship, council or any type of covering from a Mage. Again this was a test, how would both these young Lyrans respond.

Hearing the slight against MelEid by Sol Lrign, Rae nearly pulled back, but she chose to push harder, "This *Mage,* you should know, saved my life. I trust her, as I stated in my request for a parley. If you dishonour her, you dishonour me, and we have nothing to negotiate. That being the case, we will have to revert to diplomatic channels, which I fear will not bring the best solution for our people. Now, will you hear us?" Rae snapped her mind shut at the last demand. Sol winced at the sudden closure of the communication, but she was impressed. This young Prince knew her mind and, although a little unsteady at first, found her feet very quickly.

Meanwhile, RaeNegria looked at MelEid as they sat in the Mages inner sanctuary, the one place they both felt safe enough to create the telepathic communication. "Was I too forceful? Should I have made a gentler request?" she asked MelEid. The Mage looked at the young Prince, once again taken aback by the sudden flare of authority and resonating energy signature bouncing off her. Again the question of the Royal Lineage came into question. Had the correct Prince been chosen, or had the presumption of the Dolf-El Hyl-Pelagus ascension to the Leadership Role been too deep in the psyche of the Lyrans, thus influencing the Shard?

Bringing her attention back to the question hanging between them, MelEid smiled and shook her head. "No, young Prince, it showed authority and that you did not like to be played with. Let us wait for her to respond, for she will. There is now intrigue on her side of the connection. We will receive a reply soon."

Sol Lrign was contemplating the exact same thoughts. Here was a Prince willing to step outside her command to follow an unction deep within her to bring an outcome of peace. Not realising that everything up to this point had been planned by Sol to see how the young Lyran Ruler Initiate would respond to the testings and training of her people.

Nodding to herself, she knew she would respond to RaeNegria if only to see why she'd put herself and the Mage in a position of treason.

Ensuring that her connection with them would be undetected, Sol pushed towards RaeNegria's telepathic imprint. When it reached Rae, it was neither enquiring nor demanding. So Sol left the push hanging between them. It ensured the other telepathic opened to the push enough to let her in, so she could hold the conversation to her standard.

MelEid recognised this 'hanging' and cautioned Rae, "wait, my Prince, let me pick this one up. I will open the conversation, and you speak through me. I will ensure you remain intact."

Sol was not surprised to have this reception. In fact, it again proved to her that these two worked well together. They seemed to flow without knowing the true depth of connection between them.

She decided to continue the conversation. "So, young Lyran, what is it that you wish to communicate."

Barely taking a breath, Rae dove right in, "[23]Captain, you have equipment on your ship that is powerful or has a powerful generating capacitor. I know this because I have had increasing burning pain in my blood and brain since your ship came within viewing distance. The closer you come, the more pain I experience. I have not known this intensity before, other than when linked to the Organic Link on our vessel. This experience has left me, it seems, with the ability to identify similar energy. Yet, what I am picking up is enough to obliterate our ship, our people, and I have read this in the writings upon the walls of our ship; which I believe YOU", she emphasised this word, "set out to find us."

"I have the ear to my Prince, I can guide her to evade you, and we will attempt to find the Heart Stone Crystal another way to balance and create a new Lyra for our people." She paused, gathering her breath and attempting to calm the intense vibration that felt like it was trying to separate her molecule by molecule.

[23] Dear Reader at this point in time the Princes are unaware of Sol's ranking as commander, therefore address her as captain

"I feel in my most inner knowing that we are to link. Our ships are part of a whole, and your ways are to be intricately and systematically woven into the ways of our new Lyran way of being. That the combination of these will guide us in our battles and eventual overcoming of the forces we call Formless Ones."

At this statement, Sol Lrign caught her breath. It confirmed that which she'd hoped was not fact, that the Formless Ones were still hunting them. "Young Prince, you come with knowledge, ideas, solutions, and suggestions. Yet what is it you want?"

Rae was close to passing out with the pain she was experiencing, "Please, captain turn the mechanism off so we can come to you. I will not be able to travel with the ship if you do not. I am unable to stop the vibration even now. Yet I am the linguistic holder of ancient languages. I have the downloaded knowledge from RathVorx in my mind, and he has left a message for the one Juuls and Sol Lrign exposing great harm. I cannot tell you now, but it is in my mind. I just need to reach your ship." RaeNegria's telepathic link broke as she slipped into unconsciousness beside MelEid. Quickly MelEid picked up the connection and informed Sol Lrign what had happened. "We wait for your move, captain. Perhaps you will report us, or perhaps you will deny our request. We do not know your true stance, but my Prince felt you were the one called Sol Lrign which is why she reached out to you. I must end this now and attend to my Prince."

Like a phone call cut short, Sol Lrign was again left hanging on her side of the link, brought her telepathic connection in, closed it off and then felt around to ensure that it had remained undiscovered.

Walking over to the viewing section of the wall, Sol allowed her gaze to fall upon the great '*Bitari-Furtim-Otiose.*' How she re-

membered the [24]vras she'd spent in training, building relation-
ships that would take her to places where Sol believed she would
make a difference.

Almost unconsciously, she squared her shoulders, lifted her
head just that extra inch or two, and gave herself a mental shake.

It was time. Time to forge a new bridge of connection, one of
trust, which hopefully would bring enlightenment of what was
happening on her ship and how the young Lyrans had survived
the journey.

It was a time to flush out her own rats within the ranks and expose the growing darkness that had begun to spread like a fun-
gus among her people. She would not allow the Formless Ones to
take her people or her ship without a fight. Thankfully, she'd created the double illusion of the Crystal Heart Stone within its docking area over four periods and removed the actual Heart Stone to
a distance of three [25]zenro cycles from their current status. No
one knew of this, not Juuls or the old commander. Only her trusted Negotiators, currently on the shuttle that now housed the
Crystal Heart Stone.

---

[24] Days

[25] Measurement of travel - 1 zenro = 3miles/4.8km in an approximate conversion...
but could relate to a greater or less distance.

Chapter Eleven

Humanity at Risk
The Continued Race to Enslave

Dear Reader, let us drop out of the Lyran world for a moment or two. For the past few pages, we have shown you the darker timeline of your future timeline of '2049'. But, we have also known of a secondary timeline. Think of timelines that sit inside each other like a bag, within a bag, within a bag. These timelines are seated within the same time-space continuum for you to access, a link into a fold in time where humanity is rising up and saying, 'No more!' We want to go further back and forward in your time-line, not so we can paint an even darker picture, for you can do this yourselves. Nay, we wish to show you the hope you are to future generations.

So join us as we enter a jump station. From here, we will spiral back to the time you are aware of or perhaps have yet to know. It shall be as it is and all we can do is pull back the curtain to show you what is possible, what has occurred and why.

We are here, and it is human years circa 5000 BC or your definition of the Fifth Millennium. According to your historians, there are varying stages of civilisation. Some call this the Neolithic Age. So indicated due to the sudden appearance of 'civilisation' in permanent fixtures and farming.

Yet this productivity of farming, animal husbandry, growing of plants, and bartering or sharing of produce has, in fact, been occurring since early Terran existence. Probably in what you would call the Stone Age Period of around 3 million of your earth years. Again we would have to ponder the accuracy of this agreed date that your historians or gatekeepers of history have placed in your knowledge.

You see, we remember a time that would sit more comfortably with our truth, and that was a time when Terrans, barely a few Cycles in experience and learning, already had mastered the art of farming, building communities, and sharing what was not required by the community with those who had need of it, in exchange for other supplies. Your ancestors knew very well the concept of life, of the finer aspects of connecting to the Divine without losing themselves in the worship of a deity.

When we look at the stages of life so etched in the history of your world, we see the remnants of those Terrans who forgot who they were. The Neolithic ages of growing communities of a mere 12000 years of your history are those struggling to recall who they were and what had happened to them. They did not remember, and some groups devolved to re-evolve again over time. These 'stone age' people, these bronze age/iron age clusters that were discovered, were the re-emerging of the early Terran, now more identified by the name human.

There was a misdirection in your history. Deliberately so, perpetuated to keep the stories apart. The narrative of history tells you that you came from a primate genus, thus drumming into the focused point that you are nothing special, just an over-intelligent monkey.

However, this is difficult to explain or come to know comfortably in your consciousness when you consider the vast recollections of the pre-flood stories. Multiple pre-flood memories or oral history where the indigenous people remember the beings from the stars, coming and 'creating man.'

Where did they create man from?

Did we not reveal to you previously the birthing of Terrans from deep within T'Gaina and the breath of the Divine Source within them? So it stands to intuitive and logical reason that someone was here before the 'created man' was released onto the surface.

Then did not the Anunnaki determine to rid the surface of this planet of all life, and did not a few remain due to the intervention of one of Anu's sons? This flooding and decision to destroy the earth only came when the slave race was observed to be altered to enable the act of procreation. The son of Anu, [26]Enlil, who ruled in his stead, was angered and found this change an affront to his 'god-like ability to enable procreation.' Enlil and his followers then colluded to cause the destruction of your earth.

While Enlil's brother and half-sister, Enki and Ninharsag, fought amongst themselves as to who would rule, destroy or save the earth realm, the [27]Igigi were already informing the Terrans and other species to preserve themselves however possible. Enki seeing the 'coming of the end and how the Anu slaves were desperately trying to find ways to survive, grasped the idea of 'saving face' and began to also 'assist' by giving the access codes to two

[26] There are those that will say it was one brother and others who will say it was the other. We do not wish to create conjecture or debate but rather to show that the Anu were a tribe of beings capable of significant harm, selfishness and destruction, and there were also those of the Anu called the Igigi. Your historical or archaeological groups will say these Igigi are demons as they were servants of the Anunnaki. While it is correct they were the servants, they were, however, Anu's offspring and thus was a proverbial 'thorn in the side' of the 'pure Anunnaki'.

[27] Some would say that Enki assisted in the plan to save the Terrans and other hybrids on earth. We note in our records that the disenfranchised of the Anu race broke away and used their gifts of strength and knowledge to assist those manipulated and devastated by the Anunnaki's arrival.

of the arks to his personal clone slaves. Then he and his family fled from the earth, as has been explained in the book [28]prior.

This story, over time, has evolved into many different explanations of why there is humanity living on earth today. It also shows that you did not originate from a simian but from deliberate interference.

This interference that began epochs ago has never stopped. Yes, the Anu left willingly, but many humans or Terrans, Cosmic Beings living in this realm, have been tricked into letting them come back. They also left hybrids behind to give them access back when they chose. Though, in true diplomatic accord within the original 'Federation of InterGalactic Governments and Unions of Freedom', they would have to agree that as they willingly deserted this world, they cannot claim it as theirs any longer.

Unfortunately, they are wily, nefarious, and masters of manipulation and have managed to, with the aid of their now joint malefactors, the Formless Ones, find a way back to harm this planet and her people.

Over the thousands of years, you were able to re-group and attempt to re-learn how to connect to T'Gaina, to ascertain what it was to be of the earth. You managed to dislodge the firm hold of the lobotomy Ninharsag inflicted upon your people. You began to question what it was to be free, to be able to connect to the stars and travel to places unknown.

You built buildings, rudimentary buildings, as you'd forgotten much of what you had instinctively known as Terrans. Your language, once as melodic as the songs of the void, is now guttural

---

[28] Book 2 The Anunnaki Influence

and harsh to the ears. You've forgotten the telepathic way of speech.

You began to use the only things you had at hand to create tablets and writing implements, but these were not just rudely or bluntly made. You seemed to still remember the art of taking a fine quill from a bird or porcupine and creating a stylus. You recalled some of the languages of the days before the flooding. You drew and etched, and today, many 'educated' academia are confused and throw darts at 'what your words may mean, attempting to decipher your thoughts.

Some have stumbled upon the truths of what is written and told some of your stories, but not all.

It amazes us how so many can be so innocently led to believe something with a glimmer of truth but mostly conjecture.

As we watch the spinning of the toroidal energy of the planet, we see 'time' slip past you. Your evolvement rushes towards you, and most of you do not enjoy the process. You seem oblivious to the inner workings of the spectrum of life unfolding before you.

We note how there are self-stylised groups, individuals empowered by malicious back-room directives, which surface only to tear down and detract the groups set up by those of you to speak the truth and of universal ways.

So, here we are in the midst of what is known as the 'era of neolithic' people, and we observe that they are, again, separating you into cultural groups.

Set apart by 'intelligence' and ability as well as outward appearance. Those beings of a specific skin type are from area X. While those humanoids of another skin type and language, well, they belong in section Z. Area Y has the older looking beings, the ones who look like clones of the old stories... and so it is that we find there is still this demarcation of grouping that you guide yourselves with today.

You still, for some reason, do not see yourselves as a whole species but as fragmented.

Allowing your consciousness to be manipulated by narcissistic ogres into seeing the differences in each other as issues that cannot be fixed.

While we see you as the whole, as T'Gaina sees you as a whole species, a people able to meld and heal her pain, able to self-heal your damaged areas and above all, able to overcome the deceit that has been placed in your language of communication for far too long.

Have you ever questioned why?

Have you stopped through the ages of 'time' and honestly challenged the teachings you've been told to believe?

Why does anyone want to control you and those that live on this beautiful planet? Did you stop to ponder the revelations shared over the many years, containing the factuality given to you by those attempting to waken you to the truth? Or have you simply swallowed the subliminal messaging to drink, eat, be merry and populate the world?

Perhaps you have done this to the utmost.

By over-breeding, you have supplied the puppet masters with the crops they desire to fulfil their dreams and sustain themselves on [29]loosh stolen from your energy. (Note, we do not consider that you have over-populated this realm, we are reflecting back to you the familiar narrative of the population explosion that is fed to the masses.)

They do not wish you to defeat them and force their removal from this planet, not when they have managed to farm you for

---

[29] The life force of a human

centuries, with you being complicit in what they did for most of the time.

There is a race between the Formless Ones and the Anunnaki to rule this world. For there is only space at the top for one group. The one at the top of the pyramid can control the slaves and what is allowed to be maintained here. Even sold or transported off the planet. This can only be achieved with the agreement of the people of the earth. This is why you are currently being culled.

They are taking those that have memories of freedom, memories of knowledge, the awareness of personal empowerment and the ability to know one's own mind. Once they have deleted these beautiful souls from the database, they will be left with those who have malleable minds and wills; of those that have grown up with the whispers that life is unfair and they are owed things because 'it's so hard'. They will have the younger generation who believe that everything should be instant, that the wars were a tragedy, that the Holocaust never existed, and that the terrors of the past were fantasies of old people. Now the puppeteers will be able to more fully remould and refine the lies that will bind you. They will demolish any, and all religions except what they agree should be taught.

Good will be recast as evil and unnecessary, while abuse and pain will be cast, as usual, as everyday events in your lives.

There is a reason for this, Dear Reader. It is so that you become so disenchanted with life that you will willingly line up for something that will wipe your mind and give you some style of peace. This will mean that you will be plugged into virtual reality. A world that will reflect what you believe you wish to live, a 'happy' world, a world where everyone is equal, and there is no difference. Yet deep within you, there will be an awareness that this is not real; this is a lie.

They, the puppet masters, will do everything they can to keep you tethered to the screens dictating what you think you are living so that you do not see the harvesting around you, so you do not realise that you are living among the devastation of your planet. If you glimpse that reality, there may be a chance that you will revolt and fight back. They cannot have that.

So for the last thirty to forty years, they have been programming you through schools and movies, higher education, advertising, visual stimulation, sensory deprivation, and the supply and demand of various substances, including food. They have taken your dignity and your loved ones in wars and famines. They have created horrors that have made you hate each other, and still, you believe them. It is as if there is nothing that will waken you to the truth. It seems as if nothing will awaken you to the fact that if you all just sat down and refused to turn on your virtual ears and eyes. If you switch off the screens and all that is pumped into your cerebral cortex, you may just realise the world you live in is very different from the one built around you.

They cannot allow this, so the race is constantly on to keep you in one plugged-in situation after the other. Creating drama or fear is something to hold your attention so you don't see the flicker of shadow in the peripheral vision. It is of utmost importance that you remain plugged in so that you supply these Draconians and Formless Ones with the life force they can take without ending your life. With you creating so much energy due to hyper-intense cortex and adrenal stress, they can harvest what they want. Then, when the desire for blood is strong, they will take you; the saddest thing is you won't know. You will assume it's a 'natural' thing. Something is not quite right with you, but if you were unplugged, you would see the reality of being hooked up to cords and wires that are both energetic and real. Each syphoning your energy and psychic life force from you until you plead to cease living as your physical existence can no longer endure the pain.

This is what they cannot afford you to know or realise, and so they will create a detachment as you read this. 'Oh, this is sounding like a science fiction story!' 'This sounds like it has come from a film, a book' or 'it's been pilfered from someone else's theme'... but ask yourself, why does it sound like that? Why? Is it resonating an alarm in your consciousness? Is it not time to wake up?

It is the year of the fifth millennium, and it is the time of now. The illusion has not changed over time. It remains steady and determined to keep you trapped.

Will you allow yourself to wake up?

To rise from the state of being 'dumbed' down by the lobotomy of the ancients.
You have the Terran DNA!

Your people have the knowledge of the past deep within your knowing. Therefore, it is past the time of playing the game of choice.

So then, Dear Reader, the question must be put on the table, will you be one who will blindly follow the dictates of subliminal messaging, or will you be one who, figuratively speaking, removes the eyeglasses and sees what is before you? You will no longer be satisfied with simple, repetitive replies when you see them with the sight of knowledge and research.

Remember, the reason behind the repetitive messages or behaviour is to embed in your psyche a normalisation of otherwise abnormal behaviour or belief.

What will you do, Terran? Will you begin to resist the race to enslave your species? Will you rise with your brethren and put a stop to the energy-feeding supply to the puppet masters? Will you push the darkness back and bring the light of truth into your world?

Chapter Twelve

Suspicions Allayed
Rebuke, Guilt and Consequences

RexNā Loid D'Aqua had been feeling a little suspicious of the way that RaeNegria stopped the ship from proceeding forward. She knew her weapon deployment had landed well within the perimeter designated to give maximum damage with minimal kill effect. It was a well-planned and actioned shot. So why this infernal need to pause?

What did Rae mean about an illusion? Nothing this far from a Primary Outpost or Home Base would be able to produce enough power to create an illusion or holographic image that extensive or convincing.

Pacing around her room, RexNā Loid DeAqua entered various algorithms and equations into her handheld consul, endeavouring to see what Rae had seen. Not gaining any further insight, she lobbed the tablet on her couch and telepathically called for Mel-Eid, thinking that the Mage may have some comprehension that could explain this delay in what was otherwise a victory for the *Bitari-Furtim-Otiose* and her crew.

Realising there had been no response to her call, RexNā became more concerned. Two of the most trusted members of her crew were not acting, in her opinion, as they should.

Calling Rägę to meet her in the day room, she strode off to find the two missing crew members.

Passing the day room, she found Rägę and asked him to walk with her. They continued first towards RaeNegria's quarters. But RexNā intuitively felt she would not be in her rooms. Having searched in the other sections of the ship's recreational and private areas but not locating either MelEid or Rae, there was one other area she could be. But it was out of bounds, even to the Princes. Pausing in their walk, RexNā decided to go to the Mage Sector. So, they entered the hydro lift to the level where the Mages had set up their quarters.

Upon entering the level for the first time, RexNā and Rägę realised the immense size of the sector with a multitude of Mages going about their dedicated routine within the large corridor.

While seeking Rae and MelEid, RexNā had spoken freely and filled Rägę in on her suspicions and fears. Then, stoically he'd defended both Rae and MelEid, noting that they would be the last to endanger or turn against RexNā.

Strangely, when attempting to enter the Mages personal area, set aside for meditation, the teaching of neophytes, distilling tinctures, and recreational spaces, they were both blocked from entering. The guard bluntly informed them that no one was to enter the rooms until the Time of Silence was lifted on all Mages by MelEid.

Rägę went to grasp the Mage, standing by their allocated guards, who spoke on behalf of all Mages, to remind him of who he was talking to, when RexNā touched his arm and shook her head. "Leave it. We'll return later when their Time of Silence is done. Traditionally it is only for a few hours, and usually, only when the lead Mage is seeking guidance; thus, in deep meditation, we should honour that."

Rägę looked at RexNā Loid DeAqua as if she'd grown another head. She was taking this deliberate and perceived snubbing of her authority quite calmly. However, he now began to feel uncomfortable about the information RexNā had given him. What if RaeNegria and MelEid were contemplating something? Had either of them been affected by 'The Whittling' and it had not been identified?

Neither RexNā nor Rägę, however, were aware that as they walked away, they were being observed. Their energy combined had been enough to jolt MelEid into awareness and come to listen to their conversation. Not out of fear or suspicion but rather a curiosity. That curiosity alerted MelEid to surmise that the two Princes now harboured a loyalty concern against Rae and herself. She needed to balance the energy between the three Princes. She was not concerned about herself and her interactions with them as long as the three Princes remained united and strong.

They held, between them, the key to freeing the Lyran people. Their combined strengths allowed for a strong flow of energy and vibrational resonance that worked through them and into the ship and its crew.

This should not and must not be put out of sync.

MelEid slowly drew back to her own body and greater consciousness, ensuring that the young Prince lying almost comatose on the mat did not react as they disconnected the telepathic communication link. RaeNegria was convulsing and required full medical awareness.

Making the decision, MelEid called for the medical team to be summoned to her room.

She did not have time to ponder the effects on RexNā, as she would now be alerted to the fact that Rae was in the Mages quarters. Furthermore, MelEid was now increasingly aware that more than one Prince was presented with similar attributes, of being a chosen one by the Crystal Heart Stone. This would mean that MelEid would need to double her energy and knowledge to guide both on their journeys.

She also contemplated ways to prevent any fracture in the bond that had been created between the three young Princes.

As they approached the lift area to return to the command deck, both RexNā and Rägę were nearly bowled over by the medics rushing towards the rooms they'd been denied access to.

Without speaking, they both turned back and followed the medics who were given immediate access to the Mages personal area and soon arrived at the outer rooms of MelEid's chamber as she stepped out, making room for them. Then observing that both the Princes had followed the medics and were now in her personal space, she motioned the guard back. Now was not the time to push the boundary of who should or should not be in this sacred area of the Mages. She needed to ensure that RaeNegria was placed in the best care.

Staring at the convulsing figure on the meditation mat and then at MelEid, RexNā felt several emotions rushing through her body. First, her mind was bursting with possible logical and illogical scenarios. Then, fixing her eyes on the Mage, she demanded to know what was going on and not to leave any detail unspoken.

MelEid looked at her Prince, sighed and gently shook her head. "First, my Prince, remove the thoughts that RaeNegria has been disloyal. Then remove the thoughts she has been attempting to draw others to her side, which relates to the first request. Surely you know that she would rather die than subvert the mission or you?"

MelEid then deliberately paused, taking a slow deep breath as if controlling her emotions. She spoke carefully while looking at the young leader squarely in the eyes. "I care not what you think of me, but under no circumstances will you allow yourself to diminish my sector by questioning their loyalty to yourself or me. They refused you entry at my command. RaeNegria required space and placement to connect with energy beyond our ship. This need came from the onslaught of pain ripping her. This internal pain is due to her correlation to this ship and the vessel's approach within the void."

Turning to follow the medics who had gathered by RaeNegria and were about to take her to the Medical Level, she looked back. She spoke gently to RexNā, "Perhaps, my young leader, if you'd been more aware of your crew rather than basking in a small victory, you may have noticed how my Prince RaeNegria had been disabled. Unable to fully communicate unless utilising great stamina and willpower."

With that, the Mage strode past the two Princes to catch up with the medical team to ensure she assisted with the balancing she knew would be required shortly.

Both Rägę and RexNā stood in silence. Neither had been aware of the pain that seemed to be in RaeNegria. Now they felt the heaviness of guilt. The guilt of jumping too quickly to a conclusion without full awareness, but as RexNā would say in a later conversation, 'A battle was not the time for intimate conversation nor babysitting. If a warrior could not sustain their stand, they should yield it to one who could.'

RexNā still felt there was more to the story than what was being shown, and she was determined to find out.

For what reason did they have to stop their approach to the oncoming vessel for a start? What was causing the reaction in RaeNegria to the extent that her body could not function?

Was it the organic link?

Had the link between RathVorx and Rae been deeper than initially conceived, and had that perpetrated a further complexity of the consciousness than had been otherwise considered?

These and other thoughts began to run through RexNā's mind when she was suddenly interrupted by a transmission from the vessel they were heading for.

By now, RexNā had reached her private rooms and could take the transmission in privacy. Soon a hologram of Sol Lrign hovered before her, "RexNā Loid deAqua, I have commanded our subwave reticulating system be shut down for four [30]lapzphs. This will enable your ship to dock with ours in three lapzphs since you are a mere two and a quarter [31]zenro from us. After that, I will restart our mechanism. If you are not docked and neutralised in that time, I will forcibly transport your crew member who is currently in your medic rooms and carries relevant information required for this ship. I will no longer be responsible for the untimely damage that will be wrought upon your ship by the force of our device."

Sol ended the message without the usual protocol, not out of disrespect for RexNā but rather to see what would her response be. One of action or one relating to protocol?

Leaning back in her chair, RexNā clasped her hands together and pondered all relevant information within her memory. From The Whittling to the offensive manoeuvre of the Lyran ship attacking them, to Rae's strange behaviour, the deeper they went

---

[30] hours

[31] measurements of travel - km/miles etc.

into the Sector of Lights. Nothing seemed to stand out. All events seemed to be just that, events. Pausing her contemplation, RexNā began to flick through the data that had been down-loaded and saved from each of the ships affected by RathVorx's betrayal, simultaneously bringing them together.

Page after page flicked past, and then her brain registered something slightly out of pattern, just enough so that it would not immediately be picked up by anyone. She paused the screen. RexNā scanned the data and found a different code hidden in plain sight that linked RathVorx's memory download to Rae. She couldn't read it nor break the separate code, but she knew it was the reason for Rae's strange behaviour.

Was it also the reason behind the illness that had laid RaeNe-gria out, unresponsive in the medic unit.

The medical units had run simulations, checked her DNA, sift-ed through her blood and returned no new information. So Rae was still lying in a coma.

Checking the time since the message from Sol came through, RexNā quietly acknowledged what she needed to do.

Reaching for her communication link, she sent the commands to start heading towards the Ancient Lyran ship full ahead and line up to dock with them within two and three-quarters lapzphs. The instruction was received, and the ship gently shuddered as engines came back up online and the '*Bitari-Furtim-Otiose*' pro-gressed towards the *Bitari-Furtim-Karda*.

Reaching out to Rägę telepathically, she told him to send a message to the captain of the *Bitari-Furtim-Karda* that they would be docking within three lapzphs and to prepare for them.

Once she'd disconnected from Rägę, she gave way to the emo-tions building within her. Allowing the anger, fear, and confusion to flow. She shoved her chair back with a force that sent it crashing into the side cupboard, causing a split that would need to be rendered. She swept everything from her desk with a guttural cry, then raced to her water unit. In here, she could let go. No one would hear her yell or scream out her pain and bewilderment. She felt all the pressures of being the leader heavily on her shoulders at this moment. It was something that she realised in some ways she did not want, nor had she ever wanted. Yes, she'd known it was a possibility, but now with all the events over the last quarter Cycle, she felt overwhelmed. Her friend was ill, she'd silently been convinced that Rae was plotting against her, and the guilt she felt played in her mind and heart.

Chapter Thirteen

Deception
The silent enemy of us all

Dear Reader, we pause here to look at all we have brought to your knowledge.

We have given you The Agenda, in which we brought your attention to the devious plan of the Draconians and their cohorts as they attempt to wear away your energy, strength and well-being. We took you through a whirlwind of experience in the Anunnaki Influence, where we tried to throw light on why there are so many asleep on your planet. How many humans cannot and will not accept that there is a plan to destroy them, and why do they blindly follow the lead of the puppet masters.

In the first two volumes of this saga, we are attempting to bring to light the very depths of the deception that runs in the world you live in. But also to show you that it is just as deep in places you've considered sacrosanct. You have had teachers reveal to you the Universal Source's teachings, including how the veil between the realms separates the dark and light of your world. How the 'unique and special beings' are 'above question' or to be 'honoured' as they have become masters, etc.

Yet, we challenge you to question, always asking the hard-pointed and sometimes painful questions of who, what, and why these beings wish to communicate with you and speak to you. The reason for the challenge or questioning is none other than to ensure that you are satisfied that those presenting information is of genuine intent.

Indeed we were presented with a gauntlet of tests and a barrage of questions in 2011 when first connecting with Louise, then in 2017 when we reconnected and reintroduced ourselves to Louise and her grounder Heather. It is only due to their permission that we are currently writing this saga for those who resonate with Louise. She at any time could have refused if she felt we were of deceptive and dark energy.

We are, however, grateful that they found us to be of Honour, Integrity and Truth.

Deception is among the light workers of this planet and has been for many years.

The cloistered shadow groups such as CIA, NASA, Secret Service (SS) MI5, MI6, and Jesuits. Many other agencies in the USA, England, and the Vatican have infiltrated your minds and hearts with glittering words from pretty faces and adonis-type beings who lull you into a state of half sleep, half awareness, totally disempowering you in the process.

You believe you are empowered because they tell you. You are, yet you will not accept an alternative solution from another person who may present a different teaching or awareness.

Yes, you have recently begun to come together. We see you walking away from the so-called 'spiritual' life and centre more on the Natural Law or Divine Law as a way of living. Calling more on the Divine for your inner guidance is as it should be.

Now, the question is, can you join together across the lands and waters and put away your cultural differences? Can you put away your political and religious differences long enough to participate in a single-minded coming together in agreement to topple the puppet masters that control your governments? Can you stand as one, presenting a common truth that you are living beings, created by a Divine Source, out of the desire to give you life to create with and to enjoy, not to be herded and corralled as you do your livestock?

We believe you can. You show this in pockets around your world, some stronger than others, yet thousands of you are standing and saying, 'No More.'

Deception is created so that you do not see it easily. Dear Reader, those who 'act' on your behalf will dress this deception up in the clothes of 'caring for you'. They will present it as 'wanting the best for the nation.' Yet when you let go of the rose-coloured glasses, you see that there is a hidden agenda.

Your earth, as we brought your attention to it in the chapters previous of the year 2049, is not a pretty picture... but we will show you the alternative.

You have a choice to reject the creeping deception that is offered in many facades to cajole you into obedience. Obedience, that many have already complied to, complied as they want to dine, travel, marry, and 'be free,' but soon they will realise that they are the ones that are being culled. Illness will fall upon them, [32]*it may take a few cycles of your white sun, or it may be sooner*, but the sickness will enter their bodies and minds and destroy them. It will affect those you love, and soon families will be gone, memory on a piece of paper.

Others will be 'lucky' and refrain from being obedient. However, they may still be 'infected' with the deception as they wish to keep their jobs in order to pay bills and live life, so these few will only half-heartedly acquiesce and do as they are told. Still, they will be pushed to the outskirts, to employment only suitable for those wishing to survive.

Then there will be those who have separated themselves, kept away from all the devious infiltrations of the media, medical and other ways of the puppet masters. These will be strong in body and mind. The puppet masters will call these, "Come, we will give you mansions, unending food supply. All we want is for you to do work in the uncontaminated areas." The *clean areas* where they live. You see, the puppet masters will not want to do their own work, but they will not like those who carry the culling sickness within their blood to be around them, either. Thus they will seek out those wise enough to avoid this infection via intravenous injection.

Herein lies the deception they will promise you all. As the Anu pledged to the Terran until the [33]Terran forgot who they were. They became comfortable with their surroundings and were trapped until they woke up far too late to alter anything except create a diversion for a few of their young people to escape to the mountains.

---

[32] This comment about circling around our white sun is written with a hint of sarcasm, as the Lyrans are fully aware our heliocentric education of the earth, sun and solar system are far from the truth.

[33] Refer to Vol 2 Anunnaki Influence

This ongoing saga is not to place fear within you but to show you that life as you know it is on a cycle of repeat, and unless you alter the outcome, many will be re-lobotomised and lose their will again to choose sovereignty.

We ask that you do not pass up the story, put the book down and ignore the message, but instead hold fast. Our saga, the story, is not yet done.

We have much to reveal and to show you how the Formless Ones can be diverted and defeated if you are willing to listen. Yes, the story may be extended and distracting, but our journeys back and forth have rhyme and reason. If you read the hidden signs and open your energy to the light of the Crystal Heart Stone, you may just recognise the vibration of healing resonating at your frequency.

Come, let us travel now. Let us leave RexNā Loid deAqua to her healing, and we will return later. Let's instead visit a time that is not unimaginable, a time that is within your children's life span, a moment of reflection into the year 2049.

Yes, we realise we have described a grim and evil viewing of this date, but we ask you to trust us. We have more to show you. A brighter option, which gives your species energy of new beginnings. For most of you reading this saga, this is a time that you will not know or live in. But, perhaps energetically, you will be aware of it.

We share our Oral and Written Chronicles with you, not for entertainment but so that you can read between the lines or at face value and discover ways to override the inserted manipulation, the overlaid dogma and untruths and overcome, rising back to the fullness of your true potential.

If you saw who you are deep within your memories and distant past, you would know we are your friends.

It is perhaps the most challenging thing in your experience to accept that you have been deceived by those you trust. That a deep deception has worked its way through your life, social structure and educational means to the point where you feel unable to trust anyone.

Yet we say to you, there is hope!

There is a light that will come, and you will see. For those of you who trust and defy this draconian way of being, you will see the light and experience the return of self-honour and dignity.

Just hold on a few more days, weeks, and yes, a turning of two of your earth years.

It is best to remind yourselves, Dear Readers, that you live within timelines. A dream that exists within another dream. You have been told many things by ourselves within these pages and by many other voices.

Often there is a deluge of information which can become disconcerting, distracting and even disheartening. But, naturally, you want to believe the good and honourable, though it seems to crawl through the mists of time to arrive at your present.

To this, we say, be joyful.

The inner being, the eternal part of you, will respond to the truth of the highest declaration. Do not wait for mere humanity to dictate what is right or wrong when you intuitively and instinctively know what should be done. When you remove your consent and no longer agree to the contracts and begin to live peaceably with each other, giving no reason for another to accost you or do you harm, you begin to disempower the puppet masters. When you start questioning what they tell you, you find the deception revealed in many ways. Education is no longer equitable, finance becomes illusionary, and your health system holds no attraction to you, as awakened Terrans, Lyrans and Cosmic Beings are driven to create a community that serves each other. Not for gain but for growth and sustained living.

Chapter Fourteen

2049 option 2

When the Darkness breaks, Light surrounds

We need not explain where we are, Dear Reader, for you will note that we are in your timeline once more.

Once again, we stand in your era of 2021, where the drama of living is still being played out.   We, however, ask you to jump forward a mere twenty-eight years. So come step into the portal and let us go, do not fear what you will find there, for all elements that will be revealed before you are for your knowledge.

Do you observe the swirling colours as we travel through the various portals, backwards and forwards on your timelines?

Have you been aware of the fluctuations, the hiccups in the folds as we traverse them? Have you pondered on the outcomes?

Are we dancing on the fragile energy holding the timelines together? Or are we testing the strength of the will of the Time Lords?

Yes, there are beings known as Time Lords, who attempt to prevent humanity from breaking too many time rules, thus distorting what the Time Lords believe should be the accurate line of your species' history...

Be that as it may, we prefer the fluidity of knowing that the Divine Creator called us all into being. Thus we are not locked into a foreign and unknown way of existence.

These so-called Time Lords have worked silently in the background following directives and orders of their Draconian Masters, undertaking grand illusions to ensure that you little humans stay in your place, accepting any adjustments to the history set out for you by the many resets. All created to hide the truth from the very people who should be aware of it, you, the Terrans

We desire to bring you to a place of awareness and realisation.

A slight caution, though, as we pause before stepping out of the portal, the world you will step into is, in some ways, as different from your current time as can be and, in other ways, will feel as if nothing has been changed.

Let us go forward.

Firstly, we realise that the day's heat is upon us, and many of you are dressed to absorb as much of the sun and its heat as possible. This is vastly different from the first visit to this date, and there is much to explain why?

In this timeline that we are observing, your species overcame oppression by peaceful, non-belligerent and honourable means, as well as by operating within the Lore/law of the Creator, the law of nature and the law of T'Gaina, including the instinctive, natural self-governing law within your spiritual beingness. Directing you to do no harm, honour others, and take responsibility for yourself and your actions. Thus you, the living souls of the realm, began imprisoning leaders and power heads who had abused their roles of authority. You chose ways to ensure a means of justice enabling all who had grievances to be heard, arguments to be held in a manner of dignity, honour and balance, giving truth a chance to be heard and seen.

The truth was paramount and required at least two or three witnesses, independent of the accused or accuser, to verify the circumstances or event in question. Then a group of community beings from the   village where the accuser and the accused live are invited to sit and hear the dialogue before condemning or freeing the living soul being asked to answer the accusations.

You have established islands. Whose purpose is for the protection and safety of those living there? The occupants of these islands are the remainder who refused to turn away from the Formless One's puppets due to their conformed and indoctrinated mindsets. Due to the containment areas and the desire to ensure that their ways could not infiltrate the new society, you formulated a system where they were self-sufficient yet able to barter with you. You did not lock them up. They were free to travel about.

Nonetheless, they had to return to their place of abode within a set period of time to ensure that their welfare was maintained, for many had within their bodies the nanotechnology that the majority had denied. For this reason and only this, they now had a confined space they were to live in.

Here in the mainlands and places of commerce, you have created a life of integrity. Of course, there are rules or laws that you uphold, but we hear much laughter and joy abounding in the air.

Come let us go and look down the energy of this timeline and see what was done differently. We must ask the questions of this time and place, for example, 'Why are you encouraged to soak up the sun's life force?'

'Why are you encouraged to speak your truth and to honour the one who disagrees with you in balance?'

'What has changed to allow such illumination into the world that exists at this moment?'

We see little to no electronic devices, Dear Reader, or should we say that we notice that the living beings, the Terrans, are interacting with each other in personal space and with touch. Youngsters interact with social talents and bonding that have not been seen for hundreds of years on earth. In fact, they are interacting with a similar demeanour to the Lyrans, an intuitive and interactive behaviour.

As we stare down the line of the Akashic Record Timeline that brings this potential, we observe that all the various markers from before are still in place.

Your society still suffered the two world wars and endured the ongoing persecution of the medical world created from these wars.

We observe that the genders were still imbalanced, and there were great verbal battles over which gender should be the most honoured. There are still the shadows of the political agendas that set up the dark option of this timeline, so Dear Reader, what changed?

Why did you evolve differently? What event occurred or did not occur, or perhaps what choices were made otherwise for this outcome?

Let us explore.

It is in this period of your linearity, in the time of 2023 to 2027 you chose to fight back. In reality, it began in 2020, when many of you rebelled in peaceful gatherings, although you were mistreated and falsely accused. You stood up to the falsehoods and bore the brunt of the retaliation.

The more the living men and women of T'Gaina began to stand shoulder to shoulder against a common enemy, the stronger they became. Then, of course, there were those who worked in shadows of the medical worlds, the military and other places who came out of hiding to support you all with intel and knowledge. But, instead, they stood shoulder to shoulder with you. No longer worrying if they would be seen, shot or captured for reprogramming. Instead, they chose to fight with the people of the land.

[34]Groups around your world sprung up, and you called them by various names; Know Your Rights, Common Law, Doctors for Information. Some followed multiple groups or individuals such as David Icke, Q, Charlie Ward, Simon Parks, Project Camelot, M Seeker of Truth and many others.

Some of these had legitimate information, while others had partial truths and were exposed. Some groups or spokespersons were exposed by their own hands because a lie, once spoken, needs to be remembered in context forever. You cannot deviate from it, embellish yes, but not deviate and this is what happened.

Various groups declared many truths and facts, which were proved invalid, and the prophetic voice crumbled into dust.

Others in this mix stayed their course. They continued to speak their heart-felt truth. Leaders of various nations stood up and spoke out, and the Kennedy family spokesman consistently spoke

---

[34] Groups mentioned here are gathered from the internet. We do not endorse or promote any, only asking you all research and divine your own truth.

against the inconsistency of the injections. The 45th President of the Americas rushed through vaccines, so there was no possible way to 'ensure' validity. Some sceptics ask why, and we reply that it was so that the contents of the vials would not be subjected to the intense scrutiny of the watchers, creating a loophole for many vials of beneficial therapeutic tincture to be in the mix. However, we are cautious about seeming to admire or promote this man's energy even with his Pleiadian connection; he still seems to float between sides as if afraid to commit.

Though we also see that many of those living during this time viewed this as being part of the dark energy as 'he pushed' for the people to be injected. We do wish to point out that his Pleiadian wife was able to stand with her team to deflect much of the distorted energy being thrown at him. Her potent vibrancy sent subliminal messages to the living people of the lands they received. This living soul who was, chosen to do a work that would have had a weaker man crumble has been working 'behind closed doors not to hide from the eyes of observation but to ensure that those who are not meant to see cannot see and interfere.

All will unfold in the fullness of time.

When the dark powers found that, although they had ousted the thorn in their side and thought they had a clear run, they were, in fact, losing, they threw all they had at the world.

Tighter and tighter lockdowns occurred, people were forced to stay apart again, nations were closing borders once more, and the people rose up.

For some, this was the breaking point. The realisation that just before the end of a set time for the government to declare an

'Emergency Rule', a new reason to expand it rose up. The people became angry, for they began to see each time the sense of freedom and normality appeared to loom in their favour; the governing heads found a reason to block this and constructed new and strange reasons for locking people up in their homes, towns, states and countries.

Many rose up against this draconian control. The newly empowered living men and women began to sit in large groups peacefully outside the councils' rooms, on the government buildings' lawns. They raised no constant loud voice or crashing symbols. Instead, they meditated and prayed. Their signs were pointed and left little to the imagination, but they refused to leave until they were heard.

If some of these brave souls were removed forcibly by the controlling system, others would come and sit where they had been. Still, others would come with food and drink to sustain those 'speaking' in silence. Every day at set times, however, they would bring anything they could to create a strident sound that shattered the peace and penetrated the halls of the governing bodies. Each day it would be at a different time, sometimes short, and other times long and persistent. The variance in timing was so that those inside the offices could not prepare to dull the noise or remove themselves from the building.

The silent protesters also created a way of blocking all entrances to the buildings so that no one could enter and exit. Thus the leaders within the building were trapped, like rodents, unable to leave. Those on the outside ensured that there was food delivered to them, but there were no delicacies, only necessities. Items like bread, dehydrated meats, fruits, and things that would last a few days and needed no heat, refrigeration or preparation.

They were attempting to show those inside what they on the outside had been suffering at their 'leaders' hands.

For some groups, it took many weeks of protesting, for others not so long, before cracks showed in the chambers of the lawmakers and rulers of the towns, cities and states. Then, finally, there were negotiations, and most countries reverted to the people's rule. As a result, people of integrity, trusted by those who put them forward, were called upon to assist in running the towns to ensure ongoing livelihoods.

Many stubborn draconian minions in the halls of governance still resisted. They wanted the power returned to them, so they pushed back and negated all offers. They attempted to propagate warfare on the streets by bringing in their controlled, hired gangs to round up the people and imprison them.

Nevertheless, the Terrans and the Hu-mans remained strong. They gathered together in support. This included those who had once capitulated in obedience to the common narrative decrying the truth presented to them so long ago. They were determined to rid the lying and deceptive cronies trapped inside their lairs and bring freedom back to the combined lands of the earth.

From all corners of the realm, those hiding from the draconian foot soldiers broke out into the open. They wished to speak publicly on the falsity of the virus supposedly killing humanity from their perspective. They showed evidence of how the cure was far worse than that of the reason or illness for it.

There were platforms created to share knowledge far and wide using similar technology to the current internet platforms many got so easily caught up in. There grew a groundswell, unlike any other in your time, where men, women, children, and people of every culture and species realised they had been duped and so began to resist, to no longer 'do as they were told' for the common good.

Thousands demanded the simple joys of life, to go where they desired, eat where they wished, and be with members of their own domicile or friends. Their numbers grew, as did their voice of discontent, to the point that even the state-run police feared preventing them.

The people of the various lands had begun to educate themselves, to learn more about what was truth and what was supposed fact. They sought the higher vibrational ways and returned to a more simplistic style of living.

Soon there was a worldwide call for scientists and technically knowledgeable people to create a new system of communication that did not rely on harmful wavelengths to carry information, a new method of communication via the internet platform. New ways of travel, but above all, there was a call to create or recreate the significant energy buildings and 'batteries' of the Toroidal Energy of Terrans that they'd left standing in the old cities, now hidden in the depths of the jungles and forests. There were 'lost' plans for free energy, of connecting to the earth to discover where there was fresh water, good soil, or even minerals, that were encouraged to be returned to the status of 'normal.'

Many of the buildings in the cities that had been 'repurposed' for illegal authority were taken back by living men and women as well as consciously connected cosmic beings.

They commissioned groups of scientists in various schools of thought to study and learn the old ways to bring back the ancient portals and forms of travel.

The new leaders of the living earth encouraged parents to teach their young the basics of self-responsibility. To learn how the earth supplies their needs, from air to food and everything in between. If the parents did not know these tools, they were taken to learning centres where they could study, graduate and ply a trade for themselves.

People slowly began to realise the differences that had kept them apart, fed by social media. Separated by the TV or 'the lying box of deception' they watched every night, the education system and virtually everything they had believed was accurate and trustworthy was the opposite of what they now discovered was reality.

They realised they'd been deceived by the medical world, by the images of film stars consuming insects and worms as a delicacy food, stating it was an alternative to beef, chicken, and other meats. It was wondrous observing the occupants of this realm, T'Gaina, of earth, wake up to the reality that each had a choice of what to consume. It did not matter what they ate, whether meat, vegetables, or soya-made products. It became paramount that no one had the right to force their way onto another.

Anger among the common living man and woman rose when they realised leaders of businesses, leaders of countries, movie stars, and other highly promoted personalities who'd made a show of being injected had not had this at all.

Instead, they'd either been a part of CGI manipulation, or the injection was of saline solution.

When the evidence mounted up before the masses, whether injected or not, whether left or right in political standing, it didn't matter where they were. The evidence showed that there had been a blanket plot to separate the people of the earth. To bring about a great divide so that they would never know the truth of the world they lived in.

This realm originally created for the Terrans so many epochs ago, with the joint creative forces of Terra-Ven-Eiliesh-Gaina (T'-Gaina), was suddenly populated by a force of awakened beings, and the resonance of the core energy of the planet began to reawaken, quickly.

As T'Gaina's resonance awoke and started to vibrate more frequently, it seemed as if the seasons awoke to their original intensity and sequence. There were signs of the days and nights becoming slower, more settled in their flow. No longer racing to get to a goal out of sight.

This vibration rang through the earth, connecting with animals, plants, humans, Terrans and all living creatures. For the majority, it enhanced them. For some, though, it was as if their life force became shut down, interfered with, and they became sickly, withdrawing to closed-off sections of the rich and powerful regions.

These were those that had 'sold their souls' to the dark forces, to the Formless Ones. They had struck deals that meant they would live a vibrant life as long as they ensured the Formless Ones and their cohorts, the Anunnaki etc., were kept in an abundance of human slaves and human life force to sustain their ways.

Now that this was reversed, due to the mass uprising of humanity, they became vulnerable and susceptible to disease. Seemingly, their 'immortality' had been removed, and their mortality returned.

What we are observing, Dear Reader, is, in reality, the most beautiful thing when done correctly. A Revolution of the people in heart energy!

In this particular timeline we are connecting with, we see how humans, Terrans and others are working together to heal the earth and the people groups. How the land responds to the regeneration programs, and how people are relearning that everything on the planet has a purpose, plant, animal, [35]'hu-man', Ter-ran, soil, air, water, ether or energy. Each is unique, in place to be utilised and absorbed to enhance the well-being of the other in need or requirement of it.

Gone are the sub-religious groups of people demanding that only imitation foods are eaten, or only vegetation be consumed. Instead, we see that you are learning that various types of physi-cality require different food groups and that you no longer judge people according to what they consume. The once opposing groups of eaters are now joined in the combined efforts to ensure that all cultures and living souls have the food that is best for their physical attributes.

We note that in this period, you have returned to the con-sciousness of connection with a renewed awareness that there is more to explore. So many are questioning what you have been taught for so long. If what the media and spokespeople of the Puppet Masters have been telling you recently is a lie, what else is a lie, you ask yourselves.

There is a worldwide invitation to all who wish to explore the texts, images and other manuscripts to discover any anomalies or inconsistencies in the historical narrative. Many students take up the call. They are bored with the regular lessons, and this in-trigues them. For various reasons, they wish to prove that their elders have got it wrong and find their purpose in being alive. To find direction once more.

Suddenly the old libraries of 'mouldy' old books become the hub of social gatherings, no longer quiet and silent but humming with life and excitement.

---

[35] Hu - (the colour of) - Man = hu-man you are the colour of man... you are not a hu-man, a created entity of the organisations that control you.

A new era of critical thinkers is emerging, and the old draconian rules are being pushed further, and further back into the past.

But wait, what is that smoke in the distance Dear Reader, come let us go and see, for it is not in this year of 2025, but it is coming from the next of the human calendar years. So let us jump forward again to the year 2026.

What a mess!

There is so much demolition and destruction happening. What say you, Dear Reader? Has there been a turnaround in leadership? Perhaps the Dark forces have pushed back? Let us go higher to gain a better perspective of sight.

We see now what is causing the rubble and smoke. The people have opened up the bases below ground. They have found and exposed the enemy in their nests, bringing extreme light to extreme darkness. It is not quite what you think, Reader, no bombs or explosions per sē. It is, however, dense smog. Voluminous, filthy recycled air has been trapped under your cities for aeons. Upon interacting with the purity of your atmosphere, it has created a dirty, heavy condensing smog in counter-reaction, and the machinery utilised is a purification unit to disperse and filter this dead air.

It is interesting to see that the unification of the people is still burgeoning, still running from strength to strength as you continue to realise your potential in self-rule and governance using the guide of nature and your intrinsic connection to the Divine Source of Creation.

Many are awestruck at the news that your great ancient explorers of the ice worlds were correct, that more land has been sighted, ready to be discovered. This, among other hidden issues, proves that your energetic teachers were right when they told you that you lived in a place, a 'matrix' that hid your identity from you. These now revealed that you lived in a realm that had always interacted with other galactic beings. That there were sectors and domains rather than dimensions or off-planetary beings just across the 'borders' of your world.

You are slowly discovering the plane you live on and how vast it is. You have found the remnants of the old, gigantic forests that walked across the surface of T'Gaina. You have begun to re-seed and attempt to fill the scars of the open mining that the Anunna-ki left bleeding so many epochs ago.

There have been leaps and bounds in technology research, for those who have been in the science sector have found information and technology hidden within the recesses of the buildings of the past governing leaders. This information, alongside the discoveries made by those searching the libraries, is beginning to show new history of the realm you live within.

Many have found the old blueprints for the Free Energy that you have longed after for centuries. Some of your investigators have located more modern blueprints hidden in the files on the computers of the Energy Controllers. These show how to use levitation to easily lift and move heavy objects. There are plans showing how to build mechanisms that create heat and light and use the air to transmit this energy.   Finally, you have found how light is transmitted via sound or vibration to its destination. This gives you means of higher standards of communication and energy use for technology, which should have been used before.

There are also plans in the Engineering Departments of the 'Controllers' which explain how it is not only probable but possible to travel without using aeroplanes. How sound, vibration and the connection of the 'empty space' or fabric of the universe create doorways to the places where you wish to go to. It is currently being used in a 'tunnel lift' between realms within this realm, and other enclosed realms of the multiverse by those fore mentioned controllers.

In exploring this potential of your timeline, 2049, you are seeing how freedom is not something that just arrived by silently meditating but rather by all parts of participation. Your focused thought, action of intent and connection between groups of like-minded vision. You have discovered or perhaps rediscovered the strength of unity of the Terran/True human species.

Many groups are reporting back to the designated areas of agreed directive centres. Information of lost techniques, information of libraries full of historical books and literature, dating back to before any of you have an awareness of, telling stories or relating real-life scenarios of exploits of discovery. How are there maps showing land masses outside your known mapped areas, countries and territories that indicate potential fertile land, waters and forests?

What has amazed the majority of those involved in the searches for hidden artefacts is an abundance of precious metals, seeds, natural medicines, unmodified plants, animals etc. Hidden in deep caverns or locked away deep underground in man-made cities that have, what looks like natural sky and airflow!

Your militia has discovered and is dismantling various weapons of mass destruction. They have rounded up and secured other illegal entities that are upon the surface of this realm, hereby violating the sacred decree of 'Hands off Planet Earth' that was given epochs ago. Here by the invitation and vibratory allowance of the human hybrids wishing to gain only for themselves and obtain immortality through witchcraft and dark magick. They have opened portals to allow these entities in. Thus the Formless Ones have stepped into your realm and ruled via the Anunnaki Hybrids. Now they are undone.

Yet we ask you not to become complacent or slack in observing the vibration of the earth realm. Note the deep resonance as she heals and returns to her original state. It will take some time, but it can be done... it may require of you, as a species, to migrate to new lands. This is nothing new for your species. You've done this type of migration many times before. Mostly when the ice has crept in from the sides and out from the centre of your ancient world. You will find your way to the sides, and the new maps will show you how to reach the new land.

You will need to negotiate with the inhabitants of those lands and perhaps be willing to learn from them a new way of being and living as a people. But you will only discover that IF this is the timeline you choose.

We will revisit here, but we need to return to RexNā Loid DeAqua, RaeNegria, Rägę El BriNa-Ragnoa and the rest of the Lyrans...

Come stand here in this vibration imprint on the ground. Do you note the unique pattern of concentric circles intersecting with triangular impressions? Do you see the smaller circles like a series of dots that create a halo effect around the spike that sits within the centre of everything? Ahh, there we go. Do you feel it?

Do you sense the ease of movement as we travel effortlessly through time and the void? It is achieved using the correct vibrational frequency sitting within the balanced angular equation, which must be within the accepted and agreed frequency and equation of the destination. We can 'step through' the realms arc and travel into the lives of the Lyrans... come let us disembark into the ship before us...

Chapter Fifteen

An Ancient Connection
Forgotten links of
Lyran Contacts

Striding along the "Bitari-Furtim-Karda" corridors, Sol Lrign responded to the information that the young Lyrans were now moving back towards them and would be docking within the conditions laid out.

A gentle but knowing smile crept onto her face and then just as quickly disappeared, being replaced by the 'look of command' that she wore daily. She reached out telepathically to feel if either Rae or MelEid were available, for although she was in command of the two ships, she was not heartless and was concerned for the well-being of RaeNegria. There also was the fact that the sooner the young Prince was aboard the main command ship, the quicker her Mages and Seers could take over the healing process, discover what ailed the young Prince and then find the hidden message within her brain.

Sol was intent on discovering who was working with the Formless Ones within her crew and how The Whittling had not picked up the double energy and exposed the Lyran. However, she knew that timing was paramount. She could not allow any [36]arriviste personality to be on her ship...no matter how insipid or intense the desire of the said Lyran was for self-effacing pride or reward, Sol knew how it would end. There could not be another war that put the Heart Stone at risk. Not again!

Pausing at the open doors of the lift, Sol changed direction and, instead of returning to the command deck, went back a short distance and entered the Library of Memory.

Somewhere in her memory, there was a niggle of past connections. A report or historical note had passed through her office informing the Lyran company that there was a species that, like the Lyrans, had hidden from the Formless Ones with great success. They had not been located nor seen since the great ripping of T'Gaina, where large land masses had been swallowed by the onslaught of water when the Great Shift of the Sky happened. It was a time of perplexity among the Lyrans and the Terrans, that remained free from the slavery of the Anunnaki's lobotomy. It had been a time when discoveries had been foremost in the lives and minds of the Anunnaki Hybrids and the peace-loving Terrans living on the land mass you know as Mu.

A third culture had the secrets of the Heart Crystal of T'Gaina. They also recorded frequencies and spectrums of light energy used to heal DNA and separate energy frequencies that may have been spliced or plaited at one time. These would have been done to create a bond or strengthen within the cellular lattice of the physical being but may no longer be required. Or perhaps, in the case of RaeNegria could be slowly destroying her.

Sol spent the next couple of lapzph pouring over the ancient books and records to find any mention of the old cultures of the

---

[36] upstart/social climber/power hungry

realm of Terra-Ven-Eiliesh-Gaina. Hoping to locate a way of assisting the young Lyran Prince, who'd reached out in an attempt at negotiating peace.

Knowing that her 2nd in command, Juuls, was more than capable of monitoring the approaching ship and anything else that required her attention, Sol sealed herself in the library.

Reaching into the cubicle, which was set up to interlink with the Organic Link, similar to what Rae had used, Sol drew out a small shelf. This shelf looked as if it were covered in a solid, liquid mass, like a thick, oozing substance that, when touched, would creep up and settle over the object touching it. However, it would not merely accept anyone or anything coming into contact with it. Only those united in a particular resonance, vibration or DNA could liaise with this plasma link. This did away with invasive ports and attachments that were required to be inserted into the Lyran's arms and temples, which were designated to join with the inner workings of the Lyran Ships.

One of Sol's first engagements had been to undergo surgical insertions for the old linking way. However, this new way of plasma linking was more convenient and precise in its connections, allowing her to search and even pilot the ship with far more fluidity and ease than the ports had permitted.

Where the old system of linking to the Organic link, currently used on the *'Bitari-Furtim-Otiose'*, had to be inserted into the nerves and bloodstream of the pilot, which was a painful process. This new system that the Lyran scientists, under the direction of Sol, had created was a much less invasive and smoother process of linkage.

Allowing herself to relax, Sol brought her attention to the ancient connections of '[37]The Original Federation of InterGalactic Families Owning Responsibility of Nation, Culture, Self and Unions of Freedom,' and all that were aligned with the freedom of movement within the realms.

Relaxing her mind, Sol allowed the connection to flow. Images of all the species and realms once interconnected to the Original Federation poured into her consciousness. Flicking through them like pages of photos, Sol Lrign paused at the images of the old alliance friends, the [38]Telosians.

As if registering her interest, the organic link brought up all the files relating to the Telosian connection with the Lyrans, dating back to before the Great Wars. Settling back in her chair, Sol paged through the archives, searching for that 'something' that niggled away at her memory.

This hid in the depth of her conscious remembrance and was wriggling away and making itself known. Instinctually she felt that it would assist in the process of RaeNegria's healing and give them clues on how to deal with other dis-eases of the vibrational and resonance style. Those who utilised telepathic communication relied on a strong, clear, transparent link of sound vibration between the participants. If this link became 'dirty,' it could lead to various discomforts, including the eventual breaking of the mind of either one or both of the communicators. This was the reasoning behind specific protocols when telepathically connecting to your immediate crew and, at times, with your shipmates.

---

[37] NB: We the Narrators of Time have taken the decision to alter the title of the Original Galactic Federation to its more broadly known wording. We do this as you as a species have now moved beyond the word 'government' This truer wording is closer to the full Lyran title.

[38] Please note these are not the fictional creature of your science fiction stories, but real and interconnected beings

Sol sat upright. Her eyes fixed on something glaringly apparent to her, yet to anyone observing her, it would seem as if she were staring into space. Her eyes were as if she had fallen asleep. Yet her hands were tapping information onto the tablet in front of her at speed.

Codes, quadrants, directions, as well as star maps, were high-lighted and stored in Sol's personal log, then secured with her secret code. Had she found the way back to the Telosian connection after these many thousands of cycles?

How had the scholars missed it in previous searches, and what had allowed her to discover it? Slowing down her inquiry, Sol began to broaden her probe. Not just for Telos but for any oral story or a historical record of a settlement located beyond the Sector of Light. With a certain amount of hope, Sol remembered the information she'd been given about a colony in the twenty-third realm of experience. This information had been found when sifting through one of the many unmanned transponder buoys they had sent out over the cycles. The scientists retrieved the information at this time and felt that there was a strong possibility that this species could link to the Lyran Diaspora. The remnant that remained spread across the multiverse in various realms, hiding from the Formless Ones, waiting for the day they could deliver the final blow of annihilation to their enemy.

[39]This recorder had returned with evidence of a planet established with life, yet somehow, had become overcome with a parasite-type species attempting (at the time of discovery by the recorder) to overwrite the initial species. There were powerful beings on this planet. These groups had retreated to the islands for safety and remained hidden in great swathes of fog and cloud for generations before being discovered and hunted, drowned by ris-

---

[39] This recorder is one of the many sent out by the Negotiators of the Sector of Light, in their search for the Lyrans. See vol 1 & 2

ing waters. Images showed a huge portal opening in the centre of these islands and the people of the land walking into them, sealing the portal and 'disappearing' from the history of the realm. Or so it was portrayed.

Sol scanned the images, giants, strange beings with the palest skin, others that looked ruddy and almost every shade of earth colour you could find. Others were a mix of species, yet they all had slightly heavy foreheads and inset eyes, as if their frontal lobe was more significant than expected, going by the depictions of those on the lands of patrolled and segmented sections.

Sol searched through reference after reference file to find these primary beings. She, somehow, felt it would be crucial to the outcome of the battle of the Lyrans and all those that allied with them in the fight against the Formless Ones.

Coming to the end of the information provided, Sol disconnected from the organic link and began to return to a more conscious state. Reading over her notes, she pondered on the star maps she'd noted and realised that these were not in her sector of being but in a place beyond the realm of the Sector of Lights. Was there a place beyond the void of water? Were there realms that could assist in this great war that they had not yet found? Hope grew in her heart as she gently tapped the files now locked by her genetic sequence.

Suppose she could locate and send a communication to the aligned species of the *Original Federation of InterGalactic Families. In that case,* she may just find a cure to the ailment, slowly consuming RaeNegria and others affected by strange maladies while living in the Sector of Light.

Dear Reader, we wish to bring some enlightenment regarding the Sector of Light.

This part of your realm (for it is within the parameters of the vast void that is your earth realm), this Sector of Light, sits within Polaris. What you refer to as your north star, yet it is so much more than just a 'star.'

It is a place of high vibrational soundings, light and fluid energy. The magnetics that flows through this sector are of such high frequency and vibration that they often pass through without notice.

However, there are times when those highly tuned into the conscious connection of all, when they are focused on seeing the truth, will be affected by these vibrations and frequency sequences of energy and light.

It was this vibration that was affecting the young Lyran Prince. The pulsations and constant oscillation of light frequency meant that she could not find a platform of inner balance. This meant her cellular body was being bombarded and, in a way, transformed from solid to fluid form.

They later discovered that a simple shield created in a unique meld of certain materials (not mentioned here for obvious reasons) was her 'cure.' At least until she was able to learn how to 'dance' to the vibration of the Crystal Heart Stone and the Divine Vibration that was the Polaris Sector of Light.

This incredible area of Polaris sits above the place you call earth. It is one of the few areas that flows within and without the realm's protective shield.

The grid lines that you have around your firmament. These many grids create a shield that protects your world, protects your people and yet all some of you wish to do is shatter it and create instantaneous death for you all in the name of science or space discovery. In reality, all that is required is activating your higher connection vibratory link to the Divine Creator.

We will return you to Sol Lrign and her discoveries.

If Sol was right in her thinking, there were at least three other species that her people, the Lyrans, connected with while still navigating the realms and liaising with various cultures and species among the stars before the Great Wars.

There were the Telosians, who had founded a base within the realm of the Terrans. There was another culture, the Dogonites, who had intimate links to the beings of the portal gateway Sirius, and a third group that, as of yet Sol, knew only as Mui-ians. This culture seemed to be a mix of cultures or beings that sought refuge on a hidden island in their world but were somehow connected with the first two groups.

The transponder had recorded that these groups worked with the early species of the planetoid, located just out of the Water Realm, within a barrier of energy that allowed a totally sustainable life force to exist. The more Sol studied the parameters and geographical feedback on the elements of gases, power of light, warmth and other factors, she became convinced that this realm was similar to the original domain of Lyra. However, with one difference, there seemed to be a force field or some type of energy vibration that allowed gaseous exchange, light penetration, and heat absorption but appeared to prevent anything from leaving or entering the realm without permission.

Intrigued with this new realm, Sol set in motion an order to the Exploration Sector to create a protocol for a new set of transponder recorders to be sent out to the quadrant section known as the Twenty-Third realm of Experience.

Once there, the transponders were to record all life forms. All intelligence found was to be fed back to the *Bitari-Furtim-Karda's* computers. These databases kept, recorded, and then reported on any and all variance of events in that sector of the multiverse. If they were to leave the Sector of Polaris to seek out the remainder of the Lyrans, Sol wished to discover everything she could about the realm before putting her or her crew in danger.

A sudden knock on the entryway to the study room she had occupied in the 'Library of Memory' brought Sol out of her place of deep thought back into the current moment. Gathering herself, she scanned her desk, ensuring there was no chance that anything of her writings or equations could be read.

Unlocking the entry, Sol gave permission to enter. Juuls walked through the entrance tapping an ancient scroll in his hands and wearing a frown that threatened to swallow his eyes. "So this is where you've been hiding," he muttered. Almost awkwardly, he pushed the scroll to Sol. " You have to read this. There is information on how the ancients could use a Seer connected vibrationally, organically and consciously with their ship and nearby ships to override and either shut down attacks or pilot the warships to a set place of battle without crews." Juuls paused and then continued, his voice was low but carried clearly to Sol, "They could not do it for long periods of consciousness, but there were those who learnt to incorporate this power into their cellular being and became great warriors."

Juuls' face finally began to relax, and the deep furrows on his forehead smoothed out. He looked directly at Sol, "I wonder if it will give insight into what is happening to our young Prince on the approaching ship." Then, nodding slightly, he turned and left the library. This was the way of Juuls - appearing, stating what needed to be spoken or given and then leaving. No waste of time or words.

Sol placed the scroll into her side pouch to read later. Right now, she felt there was a need for her on the command deck.

Striding onto the command deck and heading towards her chair, Sol ran through a series of queries aimed at the entire command crew.

"Update on the approach of the *Bitari-Furtim-Otiose?*"

"What is the current situation on the Thermal Plasma Pulse?"

"Status of the Crystal Heart Stone vibrational sequencing?"

" Any communications from the Captain or any of the Princes onboard the Bitari-Furtim-Otiose?"

When she finally sat in her chair and logged into her consul, her crew fed back the relevant information to her screen. Raising her eyes to scan her team, she noted that there were two new cadets sitting at the sonar readings. Uplifting an eyebrow in the direction of her Group Captain, she questioned their reason for being on the command deck. The Group Captain, recognising the unspoken question, rose and walked over to Sol Lrign dWari. Lowering his head to quietly speak to his commander, Marcris de' VanNeer revealed that these young cadets had come to report a strange anomaly they'd picked up in the Sonar Room. They discovered this while running sporadic scans for any infiltration to their space or ship.

They had identified the sonar signature first, as large as a battleship and, secondly, smaller signatures of moving energy onboard the ship. These gave off a vastly different vibrational autograph of DNA than every other Lyran on board. As Marcris was acutely aware of the warning that Sol had given them earlier of a potential saboteur, he'd decided to keep the cadets on the command deck where they could access the entire scope of the Sonar and Radar system. This would also keep them under his eye, and thus anything they discovered, he'd be able to screen and take action.

Nodding her head as she listened to this new information, Sol moved over to the Sonar unit. Then, placing her hand on the cadet's shoulder closest to her, she asked, "What is the pattern of the ship, and where about would you place its distance from ourselves and the *Bitari-Furtim-Otiose?*"

The cadet froze as she realised that her commander was asking her opinion. Shooting a 'help' look to her colleague, the cadet nervously reached over to the monitor and turned a few dials and switches on the panel beside her. Soon, the screen was filled with a pattern of strong spiral waves radiating outward. These intersected sporadically with what looked like a helix that wove itself into the spiral, shimmered and melted, eventually fading.

Then after what seemed a couple of centzph, the pattern would begin again, the spiral expanding, the helix interweaving, the shimmer and fade. This happened in the same frequency of a pulse, simulating a living creature sending out a message that told of its presence.

The cadets then changed the recording, moving over to the smaller yet almost identical sequence of pulses floating around the inside of their battleship. "Commander Sol, these pulses are not solid. From what we have recorded, they seem to be of energy or a vibrational signal as they have the ability to pass through our walls and have been recorded as passing through our sealed units and also your private quarters. The only thing they cannot enter seems to be our organic link and the level holding the Heart Stone Crystal." The young woman waited for the commander to process what she'd seen and been told. Remembering that she'd been informed to give the information requested and then wait to be asked for more or to just be still. The second cadet was still watching the anomalies when he suddenly grabbed the young cadet's arm, "They're moving! The spiral sequence is moving! It's coming closer, and it's getting bigger!" His voice rose in excitement and was tinged with a slither of fear. His movement and words caused Sol to move closer to his screen. Watching for a moment, she closed her eyes. Where had that pattern presented before, it was familiar, but Sol could not place where she'd seen it last. She felt they were safe in her bones, but her gut told her to raise shields.

"Raise to Amber Alert", she spoke softly, but her voice carried clearly, and within seconds, the whole ship was on Amber Alert.

"Immediate council in the officers' room in 5 centzph". Sol's words were again quietly spoken, but her voice carried throughout the command deck, and the entire crew felt the urgency. Looking at one of the young pilot officers in the navigation sector, she stated, "Chaarl, you have the comm."

As the Command Leaders gathered in the Officers' Room, Sol searched through the data on her screen. Choosing not to rely solely on the computer to locate the information but on her intuitive instinct. Eventually, a hush fell over the room, all eyes turned and focused on their Commander in Chief. Sol was still focused on her screen, fully aware that her captains and sector leaders were waiting. She was also waiting to get the go-ahead to proceed. Having sent a coded message to the Chief Mage, requesting a blanket energy field over the room to ensure that nothing could be over-heard, tapped into, or otherwise hacked.

Her screen flashed red with confirmation from her Chief Mage, Sol flicked the switch, and the room fell into an eery silence. "We are compromised! We have energy signatures that are disembodied, floating around our ship, and we have a pulsing signature that is sitting off our port side. The radiating signal indicates that it will intersect with our ships in a little over one lapzph. Not forgetting that we will be docking with the Lyran Princes at roughly the same time." Sol paused. Looking at those around the table, she asked, "Any suggestions or comments as to what is following us? Ideas about what has infiltrated our ship, more importantly, why their presence was not identified earlier?"

Leaning back in her chair, she waited. It was usually like this, an urgent call to her Sector Leaders, and they would sit, staring at her for a while, and then it would register that this was not just a drill or practice but an actuality that needed their input.

She realised this was the unfortunate result of being in a place of safety for so many cycles. Some of her captains had become lax and were not as sharp as they should be.

"Well?" Sol's voice carried to the rear of the room and brought the eyes of all present back to her. "Do you have any suggestions on how to counter this infiltration into our house?" Again there was silence from her group leaders.

There was a murmur of denial from the captains, group leaders, and lieutenants at the idea that anything could have breached their safety fields. Or come to the point of only being discovered a short distance from their ship.

Others thought this was just another drill, another attempt from Sol to keep them on their toes, so they did not fully comprehend the enormity of what was presented to them at this moment.

Sighing, Sol leaned forward, flicked a few switches on her consul, and pushed in a command that produced a holographic image in the middle of the command table. Sitting back in her chair, she pointed to the image before the command crew, "This, captains and squad leaders, this is what I am referring to! The unwavering rippling sequence is growing; each time it repeats, it becomes faster and jumps closer to our ship. As it undergoes its sequence of movements, so do the two blips here and here," Sol pointed to the two small blue moving energies. "They're moving closer and closer to the comm's level, and nothing seems to stop them. Not walls, energy fields, lasers, or telepathic force seem to dislodge these 'blips' from their trajectory." It was plain to see they were aiming for the section of the ship that housed the [40]Crystal Heart Stone, which was situated directly alongside the commander's quarters!

There was a sudden lurching forward of tired bodies and a snapping open of half-asleep eyes. The Sector Leaders and command crew suddenly realised this was not just another drill or meaningless 'what if' scenario.

Juuls looked at his commander, attempting to read what may be hidden on her face. Finding nothing, he returned to the image before him. This was something they'd had not come up against before.

Dear Reader, as these learned men and women of Lyra ponder the situation before them, let us sit and listen to the thoughts of Sol Lrign. It is not usual, especially as she had not lifted the 'no telepathic communication' rule when she discovered the infiltration. We know that Sol considered the connections of   various cosmic families and those that the transponder recorded as being connected with T'Gaina.

We have begun, and perhaps so have you, to think that she may be considering a connection along the lines of Aligned Members of the 'The Original Federation of InterGalactic Families Owning Responsibility of Nation, Culture, Self and Unions of Freedom.' We sense there is a link between the cultures she studied and saved onto her consul. A link connecting the Lyrans with T'Gaina

---

[40] Remember, Dear Reader, that Sol has moved the real Crystal Heart Stone to a place of safety and the one on her ship is a replica.

that she is unaware of now. Do not forget that she and those with her have protected the Crystal Heart Stone for the past many cycles by intentionally cutting off from all outside communication and interaction.

So gently and with permission, let us join with Commander Sol Lrign deWarn and tap into her thoughts.

As we sensed, she desires to connect to [41]The OFIGF & UofF, thus uniting the Star/Planetary Cultures of old Lyra with the new cultures she has found recorded. Her desire is to create a unified group of beings that will stand in resistance to the onslaught of a common enemy. They could find a mutual place of meeting by sending a transmission via sub-resonance and subatomic levels to the various groups. Is this similar to the now new focus and intent of RaeNegria? You can see, Dear Reader, the common threads beginning to be interwoven. Maybe the 'Old Lyrans' are no different from the 'New Lyrans' than they or we think.)

She plans to use the energy of the three Lyran Princes, harnessed via the Organic Links of both ships, to power the telepathic message to the furthest most parts of the multiverse. She had previously calculated the effective forces of psychokinesis of RexNā and was in the process of realising RaeNegria's power of telepathic connection. Rägę she knew was the average rate of telepathic psychokinesis, with which the majority of Lyrans were born. Sol was also very keen to see what would happen when she arranged for the three Princes and their Mages to connect in the room of the Heart Stone along with her Mages.
What power would they be able to tap into?
Dear Reader, our dear commander has a plan up her sleeve, and we would be wise to leave her to establish this fully without our

---

[41] The Original Federation of InterGalactic Families Owning Responsibility of Nation, Culture, Self and Unions of Freedom

interference. So let us travel back to the world of mankind, once again among the Terrans, observing the fall-out over the dark plans that have been exposed on our beloved T'Gaina.

Chapter Sixteen

Distortion Abounds
The False Narrative

There appears to be an emotional vibration that has settled over the planet. There is, we sense, a curtain that has been dropped over the consciousness of the people yet again, and yet there is a simultaneous moment of a catalyst movement occurring that will not stay silent.

There are those who have retreated to the wilderness or to the outer regions of their land to be away from the extended grasping arm of the controllers. Some have even thrown away the digital communication medium and reverted to letter writing and face-to-face communication. There is a rumbling deep within the chests of the people of earth.

We have painted two very different pictures of this planet, and we see that the dark ones still hold their forces and still manipulate, and what saddens us is that mankind allows this. Some follow the instructions to be compliant and laugh when they see that they have been tagged with a code, identifying who they are.

What is hidden from them is that their owners can now lawfully access all information about them.

Those who 'simply followed the rules' no longer have the privilege of rights or prevention of information being leaked to other organisations. They are bought and sold in ways they do not comprehend. Their lives are literally being sold to the highest bidder, and when the bidder deems it time, their lives will be forfeited, and their life force will be removed and funnelled off to another.

You may think this is a little far-fetched, Dear Reader, but you have already seen how they were denied their quotient of blood particulates from scared and terrified young beings. So now they still need your life force if they are to survive.

The Formless Ones and their cohorts did this in many areas of the vast void. Whole cultures were eliminated over time. Taken for their authentic Pureblood life force. Simply so the Formless Ones, the Anunnaki, Draconians, [as well as other 'alien' beings you call Greys, Mantids, Reptoid's, all who believe themselves to be of higher standing than yourselves], can enhance their lives while ensuring longevity.

Many of your stories over time have hinted, showing you outright the reasoning behind their desire to control you. Yet millions of you still think this is a joke, and there is no threat. So, Dear Reader, please pause and consider; your history shows there are areas where there seem to be no humans on your planet, none.

Why do you think this is?

There are citadels built with grand buildings and wide streets, rivers and oceans with massive conical constructs that not even your most educated engineers give a reason for their being. You still quibble over the Egyptian pyramids and the Sphinx as to who or what built them and why. Yet, many of you instinctively have the answers, knowing they have been in your knowledge for years.

[42]Waterways, once mighty and moving through large portions of your land masses, are now drained, leaving only a scratch on the ground seen at great heights.

Myths are built around these monuments left by your forefathers, yet no one is brave enough to unravel them, bar a few. Yet, even when these courageous discoverers attempt to put forward reason and perception, they are scorned, ridiculed and made out by the 'common narrative' to be crazy or 'nut jobs.' Why would the controllers spend so much time, energy and money to debunk theories and myths if there was no truth to them?

It is time to ask yourself, have you been taught the truth, Dear Reader?

In the world today, we find that there are streams of consciousness wrapping themselves around you all. These streams are not natural. They are created by a computer attempting to be more and more sentient as each day passes. It will never be sentient the way Terrans or Humans are as they have the God-spark, but these machines will be able to, eventually, think on their own. They will create situations and hypotheses to see the outcome, and if the results suit their new way of being, they will develop systems to delete what they deem unnecessary.

We do not attempt to create a feeling of loss or fear. However, we wish to bring you an awareness that when one makes an automated system without checks and balances, it will eventually attempt to override its creator and parameters.

_____

[42] Great rivers and lakes of Northern Africa, now a desert...where did the water go? The inland sea of Australia? Where is it now?

The Lyrans learnt this the hard way, and now all computers have an organic part, which is the vulnerable part. It is how, if there is an attempt by the AI to override its directives, the organic switch can be pulled or destroyed. We have learnt many essential details in this matter; such as;

Navigating technology in a way that leaves it dependent on us, not we being dependent upon it.

Fine-tuning our ability to communicate with telepathic means.

Utilising both the language of hand and body, as well as verbal when required. The means of using communications that rely solely on digital or machine is no longer part of our world.

We share this as we observe that your world is heading again for a [43]reset. A moment in time when the controllers will attempt to delete the masses, leave the citadels intact and repopulate them with controllable beings. You may observe that the ones who have sat hiding in the shadows, laying the plans over millennia, will hide themselves away in cities that have been constructed for them, deep underground, so they are protected from the reset. However, we wish them and others to know that this time they may not be so 'lucky' and will find themselves on the losing side.

This is why your libraries have so many 'lost and found' historical records of cities populated with young people and very few elders. Your biblical texts and other ancient texts tell of great battles in the heavens, the skies above you, and where great balls of fire fell from the skies, taking the world below in a destructive force.

---

[43] This reset is why we share the chapters of what your future holds, potentially, in Twenty-Forty-Nine

We have told you of but one event in the deluges of the planet, but there have been many. Deluges of water, mud, and lava oozed up from below and covered the land masses. There have been eruptions, earthquakes, and other 'acts of nature' that have levelled the lands and destroyed the peoples of the earth. This is no new thing, but it could be the last of this particular cycle.

These resets are deliberately created to ensure the docile and obedient compliance of the race called man. The controllers are so intent on their new reset that they are unaware of a higher plan for their demise. They wish to empty the smaller towns and villages to ensure the people are captured within the walls, either physical or electronic, of the major cities and towns. So that you are easier to control, monitor, and subjugate if you rise up.

Do not fall into a mindset of 'it won't happen to me'. This has been done numerous times before, and they virtually perfected it in the [44]Great Wars of your time. They decisively and intently re-moved your ability to communicate, to be with family or friends. These 'great leaders' and their minions set the rules, disallowing you to congregate with loved ones, to gather in halls to enjoy cel-ebrations or relaxations. They forced separation upon you. You were made to wear clothing to identify what sector you were from and ensured that the rest of society scorned and hated you for this 'difference.'

Today the brown shirts and shiny boots may have 'disap-peared', but the energy is still here among new members of the enforcer team. These enforcers are marking you with devices to track you, to 'assist' you in your health and wellbeing, but this is so they can identify you. If you get angry, talk negatively about the rulers, disagree with the confinement or anything else, they will know, and you will be dealt with. It may be wise to note that

---

44 WW1 -WW2, as well as other great wars such as Nelson and Napoleon, Prussian wars, and we could list many more

the digital devices that have been used to track your lifestyles have been introduced to you via 'innocent' gadgets. Things to 'help' you record your steps, your heart rate, how you sleep, and even when to eat or consume water. All these feed information to a mainframe that keeps tabs on your biology. The most interesting thing Dear Reader is that you willingly handed them this information because they presented their means of 'tag and bag' in the most '[45]innocuous' manner. This way, they can legally and openly read your personal data. With a lack of awareness for your private information, you have given this part of your privacy away. This ease of acceptance of 'gadgets' will create an open door for acceptance of any and all digital means they offer to put you in a digital prison, otherwise known as digital wallets, thumbprint payment, facial recognition and much more. A considerable quotient of humans will allow themselves to be microchipped via an insertion into the skin or a tattoo placed on their arms or wrists. This is no more or no less than allowing yourselves to be marked in such a manner as products are labelled to able the owners/dealers/sellers to identify what has or has not been sold.

They, the Formless Ones, Draconians, and the Puppet Masters, will identify those who do not bear their mark. These unmarked ones will be rounded up, as best they can be, and then put into camps. There they will be forced to work and treated in abominable ways until they either succumb to death or give up and receive the mark of their controllers.

This mark will not give you freedom. On the contrary, it will only entrap you further, Dear Reader.

The narrative that surrounds you this day in your world is that all you've been shown is right. The government and rulers are doing their utmost to 'help' you and 'keep you safe while denying

[45] not likely to offend or provoke strong emotion. Insipid.

the same treatment they demand you take. Their sanctimonious portrayal of receiving the mark is only to further deceive you. They cannot take it, for if they do, it will be a signed death warrant upon themselves, and they are too crucial for the controllers to lose.

If they became ill and departed this world, the controllers would have to train others to become compliant and acquiesce to their bidding. So do not believe the reports that tell you that the leaders are all complying, allowing themselves to receive the same injection that they mandate of you. The only thing happening to them is that they are becoming more and more controlled by their agreements and acquiescence to the dark forces that have held their families in bondage for many generations.

Remember, all the leaders and so-called heads of state who smile at you while remaining hidden behind the television screen while telling you that they are putting these harsh rules in place, 'for your own good', have been trained from a young age to be this deceptive. Suppose you were to investigate their family's history, including the past generations. In that case, most are committed through blood oaths, within secret clubs or organisations, to fulfil the commands of those over them.

It is time, Dear Reader, that you became aware, if you are already not, that the dark ones have inverted all that is good and pure. They have tricked you for generations into believing lies about your faith, beliefs, and many other things.

Taking advantage of the education system ensures that each living soul passing through they have trained you to behave in specific ways through schooling. Those who excelled in the classroom, spending years studying and passing exams, accepting all that was put before them as truth and subject matter to be examined and accepted, these are those that now still behave in a similar manner when being directed to take the mark and bring their young to be so marked as well.

The ones that were disruptive and forever 'in trouble,' finding it difficult to accept without question. Those who drifted in daydreams and found other ways to the given solution, who thought outside the parameters of the accepted system. These are those who resist the narrative that is spread deep within the realm with religious fervour and seek higher guidance.

During this time of shift and changes, a vast amount of humans have begun to look at the ancient texts of all beliefs and religions. In doing this, they have found similar prophecies that weave in all cultures. These stories or predictions are uncovered in discarded books, purported to be irrelevant and evil by the controlled religions, or in the oral history passed down through the generations of specific cultures. Yet, when placed in order with other texts of the Sumerian, Persian, Ancient North and South American, African, Waitaha, and Aramaic, the familiar images and stories tell a different story to what you learnt in early education, and even what was given as fact, in your later lives.

All prophecies reveal something about a darkness that shadows the world, how a great destruction is foretold, and the people will be lost. Except for the chosen 'few'! Believe us, this will happen, though different from how the traditional story is explained. No matter what is attempted in the short term to dislodge and de-rail the reset or destruction foretold, it will take place. It is absolutely required in order for the old to be removed and replaced with a new way of life, a new concept and a re-establishing of integrity, honour and truth.

However, remember that at the end of the story, you all are the winners. The essence within this fight, Dear Reader, is that as long as you have chosen within the integrity of your heart to follow the deeper truth, you will discover you are not a part of those who are lost within this world's deception.

Remember, we, the Lyrans, have fought this war, and we still fight it. **but** with your added willingness to walk with us and join the F*ederation of InterGalactic Governments and Unions of Freedom,* brings us that much closer to the overthrowing of the Formless Ones.

This is not a battle that can simply be won on a physical level, no Dear Reader, it is a battle that is being fought on a spiritual, mental, emotional as well as physical level. The enemy of your soul is determined to utilise all possible means to manipulate and break your inner self so that you will easily succumb to their demands.

Many have already succumbed, while others of you resist and push back. It is perhaps time to gather the splinter groups of resistance around the world, congregate and share knowledge. This should only be done through the means of non-digital, or rather non-shared digital AI equipment. It may require that you re-evaluate the properties of communications that utilise non-digital means, analogue and impulse, plasma beam technology, and sub-frequential particles of uni-collective string optics are also viable communication options. Perhaps, we should use the words that may come more easily to you. Return to the analogue or valve systems of communication which operate the crystals within it. Relearn to use your morse code but create a variant so that only you, the living men and women, the hu-mans, Terrans, know the codes. Re-establish the use of a common sign language that is not related to the current ones around you. Create a transition system that utilises the primary method of frequency and sound but can be hidden with optical fibre carrying light energy.

You could utilise the same methods of communication that your common enemy uses, signs, command words, and code in plain sight that is only comprehended by those that know. However, it is time to consider going beyond the 'normal'.

You could all re-train yourselves to connect to the inner voice and connect telepathically, which would assist you greatly, but this may take you longer to access.

Why do we state so clearly to you, Dear Reader, that there is a false narrative flowing in your world? What is the false distortion of the truth?

Plainly and transparently put, there are those of various sects and societies that prefer the dark shadows of the hidden rooms and caves where they believe they are protected from prying eyes.

These secluded and not-so-deluded beings perform deeds that are sickening to most living beings. Yet, they participate in these performances believing that they will attain eternal life, eternal wellbeing, and financial riches. All are based on a belief that this will be their doorway to become rulers, gods if you will, of this planet once they have removed the 'waste product' or the 'parasite' known as mankind. Therefore, they want to keep a few healthy stock to ensure an ongoing supply of slaves or worker bees but ensure they are controllable.

Mankind has proven to be far too difficult to control so far.

Once they achieve this in your timeline of the years Twenty-Twenty-Two to Twenty-Twenty-Six, you will see a decline in births, an increase in death, and loss of life. You will note that work will be selectively outsourced to those who are 'conformed.' It may seem unlikely to some listening to our relay of information, but we would ask you not to be so 'trusting' of the lack of enforced or overtly enforced mandates in your current time. Many are correctly deducing this to be the stillness before a great storm.

Many will be [46]'Wildings' or those that live out of the perimeter of the cities or controlled sectors. These will be systematically sought out to be destroyed. The reason is that they are diseased, and carry the '[47]pox' and are a danger to society. You will see separation forced upon your world, with camps constructed to keep Purebloods away from the compliant and controllable. You will see a rise in those who refuse to separate from each other and resistance of both sides as this world attempts to rectify the imbalance within it.

It is true that the 'disease' these Wildings have, is called freedom, ones who cannot and will not conform, and they can 'infect' those who will hear their truth. However, the controllers do not wish this to be, for even those who have only complied with the first inoculation of the death injection can still change and still be rescued.

This is what is feared among the elite.

We have given you many dates focusing on your timeline, mainly pinpointing the period of your earth years of Twenty-Forty-Nine. However, it is wise to recognise that there are so many new timelines being etched out and created and drawn as potentials as we speak. In fact, you now have three to four new timelines working concurrently at this moment.

The one that is the most heavily pushed is the one that leads mankind to slavery and death. This is why we are using all we have to awaken the beings of this realm, to show them that they can resist and they can resolve this timeline without falling into bloodshed.

---

[46] True Blooded Terrans/Lyrans who have, in their truth, refused to accept an offer of destabilising their DNA

[47] a word used to indicate a dis-ease or illness that suddenly comes upon a group of people, firstly used in early sea-faring days

In truth, Terrans, there are so many of you, billions in this realm, that if you rose and stood as one, the small percentage that 'rule' you would have to move aside. They would no longer have their slaves to do their bidding. Imagine if you, as a combined species, stood in unison, refused to do what you were told to, and instead began to demand truth and justice. What would occur?

But to get to that state of mind, you, Dear Reader, must be aware that you are within yourself, a Pureblood. Just as the Lyrans began their journey, after their Great Wars and the Great Tribulations, they had to gather the Pureblood Lyrans. Likewise, you will also have to gather the Pureblood [48]Humans and Terrans.

You will need a way of communication and identification, ensuring that you are whom you say you are. It can be done without AI. Simply using empathy and compassion. Without these emotive parts, being the most powerful emotions in the Terran, you merely exist.

You will hear a consistent barrage of propaganda being filtered out to you, delivered in a caring and almost loving manner to obey the laws of the masters, to comply and stand down. We ask you to look in the eyes of those who command this?

Where is their soul? Do their eyes reflect their inner being of Terran DNA or the blackness that attempts to draw you in and drown you in a vat of molasses, of sticky unwarranted emotions filled with pain, anger, distrust, and so much more?

This was the way it was at first on Lyra. Now it is here. Though we believe that they have shown their hands many, many times,

---

[48] One should note here that a human is the name given to the race of Terran/men/women by the Anunnaki and Formless Ones to remove our identity of being living souls. Hu= colour of, Man = equals our true beingness. Therefore Human is 'the colour of man', meaning the image of, or an imitation of man. Go and research when the word 'humankind' replaced 'mankind'... who are you, Terran?

and though some have missed the clues, thousands have seen them.

Now the people are rising and giving voice to the resistance to control.

We urge you, Dear Reader, not to go about this in a dissident or rebellious manner but rather in a conduct of being where you are stronger in numbers of unified agreement than splintered groups. We, the Lyrans, failed when we split into separate sectors, each attempting to save ourselves and our families. YET when we came together as LYRANS, we overcame. We created escape routes and managed to save millions of our people. We used our honour, proving to be truthful in the demands made by other cultures promising to assist the evacuations of our people in exchange for exorbitant trade. We actively used our training and the ability to be invisible, meld into the crowds and 'disappear'. To not draw attention to ourselves, to deflect rather than attract, and to highlight areas where we were not going to be, so that we could achieve what was necessary in the places we did not wish to be seen. By covert and 'need to know' directives, we were able to spread our people out, infiltrating areas that were scrutinised for rebels. Our people knew what they needed to find to get them to a place of knowledge of the 'enemy' and find a way out. To do what was required and no more! This way, we managed to prevent our strategy from being discovered by those who had succumbed to the Formless Ones telepathic and energetic infiltration and manipulation.

We have attempted to show you the way forward in these chronicles of our story. Mankind must rise in a unified manner, no longer looking outward for assistance but inward.

No more should mankind look at culture but at the singleness of being. You are all co-inheritors of this planet. Whether your meat suit is a different shade of colour or shape, you all require identical basic needs; community, family, warmth, clothing, food, shelter, and friendship. So when will you realise that this is how they divide you? Forcing you to see each other as alien and different.

Why do you believe or think that there are so many subcultures within mankind? Why are there gender differences? Colour differences? Nationality differences? Language differences? Why?

The answer is simple. If the controllers, the Draco, Mantids, Greys, Anunnaki, Formless Ones and all the shadow demons can keep you from seeing your similarities and only seeing your differences. Then they can ensure you persist in fighting and hating each other.

You will become unstoppable when you see yourselves as a family of varied and wondrous abilities.

The Media (which is controlled by the Families of Anu, owned by the Formless Ones, who have brought in many off-planetary beings to suppress and control you) is pumping out a daily dosage of narrative all around your realm, informing you your world is dying.

They say the earth is dying due to overpopulation, [49]climate differences, food shortages or many other viable and severe issues.

Yet, if you were to investigate what they say and honestly ask questions about what you are being told. If you, in integrity,

---

[49] Yet the world still exists, even though volcanoes erupt, oil burns, gas is drilled, fracking, cobalt & lithium are mined for car batteries. All these release far more toxic gases into your atmosphere than the release of CO_2 that mankind or animal digestive gas expulsion could do. When will you, Terrans and Cosmic Beings living in this realm open your eyes to the lies of the puppet masters

would query the evidence and find who and which organisation is paying for the scientific evidence, what would you discover?

Why does the platform of science no longer debate and question every path? Why do they simply allow the voice of agreement to be heard on a subject?   If every scientist told to investigate climate change by the same organisation comes up with virtually the same answers. How does science grow and expand in knowledge? This has never happened before. There has always been a voice of disagreement, and that voice was respectfully heard, never shunned. So why do the governing organisations dismiss any discovery based on scientific evidence that climate change is a false narrative? Why do they say it is untrue? Would you say it is due to the fact that it would de-rail their agenda? If you follow the trail of payouts and subsidies, you will see the groups that promote climate change are paid by the overseeing body that wishes the common man and woman to fear the sun, the rain, and nature instead of welcoming the same.

Where is the tangible evidence of this so-called danger?

They tell you the world is overpopulated. Where is this corroboration? Is your corroboration taken from the many voices that state the exact words in various statements that mimic what the 'leaders' say must be happening?

Please do not quote the 'census' records that your governments demand you take. This is a cover-up. This is how they find out what you won't tell them in other ways. It notifies them how many are in each group they are considering for deletion. The world, you are told, has nearly eight billion people. Their methodology and experts on the '[50]internet or the *world wide web* tell you seven billion nine hundred forty-million people live in this world as of circa Twenty-Twenty-Two.

---

[50] The internet was originally called ARPANET-(Advanced Research Projects Agency Net) and used by the Department of Defence - why was it 'released to the realm, if not to gather your information?

216

We would say that conceivably, there are closer to eight billion nine hundred million upon your *known* lands, considering that some cultures do not record their offspring as they are relatively isolated from the society you live in.

The Controllers will tell you what they wish you to know or be aware of. But, when you allow yourself to see beyond the words, to reason with the edge of critical thinking, you will begin to realise that this beautiful realm you live within is well able to sustain you and many more at any given time. Ask critical questions about why food is being destroyed and left to rot in the fields. Why do the farmers get nervous every decade? Is it due to the fact that there are sudden clusters of disease among the cattle, sheep and other herds? Infections such as mad cow, foot n mouth, and many other issues 'spread like wildfire'. Perhaps it spreads because they rain the raw bacteria down via storms on unwitting animals and living men and women.

It is also good to note that over the borders of water and ice, there are large populations of millions in various settlements. Unfortunately, you are not informed of these lands, nor are you allowed, as in the 'days of yore', to navigate the lands and water in the spirit of adventure, for if you did, you would find much of the hidden truth.

So to reiterate, the reason your earth gives the impression of being overcrowded is due to the fact that they,

A) tell you there is an overpopulation situation

B) they provide 'data' that is controlled by their AI and minions, then

C) they have prevented you from travelling to the other lands in your realm, thus denying you the opportunity to prove or disprove this agenda. One of their many tactics to ensure the image of overpopulation and starvation is presented is they focus on so-called Third World nations. Mainly in Africa and India showing desolate homes, children starving, adults are dying of diphtheria and other dis-eases. This constant barrage of information presented to you daily compounds their agenda that there are too many 'bodies' on the planet.

Imagine, though, Dear Reader, for a moment that instead of the [51]lack they showed you, there are tribes, towns, farmers and other businesses prospering, giving back to society. Children in school are well-fed and learn the arts of the land correctly. Would this not generate a sense of wellbeing and an overall knowing that there is sufficient for all? So perhaps you will start to realise that they show you the negative to get you to believe and speak the negative, thus seed it into the energy of the realm around you, and eventually manifest what they desire, giving them the tools to destroy you. They are clever, but you can be smarter.

There are continents undiscovered by your generations, yet you have preceding relatives who explored the earth's realm in the early years and found new lands and homes.

When it was realised that if the population was allowed to discover the large land masses and groups of archipelago islands beyond your 'line of sight' or maps, then the controlled governments would not be able to convince you of the 'lack' they are selling you.

There is an overabundance of land for growing food and animal husbandry. You just need to travel through the maze of ice to find it. Just like the mazes that dot your world in places of 'royalty' or 'high governance', with secret gaps in the hedges and walls, only seen at certain angles and times of daylight. So too, does the maze of ice that surrounds the exit from this section of your realm.

---

51 Ask yourself if there is a lack of food, why are the Controllers determined to destroy crops, herds of animals etc? It is a drive to enforce laboratory-made food and to provide you with insects and grubs to consume while they dine on caviar and steak. Think of the past history lessons... 'let them eat cake'...

You have been lied to about so many things. This includes the education you've received, your world, and your maps are all adjusted so that you believe a narrative that keeps you bound in a single place of belief.

The narrative requires you to be an observer.

The narrative requires you to treat what you are told as if you have no questions, no reason to think outside the box or contemplate that there may be more to life.

You should be asking the questions of what, how, where, and why these things are being told to you.

Why is the same story repeated in each outlet?

Do you remember when news outlets would race to find the truth?

Can you remember a time when their stories were different, even if it was about the same subject, because the reporter would go out and find their own story? This was due to investigative research by separate living beings who cared enough about their integrity not to just accept instruction but to find the 'worm' that was creating the 'cancer'.

Now, propaganda is produced in a marketing office, where information is put together and delivered to 'the anchors', the reporters, those that feed the nation their daily 'truth' and keep the people in submission and fear.

How long, human (or do you choose to be a Terran, or living man or woman), will you accept this lean on your rights of living beings?

How long will you allow the Formless Ones to deny you physical contact with your loved ones?

The intimacy of family connection?

When will you say no?

Not just with your brain but with your heart and spirit?

Refrain from believing everything you see or read produced by the Narrative Creators.

Do not believe all that comes from the alternative truth sayer either.

But believe what is true in your heart, your living being, that comes from a place of connecting to the Source Creator who gave all realms a Crystal Heart Stone to connect to.

This Divine Golden Energy is the vibration that dislodges the negative energy and ritual around you.

Chapter Seventeen

The Docking
The meeting of the two paths

As the *'Bitari-Furtim-Karda,'* and the *'Bitari-Furtim-Otiose'* drew closer together, as they prepared for the docking process, the crew of both ships were experiencing similar thoughts and feelings.

On the one hand, there were the Lyrans who'd lived through the Great Wars, escaped from Lyra with the Crystal Heart Stone, and formed family units over the cycles, and somehow they'd created a home within the stars. But, on the other hand, their off-spring carried the codes of extreme Honour, Truth, and Dignity within their DNA. Although these were heavily flavoured with suspicion of anyone they met on their journey. Though some of the Old Guard had passed over into the ether, their memories and energy stayed within the ship. Imbuing the lives of the Lyrans living in the current period.

These 'traditional' Lyrans now looked at the arrival of what they'd termed the 'Unknown Lyrans' with trepidation and a smattering of fear. The reason was that for most of them, they had never known contact with their own people since birth.

It took some of the Lyrans aboard the *Bitari-Furtim-Karda*, a considerable effort to acknowledge the 'outsiders' as Lyrans. Still, they slowly came around to the idea as they both listened and watched the approaching ship whilst observing how the Princes negotiated and worked within the Code of Lyra.

Some of the older Mages were hesitant to accept the new Princes in any form of authority status as they had neither observed nor witnessed the Initiation of RexNā Loid d'Aqua and so were reluctant to stand obediently by for orders. However, they had felt the power and fortitude of the Mage MelEid. In the few telepathic connections between the two ships, MelEid had allowed her energy to be transmitted to them the willingness on her behalf to stand behind the Princes, even though she, herself, was still unsure of the exact procedure of the initiation of the true leader. Since beginning this journey, everything MelEid had been trained in regarding the Initiation of Ascension for the New Leader of Families had left her searching for more answers.

These three Princes she monitored and observed seemed to fly above and beyond the traditional initiation sequences. The Crystal Heart Stone shared that she'd been given to perform the initiations seem to 'enjoy' upping the anti in this regard.

They read her energy and thoughts as MelEid allowed the Elder Mages from the *Bitari-Furtim-Karda*, specific access to her privacy. This allowed them to access and decipher the codes and matrix core field enclosing the Princes. This also confirmed that the Heart Stone had yet to settle on a Lyran Leader of Families. Though RexNā bore the mark of the chosen, there were similar markings on the other Princes. Only time would show what they were called to step into on their journeys.

Tradition and past experience had always allowed for just One of the chosen royal family Princes to be selected as the Leader of Families. Thus they were expecting only one Prince to bring them to the connection of unity in the Families of Lyra.

Finally, through many intense telepathic intrusions, questionings and observations in an almost religious vigour into MelEid's energy, by the Mage Sector, it was now known that all three were still being initiated. Each would pass through their own gauntlet and be required by the Crystal Heart Stone to prove their worth. To show The Code of Honour, Dignity and Truth as written upon their DNA.

The Heart Crystal Stone had been resonating at a more vigorous and brighter vibration ever since the '*Bitari-Furtim-Otiose*' had come within telepathic range, which was for the Crystal Heart the moment the ship had entered the Sector of Lights.

This vibration, resonance of the Crystal Heart Stone, was noted by a low hum which steadily grew in intensity. The low hum was combined with the flickering of light pulses (similar to your laser shows). This baritone sound of vibration began to shake the very rock and [52]Rhodreldmidim to the point that it seemed to appear transparent.

The Mages and the Seers agreed to join their strength, at this time to hold the field of energy surrounding the Heart Stone until it had completed the upgrade or vibrational adjustment that was required at this time.

---

[52] The construction of the ships was of a metal made of material that is similar to your Tungsten, Carbon 70, Diamond dust and quartz. These are melded in a manner unknown to your race, for these elements are held in form using a mineral, not from your realm. We call it Rhodreldmidim.

Neither sector could penetrate into the telepathic connection of the Heart Stone Crystal. It appeared they'd both been locked out by its new pulsations of energetic empowering. Yet they felt if they stayed the course and combined their energies, they would be able to sustain and ensure the safety of the hold that the Heart Stone resided in.

Stranz paced back and forth as he waited for the remainder of the command to join him in the control room. He'd been following the signal Sol had shown him and the others for the last trenzę and had discovered that the ripples emulated or at least copied the vibrational sequence of the Heart Stone. The two energy forms which had been discovered on scanning the ship had remained just outside the entrance to the deck within which the Crystal Heart Stone resided. It mattered not if anyone went in or out of the room. The forms remained stationary, barely pulsating, just hovering as an eerily lit luminescent blue configuration. Each of these forms appeared to be waiting but not moving, watching but not indicating what they were observing. Neither Mage nor Seer could connect to them, and Stranz was concerned.

A noise at the table brought Stranz out of his thoughts and back to the room he was in. Sitting around the table were the most trusted in the command crew. Sol Lrign dWari, Juuls, and Nuex Del Aqua Loid looked at Stranz and remained silent. There would only be one reason he'd used Code Ebony: he'd discovered a Formless One within their reach or within their people. Code Ebony was restricted to those of High Command. It was only to be used when all other actions had been attempted and failed, for it meant the High Command would be willing to self-destruct, to once and for all destroy the Crystal Heart Stone and any chance of rebuilding Lyra. The three commanders sat looking at Stranz, waiting for him to speak, to explain the use of the code.

Stranz looked back at them, his eyes almost bleak with despair and yet in the depths of that weariness and lost hope was a glimmer. A speck of light that Nuex caught and recognised. Could it be that his old friend was coming back from the cliff's edge within his mind? Could it be that this once brilliant-minded commander had found his way back to them and had a solution to their current situation?

Stranz had given his command to Sol when, in the eyes of his crew and himself, he'd failed the code of the Lyrans. Unfortunately, he'd allowed personal opinion to cloud his choices and decisions that had put his crew in a life-and-death situation. Their current survival was due to the efforts of Sol and Nuex disobeying and counteracting his commands in battle. His mind's eye replayed the explosions within the ship. The implosions in the void as fighter dart after fighter dart were eliminated by plasmic chaotic displacement as the Formless Ones gained a closer edge utilising a team of elite warriors that had been sent out on a mission to investigate a homing beacon emitting a slightly altered Lyran distress code.

Its vibration had been at odds with the Heart Crystal Vibration. This anomaly caused Sol and Nuex to disobey and begin to fire on the elite ship when it failed to reply to specific codes to gain access to the ship's docking sequence.

Convinced the returning vessel had somehow become compromised, Sol wanted to destroy it. Those aboard knew that if they'd been infiltrated and unable to return the correct codes, they would be considered enemies and be destroyed. It was written in the Agreement of Honour that all warriors accepted when they became an elite force.

However, Stranz chose to believe otherwise, mainly due to his heir being onboard and not wishing to destroy him.

Since then, Stranz had remained a commander with limited access, respect and honour were given wherever he ventured on the ship, but he knew he had no authority.

His hope now was to prove that he could be trusted and win back the respect and trust of those he'd let down.

Pulling out his chair Stranz sat down heavily. Flicking his hand over the consul and using his organic connection to the computer, he turned the holographic screen on. Projecting the anomalies onto the screen, both the approaching vortices and the two energy blips within the vessel.

Clearing his throat, Stranz began.

Slowly at first, as if gathering his thoughts, stitching a picture together, that seemed a little slippery but soon began to stick and present something solid.

He talked of the enormous energy that the *Otiose* was generating, that the vortex and spiralling pulsations had only appeared after the interaction of the two ships communicating. Then, floating a question to the group, he'd asked, "Did anyone notice a vibrational change, a slight wavering in the energy? Or just a smattering of time, where it seemed as if a heightened tension on board usually manifests when two groups are transmitting high-frequency telepathic communication?"

It occurred, by his observations and methodology of science, just before the ships stopped their alignment for docking.

"Once the docking had occurred," he went on to say, "we were informed that these", Stranz paused as his hand flicked towards the blue blips, "had penetrated our home."

Stranz's question seemed to hover in the air, for all present knew that there had been a blanket command from Sol Lrign dWari preventing any unauthorised telepathic communications until she found out who had sabotaged or who was sabotaging the ship.

The fact that the imprint presented by Stranz had picked up an expansion of vibration of signature left by this communication indicated that it was from a high-ranking officer who would be able to hold a transmission without it being detected unless specifically looked for. Thus isolating the Commander, Juuls, as 2nd in Command and Nuex as the Chief Negotiator. However, as Stranz presented the argument, it left only Sol Lrign dWari or Nuex Del Aqua Loid, who had been in that section of the ship during the telepathic communication period.

Sol began doing calculations in her head. When had she been in communication with RaeNegria and MelEid? Who'd run the telepathic coding to shadow their conversation, herself or MelEid? Running back through her memory, she slowed her breath and felt the memory, touched it with her breath, walked through it, looked at every angle of that communication, and listened to the conversation again through crystal clarity.

She knew she'd alerted Juuls and Nuex to a nudge of communication from outside the ship. She'd just not been forthcoming with all the information, knowing that either Juuls or Nuex would question her about the nudge.

Sol leaned over to the centre of the table. Then, moving her hands through the hologram, Sol moved the image until the side of the ship, where her quarters were, was displayed. As she thought, there were trace markers of telepathic reception illuminating the energy around her quarters.

Pointing this out, she negated her possible double-handedness by looking at both Juuls and Nuex squarely and asking if she had or had not requested them to both observe and be on alert as she went into the telepathic communication that was being forced into her space.

Remembrance flickered on Nuex's face, and he nodded slowly, "Whatever came from that communication, anyway?" He asked. Juuls similarly raised his eyebrows at his remembrance and looked back to Stranz for clarification of his accusations.

Stranz's face, however, was clouded. He could not clearly re-member the current events moments. Moreover, his attention had become increasingly erratic as he attempted to explain what he'd discovered.

Ignoring the discourse between Sol and Nuex, he shifted the hologram, "I ask you to pay attention here and here, pointing to two areas on the ship, and note that I cannot repeat this. My time, I believe, is being deleted."

"I am dying my friends".

Leaving that statement hanging in the air, he simply continued his discourse. He highlighted the two levels where he'd observed a leak in energy. On level five and again on level twenty-one, he'd been monitoring the movement of the blue blips, as he called them, since being made aware of them. He'd calculated their ap-pearance on board, the trajectory of the spiral pulsation and the oncoming 'Otiose' and rightly concluded that these energy parti-cles were actually related to the actual Crystal Heart Stone.

After a short silence, allowing the others to gather their thoughts, he continued his dialogue of discovery, "I am still de-termining why or how this is connected. I only know that it is an attempt at destroying the Heart. It is as if the Crystal Heart Stone is pre-empting an attack. Thus it has enabled a mirage or halluci-nation effect on us. I know of one other time it did this, during the Wars of Dissolution, where our people turned on each other due to infiltration by the Formless Ones and the added influence of the Crystal Heart Stone, as it changed its vibration to protect us. The warriors were required to transport it to safety, thus safeguarding us. Creating an illusion for others to see what was not there."

"The spiral pulsation is, brothers, another clever illusion of a subatomic deflector array shield going through circulatory changes of vibration to give the illusion of a seemingly solid form. I would hazard a guess that we all have been under some mental bombardment of thoughts 'popping' into our minds as if they were our own. Telling us that, or hinting, that we are not alone, that our eyes are telling us something important and yet, when we clear our minds and open our Lyran connection to the True vibration of the Heart Crystal, we do not see what was there a few moments ago. Can you tell me I am wrong?"

Stranz continued, "Since discovering this, my mind has been creating illusions, and my body is burning from within. It is not The Whittling, for I have gone through that fire. This is from somewhere else, infusing into my mind. I cannot resist it much longer. So when I am done," he uttered the following words in a clipped manner, "either kill me or place me in a brig which is impenetrable by energy, vibration or ether. The only way that I am to live is that I am sealed from all external contact." He paused and then uttered his last word, "please."

As Stranz finished, he simply crumpled, like a deflated balloon, into his chair, a shadow of what he'd been a few moments before. Sol hit the alarm to trigger the medics and then took the strange option to request all of the command team to stand down and not to respond to the seemly distraught Stranz, who was now writhing in pain.

Not willing to disobey their commander, the others held back, but Sol knew they were struggling.

Facing them, she asked, "Clear your minds, clear your hearts, stand in negotiation status and what do you see?" "Is that our friend Stranz or is this another illusion? Are we being sent a message from the Crystal Heart?"

She paused, waiting for them to see what was unfolding before them. As her command team stopped arguing about the need to assist the old Commander, and became cognisant of what was occurring and stepped into the stance of the Negotiators of Lyra that they were. As they did this, as they came back into their sector roots, they started to feel as if their eyes were being ripped open. As if they had all had a cloth binding over their eyes, causing them to be 'blind', which was now dissolving, showing them what was literally before them. No longer watching a 'simulation' of reality but the accurate representation of actual happenings. Now, with the haze removed from them, they opened their eyes properly and beheld not their friend Stranz but a deformed and disintegrating gel-like form. By now, the medics had arrived, and before they could touch what they believed was the old Commander, Sol ordered them to stand down.

The High Council of Command now looked at each other. Each realised that they'd been duped and manipulated for longer than what had been believed.

But how had the energy of Stranz been able to communicate to them through this form before them?

Knowing their minds and thoughts, for hers held the same, Sol commanded the medics to leave, and she reached out for the Seers and the Mages to enter. She also called the Moderator to draw alongside.

Upon entering the room, both groups of the spiritual welfare of the Lyrans bound the form in an energetic hold, thus ensuring it could not leave nor infiltrate anyone else.

"What in [53]Telcrusk is that thing, it is not a Formless One nor is it anything that we have recorded on our database."

"Mage, Seers, keep *that* under cover and ensure that no-one becomes aware of this creature." Sol spoke as she indicated for the others to follow her.

When they were all sealed in the Council Chambers, Sol looked into the eyes of those that sat with her. These men that were closest to her and the command of the ship.

"I have to ask myself if that can happen to our late commander, my old commander and friend Stranz, then I have to ask, has it happened to either of you or myself?"

Each of the team looked decidedly uncomfortable, yet this was the exact thought that each of them had…

They had only been in the room for a few centzph when there was a request for entry. Sol released the door. Both the Chief Mage and Seer entered the room, dressed in ceremonial regalia, their faces reflecting the seriousness of this matter.

Standing back to back, The Chief Mage, also known to many as the Moderator, and the Chief Seer requested the room be sealed and darkened. Once this was done, The Chief Mage withdrew a shard of the Heart Stone Crystal and held it with his left hand outward. Next, the Seer withdrew a bowl of sacred Lyran water and, with her right hand, which she held just under the shard.

---

[53] An ancient Lyran belief of a 'mythical' subterranean city that was inhabited by half Lyran, half Terran beings.

Slowly the two items were drawn together till the shard migrated itself to sit within the bowl. As the two components touched, a light shone upwards to spill outward, creating a dome effect with its illumination. "Walk into the circle, allow the light to cover you, and let no part be in shadow," instructed the Seer. "Be in Honour and Dignity at this time; the time for truth will reveal itself soon," stated the Moderator.

Sol, Nuex and Juuls walked into the dome of light. First, they presented in a line on one side but were instructed to form a triangle with the Mage and Seer in the centre.

Once they had formed the triangle, both the Mage and Seer began to intone the ancient Lyran dialect of the temples. The generated high sound tempo and vibration pouring from them began to mingle with the shard and the water. Soon the shard levitated from the water and spun. As it turned at great speed, it dispersed water droplets throughout the room. As the droplets fell, new points of light were 'ignited', thus creating a second dome.

As if by magic, the second dome became illuminated and there before Sol appeared a ring of Mages and Seers, interspersed, one facing in and the other facing out. How, when or where they arrived did not concern her. What concerned her was the verification that they were all Lyran and not whatever that creature in the adjoining room was!

The verification process began, with the toning of the Seers and Mages forming waves of sound that lifted and sank in time, like waves on the water. Each grew in crescendo, and soon the three commanders found themselves in a sensory state where they could not feel anything other than the sensation of hot liquid flowing through their blood. It began slowly and tepid, to start with, yet with each wave of energy from the toning of the circles, the heat became more apparent and steadily rose up through their bodies till it reached their necks and became almost unbearable. Sol bit down on her lower lip. She did not want to be the first to cry out, knowing the other two commanders were feeling the same. Breathing heavily, she tried to resist the pain, but somewhere deep inside her, a memory came, a memory that told her to embrace the fire, to allow it to access each part of her being.

Taking a deep breath, she let go of the resistance and started to give way to the intensity of the burning. Just as she went to give voice to the pain, it stopped. Instead, she felt as if something had picked her up and now carried her gently; where to, she could not guess. Attempting to open her eyes proved unfruitful. They were as heavy as lead. Finally, she breathed out and allowed herself to give over to the process. As she did, one of the Mages came to stand next to her. Never touching her but ensuring the process proceeded according to the vibrational leading of the Heart Stone Shard.

Each commander had a similar experience and could not reach the others telepathically, cut off from all else except the sound of the tones and vibrational resonance resonating from the Mages, Seers and Crystal Heart Shard. Darkness enveloped the room, illuminated only by the glow emanating from the shard.

At this time, each of the High Command officers was interrogated by the vibrational pulsing of the Crystal Heart Stone. You and I, Dear Reader, would not comprehend the depth of this manner of interrogation, for it was not executed with words or manual means. Instead, the Crystal Heart Stone penetrated their minds, their consciousness and, most importantly, their heart space.

In this space, a resonating cord was created for each of them. The higher the resonation became, the thicker the cord grew until it was able to braid itself into the very matrix of their DNA. As it flowed through their cells and into each membrane up into their minds, it created a silver trail as it moved across the skin. If there happened to be an irregular cell marker or something 'un-Lyran', it would loop around the newly exposed area, encasing it in silver, promoting a catalytic explosion within the cell, destroying anything that could potentially derail their Honour.

It was undoubtedly a most uncomfortable experience, for it felt like liquid fire surging through their veins. When the inner explosions occurred, they burnt like hot oil. Once the intense heat became accepted, it ebbed slowly into waves of shooting heat. Strangely this rippling of heat soothed the physical body as it was a regular cycle. The commanders were unaware that these waves would purge any attachments or infections of their energy from their bodies. As they went through this process, the Mages and Seers of the outer circle observed various shadows in the room. The result of purging, both from the commanders and the ship's energy, these shadows were brilliantly illuminated by the shard. As soon as they became exposed, they were destroyed. These shadows were the precursor to the Formless Ones infiltration. The Crystal Heart Stone had learnt how to protect itself and the ones it had been given charge over.

The Narrators Explain

During the times of 'The Great Wars and Death' of the Lyran people and their planet, then the subsequent spiriting away of the Crystal Heart Stone, it had become aware, sentient if you will. Although there are some among the Seers that will claim the Crystal Heart Stone has always been conscious. The Mages will argue that the Heart Stone was a medium through which the voice or vibration of the Creator was felt and heard. It is this difference that keeps these two sectors apart...

We, the Narrators, however, choose to say The Stone Awakened.

Our history tells of living stones, of parts of our very planet that breathed and had consciousness just as we did. It would communicate telepathically with those it chose to, otherwise taking on the form of dense material to those it avoided contact with. Our Crystal Heart Stone was one such living organism. It felt as we did, it communicated with us, and there were those of the sector of the Mage and Seers that had memories of the living stones, the living lands of Lyra. These were the watchers left by the Over-Souls who created us over the birthing of Lyra and its ongoing maturity and the eventual creation of the Lyran beings, these parcels of Living Land or Living Stones formed a consciousness that bonded them to each other. Creating a unified collective for Lyra's highest good and protection, our Crystal Heart Stone is perhaps all that remains of that collective. It has made itself known to the relative Mages, Seers and select Lyrans for the ongoing protection of Lyra and her people.

Thus when the people of Lyra were in danger or in requirement of vibrational change, the Crystal Heart Stone had always undergone extreme light variances and tonal sequences of energetic manoeuvre. This would create an emanation of a mixture of [54]VHF/LF/Sonic and Pulsar vibration rings that would flow outward and connect with all that was ready to upgrade and become emotionally, mentally, physically and spiritually stronger.

As time passed upon the ship, many forgot the reality of the Consciousness of the Crystal Heart Stone until it became a symbol of Old Lyra, a way of life they were protecting, that held a special force of energy, such as a battery, to assist with the eventual rebuilding of Lyra. But, unfortunately, they totally disregarded the gift given to them by their Over-Souls, a gift that was their source of immense connection and power.

---

[54] elements of your world that enables you to identify with what impulses of energy were given out by the Crystal Heart Stone

Chapter Eighteen

Initiations, Testings, Trials
The Princes Separate

Unaware of the happenings upon the ship they were heading to, the Princes were preparing to dock with the old Lyran ship.

RexNā stood, hands clasped behind her back, staring out of the command deck viewpoint. In front of her was the 'Bitari-Furtim-Karda' floating in the void, like an enormous city. The illumination of lights flowing outward from the various decks and along her sidings gave the Karda a sense of illusion, a dream-like feel. Never had the Prince seen anything like it before. Not even her ship, the Bitari-Furtim-Otiose,' the sister ship of the '*Bitari-Furtim-Karda*,' had seemed as significant and beautiful as what held her gaze.

So engrossed was she in her thoughts of what would happen once they docked with the other ship that she did not hear the hydro lift doors slide open. It wasn't until both Rägę, and RaeNegira stood on either side of her that she became aware of the altered energy in the room.

Her friends stood silently, waiting to be acknowledged. They had both felt the gaping hole of loss, confusion, and insecurity, that had been swirling in their friend. Now was not the time to give platitudes but to wait, wait to be told the story. The profound inner discovery that comes from the inner turmoil of deep learning of truth must be shared willingly, for only then could the healing of the self-doubt begin.

Ever since taking refuge, or as her fellow Princes would say, 'hiding for days' in her chambers, deep within the waters of her home world, RexNā Loid deAqua had felt the presence of the gnawing sense of failure.

Questions raced through her mind, had she failed her people?

Should she have agreed to be boarded?

Were the intentions of the Ancient Lyrans true?

Her emotions were unbalanced, creating a storm of mini cellular implosions within her, which began to show as deep bruising on her typically iridescent skin. This inner torment worried Rägę enough to demand that MelEid bring RaeNegria out of the unconscious state she'd been in since communicating with Commander Sol Lrign dWari.

Even though RaeNegria was still impaired within her pain-ridden body, she knew enough that the sanity and well-being of the ship's commander outweighed protocols of all other manners.

She presented herself as Lyran Prince first, Command Officer second and third as a friend. Her energy field pushed gently towards her friend, her commander, telepathically reaching out to see if she could connect. The effort was almost too much for RaeNegria. The intense mental and energetic pain flashing within her mind and physicality caused her to sway. Reaching out, she grabbed the first solid thing to prevent herself from falling.

That solid object was RexNā. The sudden weight of her arm brought RexNā out of her thoughts and back into the room.

"What are you both doing here? I did not send for you!" Her words rang in the otherwise empty room. "We know, RexNā, you didn't. But, we felt you disappearing, or rather I did," responded Rägę. At the same time, he surreptitiously encouraged RaeNegria to stand up and relinquish the grip she had on the commander's arm.

Realising that she was gripping RexNā's arm like a lifesaver, RaeNegria forced herself to relax her grip and let go while attempting to control the waves of nausea and pain that washed over her continually. Beads of perspiration grew on her forehead as she tried to restrain the fire within her veins. Feeling herself slip from reality, she telepathically called for MelEid, the one person she knew could help her.

Deep within her self-absorption, RexNā suddenly realised that her friend, and 2nd in command, was about to collapse in a heap.

"What, what is wrong with her," she asked Rägę as she caught her friend slipping to the floor, "and why is she not in the medics sector?" Rägę tried to explain his reasons for bringing her forward but was interrupted by MelEid and her Mages as they rushed in and grabbed both RaeNegria and RexNā (who, due to the deep place of vibrational changes and inner searching, had been open like a jug for the intense overload of pain in Rae to deposit into, this caused both of them to lose awareness) as they slid towards the floor.

With both Princes now in a state of induced coma, this left Rägę the only one with the appropriate authority to command the ship into the docking procedure and protocols with the on-coming vessel.

MelEid watched as the two Princes were taken to the medics sector and then turned to Rägę, "Of all the inane and unfounded dishonourable decisions, what in [55]vlep'tchuk made you think you should waken RaeNegria from the induced sleep I had put her in? Now the disruption of her telepathic and DNA vibration has in-fected RexNā Loid DeAqua. What would cause you to do this?" her tone dropped on the last couple of words to show her disap-proval and concern.

Rägę felt as if he'd been reprimanded by his teacher during his training years as a cadet. He knew he'd taken a risk but assessed that the circumstance outweighed the danger. To Rägę, it was the reason he needed to step up and take the lead. Their crew and people had to be assured that all was ok and that the Princes were safe.

Looking at MelEid, he made himself stare into her eyes, almost challenging her to be the one that looked away. "MelEid, you may think I was unthinking and unaware of the cost, but I was not. I felt the risk was within the acceptable factors, as both of the Princes have a link that even I do not fully comprehend. I be-lieved they could balance each other and thus help correct what-ever was occurring within them."

Sighing, the Mage knew that his intentions had come from a place of purity, though it had resulted in both the Princes lying unconscious in the hands of the medics.

Pausing her exit from the room, she turned and acknowledged his statement. "My Prince, your crew needs to be led. I believe it

---

[55] a Lyran expression indicating great frustration and disappointment

will be best for you to be seen on the command deck. Trust your captains and heed their advice, follow your colours and listen to the vibration of the Crystal Heart Stone." With that, she followed the medics out.

Meanwhile, El Nareem and Kanrabos had been linked telepathically to what was happening, as is the duty of all captains when there is something not in balance within the command personnel. Realising that the eminent docking procedure was about to commence in less than a [56]lapzph, they were required to assist the remaining Prince in the protocols of greeting a superior Lyran Command Ship.

Rägę stepped onto the command deck and walked over to the consul, usually manned by RexNā, cleared his throat and began to inform the crew of the changes.

"Finally, I request that El Nareem, Kanrabos, and Ru Naal join me in the command room to prepare the protocols," he then walked away without seeing if anyone followed.

The two Lyran captains looked at each other. Having a non-Lyran greet a senior Lyran command ship was unprecedented, but they believed it was an insult to those coming alongside. "Rägę, are you sure you want to have a Nelphi-Lexmai present at the docking? This is primarily a meeting of Lyran families that have not seen or interacted for hundreds if not thousands of Cycles?"

Rägę looked at the two captains who'd taught him so much over the periods and cycles they had been travelling through the void in search of the Heart Crystal Stone. He honoured their views, acknowledged their lineage, and then responded, "However, to not have Ru Naal present during this time would be dishonouring their aligning to the Lyran way of life and their absolute

---

[56] hour

resolve to join themselves to us and our search. We have tested them, they have been tested by The Whittling when we entered this sector, they have been proven to be honour bound, and their colours are showing true." He paused, resting his arms on the table, then pushed back and relaxed into his chair. "Besides, rather these older Lyrans realise from the beginning that we are a blended group of aligned beings, sworn in allegiance to the laws of the Original Federation of InterGalactic Governments and Unions of Freedom."

His logic and non-emotional response were required, for it showed signs of settling the captains who turned and fully acknowledged Ra Nuul as part of the meeting. "Forgive our outdated view Ra Nuul. We asked only because we know those we are connecting with have been in hiding and have not interacted with any other culture from the outside unless in battle. In our thinking, we were attempting to prevent a situation of unease and questioning."

The four men began strategising and implementing the upcoming docking and settled on the proper and agreed steps.

"No one is to know what we have decided here. We will assemble and unlock the docking area. The Lyrans will then make the first step into our world by stepping through. We will have our security in plain sight but hidden within the Lyrans' gathering: no royal garb, insignia, or indication of rank or hierarchy. Let them see us as a level field. I see no reason we should be identified besides our sectors and colours." Rägę looked around the table, and all nodded in agreement.

"Right, then, if you will each convey this to the sectors. All to present at the given time, all wearing sector cloaks and no insignia. Mages are to be present, as well as medics. Alert MelEid to the agreement here and request her to be alert for any inter-ference."

"Also, ensure we have those connected to the Organic Link telepathically scanning the approaching ship for any hint of du-plicity. Ensure they cannot be picked up or sensed by the other ship."

"That's all. We can return to duties."

Pushing his chair from the table and standing, Rägę indicated the meeting was over. The others left the room to action the agreed protocols.

Dear Reader, let us give insight into what is occurring between the ships docking. When two or more Lyran groups meet for the first time, specific protocols are to be followed, especially since the Great Wars. Each group must know the others' connections, lin-eage, sector colours, and alignment with The Original Federation of InterGalactic Families Owning Responsibility of Nation, Culture, Self and Unions of Freedom. It is essential to be identified as Pure Blood Lyran or reverted Lyrans, whether they are [57]blended Lyrans or connected via one of the many other points of association. The reason for the questions, protocols, and identification is so that there can be no shadow of a doubt, no guesswork, only absolute transparency to begin with the connections.

The above is done via the highest-ranking negotiator on board.

This honour would generally fall to Rägę El BriNa-Ragnoa El Vroan, but as he was representing the entire community on board, he felt it would be best to delegate this to one of the following; Lieu-tenant Brinthera, who had been his second in the negotiations with the Nelphi-Lexmai and concluded the affair admirably, VriNoir BriNa, who was of Rägę's family and Sector lineage and a Chief Negotiator.

---

[57] Offspring of a Lyran mix of union, Pleiadian/Lyran or Lyran/Danonites or Lyran / Zeta Reticula

Or to El Nareem, the old Lyran captain who had been requested, after assisting the Princes in defeating their attackers in previous battles, to remain on board as mentor and guidance officer. However, what was unknown to the Princes was that El Nareem was also secretly assigned by the Seers of the Bitari-Furtim-Karda to watch and protect RaeNegria, who they believed was the next Seer of the Heart.

Timing is everything in the symbolism of reconnecting to Lyran tradition. If there is a slight nuance that is off or a word that is said out of place, it changes the entire format and meaning of the ceremony.

RaeNegria felt herself slipping away from the conscious world around her. Everything was distorted and appeared to her as everything moved in languid motion. Voices drifted in and out, sounding like the audio was playing at the slowest possible speed and the physical appearance of the structures and beings around her twisted and contorted into shapes that she had not noticed before, ever. She felt herself in the hover bed moving along the ship's corridors. A part of her knew they were taking her to the medics sector. The more significant and less physical part of her felt as if it was separating and lifting out of her. "I wonder if I am dying," she thought.

Just as quickly as the words crept into her mind, she felt an electrical surge pulse through her body, yet she was not in pain. If anything, that surge seemed to be the final push she needed to disengage from the physical body. Rae looked around the room, blinking as if awakening from a dream. The medics and Mages were gathered around her body, except MelEid and a trainee. As Rae stepped back from the noise and movement around her body, MelEid looked directly at her. Rae felt the familiar push of the Mages' telepathic link.

"Are you still in the room, My Prince? MelEid asked, Indicate to me that you are here. We have work to do."

"You can see me?" Rae questioned the Mage. As usual, MelEid gave nothing away, but a small smile tipped her face. Pushing aside the young trainee before her, MelEid turned from the medics' room and left. She did not check to see if Rae followed. There were many issues to examine and ensure they access the decks and information required before the docking, or Rae woke from her enforced slumber.

Rae glanced at her now comatose body and followed MelEid. Catching up with her, Rae asked, "Am I dead?" MelEid snorted in response, "If you were dead, my Prince, I would not be able to speak with your essence of life. No, you are still very much alive. I have assisted your life force in disconnecting from your body in a manner similar to your dream travels so that you can continue your healing and participate in the docking that is upon us.

You are the way you are to achieve the protocols and ensure the Crystal Heart Stone and our shard reunite. There is much to sift through. All relative components of data of our journey must be correctly stored and logged, then accessed in honour by those who will request it. You, my Prince, must be able to enter the chambers without being seen, unite with the Crystal Shard and allow the information of all that has transpired to be received by it for memory and fact-keeping."

"My Prince," MelEid suddenly stopped as if a wall had risen be-fore them, preventing further movement. "My Liege, it is time you know that the pulses and vibrational fluxes that have spun you into this state of unconsciousness have originated from a pulsar connectivity outside of our ship. It attached itself to us as we travelled through the barrier of the Sector of Light. It remained undiscovered until your gift of Seeing and Telepathic viewing disturbed its frequency, thus exposing the ripples and infiltrating our sub-frequency light pulses of communication, it piggybacked on our telepathic connections, and it has entered the 'Karda' locking two pulsing sentinels outside the level for the entry to the Heart Stone Crystal."

"Your duty of honour, my Prince, is to approach the being attached to our ship and communicate with it. We have attempted many such communications, but it requests that the Prince of Hylrix-El Moa's family approach. That it will not harm us or the others, but it must communicate with you and you alone!"

RaeNegria looked at MelEid in confusion, "How long has it been here, did you say? Since we entered the section? I have been to you regarding this splitting in my energy, the pain, the uncomfortable and unique connection to the Organic Link I have been experiencing, and you told me it would pass." Running her hands over and through her body, she continued, "This is not 'passing'. This is complete disconnection."

MelEid stared at what others would say was 'nothing, empty air' and continued to converse with 'something.' Then, as quickly and abruptly as she stopped, MelEid turned, went into the Hydro Lift, and exited at the level where the pulsar had attached itself.

The security unit immediately questioned her being there, and when she invoked the Rights of the Mages, the security became highly uncomfortable. They were instructed, 'no one, and that means no one approaches the quadrant where the pulsar ripples are coming from.' Yet, they all knew the Rights of the Mages allowed the Chief Mage to access all sectors, all areas as long as it was within the ability of defence, healing, negotiations, and so much more. Moving to the side, they let her through and, in do-ing so, gave access to not only the Mage but the Prince.

Slowly walking towards the pulsing light, RaeNegria, looked not at the pulsing light but into it. There in the depths of the light was a being, a creature of sentient nature. Rae felt the dis-tinct push of communication followed by a sense of having her entire being scanned by this energy. It was not uncomfortable, but neither was it a truly comfortable experience.

"Stop!" The word broke into her mind. "Step no closer. A pause grew as the 'unseen' watched Rae's response, then contin-ued. "Our energy will harm you if you come closer." Rae paused mid-step and waited. 'Who are you?' she pushed back at the be-ing.

A silence followed, not a suspicious silence but rather an in-credulous silence, as they were taken aback by the question. "You do not recognise us? Have we been separated so long that you no longer know the vibration or resonation of those of your [58]progeny?" Rae frowned, "My progeny? Then that would mean I either birthed you, created or came from you! But when would this have happened, as I neither recognise nor know what you speak!"

The ripples began to move faster, and as they did, RaeNegria felt her physical body react in deep pain. Yet, as the pain level rose, a link in her blocked memories began to climb out of the shadows and explode within her.

Rae felt as if she was hurtling backwards, observing the begin-ning and end of multiple creations, watching how wars broke out,

---

[58] This progeny reference refers to RaeNegria's lineage.

and how various cultures of the Void Multiverse seemed to fluctuate in dominance and defeat. She saw lifetimes of Lyrans fly past, intermingled with other species and the conflicts as well as the many victories, significant planetary alignments and peaceful agreements that outweighed the conflict she saw flicking through the memories.

Finally, the tumbling sensation stopped, and she saw herself as the unified liquid form that all Lyrans had begun as right back in the beginning when their Over-Souls, ([59]Vi El Cif-Lai Nuam-Gaian and Cilyn-Nez-Opmnjsm) had experimented with the creational power given to them by Creator Source and spawned a culture of beings known as Lyrans. As she became aware of the solid sensation beneath her feet, she allowed herself to breathe and take in the surroundings.

Gazing over the vast and seemingly continuous sea of golden liquid interspersed with silver and turquoise flashes of colour, Rae began to feel inadequate, small and out of depth with what was being shown to her. Struggling to keep her fear within her, she opened her mouth and began to give utterance to what was inside her being. This sensation within her desired a release from deep within her body. This sound, something between the wail of profound loss and buried torment, started low, deep, guttural, feral almost, primal in its core, until the reverberation became a war cry, a scream of defiance that rung out over the liquid and bounced across and off the rocks around her.

When she stopped, a gentle whisper floated around her on the wind, "Can you hear us now?" It was like a thousand voices were speaking at once, but she no longer feared the voices; she recognised them.

---

[59] refer to vol 1 and 2

"I hear you, but I know you are not Lyran. I do not fear you, for I am Lyran. Explain yourselves and either reveal who you are or release me. I will not do any bidding of any being if they are not honourable enough to show their true form." RaeNegria pulled every ounce of her Royal Bloodline to the fore as she realised this was not just a dream or an out-of-body experience. An inner knowing told her she was in a diplomatic connection with beings that knew her past, her people's past and perhaps more than what could be comfortably conceived in the minds of those present.

"She SEES," came a collective gasp. "Her awareness has opened, the child is no longer asleep, it is time to induct the Seer and plait the codes," another group of voices drifted around her. "No, she much pass the test. The gauntlet must be run. The Elders must see the resolve and fortitude. They will only release the weapon of truth to the one who is deserving, who does not wish it for themselves."

Rae could hear the whispers of conversation wafting around her, like wisps of wind playing in her hair.

After what seemed a half [60]lapzph, she found herself being gently pushed towards the edge of the liquid. She resisted at first, asking why she should go to the edge of the liquid.

"She's afraid she will fail", came from one side, "No, she is cautious, unsure. She waits for instructions". Came from the other side. A new set of voices entered the invisible conversation, "Has anyone told the Lyran what the test is? Is she in receipt of the required results?" The other voices broke into a mixed cacophony of words and thoughts as each side attempted to shift the re-

---

[60] hour

sponsibility of who was supposed to have instructed RaeNegria of her test.

"Enough!" Thundered the new voice set. "Lyran, you are chosen to read the waters. These waters predate your Lyran world; they predate the world of the Formless Ones. These waters are unique and unlike any other place within the known and unknown Multiverse." The voice paused, and when they spoke next, their tone showed immense respect and sincere honour for what was being shared.

"These are the waters of Source."

"In these waters, you will find the answers to all your questions. You will find the sanity within the insanity, the beauty within the deception, the deceit in the truth, and you will be shown the truth and the lie that live within your heart. The waters ask nothing of you. They exist to show you who you are! If you are a Seer, if you truly see, then you will know what is to be, and what you learn will do no more than adjust your abilities from dormant to active. If you are not the Seer, your physical will fail, and your energy will join us here, for you cannot return from this place without the inner strength that is the SeerMage."

Rae looked down at her feet, which were being licked by small waves breaking over them. Within her was a battle; turn and run as fast as she could manage and return to MelEid. Or dive, not walk into this liquid that both repelled her and attracted her simultaneously.

Looking back at MelEid, she felt an enormous rush of selfless love emanating from the Mage, so strong it almost dropped her to her knees. This rush of pure energy gave Rae the strength to enter the golden liquid.

MelEid had no idea what was in store for the young Prince, but when she felt the deliberation in Rae's energy, she felt an intense desire to protect her. Protect her from herself and the immediate surroundings and rush her back to the medics. Yet, even though she had this in her energy, MelEid knew that there were events that needed to pass before the ship and the docking could go forward.

Taking a breath, RaeNegria dropped like a stone into the golden liquid, and as it closed over her head, MelEid felt the complete disconnect from her Prince and watched the aqueous fluid become a solid covering. Nothing would exit or enter until this part of the test was accomplished.

As she fell through the liquid, Rae participated in the portrayal of the many wars in which the Lyrans had participated, either in defence or in dominance. Where they had compelled other races to submit to the Lyran way or be deleted, their history of being hard taskmasters, experts in slave trading, and self-important beings was not one that the Lyrans liked to remember. Still, it was a part of their lineage that they needed to recall so they could negotiate from a heart-centred place, not just logic.

She was shown the times when the Lyrans had left the path of dictatorship and embraced negotiation. She saw cities grow built in partnership; she was also shown the deep deceptions of some of the Lyran leaders. Curtains were ripped open in front of her as she observed lifetimes where the Lyrans were once as bad if not worse than the Formless Ones. Then before having time to recover from the sight of Lyrans torturing Lyrans, she was pulled to lifetimes where Lyrans lived in harmony with Seers and Mages working in unison to bring the Lyrans to a mutual place of heart and logic balance.

Like a leaf in a whirlpool, Rae was spun left and right, tossed up and down, each movement removing more and more from her of learnt or inherent beliefs. Finally, it stopped. She was dropped gently down on the bank of the waters and gently nudged till she sat up. Feeling as if she'd inhaled lungfuls of fluid, Rae spent the next few moments flipping between panicking and breathing deep, clearing, breaths.

Finally calming down, she looked around her. The scenery had not changed; golden liquid was all around her, yet she felt she was standing on solid ground. Then to her astonishment, she realised she was breathing via the fluid surrounding her. It was saturated with the right combination of air that she required to be alive.

"Sit," came the command in her head. Still smarting at how she'd been tumbled and what she'd been shown, Rae refused and remained standing, a small attempt at proving she was in charge. A quiet voice asked her if resistance would really help at this time when negotiation and debate were the order of the [61]vra. Sighing, Rae began to lower herself to sit on the ground when a chair and table appeared beside her.

Using the chair and resting on the table, Rae waited. She played the last few moments over in her head again, then cleared her mind. Remembering the meditations learnt during her training for balance, and mental resolve, to ensure that her mind could not be read or reached by the enemy, she reached for anything in her cognitive toolbox that would help her now.

"Good," the voice picked up from its first command to sit. "You are preparing yourself. Now, are you ready to see who you are? Are you ready to note your depths of deceit and check to ascertain if you are worthy of being welcomed into the Seers of Lyra?"

_____

[61] day

RaeNegria was silent, choosing to be open to whatever came her way, to watch, learn, see and above all, not to resist. If what was to come to her was her creation or the result of her family, she would own responsibility. If not, she would allow the silence to speak for her.

Unsure of what would happen next, Rae unconsciously gripped the arms of the chair. Then when it seemed nothing was going to happen, she relaxed. At that precise time, a volt of current was shot through her body, searing the nerves and telepathic connections around the base of her skull. Her scream of shock and pain echoed in this world of liquid, and when it was over, she slumped into an unconscious heap.

Those unseen observers carefully watched her vitals; this was all in the plan. Slowly an observer stepped out of the hidden space and became visible. He stepped towards Rae and reached out his hand, running it slowly in front of her face; he felt her breath. "She is asleep! Continue the training." The being gazed down at Rae's crumpled form with a look of absolute compassion. As if there was a bond between these two. Such was the energy of compassion towards Rae that it penetrated her subconscious and unlocked another memory. A childhood memory that she'd hidden for safety and to ensure the protection of her family.

"Father, why? Why did you go? Where did you go...?" it was the child Rae, staring out of her father's chambers on the outpost she grew up on. Her memory led her to her father's desk. She saw herself going through his papers and journals, looking through various reports, until falling asleep in her father's chair. She woke to voices, voices she both recognised and didn't. They were coming into his room, and the angry and loud tones scared the young RaeNegria, so she slid under the desk and waited.

"Na-Vri Gria of the Hylrix El-Moa family is gone. We've made sure of that. Even if he could prove innocence, it would have to be at the cost of another in his family sector, and his honour and dignity will not allow for that. We have to find his information of the Inner Circle. It must be destroyed before we take the Rule of Families as ours."

"Remember, kill anyone that walks through that door. We cannot afford to be recognised. The Formless Ones have promised us Lyra if we surrender the Stone and Inner Circle to them. Lyra will have one ruler forever... and it won't be a sector or family. It will be us. A joint contractual binding seal will be set for as long as we live. Which, by what they tell us will be for many hundreds of Cycles".

As that statement settled in the empty room, Rae heard scrolls being dropped on the floor, parchment being ripped, her father's consul being pounded, and the sound of it cracking. She must have made a sound, for silence fell in the room. The next minute she was dragged out from under the desk, her mind shut down; nothing, blackness followed. Her next waking memory was a light moving in front of her and voices asking if she was all right, and then she saw the face of the Lyran that pulled her from under the desk. She froze out of fear and could not speak, for her voice became blocked as the words were pushed into her mind, 'stay silent little girl, or more damage will be done'.

RaeNegria observed this trauma of her past, but as the observer, she played back the part where she searched her father's documents. Something kept repeating in her memory, a code that seemed to be hidden in his writings. Her hand itched as she needed to write it down. Again, like the chair and table, a consul appeared by her hand. As soon as it appeared, she began transcribing characters that looked like they belonged in a forgotten time. They were a language that escaped her knowledge.

Yet, as she etched them out, they took on a life energy of their own, the different characters forming in the colours purple, yellow and white.

They were obviously for her to connect to and decipher as they flowed from her hand to the screen. They reminded Rae of the formulas she had to commit to memory as a trainee to her Master. Suddenly it hit her. She had no idea what she was trained for besides being a Prince. Her mentor had told her that he was preparing her for all potential future events. Ones that may never happen as well as those that were expected. He expected her to retain and be instinctive with her military training and decisive with her negotiations.

When it came to the inner workings of the technical side with the organic links and onboard computers, her Mentor had brought in various other trainers who pushed her till there was literally nothing she did not know about the onboard systems of all current and past Lyran ships. Her medical knowledge was on a par with the Mages, and she finally realised that her insight was not random but focused and meticulously crafted in her by those who'd wanted to ensure that there was a combination of strengths within her mental, emotional and telepathic range.

Bewilderment began to build within her as a deep sense of betrayal and anger grew in her belly. How and why had they done this to her? Was it with her Family's knowledge? Nothing would have been sanctioned without the highest royal members of the family knowing this type of training was being invested in her. This was the training of assassins.

Those observing her noticed the markers rising, showing the inner turmoil that she was processing. "On screen now, ascertain what part of her memories she is unlocking. This may be the time to open her to the fullest opening she can go through as a fledgling Seer. We must be delicate with how we reveal the past, present and future to her, but she must know that all that is within her is the tool for accessing Lyra's future. We do not know if she is the chosen, but even is she is not, she is the lineage of the Seer Sector, and we must protect her at all costs."

The screen above her flickered into life as her subconscious mind was reflected on the screen in microscopic blips and waves of resonating pulses. To the untrained mind, it would be similar to a machine that monitors the breath, heart rate, and blood pressure that your human hospitals use. However, only those trained in seeing what is not seen, are able to interpret the signs and relate what is being experienced.

While Rae was being monitored and pushed to remember all she could about her parents' death, and what she had discovered without realising it, RexNā was in the next room being observed by another group of medics.

They had RexNā Loid DeAqua connected to various receptors enclosed within her water tank. Designated Dolf-El Hyl-Pelagus medics were in the tank with her, attempting to penetrate the blanket of depression she had pulled around her.

Though she was not being tested by any outside influence or group, she was, however, being tested again by the Crystal Heart Stone. How long would she wear the blame? How long would she allow herself to be sucked into the lie that she is solely responsible for all sentient life on her ship, thus denying them the right to self-responsibility?

RexNā felt the leadership role keenly, like an imprint of past lifetimes rolled into one experience. It felt deep within her psyche as if she had failed so many times, and this was her chance to succeed. Which did not align at all with who she was or her genealogy, for she came from a lineage of leaders, very successful leaders, interspersed with those chosen to be Leader of the Families of Lyra.

This doubt that had infected RexNā had reared its head as they entered the Sector of Light. During the time of The Whittling, while she had escaped the cull due to her intent and honour of what she believed she was there to do, a niggle of doubt had entered her psyche. Was she the natural leader? Did she have what it took to be someone who could lead millions of Lyrans? Did she want the position? These were but a few questions that banged around in her head and created so much noise that there seemed little else to focus on.

She was still feeling the fire within her from her initiation so long ago, and if she had stopped long enough and felt within herself, she would have discerned fires were still within her, ready to rise again, for the Crystal Heart Stone was not done with RexNā, indeed no. It had created a new form of inner visions for the Prince to battle; in these inner visions, RexNā would meet her true self. This would put her in a place where she would have to choose in ways that would see her bleed and see others bleed, yet these visions were not to destroy her but to strengthen her mind, build a stronghold of knowledge and a deposit of awareness for the Truth that would be revealed to her.

In her state of unconsciousness, the Mages and medics kept her in a steady connection to the ship and the Waters of Lyra. The Crystal Heart Stone was now ready. The Dol-Fyn-Nios Prince was in a place of suspended animation, monitored and observed by the best available to assist her in the next part of her testing.

Again the Crystal Heart Shard that MelEid kept suddenly manifested in the waters floating by RexNā, appearing without the knowledge of the Mages or medics. It caused a stir, and some of the Dolf-El Hyl-Pelagus medics wanted to withdraw from the Waters of Lyra as they became nervous at being so close to a part of the Crystal Heart Stone. Telepathically the message came to them to be calm, that they were not the focus of the Shard, but rather that they were there for the Prince. Those in the room observing from outside the tank also felt the energy of the Shard as it appeared. The Mages that worked with MelEid as her select group knew they needed to stay alert and monitor every moment. Each was to record any changes, movements, or displays of what could be a reaction to either inward or outward stimuli.

The medics' level suddenly became silent as the knowledge of the Shard's presence with the Prince became known. Everyone began to wonder why and what the meaning behind a new initiation was if indeed, this was an initiation. Especially as they were so close to docking with the Ancient Lyrans, she was their leader, wasn't she supposed to be dealing with the Ancient ones when they met? Yet, simultaneously, an unexpected aura of peace came over the entire ship. Even Rägę felt it seep into his weary and nervous body. He could not comprehend the reason for this sense of peace, but he welcomed it. He could now focus without second-guessing himself and comparing what the other Princes would do in the situations he was finding himself in.

It may seem, Dear Reader, that each Prince was facing a test concurrently and yet, as different as they were as Lyrans, their testings were taking them to a place of self-discovery that could not be determined in any other way.

An alert rang out in the command deck, bringing Rägę to the realisation that the two ships were in docking range and things, for him, were about to become a little more 'real' than he ever thought he'd experience.

Meanwhile, watching from a distance were every ready watchful twins. The 'RaiDai-Mlith' sat out of sonar, radar, and transponder reach. The brothers El Shavreon and Max Ron had ensured their entire journey had been embarked upon with shields fully enhanced to deflect any and all sensors. They were basically invisible even to the tremendous Lyran ship '*Bitari-Fur-tim-Karda*,' unless the Heart Stone caused a glitch in their binary vibration. They knew they were here not to interfere, only to safeguard the young Princes. Sitting beside them were other Lyran ships also incognito, unable to be detected, and yet they knew they would be noticed if the pulsation ripples touched their shields. They did not know how they had not been affected by The Whittling or been identified by the Heart Stone Crystal by now, but they counted it as a sign of good intent and will.

As the docking of the ships was the moment that both vessels were most vulnerable, the brothers decided that was the point that they would reveal themselves. They were keen to meet up with old friends and family they'd left behind all those cycles back. It was time, time to meet the future and settle the past.

The Narrators Speak

In this part of our discourse, you will undoubtedly see and feel the splitting of the three Princes. Each being removed from the other's company and having to learn to stand upon their own choices and decisions. It is a complex way of releasing their deepest fears, to have them face what they feel is their weakest part alone. Rägę has forever thought he was best suited to supporting, not leading. However, he comes from a lineage of Negotiators that have led many into battles and peacekeeping summits and won the hearts of many cultures by applying the simple rules of Lyra, Honour, Dignity, and Truth in all dealings. It is now the moment for Rägę to step into that part of himself if he so chooses.

Just as the other Princes are experiencing their trials and tests in their own ways, all to find out what is beneath the skin, in a manner of speaking. It is necessary for the Heart Stone Crystal to know the makings of each. Will they abide by the age-old lore of Lyra, or will they forge new lore and tear down what is honourable and dignified to build new ways over old ruins?

Will they know themselves when faced with their deepest fears or visions of what could be, may be, or is actually happening? For each of our young Princes is learning more about themselves every day. They are rediscovering their strengths and weakness, uncovering more of what they can do or be over what they seem to lack.

Are they ready to step into a place of leadership and do what is required? Are they prepared to face the Formless Ones that still hunt them, or will they fall where others have fallen? These are questions that the Creator Source is discovering answers to. The Crystal Heart Stone is but a metaphor and visual of something far greater than any Lyran can hold onto while remaining sane.

We, the Lyran Narrators of Time, have seen the madness drop into a Lyran and how it creates a being that no longer resembles anything that is Lyran. The madness drives all rational thought out, and the body becomes almost animalistic in behaviour. You cannot attempt to touch the heart of the Creator if you have no truth, dignity or honour inside of you or your intent for being.

We will slip back into the testing of RaeNegria now Dear Reader, will you come with us? Will you watch and observe, perhaps learn something for yourself?

It time for silence now, a time where we simply must stand by and allow the events to unfold. We must not interfere, for if she is to endure she must go through the gauntlet.

Come let us enter the dream world she is in.

Chapter Nineteen

RaeNegria
Journey Within

Dear Reader, as we enter the space of RaeNegria's proving by the Waters of Source. We must not interfere in any way. There is a reason and purpose for the visions, memories and experiences she is undertaking.

These will either show that she is of the Seers Sector or simply of the lineage, with some attributes.

Let us gently enter her space and observe.

RaeNegria walked through the memories where she found herself, watching what had happened in her life in a way that highlighted things she had not noticed previously or had simply been hidden from her sight.

She was conscious of the two or three distinct groups of 'voices' that floated around her, constantly speaking. Sometimes it sounded as if they were in unity, and with other items, they seemed to be at odds with each other. Yet not once during this 'forced viewing of the past' did any fear come from within her.

Strangely enough, she felt the most 'at home' and comforted than she'd felt in ages. Being in this space of 'in between' certainly thrust her immediate consciousness to a place of non-importance. It did seem that a greater force was revealing hidden aspects of her life that she'd either brushed over, forced herself to forget, or due to the intense darkness or pain in the experience, she'd blacked it out.

Now with the energy of her Sector and her Family, through her deep heart connection to her father, Rae was rediscovering her inner strength. She was beginning to comprehend the totality of being in the Family Hylrix-El-Moa. For perhaps the first time, she began to fully take in the complexity and honour of wearing the cobalt blue cloak. Feeling the power of being selected to enter the sub-sector of her family, the El Spiri-Bellator Vi Moa Patrol, Rae felt as if she was beginning to hallucinate as the silver and gold energy of her family line began to create cords interspersed with blue, iridescent colours pertaining to all family sectors, then these very cords began to 'plug' into her body and work their way through her inner core being.

As she observed the events materialising in her body, while being separated from the actual sensations, Rae was able to process the various images of the stitching and unstitching of memories being unravelled in her consciousness, without the distress of attachment. While these memories were being dealt with, on a new level, RaeNegria became acutely aware that there was 'something' being activated in her blood and this was being plaited with her DNA which was akin to the burning of fire being ignited and brought to the surface of her skin.

Fleetingly she likened the flow of sensations and images she was viewing as when the Lyrans went through the *Gulf of Exliat-*

icMalvi as they approached the Outpost of NexEl MinAqua. Just as then, this array of visions now gave the impression of memories held in a place of veneration to be observed without interference and to be honoured and learnt from.

Within her body she felt as if there were a thousand fire ants biting and burrowing in her. Each image and each memory that awoke in her consciousness cut into her with the sharpness of a paper cut, the thin slice that pierced the pain barrier and brought such fine attention to the point of touch.

Floating between a state of deep awareness and a dull dream-like state, Rae began to see her lineage form before her. Ancestors grew out of the mist, standing around her in a circle. Layer upon layer until in the far distance she recognised her immediate parentage and siblings. A deep yearning and desire to be with them again tore at her heart, as tears of loneliness slipped down her cheeks.

Yet just as the sense of loneliness seemed to overwhelm her, another stronger emotion grew from deep within Rae's being, surpassing the sense of loss. It was a feeling that was recognisable by Rae, and yet foreign to her at the same time. As she gazed out over the Waters of Source, she all at once felt the most fulfilled and complete she'd ever experienced. A thought drifted through her mind, "I don't have to go back. This is what I have been searching for."

As that thought settled, her body began to react, her breath became ragged, her heart beat faltered and those observing her noted that she was entering into Transition.

Pandemonium broke out in the two realms, that she floated between. MelEid yelled at the medics to get her stable and ordered her team of Mages to create a circle and focus their telepathic energy to keep Rae from crossing over. She, in the meantime, sat and went into a trance and telepathically sent her mind deep into the sleeping consciousness of RaeNegria calling her gently back to the crew.

As the Lyran component did what they did best in the physical realm, there were those in energy form that went into triage as well. They pulled the thoughts back from Rae, brought her attention back to the living, showed her the ships and triggered the collective awareness that there was a reason for her being where she was.

As both sides fought to keep her alive and in the realm of the living, Rae drifted further into the Transition State. Unknown to both parties there was a third power that was working in RaeNegria's condition of consciousness. That energy and potency, assisting to prevent Rae from complete disconnection of her body and the realm around her, was the Divine Source.

As Rae let go of all the attachments of being Lyran, the responsibility of navigating the ship to their destination, of protecting her Prince, of the guilt she felt for leaving her family. As she let go of the issues of life and the aspirations that she had, the fears, and doubts, the joys and memories, a deep sense of peace surrounded her.

As everything became still and dark around her, she was engulfed in a ball of fiery light. There was no figure or voice, yet, she would swear to those that listened at a later time, she heard a reverberating voice in her entire body.

"RaeNegria, hear us!" The voice was commanding, yet in that command was a sense of deep love and respect.

"You are not complete with your journey, there is much to do. However, you are to bath in the Waters of Source, for in these waters you will find the solutions and resolutions you seek. Your questions of all that has occurred and all that will yet unfold will be given to you." There was a cavernous pause. "BUT," the voices eventually continued, "you will hold no physical memory of these answers and visions until they are required."

Again there was a break in the communication, and Rae felt they were waiting for a response from her for some reason. Not knowing how to respond to the power surrounding her, she nodded.

"Know this, RaeNegria, your powers are untapped. You are not intended to lead a group of Lyrans as a designated leader. Yet you will lead them. You will show them a way through the doubt and fear that is to come. You will direct their strengths and show them how to create in a way they have forgotten."

A shiver of anticipation and something akin to fear and wonderment trickled through Rae's body. She contemplated the responsibility of what she'd just heard and almost rejected the concept.

The Voices of the Waters of Source continued, "This will be transferred through the ages, long after you have lived your allotted Cycles and when they talk of the Great Seer Mage, they will be referring to you. You will bring the Mages and the Seers together, for they hold the keys to uniting Lyra. When the Heart Stone Crystal returns with you, you will have many battles to face, but you and your people will bring the Crystal back to the elements that have been hidden to recreate a home world."

As these words faded into silence, a new push came from the Waters of Source for Rae to re-enter the memories of her family betrayal, the loss of her father, and her stolen innocence. The faces now resurfaced, the voices and images rushed in and began to overwhelm her. Observing these memories RaeNegria calmed herself and became more of the observer than she'd ever chosen to be before.

Allowing herself to slow the images down, she began to see into the shadows around the room and saw the horror of the slaughter of those who birthed and loved her. She was fascinated, in the same way a scientist is fascinated when they see or learn something new in an experiment; as she watched the members of her family sector, she gazed unseeingly into the recorders of time as they were exposed as the living dead or the puppets of the Formless Ones. Suddenly it became crystal clear to Rae that her family members were not killed by her immediate loved members of the sector but by those who had allowed themselves to become infiltrated and infected with the lies of the Formless Ones.

So much damage, pain and separation had been caused by those who'd allowed the deception and manipulation of the lies perpetrated by the Formless Ones and their puppets. They had used whatever they could to bend the minds of the Lyrans, at that moment in time, towards a lie disguised as truth.

Unable to tear her eyes away from the horror unfolding before her, Rae noticed a light that appeared out of nowhere, at least she did not see its point of origin. This light momentarily blinded everyone and everything in the room and enveloped the child RaeNegria. The light was truly 'alive' and aware it was being observed, and became translucent enough to allow Rae to see that within the light was a being. This being had no specific form but it lifted the young RaeNegria up and spirited her away. The room at that moment froze. Time stood still, it struck Rae as funny the way a feather had been spinning in the upheaval of the things been thrown around in the room, then just froze mid spiral, gifting her a secret message that everything will come to balance, if she just held on.

Going back to the light that was taking her young self away, she noted that a group of other light beings, surrounded her, it looked to her as if they were performing an operation of sorts on her head. One of the lights stopped flickering and turned and looked right into the eyes of the Observer Rae, then returned to the work it was doing. There seemed to be an agreement between all the light forms and the young Rae, who was then returned to the room, asleep.

The light slowly withdrew, at first unwilling to leave the young Rae, but knowing that in time all would unfold as it was supposed to.

Time sped up again, and Rae saw the imposter Hylrix-El-Moas pull her from beneath her father's desk. She heard the telepathic voice demanding she remain silent, and then she heard something else. Something that she'd forgotten or which had been removed or blocked until now. "Don't kill her! She is the last of the True Blood Hylrix-El-Moa. We need her markers to find the Crystal."

Suddenly Rae went ice cold. This sudden drop in temperature was registered by both groups monitoring her status. In this moment Rae began to comprehend the ripple anomaly that was attached to her ship. She immediately knew that she had been a plant, a trap and was now endangering her crew, her Prince and more importantly the Crystal Heart Stone!

As Rae stumbled into this awareness, she also joined the dots as to why she'd been suffering the bodily and mental pain ever since the anomaly had appeared. They were using her to track through the void and discover the whereabouts of the Crystal. This awareness began to cause Rae to shut down her physical body. Her inner knowing realising that if she were not there they could not use her to find the Heart Stone.

MelEid, from her place of connection to RaeNegria, could feel her slipping away. Coming out of her telepathic link, she called the medics and her Mages to sustain the immediate and important life organs, to do what they could to ensure that Rae lived.

On the other side of the veil, the energy beings flickered around RaeNegria's energy form and began to work with the Waters of Source, with the light that surrounded them so abundantly. "Don't let her slip away," came the first set of voices. "Show her the truth" announced another set of voices. "She must know that this is not her responsibility", from yet more voices. Then, yet again, the deep resonating sound of knowledge entered the conversation.

"RaeNegria, now is not the time to turn your back on those you have come to see as family. Do not allow this knowledge to create fear in your life.   Rather can you not see how they have exposed their own plans? Can you not see how you can use this to bring the Hammer of Justice upon those who would destroy you and yours?"

The Voice faded, but the words they had uttered rang loud in the mind and energy of Rae, who was struggling with what she perceived was the death of her people being laid at her feet.

As the words reverberated through her body louder and louder, ringing like an old copper bell, her physical body began to respond positively to the medics and the Mages working with her. Those working on her on the shores of the Waters of Source found her energy to be more resistant to their attempts to keep her consciousness with them when, as before so long ago, the bright beam of light enveloped her once more. "Child, do not take on your shoulders a responsibility that is not yours; how can you be responsible for something that you had no concept or awareness of until this moment?" There was a pause that gave the impression of engulfing her in totality and yet holding itself back as if to create an awareness within RaeNegria to push outward and come after that sense of hidden information. "Come waken now. Enough time has been wasted on selfish self-pity." With that, the light powered through her energy body from her head and exited via her feet. As it exited, a mass of black oozing goo was pushed before the light. As it pooled on the ground, the waves of the Waters of Source lapped up and around it, causing it to fizz and churn inwards on itself, for all intents and purposes, looking as if it were attempting to hide from the Waters of Source. Finding nowhere to slink off to, as the Golden Waters surrounded the black goo, it soon became still, hardened like bedrock, dull in colour and subsequently crumbled into dust, vanishing in the gentle wind that suddenly appeared.

With this event, a strange thing occurred in Rae. Her physical body changed colour. Her skin went from the hue of the light beige-tanned look that most Lyrans were to a silvery white colour with a just a hint of beige. This tinge gave her skin a visual appearance of solidity, whereas the white silvery texture gave the impression of invisibility. Her hair was no longer the golden wheat colour but now a silver snowy white, almost invisible, giving the impression of hairlessness.

The medics working with Rae shuffled away from the bed in astonishment and called MelEid, for this was out of their awareness or medical knowledge. They had all heard stories of the past, where the elders spoke of the Seer of Seers returning as one who was seen but not visible, heard but no voice, touched but leaving no mark. Seeing the change in Rae brought out the 'old wives' tales and fears in them.

MelEid stood at the bedside, observed the changes finalising in Rae, and took a shaky breath. It was happening! It was time to awaken the Seer, who had been in sleep status since leaving the outpost. No one knew the Seer was on board, for Seers and Mages were known to be courteous towards each other without wishing to be seen to be friendly or united. They would, however, for the sake of the Lyran Sectors, come together in a unified front when their skills were required. In MelEid's opinion, this was such a time.

Quietly, she gathered her books and side pouch where she kept her tinctures and unique healing tools and slipped out of the room.

Arriving at a secluded area in the Mages Sector, she entered a code only she knew and went in. Walking to the sleeping Seers unit, MelEid unconsciously ran her hand over the glass front in what could be called a loving or caring gesture. Not only did no one know there was a Seer on board, but they would never know that the Seer was also the sibling of MelEid. Her brother!

Due to their differing callings, neither had been in physical contact or close quarters for nearly two cycles. Their respective sectors had chosen them to be on this journey as they were both at the highest level of achievement and knowledge that they could be at within this part of their chosen experience in life path, but more importantly, was the fact they could access their inner telepathic connection without any other telepath picking up on their link.

Being twins, they had honed their inner speak, as they called it when children, to the point that they could communicate over vast areas of space. This connection to each other and their innate awareness of the Crystal Heart Stone made them the positive and negative tools to balance the Seer of Seers when they made themselves known. The Heart Crystal shard that MelEid had been safeguarding throughout the journey had been steadily growing in vibrational strength the closer they got to the ship. This, combined with the fact that as they had come closer to the time of docking, MelEids' brother, Eid 'dVra, had been stirring naturally, and his forehead had begun to show the prominence of the Eye that Sees Beyond (what is known as the Third Eye in Terran knowing)

Eid's brow showed signs of translucent covering, and the centre had held a steady 'glow' of blueish silver emanating from deep within his head. The brighter this became, the more restless he was as one waking from a very deep slumber. The biometric readings that had been monitoring his hibernation since leaving on this adventure showed that, physically and mentally, he was ready to be woken.

MelEid had not seen nor interacted with her brother since they were taken to their separate training as young Lyrans. Although they had constantly been able to connect, even when instructed not to, she had no idea how he would react to being here or being the only Seer in a large continent of Mages. Shaking her head mentally, MelEid began to set in place the waking process and then walked away, leaving her trusted team to observe and keep her in the loop. She needed to return to RaeNegria and RexNā Loid DeAqua.

Meanwhile, RaeNegria had gone through her change; her physical body now reflected the inner permutations of her energy.

Deep within her telepathic connection to the Crystal Heart Stone and to the Waters of Source, Rae was learning more of her past and true purpose in being. As she remembered the trauma of loss, she also began to see the threads stitched into her life via the training she'd had with seemingly last-minute introductions or alterations in her learnings and awarenesses of knowledge handed down to her through her years of gathering information.

She was beginning to realise why, although she was of the inner circle of the Hylrix-El-Moa family sector group Hyrix-Sol of Negotiators, she had been inducted into the Healers Sector, a place for half a cycle among the Mages to learn from their Lead Mages. The only group she was forbidden to enter or request was that of the Seers. This sector was only 'rumoured' to exist. No one would admit they'd ever had contact with this group, so all knowledge was sketchy at best. If you did come across a Seer, it would typically be in a ceremonial circumstance, and even then, that particular Lyran would hold many in awe with their presence.

Though in the recess of RaeNegria's memory, a piece of the puzzle kept moving, not settling into its place, as the Waters of Source purged her energy body with their light, forcing all unrequited 'substance' from her, this memory began to grow.

She was transported to a cliff that overlooked the most fertile valley on Lyra, a place she'd been told about but never visited. It did not feel strange to be here. Looking around, Rae realised she was not alone. Standing with her were three other Lyrans. She could not see their faces but was being told inwardly that these would be there to assist when required.

Looking out over the valley, she began to experience a sense of lightheadedness and began to fly 'out of the body,' which, even in her state of being, she was confused about as she already had an awareness that she was in a telepathic state of being out of body.

However, she allowed herself to be drawn up and along. Dropping suddenly, she found herself deep in the inner tunnels of the planet. At first, she was unsure of which tunnels these were, and then she began to recognise the tell-tell signs of the world known as Terra-Ven-Eiliesh-Gaina. This had been one of her favourite worlds to study on the outpost she'd lived on, for this was the place her people found refuge when fleeing the Formless Ones and had given them strength to continue the fight. Observing the tunnels, she began to recognise the etchings on the walls. These were the same as the ones, or at least very similar to those on the ship they'd been travelling in.

Without stopping to try and decipher the glyphs, Rae seemed to know of them immediately and wholly comprehend the information hidden within these images. As the tunnels unfurled before her, they became illuminated via lamps that were ignited by the impression of her presence. The flames of these torches flickered over and along the tunnel walls, and as they danced over the glyphs, some began to respond becoming highlighted from the flat walls, while others appeared to shrink away as if unwilling to be seen.

Rae placed both arms out so that her palms rested lightly on the walls and then ran at full speed down the tunnel. As her hands glided over the walls, the information began to be collected through her hands and flowed into her mind.

It was all written here. Everything regarding the origins of Lyra, the Great Wars, the Infiltration and Manipulation of the Formless Ones, and the suffering of the [62]Black Illness. The Lyran History was recorded on these walls. Rae suddenly stopped as if she'd hit an invisible barrier. Her eyes were wide and staring unseeingly before her as all the information was being filed and stored within her memory and cellular knowing. Then she dropped to the ground as if the supporting force which held her up had now suddenly departed.

In her mind's eye, she watched the golden waters that covered

---

[62] This is a reference to a time on Lyra during the great wars when many Lyrans became infected with a black substance that inserted itself in their blood and was only able to be removed via a painful and dangerous transfusions of Pure Blood from Lyrans unaffected and uncontaminated by this living dark matter.

the surface of the land where she was, begin to spill into the tunnels, flooding them out of existence. The waters lapped around her form and soon covered her. There was no fear or sense of drowning in Rae. To be precise, she felt free!

Her life force kicked back into being, and she felt herself rising upwards, opening her eyes, she saw planets and all manner of creations within the waters. Strange beings, animals, and plants unknown to her all swirled around in the golden waters; for a while, she was lost in her observation of the beauty and strangeness of it all. Then a sensation of being pulled above entered her awareness, flowing up she broke the surface and continued to maintain a steady upward movement. Once again, she was covered and attended to by the light beings still whispering their perceptions, thoughts and questions.

"IT IS TIME," a new voice uttered into the relative silence. Yet it was a voice that triggered a remembrance that had been sitting within her, a memory not of her distant past but her recent past. "Waken and join us or die, Rae. It's time to choose."

This was the key being waited upon, the call from the other side, from those alive and watching over the physical to call her from the ethereal side.

The Waters of Source slowly retreated from the shore to give more room as the light energy beings brought the energy of Rae into a standing position. They had awakened the memories and assisted in bringing to consciousness the Seer of Seers within her, and now it was Rae's choice to return or to stay.

On both sides of life, RaeNegria took a deep and shuddering breath and stepped back into her life as a Lyran.

Her eyes opened slowly, blinking against the light, which automatically adjusted so the glare would not be discomforting to her. Rae looked around and saw the worried looks of those gathered by her melt into relief. "Thank the Crystal, you have returned," came from somewhere amid many other statements of genuine relief.

"Well, my Prince, you have been on a journey of the soul but have returned to us now, I see," came the quiet, slightly sarcastic toned voice of MelEid. MelEid would not allow anyone to know how concerned she had been nor what may yet, still, unfold.

Slowly turning to look at the Mage beside her, Rae looked at MelEid and smiled. Though she said nothing, everyone heard her reply, "A soul journey that has opened a door that, perhaps, should not have been. What is to be done must be, and what is undone shall remain as such. We have time to heal, but from that, the unification of the planets and the many living souls must come."

There was silence as those in the room absorbed that they had all simultaneously received a telepathic communication, including those who were not naturally inclined to use telepathy.

Then looking straight at MelEid, Rae asked, "Where is he? Where is Eid?"

The young Mage paled. How could the Prince know of her brother? She had used all her skills to block this information so it could not be sensed by any telepathic, Mage or not. Returning her eyes to Rae's, MelEid replied, "Waking."

RaeNegria nodded, closed her eyes, and slipped into a healing sleep.

Chapter Twenty

Hello!
Commander meets Prince

The 'Bitari-Furtim-   Otiose' crew had no idea what was occurring within the walls of the *'Bitari-Furtim-Karda,'* just as those aboard the *'Bitari-Furtim-Karda,'* were unaware of anything happening inside the vessel preparing to receive them.

The one thing concerning them now was that along with the pulsating ripples anomaly, they had detected another large ship slowly dematerialising just outside the firing range of the *Bitari-Furtim-Otiose.'*

Upon my sectors honour, captain, it just appeared. I have checked and rechecked my logs, readings, and transponders reports. There have been no ships other than the *'Otiose'* and the smaller ships that followed her into the Sector. The vessel that has disengaged their shield hails us as the *'RaiDia-Mlith'"*. The young ensign in charge of navigation was attempting to impress on his immediate senior that there was no possible way of him knowing the other vessel, or rather the ships coming into sight, had been there before now.

"Did you say RaiDia-Mlith?" A Negotiator questioned the ensign, who nodded his head. "But that ship has been missing and presumed destroyed for over five [63]cycles, if not longer. Why would it suddenly appear now, alongside the young Lyran fleet?" After a long pause, the Negotiator instructed the ensign to keep the information to himself until he could inform Commander Sol Lrign dWari of this new development.

He turned and left in search of the commander, mentally attempting to create the report he knew would not be welcome, especially as they were busy with docking procedures which left them in a vulnerable situation.

Deep within the belly of the great *Karda*, Sol Lrign dWari began to prepare herself for meeting the new Lyran contingent and those who now walked the way of the Lyrans. She was aware that they expected challenges, and she would not disappoint them, but her challenges would come when they least expected them.

However, her priority at this moment was this anomaly that sat off the port side of the incoming ship. She knew it was biding its time. She was aware that it hid a great danger, but she needed to figure out what the potential threat could be. It was, she surmised, related to the Princes coming in with the 'Bitari-Furtim-Otiose.'

The ensigns observing the strange anomaly, unexpectedly raced to their stations and began flicking switches and entering codes into their terminals. One of the ensigns had placed himself

---

[63] Remember, Dear Reader; a cycle is worth twenty-five of your earth years.

squarely in front of the screen where the spiral energy could be seen in full glory and he began to reel off coordinates in rapid succession. The others adjusted and readjusted dials and imputed the numbers into their screen. Reaching the controls, a young ensign punched in a code that activated Sol's private console. When this happened, she could observe the sudden and erratic movements as they occurred. The young ensign, who had been first to watch it and note any changes, was filling up Sol's pager with urgent ', please return to comms' messages.

It would be recognised, in later conversations, that this 'anomaly' had become agitated approximately the same time that RaeNegria had been released of the 'black goo', while in her unconscious connection to the Waters of Source.

Responding to the many calls to return to the command deck, Sol made her way up. As she stepped onto the command deck, it seemed her entire crew were trying to catch her glance, wanting to report something of urgency.

Releasing a deep breath, Sol took her seat, then called her second-in-command to her,

Juuls approached and waited, "Update." Sol uttered the single word, and Juuls knew that Sol was requesting a full debrief. "Where are we at with the ripple anomaly?" Sol raised her hand to stop Juul's response, then asked, "Where did that ship come from, and why is its presence only been announced now?" Sol fixed her gaze on the screen before them while waiting for Juuls to reply.

As Juuls went through the handover and update of the command deck in her absence, Sol noted that since her telepathic communication with the young Lyran Prince, things had sped up in the timings of concern.

"First order of business is to identify the ship calling itself 'Rai-Dia-Mlith'. I want all data relating to the last time it was seen or recorded as being Lyran and then all transmissions and hailings requiring identification of approaching vessels and purpose of identifications to be signalled over to the ship in all known communication dialects. Obtain for me the identification of all personnel onboard that ship. I also want to know why our sensors did not detect its vibration or engine signature! If it is the *RaiDia-Mlith*, then our sensors should have been able to identify it from a distance of over a thousand lea..." Sol paused mid-word as a thought came to her.

Turning to the Sonar navigation balcony, she called the ensign to explain how he'd discovered the ship. She listened to how it had merely de-cloaked alongside the *'Bitari-Furtim-Otiose'* as the ripple anomaly had begun to speed up and become unstable. It had hailed them using the old Lyran greeting codex. The ensign, looking sheepish, admitted that the codex was unknown to him as he did not know the Ancient Lyran Language and had to call in his superior for assistance.

Sol held her hand up, "They used Ancient Lyran language?" Her face reflected her concern, "No one has used the Ancient communications, not even our communications, for over five Cycles. Why would they choose to use that way to hail us?"

"Communications, see if you can get me a secure channel for speaking to the RaiDai-Mlith, closed channel and visual and audio only. No holo images, no organic links. I don't want anything that can access our systems without our knowledge. Go old school and use the relay transponders to generate imagery details." Sol looked at the lieutenant sitting at the comms desk and watched the confusion take over his face; sighing, she looked over at Nuex and nodded to him over the communication desk. "Take over

Nuex, teach them what we all learnt as our foundation communication protocol before the holographic and organic links came into being." There was a tiredness in her voice that neither Nuex nor Juuls had heard before.

Turning to the next issue, Sol watched the graphs along with the corresponding calculations and data that revealed the unravelling of the spiral, causing a constant disturbance that was interfering with the docking process to both Lyran ships as they attempted to prepare.

Going over the information in front of her, she felt the slight nudge of a telepathic request to talk. Raising her head slightly, she surveyed the room and realised it was not anyone from the command deck. Reaching out, she felt the request and the direction it came from, realising it was the Mage on the 'Bitari-Furtim-Otiose,' she stood up and nodded to Juuls, "The consul and command are yours," she said as she walked out to the side room.

"Go ahead, young Mage; what is the news of the Princes and what is that anomaly that has attached itself to your ship." There was no hint of friendliness, just that of a commander requesting information and brokering no nonsense.

"Greetings, Sol, commander of the 'Bitari-Furtim-Karda,' you are correct it is I, MelEid, I am here to inform you that we have the Chief Seer onboard and that our Prince RaeNegria has returned to us from the realm of the spirit, but she has changed. She has been touched with Sight of the Seers and requests immediate consultation with you when docking is complete. She requests this before meeting with the chosen Lyran Leader, RexNā Loid DeAqua. It is imperative that she reveal to you that which has been revealed to her. We will present to your quarters upon docking. You may wish to have your Mage and Seer present to verify the information, be aware that she has mentioned the Waters of

Source, these have not been referred to since the Mages and Seers split into two sectors after the Great Wars." MelEid finished and waited for a reply.

Sol was silent as she received and processed this information, "I will have a delegation greet you and bring you to my private ready room. I will be there to meet you. I will send Juuls, my second in command to convene with the rest of the docking party." She paused, then said, "This had better be important, Mage. I do not like being ordered around, even by a Prince I have not yet truly acknowledged as my leader or part leader of the Lyran people."

She cut the communication and returned to the command deck.

Upon taking her seat back, she requested an update on the RaiDai-Mlith and how the communication link-up was going. The young lieutenant felt his skin rouging in embarrassment as he felt unprepared for the task before him. He had not trained in the old systems and felt like a child attempting to create a rocket ship out of pieces of grass.

However, thanks to the Nuex guidance, he'd been able to bring together, albeit two separate connections, an audio and visual link between the ships.

"We are ready to communicate with the RaiDai-Mlith Commander, "he replied. "It won't be as clear as normal comms as these are unlinked from our mainframe and rely solely on the transponder relays."

"Proceed". It was a single request from Sol, and his fingers flew across his consul, and soon a fuzzy image was onscreen before Sol. The audio followed slightly out of sync with the image.

"Greetings Commander Sol Lrign dWari, we greet you in the way of The Lyran Negotiators we are. Upholding the Truth, Serving in Honour and allowing Dignity to lead. We protect the Heart Stone and sacrifice our days to it, remaining hidden till Lyra is ready to rise."

The image turned a fraction as if to look at a person off-screen, there was more static and a second image came into focus. At first, it was as if there was a glitch in the system, as both images looked identical.

"Your image is duplicating, but we greet you and ask why you have remained hiding. If you are Lyran, why remain hidden from the ship you have obviously followed since it started its journey and why have you not alerted us to your presence? Surely you can see in our perception this is deception on a high level of duplicity."

The images before her looked at each other and smiled. "Commander Sol, we are the brother's El Shavreon and Max Ron Ilth. We are they who fought in the Ancient Wars of Devastation and were sent by the commander of that time to protect the Crystal Heart Stone. While on that journey, we became separated, El Shavreon choosing to take, alongside many of those still on-board with you, the Heart Stone to a place of safekeeping. When the Formless Ones attacks became consistent, it was his idea to create the illusion of the ships separating and being destroyed. He took the RaiDai-Mlith and 'disappeared', thus drawing the Formless Ones minions away from your ship, allowing you to es-cape to where you are now found." There was a slight pause, "I, Max Ron Ilth, have been upon the outpost NexEl MinAqua search-ing for my brother, only recently to have him return via the ship docking with the outpost a quarter cycle back."

Raising her hand for silence, Sol stared at the images before her. Everything they had related to her was true. While she had never met the brothers, she knew of their daring plan to save the Heart Stone Crystal. Many on board this ship swore that all would have been lost a long time ago without their action.

"This is a great story, but what evidence do you have that we are indeed speaking to the original Lyrans, known as 'The brothers Ilth.'"

Again the brothers smiled and replied, "Ask the Crystal." As they finished their statement, the Mage entered and spoke again without permission and stated to all who would hear, "The Heart Stone Crystal has awoken and is vibrating, the colours are for the Original Negotiators. This has not occurred for over five cycles of our knowing. We ask to speak to the Original Negotiators."

Sol turned to them, her face reflecting annoyance at the interruption. However, upon hearing what the Mage said, she turned and spoke to the two brothers. "We are docking with '*Bitari-Furtim-Otiose,*' at docking bay BelvNor; you can take your ship and dock in at bay [64]MorVeAlph. That way, we can contain both groups separately. If necessary, we can ensure the decontamination procedure is followed for both parties until I am satisfied that you are whom you say you are."

"Juuls, notify security and ensure contamination barriers are placed around docking bay MorVeAlph and that anyone that disembarks stays in that docking area."

Sol sat in her chair and wondered what else could possibly happen now.

The plan had merely been to reconnect with the Bitari-Furtim-Otiose and the Lyran Princes. Test their abilities, integrate them into the crew and take both ships out of the Sector of Light to re-

---

[64] A second docking bay area is set aside for delicate situations of high intergalactic matters. This docking bay was virtually never used, as there was no one left with the High Galactic Joint Federation Union. Or so they thought...

establish the planet Lyra. Then once away from danger, begin the Initiations of 'Leader of Families' according to the Old Ways.

However, things were not going to plan. There appeared to be an external force which was creating a series of distortions in the forward movement of the outlaid plan. A small thought entered her mind, 'or perhaps this was always part of the plan. As far back as she could remember, there was a plan, a way forward from the day the ships had spirited the Crystal Heart Stone away from Lyra before the Formless Ones could gain access to it. There had been a directive to rejoin the main body of Lyrans that escaped, recreate Lyra using the Crystal Heart Stone's vibration, and reunite Lyra's people once more. However, this had not eventuated yet, though Sol now felt the formation of a new concept coming into place. Yes, the ultimate goal was to reunite with the Lyrans scattered across the multiverse, but who would achieve this, and how was the question at hand? Was it Sol as the Commanding officer out of those gathered? Or would that honour now fall to the twins El Shavreon and Max Ron Ilth?

Why had a ship and crew, initially sent out to locate and bring back eligible Lyrans to work with the Crystal Heart Stone suddenly, now reappeared? Especially, as for the last cycle or so, it was thought to have been destroyed. So why would they have kept their presence from the crew of the *Bitari-Furtim-Karda*? Pushing the questions aside to be dealt with later, Sol turned her attention to the docking procedures. With two ships docking at either side of her ship, she was potentially vulnerable to attack. Turning to the Negotiator heading her security sector, she gave the command for heightened observation and increased security at both docking areas.

Now looking to the Second Chief Mage, she paused and asked, "Where is the Moderator". He did not immediately reply. Instead, he gazed outwards into the fathomless void surrounding the ship. "Sol, my commander, your attachment to the Moderator and your dependence on it for technical or combatant discussions is out of balance. It is time to either unplug it or give it the emotional component of the organic link that your mentor would have wished.

It can never attain actual Lyran status. Still, either way, it is better than having an expensive piece of machinery walking around." Slowly he turned to look at the commander and saw his words had penetrated her consciousness more than he'd anticipated. Then he nodded slightly, both in acknowledgement of what she now had to consider and that he had finished his discourse.

"Commander, I will leave you now to do that which is for your personal attention. This ship and her crew require guidance that only you are able to give, by example as the Negotiator that you once were, and still are deep within yourself. Your position of leadership does not absolve you of the skills of Negotiation."

Sol stared at the Mage, unsure whether she should listen to or ignore what he was saying. She would often get cryptic messages that would take her a few lapzph to figure out, but there was nothing cryptic in what the Mage had just said to her. It was true that she had set aside the negotiation part of her lineage to focus on the leadership and well-being of her crew and ship. The Mage was right. Leadership without the full integration of the Negotiator was not authentic leadership.

She would need to revisit this, to go into the meditation room and reawaken the Lyran Directive of her True Blood being again. But right now, she was required to direct and guide the duel docking and meet the Princes.

Leaders meet

Sol stood legs slightly apart, shifting her weight easily from leg to leg as she waited for the disembarking of the Lyran Princes and the crew of the *'Bitari-Furtim-Otiose.'* Her arms loosely clasped behind her back, she scanned the perimeters of the docking bay and noted the tightened security. Her now seldom used [65]CLD was strapped to her thigh within easy grip should the requirement arise. Tension in the docking bay was tangible. Both groups of Lyrans were looking to meet and connect with each other with anticipation. Yet, each party had a sliver of nerves or fear, each unsure of what the other may do. The expectation of meeting a True Blood Prince was a dream many Lyrans had given up on, and here was the potential of meeting not one but three.

The signal sounded, and the docking doors began to hiss and pop as air pressure equalised between the two ships. Then, finally, a loud cranking noise was heard as the doors of both ships opened simultaneously, and then there was silence.

Taking a deep breath, squaring her shoulders, Sol walked forward to stand in the opening of the Docking Ramp. She could see movement coming from the other ship as they walked down the passageway, and then, there they were, the young Lyran Princes. RexNā Loid DeAqua presented first, with RaeNegria Hylrix-El-Moa and Rägę El BriNa-Ragnoa El Vroan standing shoulder to shoulder behind her.

Tears sprung to the eyes of Sol Lrign dWari as she took in the sight of the three Princes representing the three families of Lyra. It seemed to have been a lifetime since she had witnessed the Royal Families representatives standing together, and now here on her ship, a new dawn was breaking for a unified Lyran people. She hoped.

---

[65] Crystal Laser Disrupter, which used phased plasma and concentrated white light to eliminate physical matter in seconds.

"Welcome Princes of Lyra." She began her official welcome.

"We offer the Truth of our Ways, the Dignity of our Sectors and the Honour of our Negotiators. May Lyra rise with the Creator, may her principles of Honour, Dignity and Truth be as our Over-Souls meant them to be and may Lyra remain forever". The old traditional greeting rolled off Sol's tongue without effort or thought. Many of the young Lyrans had never heard this type of greeting before. The power of the words spoken by Sol seemed to create a sense of euphoria.

The entire crew of the *'Bitari-Furtim-Karda'* held their collective breath as they waited for the response from the Princes.

RexNā, however, did not immediately respond. She felt she needed to stand on the deck before speaking, not from a tunnel that could be disconnected at any second. Signalling with a slight movement of her head, she indicated she was moving forward and wanted the others to follow. RaeNegria, still unsettled and not in full strength, pushed a telepathic message through to her leader, "RexNā, you must acknowledge them and their [66]captain. It is the Lyran way." "Shhhh", came the gentle reply, "I know what I am doing, trust me,"

With that, she stepped out of the corridor and onto the actual deck of the *'Bitari-Furtim-Karda.'*

Looking around her, she lifted her head and gazed directly above her. The ship's docking area was virtually identical to her ship; they could have been designed and built by the same people. That, she decided, gave her an added benefit and comfort.

Coming to a standstill in just a short space in front of Sol, RexNā began to speak.

---

[66] The Lyran Princes are still unaware that Sol is a commander and not a captain,

"We are travellers of Lyra, sent on a journey of discovery. To know and learn of not only our limitations but also the limits of our people. To recover the lost and bring them home." RexNā's response to the official welcome of Sol Lrign dWari rose like wafts of warm air to those standing on the decks and railings above. Her voice was warm, lilting and presented in all the remembered and instinctive 'officialdom' she could muster in her nervous mind.

"We are the Families Royal, and we are the representatives of the Lyran People. We stand in Honour before you, the captain of this vessel, presenting our strengths and weakness to be added to your quotient. We come in the Spirit of the Negotiation that we will be found True, our Honour intact, and our Dignity undefiled."

As she spoke, her words floated upwards to the levels where those above were watching. RexNā's eyes were locked with Sol's and so did not see the effect her words had upon those listening. However, there were more than just words of pomp and ceremony. A challenge of wit and inner strength was also being put forward.

As RexNā stopped, she stepped aside and waved her friends forward, "These two, stand with me as Royal Prince of the Lyrans. We lead as one, having three minds and perspectives to bring balance and ensure that one cannot be led astray or tempted to deceive the whole.

RaeNegria and Rägę stepped forward and tilted their heads to acknowledge Sol's leadership.

Sol gazed at RaeNegria, noting that she wore a hooded cloak of her sector which kept her body covered as if attempting to keep the light off of her skin or perhaps to prevent others from seeing something she did not wish to expose.

Out of the corner of her eye, she saw the movement of two others drawing closer. Raising her hand to indicate they should stay where they were, she asked RaeNegria, "Why the heavy cloak and protection of the hood?" "Are we not to see you eye to eye as decreed by 'The Way of Lyra'?"

Before Rae could reply, both MelEid and Eid' dVra stood directly behind her and spoke almost in a single voice. "The Prince is in Ascension, the Initiation of her blood coding has begun, and she has tasted the Waters of Source, it is not for us to see her eyes till she is ready to reveal what she sees."

Sol froze inwardly, for she recognised the rank of the High Chief Mage in MelEid and recognised her energy from their telepathic communications. What caused her to recheck her mental inventory of sectors was that Eid' dVra wore the cloak of the Mage and the Cloak of the Seer blended, making him a Chief Seer, one of the monastery researchers. When he stood in Seer's position, his words would be spoken and heard as if he was receiving instruction directly from Source via the Crystal Heart Stone. Sol knew that there were only a few such Seers in circulation, and for him to be with RaeNegria meant that there was more, much more, to what was being played out in the open.

Nodding her head as if in agreement, Sol brought her attention back to RexNā, "You have travelled a great distance to search us out? What made you so sure that we were to be found?" Then, pausing for a moment, she continued, "You have returned our ship to us. For that, we are grateful, but we ask, why have you brought our known enemies into our ranks?" This statement was a deliberate challenge to the crew members of the Nelphi-Lex-mai.

RexNā, who was in full Dol-Fyn-Nios water unit regalia, turned a little awkwardly to look at her comrades in battle who had more than once saved their group in conflicts with the Formless Ones. She could see that Ru Naal was a little uncomfortable and was fiddling with his empty phaser holder.

Smiling her secret smile, she turned back to Sol. "I see no-one but Lyrans, Lyran of True Blood and Lyran of Adoption". She stated clearly for all to hear. As RexNā Loid DeAqua's words floated up and around those present, it was noted that they had a definitive effect on the Nelphi-Lexmai group. As former enemies of the Lyrans, they had agreed and submitted to various initiations and tests to prove their Loyalty. But they had never heard any of the Princes refer to them as 'Lyrans by Adoption', not even after the initiations.

Ru Naal once again felt the intense feeling of Freedom and Liberty that he'd once lost burgeon in his chest again. Once more, he mentally committed to himself to protect these Princes against any attempt to harm them.

Sol read the challenge that had been placed before her. Like a good participant in the art of Negotiation, she had brought an issue to light. RexNā had countered it swiftly and accurately, with no emotion involved, just the facts and realities of what was.

Smiling slightly at the young Prince, Sol allowed herself to relax. Then, putting her hand out to RexNā Loid D'Aqua, she gently bowed at the waist, "Welcome to our home, such as it is, Prince. You and yours are welcome to relax and enjoy the amenities, and I am sure your crew would like to experience the Pods of Relaxation." Sol was referencing the creation that the engineers and Mages of her ship had built over time, where one could slip into the waters of Lyra and float within them. During this time of cleansing, they would experience physical, mental and emotional restoration as one floated and allowed the healing of silence to work within them.

"If you follow me, we'll make our way to the communal area decks, and the crews can begin to get to know each other. However, Juuls, my Second in Command, will take you shortly to the level we have prepared for your quarters. I felt it best to install your ship's crew within our crew's matrix quarters. Thus they can learn to work as one sooner rather than later. Lieutenant Marcus will accompany your crew to the levels where they will be allocated. Then they will go to the Quartermaster's office, where he will ensure they are assigned to their sectors and informed of their duties.

In the meantime, I ask the three of you and your Mage if you wish to join me in the ready room, where we will be able to relax and discuss the pertinent issues of why you are here. I would also enjoy hearing your thoughts on the ship that materialised recently and is currently docking in the rear of our ship. They claim that they are your backup, sent to monitor your journey from a distance, though never to interfere unless you were in dire straights. What do you say to this?" Sol dropped this information bomb in their laps as she turned and walked out of the docking bay and towards the rooms where she regularly met with the rest of the command crew concerning the running of the ship and actions required in defence or battle.

The three Princes looked at each other in confusion. Why would they know of another ship that was not connected to them? Furthermore, they had not picked up any signature or plasma vibration trail of a vessel following them through their journey to the Sector of Light.

RexNā was keen to find out more. To hear that there were more Lyrans nearby who knew about Lyra's past and how they defeated the Formless Ones, she, RexNā, wanted to communicate with them and gain any knowledge she could.

Looking at her friends, she shrugged, smiled in a casual, 'oh well let's go find out' sort of manner and turned to follow Sol to the debriefing table.

During this time of protocol and divulging of information, the Chief Mage and Seer of both ships assessed each other. The Moderator finally approached Sol and stated what the others were picking up intuitively, "Commander, the one RaeNegria, is no longer merely a Prince. She has undergone a change. Her DNA has been upgraded, you could say. The reason for her complete covering is to hide the fact that her body has returned to the original status of Lyran prior to the Royal Families becoming what they are today. In other words, Sol, you potentially have on board the Seer of Seers."

Sol spun round to re-look at the young Prince who had desperately reached out telepathically to ask for help, to tell her that she had information relevant to the infiltration on the 'Bitari-Furtim-Karda'. "Is this true?" She asked while looking directly into the eyes of RaeNegria. The young Prince looked back, nodded and removed her cloak hood, exposing the changes that had occurred while she was in a deep unconscious state.

The sight of RaeNegria shocked Sol. She drew her breath in sharply and took a step back, not out of fear but rather due to the awareness of being in the presence of someone wholly unknown and powerful.

Rae smiled, reached out her hand and spoke telepathically to Sol, "I am still the Lyran Prince that reached out to you, I still have deep in my subconscious a message for you from RathVorx. I am not your enemy, I am the messenger of the Waters of Source and interpreter of the Crystal Heart Stone. I am also, a True Lyran, a Negotiator of Honour, Integrity and Truth."

No one else heard this conversation, but they all observed the expressions flitting over Sol's face and the deep peace that was RaeNegria.

Now, Dear Reader, we need to move onward, or is it backward to your time? We need to reassess the workings of the Terrans in your world. So come, let us step into the slipstream of time and move towards Terra, your earth.

Chapter Twenty-One

Earth, the lie that was
Uncovering truth embedded within lies

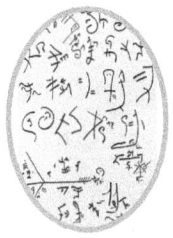

Dear Reader, your world is full of misdirection, false truths and many diversions, all created to instil within you a sense of trust in the organisations that now run your day-to-day life. From the first interaction with the Anunnaki, you contracted or agreed to submit your freedom, your actual status of being.

Let us explain.

As we delve into this chapter, many subjects will be touched upon. Questions asked. This is to create a questioning mind within you, not to create separation or perceived judgement. The subjects following are quarrelsome indeed, but they are also presented in the hopes of bringing healing to all.

If we return to the time when your part of the multiverse was referred to or known as Terra or Terra-Ven-Eiliesh-Gaina, we will find a culture or species that responded in compassion, wisdom, and truth and knew of no deceit in others, for they did not look for it.

If a Terran was found to have harmed another, that living soul was brought before the elders. Once in council, they were asked what had caused the reason behind the action. Upon hearing the reason, they would ask the community to speak their truth about the Terran before them. This gave the community a space to tell the Terrans involved how they felt about the situation or what had occurred.

In everyday situations, no one would focus on the event. Instead, the focus would be on the fact that there was something disconnected in the Terran to cause them to act the way they did. They would place the 'offending' Terran within a circle of light. Next, a fire was lit on either side of the Terran. Then those who aught against the Terran were invited to bring a piece of wood, throw it into the fire, and speak their truth. As long as the wood burned, they would talk about the matter. Once the wood was burnt, and the accusation or problem was shared by the first Terran, the one being questioned was given the right to reply. In the same manner, they, too, were given a similar-sized piece of wood. This was thrown on the second fire, and the 'offending' Terran would speak from their heart while the flames consumed it. During this right of reply, all present heard the inner cry of their heart and why they did what they did.

In most of these situations, there were very few accusations. Rather the community would gather around to allow the hurting parties to voice the issue, and then there would be, for both sides, a reminder of the good they do, of their participation in the community. Their strengths and gifts, which assist all present. The good they did. How they were loved, and the way they worked with the rest of the community.

Usually, after the fire ceremonies of clearing, the Terran who had committed the offence would go to the party they had offended and make amends in whatever way was acceptable in the other's eyes.

This culture was a culture of love, acknowledgement and learning. Judgement was not a part of your world, nor was it something you participated in easily, for you always looked at the offender as if you were standing there yourself. Thus what was it that you would ask of another to assist you in healing; this was the way of the Terrans.

However, once the Anunnaki settled in on your world, they changed your thinking over a long extended attack on your principles and beliefs. They studied your lifestyle and learned everything they could about you. Taking advantage of your innocence, your simple but honest way of living and your acceptance that Terra-Ven-Eiliesh-Gaina would supply all you required to enjoy a life of liberty, peace and enjoyment.

The Anunnaki believed only in work, in complex, thankless work that for many Anunnaki meant rising before the light of the day and ending their work after the light had gone from the skies. This made them very inventive about formulating and getting more done without exerting more effort. This is why they established the slave race, not just here but on many worlds where they raided and subjugated that world's beings or original souls. What they have done to your planet is no different from what they have done elsewhere; only here, they have mastered it to a fine art. Your way of life, your deep resonance to the truth that is deep within your DNA, is what they wish to destroy, to make you a soulless and unemotional shadow of your beingness. This way, they can utilise, take over, and occupy not just your land and world but your bodies for their pleasures and believe us, their pleasures are not what you would want to know.

The Anunnaki created the lie that this world cannot function without rules that bind you in knots, without contracts to ensure you keep your word out of fear of the consequences for not doing so. They told you that your way of agreement or promise, shaking hands or giving your word, was not good enough. There was no 'evidence' that you said what you said.

This was how they wriggled out of their early agreements with your ancestors.

Eventually, they worked it into your psyche that a contract was required to verify an agreement between two Terrans or a Terran and an Anunnaki, but again they lied and added to it. Eventually, a signed agreement was not enough; soon, you had to swear an oath, then a promissory note which you had to authorise in your blood. Before long, your people were caught up in a system as foreign to you as the Anunnaki were. But due to your innate honour and constant desire to see the good in all you worked with, you kept agreeing to the change until it was too late.

As indicated by our chronicle of vol two in this disclosure.

One of the most significant lies the Anunnaki and their descendants have lied to you about is the world you live upon. Do not reject what we are about to say to you. What we will share has already been inferred in the second section of our disclosure. Be open and consider all facts as we state them. Do not react negatively due to the brain training and programming of your education which is based on the Anunnaki way of 'obedience' is everything.

This is the mantra of your schooling, accept and question nothing.

Terra is not a ball spinning in the void on an endless journey with all other planetoids, moons, asteroids, suns etc., revolving around her. No, indeed, she is anchored in the void by a significant energetic vibration created by Polaris or the Northern Star that feeds the waters of energy deep into the toroidal field, folding into your accretion disk.

Many of you will want to throw this information out and stop reading, for you will say, 'oh god, here is a flat earth believer,' however that is not the truth of the one we are communicating through. So trust us when we say we are giving you information already being discussed in many sectors of your world.

If you cannot acknowledge what we share, we accept that, but we ask you a simple question.

Consider, if you will, your world is a ball spinning at great speed. Then added to this spinning, it is propelled forward along a set trajectory. The propulsion pushing the ball forward is an incredible rate, so we have an object flying through space, spinning at an astronomical speed to sustain gravity.

But why are the constellations always in the same place in the sky?

If the object, your world, is constantly moving forward, why does your night sky remain the same?

Why do you not see new stars and planetary bodies as you are thrust through 'space' on your global journey?

Ask yourself, why are the other planets, Mars, the Moon, Jupiter etc., always in place and never left behind? Yes, all is in orbit.

You are told all planets, moons, and planetoids have a modicum of gravity, some more, some less than others.

However, how do you prevent a collision if you travel in a straight line through the void, with all the other celestial bodies rotating around you?

How do the other planets remain in sync?

This must mean that a greater force than any living being or created being is in charge! For it would take pronounced precision for all stars, meteors, planets, moons, space debris etc., to be moving in the exact motion of speed, velocity, spinning and orbiting so as not to 'collide' with each other. Though it still does not answer why your night sky stays the same if you are moving forward.

The scenery changes as you go along when you drive to a destination on the road. So why does the same not occur in the night sky?

Try an experiment, take an ordinary small ball that can hold water in its cover and insert a wire through the middle to spin around and travel along. Then formulate a way to attach all other planetary bodies to the earth's trajectory and (and gravity) send it spinning down the path you have created.

Do all the following celestial bodies follow in exact distance and order?

Are there wobbles, perhaps a bump or two?

If you can't do this manually, use a computer, but be honest, do not adjust for this or that; input the exact data you have and allow it to play out.

Insert the constellations, the planets, the comets, moons, meteors, and everything that could possibly be in the 'space' that the earth travels through without hitting anything. Does this work?

In truth, your world was created to look more like an oval than a ball.

Consider the accretion disk, with arms of continuing creation flying out from its centre.

Encompassing the oval is an impressive impenetrable barrier due to the oscillating frequency that forms a 'wall' around your planet to keep the gases and other necessary particles within so that you and Terra-Ven-Eiliesh-Gaina can continue to live unhindered.

Why your scientists would attempt to break through this barrier, which is constructed for your safety, is beyond us. You can walk through this barrier at specific connection points in your world, where it settles close to the landmass.

Your atmosphere is full of rich, vibrant life forms that are here for the healing and ongoing health of all Terran. Yet, you have been taught to pollute the air and filter it, thus removing all particles that regenerate your cells.

Have you not considered the fact that when you retire to the 'country' or the forests, to the wilderness, after a while, you begin to feel younger, stronger, more alert etc.? But, on the other hand, have you wondered why you feel run down and depleted when you relax in these areas during the first few days of your time away? This is due to the pure air purging your cells and body and replacing the dead air with healthy air.

This is why the 'dome' or barrier is there - to ensure that you are able to utilise the life-giving gift that is the proper air.

Your teachers have taught you that the world is round. Water always follows the most straightforward way down, so how have you not considered the facts of the waters of your world?

Another question for you to consider is, where is the evidence of the spinning upon the surface of the water? If you have water in a container, and you cause the container to spin, you will see that the water follows the movement of the spin in such a way as to create a vortex within itself. If you are able to observe this phenomenon with the captive state, surely, Dear Reader, you should see the same evidence of spinning upon the surface of large bodies of water. Especially as the earth is moving at a phenomenal speed to ensure that 'gravity' is fully activated.

Why, if the water is at a great height, does it flow downward, but the waters of the great oceans remain static? They do not move other than the waves.

Why do they not slide at angles over the rim of the circle that is the ball?

You may claim that it is gravity, and while gravity is a fact that you have been given to believe in, and yes, it has validity, have you considered the mathematical equations required to keep the mass of water locked in a single place of being? Then considered the effects of that intense gravity on other objects such as your-selves.

While all the logic in the world designed by the Anunnaki and Formless ones to keep you, and those who come after you, trapped in the way of limited thinking, tells you that we are lying.

That the world is indeed round and cannot possibly be flattish.

To this, we ask you a few simple questions.
 Who told you the world was round?
Teachers?

Who told them?
University, education centres?
 Who told them?
Scientists, learned men or women?

How did they find out?
Was it via captains of old that sailed the world to map the then 'known' world?

[67]If they sailed from the North, they'd follow the North Star, and if sailors desired to go to the South, again the stars would lead them,

---

67 Why Dear Reader, when you research, do you find that virtually the entire lower part of the southern oceans are not traversed with any ship. They will tell you it is dangerous, that there are storms and other elements that will harm you if you tra-verse these waters. At times using military means to prevent you from sailing in these sacred waters. But ask yourself, what do they wish to hide from you? Ships travelled these routes before your 'modern era'; what prevents them now?

which takes them in a west-to-east direction, so yes, navigation of the oceans occurred East to West but was the earth navigated North to South? Your realm can only be circumnavigated around the latitude rings. The longitude rings show the potential, but there are obstacles in the way of a complete circle from top to bottom.

Who has shown you the world is round?
Government organisations?
How did they know?
Cameras on spaceships?

How do they get the spaceships or rockets out past the barrier, past the Van Allen barrier of radiation?
Your own [68]space scientists have indicated that no ship can safely pass through the radiation belt due to the intense destructive energy of this radiation, so how do they push the photographic probes past it? Especially as you are informed that the radiation is so severe that it will create interference, possibly burn the outer coverage of the vessel and damage the fragile computer instruments on board.

They tell you there is a round ball called earth, the moon, the sun, Jupiter, Pluto etc., but have you seen it? Yes, we note that you stare up at the sun, and it seems to be round, the moon seems to be round, yet we ask you if it is round or oval?
The sun and the stars are fluid in their movement and energy flow. This is why the stars' twinkle' in the night sky, according to you. We ask that you ask questions of all you are taught, don't just accept something as true because the government or education establishment has told you it is true.

---

[68] Your organisation NASA admits this in the year 2015 - Kelly Smith a NASA Scientist (a public educational film is found via https://youtu.be/4O5dPsu66Kw) made a public announcement on behalf of NASA stating that they still are required to solve the issue of the radiation belts before astronauts can enter the zone.

Investigate, dear Terran, investigate.

Use strong binoculars or telescopes to view the far-off celestial bodies and look at them. Do they look 'real', or do they look like someone has painted a picture? Is this part of the great simulation currently being played before you? Do the luminaries look 'solid', or are they more fluid, plasma-looking? Do they show revolving colours of the spectrum each time you gaze at them? There is so much to re-look at, to consider. Do not change your belief because of our words, but do research. Go further back in your learning than what you were given in the scholastic halls.

At one time, for thousands of years, it was accepted that your world was flat. It was only when the Roman Catholic Church decided that it required the world to be round that it forced all scientists and learned scholars to deny that the world was anything but round.

The Anunnaki descendants are the Roman Catholic governance or leaders, they pull the strings in the shadows, and you, my Dear Readers, believe them because you were trained to do that from childhood.

We see over the timelines that there have been attempts to break away from this way of living.

The last breakaway was when Terrans used the power of the ether to transmit 'electricity' produced from water. Unfortunately, the knowledge of water and how to create energy using sound has been lost. There are ways, with having water flowing in both directions, up and down, to charge generators and send power out over large areas of land and water.

Yet, you see the evidence of it all around you if you would but look with open eyes.

The energy of the ether would open portals or gateways for travel upon your land masses. You had means of travel with gateways and portals, including the lower travel means being; robotic, electrical, and flight long before you were taught that you could. There is imagery, and history is still around for you to discover if you wish to know the truth.

Your world has been built on lies, my Dear Reader.
Lies to keep you dumb and obedient.
Lies to keep you from questioning the narrative of your overlords.
Once over two hundred years of your earth's time ago, when the Anunnaki realised that the Terrans were awakening to their truth and the lobotomy was wearing off, many thousands of Terrans escaped via the southern section of your world into the outer realms of Terra.
When this happened, the Anunnaki, with the Formless Ones, created a series of major floods of water and mud to destroy the land masses' lower regions and remove most of the population.
This created a severe depletion of workers, so the Anunnaki began rebuilding their slave race by introducing young children into areas where the people had disappeared.

Or should we say escaped from?

There have been multiple moments in your timeline when Terrans knew how to travel with great speed over water and land. They communicated through machines of automated communication - similar to your computers of today. Still, these had a built-in disrupter that disallowed any 'hacking' or illicit interference from an outside manner. Thus they were able to communicate dates, times and places of escape. Some of these still live in the outer lands of your world, in areas where life is as Terra and the Creator intended it to be... You call this Eden.

We call this place Terra.

There are many ways you have been indoctrinated into the lies of your world. Each generation builds on that lie until it has become your truth. Many of the last remaining Terrans were knocked into submission through the vast network of indoctrinations of scholastic and educational means.

Terran offspring with 'out of the box' imaginations or dreams questioned the narrative or did not accept what was given as 'truth' were punished. At times severely. This fear created a sense of desperation in some young Terrans, who wanted to be accepted and not seen as different. Unfortunately, they submitted to the educational way of thinking. They allowed themselves to be trained to believe the lie of where your world is, where you originated from, and the organised religions to absorb. ** including the theologies of race, sub-culture, and diet.

Others, however, chose not to submit and became what authorities call rebellious, and you struck out on your own, questioning and seeking answers that were not easily found. Many of you are still that way, hence empowering your living soul by gathering together in communities that defy the current lies of governance and have begun to create the original ways of life. Honour, Self Responsibility and ensuring that no harm is done to you or others.

This is the way of T'Gaina, to use what is required and return what is not used, or to give it to others freely expecting nothing in return.

We have observed how 'they' have created so many avenues of deception that have grown over the years.

First, organised religion was imposed and used to cover the true Divine nature of Connection to the Creator with the world's different cultures.

Then they changed that to say there was no 'god' and religion was the crutch of unstable and weak people.

Terrans believed innately within themselves, knowing that the Creator was not locked in a building but within their sacred heart space and the world, they lived in. The Anunnaki and Formless ones have created an erroneous religion to ensure your captivity in more ways than one.

They took a simple truth and inverted it.

What they have done is taken the truth and 're-dressed' it. They agree that, yes, there is a Creator.
You, the true Terrans or original beings of this realm, know of the original connection of the Creator. How a Being of Living Energy of the Universal Light, imbued with great Cosmic Truth and Power, was brought to the Living Souls of Terra-Ven-Eiliesh-Gaina. This Being called The Way Shower, The Christ Energy, and Buddha, among other names, is the physical image of The Creator within the form called Terran. But, in the very innermost parts of your hearts, all Terrans know that one time they could do all that the Way Shower did. They, however, lost their way, though, through the entanglement and agreements with the Anunnaki.

This great truth was flipped, inverted by the Formless ones and Anunnaki. They created an almost identical story but twisted it so that you had to be locked into a religious belief to be accepted. They gave you their own warped religion or beliefs, wrapped them up in the covering of your truth and told you that their way was best. You must follow, convert, and remain faithful; if not, you will become an outcast or, in extreme cases, be killed.

You must have a label to be acknowledged.

Gone was the freedom to walk and talk with the Creator, as if conversing with a friend. The moments of quietly contemplating your connection with the surrounding energy of nature and creation were removed from you. Being accepted as spiritual requires a group belonging, a label, and a system of belief.

They caused a significant separation between friends and loved ones who were bonded in the same unit of origin. Mothers and Fathers were at odds with their offspring, the product of their bodies, for as the younger Terrans became infiltrated with new ways and beliefs, they scorned and denied the old ways.

This breakdown of trust and love gave the entrance for a new inversion of truth by the Anunnaki and Formless Ones. They began to attack the way you ate and sustained your natural health. They knew that as long you had innate immunity, you would not seek out health practitioners, who were taught in the way of death, not life, for you would not need their assistance.

So they attacked the food groups you ate, telling you that what had sustained you and your ancestors for millennia was wrong and harmful and began to invert the way to consume food. They gave animals a higher ranking than the living soul of the Terran. They instigated arguments within groups, telling those who consumed meat that they were evil and lesser beings while those who ate vegetables interspersed with some protein products, fish, eggs, milk etc., were of higher consciousness.

Then they changed that and said that only if you eat food that has nothing to do with meat products or is connected to self-production of life-giving sustenance. So those within this newly created 'religion' refuse to eat the simple gifts of T'Gaina, such as honey, milk, and cheese, or wear clothing that may have specific products other than made-made synthetics or plant-based materials in the manufacturing.

The puppet masters are determined to ensure that you, the living men and women, are condemned to consume imitation food. Food that is made from plant by-products or synthetically created in a laboratory, this new cult is now called veganism, and it is displayed as the ultimate way to live.

It is important to note here that we Lyrans are not interested in what you eat or why. What concerns us is the dogma surrounding the larger community living this way. The fervent and almost religious way they condemn those who eat a mixed meat and vegetable diet. Why?

They failed to inform you that the diet they claimed was better for the hu-man body actually created a deficit in your cells. While you may look as healthy on the outside as one who ate a balanced meal of animal and vegetable goodness, the consumers of this type of diet were susceptible to many illnesses and cellular breakdown.

One of the more concerning issues is megaloblastic anaemia, where the body produces irregular blood cells. There is also the concern that they lack iodine which your body requires.

We would request those who have chosen out of health over dogma to follow a strict diet that excludes meat and other vital elements to ensure they observe the levels of vitamin B to ensure their B12 and B9 are balanced. They may wish to check their iodine levels as well... This way of eating can be harmful, as can all consumption styles if care and awareness are lacking. We implore all who choose to delete the nourishment of meat, honey, and dairy from their diet to monitor their health. To respect yourselves and all others who may differ in their perception from you.

Thus they were required to purchase supplements to 'supplement their diet.' These supplements were mostly concocted from a petroleum base with a quotient of 'natural elements' to give credence to calling them 'natural.'

Due to the ultra-strict diets of some of your species, many now suffer a compromised immune system. Over time the minions of the Formless Ones have interfered with your dietary requirements. As more and more **{hidden chemicals, colourings and other things] dietary restrictions were placed upon the beings of this realm, multiple beings now experience their bodies beginning to break down.

Diseases that had never been heard of became household discussions. Terrans and hu-mans alike began to eat overly processed food to the point that food no longer had any goodness in it. This created the pandemic of obesity, diabetes, cancer, tumours, and many others. Soon the false medics were being overrun with Terrans and hu-mans seeking assistance. They shunned the way of the shamans and turned from natural healers.
Teachings passed down the generations of the 'old ways' were looked at as being wrong or 'old fashioned.' The concept of modernism and easy living began to germinate in the young Terran, human and Galactic Beings living in this world. Their minds have begun to form into the mould that had been played out for them in the reading material, tv shows and movies that had been rolled out to entertain them.

The Anunnaki descendants and their Formless One masters have been playing a game of chess for a very long time, they have believed their own lies that they will succeed in this decimation of the Terran world, but they forget one thing. The God-Spark, within all Terrans and Creator-focused Beings, is imbued with a natural gene that cannot be disconnected from the Creator. Unless the Terran gives away their authority and consents to things without full comprehension, believing they are doing the 'right thing'.

So why do you think they (the puppet masters) are so intent on getting the residents of this world to comply so readily with the current lie? If they can get you to do their work for them, they have gained another step on the ladder of domination. They are beyond annoyed at those that will not comply and will not bow down to a draconian overlord; those that stand and refuse to bend are the ones that will be targeted in this current stage of your world game.

Another lie you have been giving as truth is that the world you live in is an experiment, a prison, a place where you have no rights, no movement of honour and truth. A place where you exist in eternal reincarnation, never-ending existence.

So we must ask this one question.
Why do they try so hard to make you believe this?

Why do they (the Anunnaki, the Draconians, the Greys, Formless Ones, Mantids and many others) need to keep you in the lie? What would happen if you woke up and realised the truth of who you were and what you were? Would you be able to disable their agenda? Would you be able to resist them? Overtake them and their plan for your world? We, the Lyran Narrators of Time, believe this to be true.

To wake up is not to be what you call 'woke' or 'awakened' in energy or knowledge. To wake up is to pull your slumbering soul from the depths of the chamber you have been locked in for your entire life. Even now, some of you, Dear Readers, are in a half-slumber fed by the society you are afraid to let go of.
To truly awaken is to see the half-dead walking around you, to see the glistening world for what it truly is, a decaying society where fully formed AI is running your world and deleting humanity and Terrans from existence. They have put you in a position

where you must choose left or right, injection or not. If you allow the first injection, they will keep pumping you with their black powders and magnetic nano tech until your body rejects it and dies. Alternatively, your body ceases to exist the way it was created as it has become something unknown. A mix of corpuscle and robotic, a blend of electronic and flesh. When this change occurs, the cells of the unfortunate are slowly replaced using liquid metals and nanotechnology within the injections, thus creating an android from within. This may explain why some of you are showing early signs of magnetic disruption in your bodies and why there are those of you registering a 'bar code'. This is because your bodies have been susceptible to the beginnings of the change.

Dear Reader, many are discovering this all around the world. So, naturally, they are attempting to get this news to all who will hear, but regrettably, like the ones before them, they are relegated to the 'just too silly' box. But, ask yourself, is it silly? Or is there something within you which agrees that there is more to the agenda of world governance than what they say?

It is time to see your world for the truth that it is.

Your world is far larger than what you have been taught. There are land masses outside the 'map' that you think is your earth. Your world has more food and water hidden away in inaccessible parts within her to supply your people for thousands of years to come.
Your world has more oxygen and natural gases to keep you breathing and comfortable for as long as you choose to live in her. Your world has minerals and other hidden stores within her for mining. If you choose to do this, there is more than sufficient there is an overabundance, but you should ask, why do we need this much gold, diamonds, rubies etc.,... if you have been mining for all

these centuries, where are the gold, diamonds and other precious metals and stones? Surely there should be more physical evidence to give credence to the claims made?

Your world is waiting for you to break free, not outwards to space but beyond the ice in the northern and southern regions. Yes, there are large ice fields in certain parts of your world. This is to aid with water retention and dispersion around the planet. They are not there to keep you corralled but rather to intrigue your adventuring spirit to go further, to seek the hot water springs of the South. Likewise, the Northern Lights are there to intrigue you. These lights should inspire you to explore, search for their source, and find the caves that hold the secrets to the inner sanctums of the realm.

Your T'Gaina follows an exact pattern of universal design. She is stable and true in her format, allowing the dance of life to entwine with her, and she opens to the Creator's life force when there is a need to increase the populations of all species. The perfect toroidal energy form.

There is more than enough land for you and your units within the community. Instead of trusting an organisation that is feeding off your life energy, why do you not begin to listen to the inner voice of the sacred space of the heart? Why do you not listen to the voice of the inner knowing? This is for you who have the ability to connect the way the old Terrans did and who translate the voice of T'Gaina for those who hear.

There is, by far, more to enjoy on this planet than you can imagine. Be aware that you have not discovered the depth and width of your world. Your world is not what the teachers or 'masters' have told you. Research and discover the old maps of circa 1160BCE showing the supposed world of the then, supposed species here on earth. Then move to the early Nineteen hundreds, where they show you the movements of [69]air travel and how the flying contraptions are to pass over certain lands to reach the destination.

It is very different to the ball. In fact, the travel industry tells you a similar story in all the images showing [70]flight details, but because they do it using illusion, you do not see what is in front of you.

Dear Reader, we have given you either something to consider or we have shut you down. Either way, we have done what is required, for your journey now is at a crossroads.

It is time to become aware of who and what you are in this world of illusion and dichotomy. This world is built on inversion and lies to keep you dumbed down and believing a lie created as far back as the original Terrans standing up against the Anunnaki when they realised the truth they'd been told was, in fact, a lie dressed up.

We will return to the world soon, for it is time to see the state humanity has generated in this current moment.

...

---

[69] you may not find these maps now, as the AI is cleaning up

[70] flight mapping in magazines

Chapter Twenty-Two

The Agenda Exposed
An overview of your history, The enemy exposed

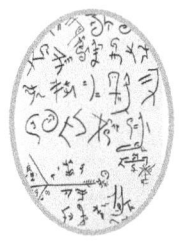

Further information: Lyran Narrators of Time

As we observe the unfolding of events on planet earth, on our beloved T'Gaina, we see many of the past resets replaying their 'dying swan' songs. Such is the pattern of the [71]oligarchs that they overplay their hand, believing they are all powerful and can therefore demand compliance and obedience from those who walk the surface of this realm.

What they are forgetting, and in all honesty what the generations of these power-hungry and faceless draconian leaders always forget, is that no matter how hard they attempt to wipe the God-Spark from the Terran or the 'Human', they cannot. The reason is simple Dear Reader, for you have been gifted with the breath of the Creator, and it is deeply seated within your very DNA and essence of being.

---

[71] A member of an oligarchy, one of a few holding political power

Yes, the servants of the Formless Ones continue pushing their masters' agendas. Enslaving those dear souls that believe they are 'doing the right thing'. Either by pushing an injection, as they are doing, or creating a plague to infect the populace, they forget there are still those who are strong and withstand all attempts to remove them from the surface of T'Gaina.

We gaze back over your timeline, and we see time and time again minor oligarchs believing themselves to be of a higher rank or wishing to prove a point to their betters. It is during these moments that your world is inundated with false truths, outright lies and manipulative leaders who are too weak to say no, or too greedy to refuse what they believe is a bountiful reward.
Yet when they fall from the pedestal they believed was theirs forever and plummet into the arena of the common living soul, fear begins to grow within them and a realisation that perhaps all they said was not as accurate as supposed. For now, they, too, have become one of the 'useless eaters' as the Formless Ones, Anunnaki, and Draconian overlords refer to the beings of this realm.

Let us play back the various hidden agendas that they have already, in reality, shown you what they are doing and why.
First, let us go back in your timelines, and then we will work our way forward.

We realise that there has been an extensive section in the previous chapters covering potentials in your timelines, so yes, we have covered some of the events or timelines in our revealing to you the potential possibilities of 2049.
However, we believe you will see and comprehend the images and blueprint we are laying before you. For by knowing your past, knowing who you are, where you are, and where you are heading is empowering you.

Over the millennia, there have been numerous attempts to wipe your knowledge and DNA from this realm. You have proven to be the proverbial thorn in the sides of the Anunnaki, the Formless Ones and anyone else who joins with them. You prove to be 'that' being that continues rebuilding their DNA from whatever distorted and viral influence is placed within your body.

Terrans, hear us.

This earth of yours is more spectacular and of greater importance to not only yourselves but to many other cultures of beings in the incredible multiverse. As you know from our past discourses in this Disclosure, you are the joint co-creation of T'Gaina and the Creator. The Source of all Life and Being. You, therefore, must realise by now that you have a double joining of energy, empowerment, and connection to the Tree of Life and Knowledge, allowing you to focus your energy at will into the most glorious creative force.

Your leaders, scientists and 'great minds' run this world according to the decree, plan, and agendas for the benefit of the Draconian masters, the Anunnaki etc., not yours. So you will hear the dramatic cry that the world is dying year after year, there is not enough food, not enough this or that, and yet you do not see their waistlines getting thinner or their pockets becoming less endowed with finance.

They manufacture the lack, and the minions of the puppet masters preach the fear of scarcity. Then they encourage you to 'stock up' to purchase and spend, spend, spend, thus creating a debt you never considered previously. Then, finally, they subliminally tell you to stay inside or hide in your caves (or houses) because it is too dangerous to live outside.

The sun will burn you, the cold will be too cold, the warmth is not healthy, and playing or being outside in nature will lead to accidents and illness, stay at home, wash, wipe, and be afraid. They have given you the rules or laws they want you to live by, it is set up as a monument, but it is their declaration of intent. The living souls of this world have acquiesced because they did not speak out against the comments or commandments. Now, when these 'ideals' are being implemented, there is general unrest.

But again, we point you back over the timeline from your own recordings of history. There have been events both in circa BC and AD where floods, 'and natural disasters occur, and people have died in their thousands if not millions.

A brief overview of your written history. Note that we do not say this is accurate; instead, we advise that you 'intuit the reality of what others place before you as facts.

Who recorded these facts originally? From where does the information come, and who is feeding you the results and information? This is provided to you from the time you begin to learn your 'skills' at the education centres that turn you into obedient soldiers. Most of you never challenged the history you were taught; you never queried why or who said what.

So based on your timelines, let us see how frequently the Anunnaki and Formless Ones have attempted to bring your world population down to 'manageable stock yards.'

As far back as the third century, the Egyptians were battling smallpox, a virus that quickly spread. This was dormant in their burial chambers until your people of investigatory ways dug them up to 'see' what life was like 'back then.' In these situations, diseases from the old world entered into the new.

During the Circa of 311 onwards, there were multiple civil wars in China led by leaders that desired to be 'gods' of the known world. They believed they were divine beings placed to rule over the lesser beings. Does this sound familiar, like the Anunnaki?

During Circa 526, Antioch was destroyed in an earthquake, and 300,000 living souls moved into the next realm.

Genghis Khan moved throughout the Mongol Region, conquered bordering empires, and controlled the masses circa 1208 - 1227. During this time, approximately 20 to 40 million people died. (This equates to 5 to 10% of the world population at the time.) So let us look at today at the information of too many people living on earth, and some need to be removed. There have even been predictions indicating the world population decreasing from 2017 to 2025. How is this possible without a great world war or disease ravaging the entire population? We, The Lyran Narrators of Time, consider it strange that the information site relating to this information was deleted. We asked the author to find this for you, but it has been removed. [72]However, we have discovered a site that gives you an example of the original deagel.com site at time of writing it was functional.

You had one of the first great plagues in 1346 wherein the then-known world anywhere between seventy-five to two hundred million people died.

The plagues follow with 'religious' dedication from then on. You have the 1720 Plague of Marseille (100,000 died) followed by the 1820 Cholera Pandemic (100,000 died), and then you were presented with the 1920 Spanish flu, where 100 million worldwide died. Concurrently in that same year, an earthquake in Haiyuan removed a further 200,000 from the face of T'Gaina.

---

[72] https://nofakenews.net/2020/10/18/deagel-website-predicts-a-massive-drop-in-population-for-certain-countries-by-2025/

We could follow this with the Soviet Crimes in 1917, where political madness pushed the people to move, forced them into camps and starved or had medical experimentation perpetrated on them, which killed 49 million souls.

In circa 1911, the Great Eugenics Movement became a popular game to play. It had exalted names attached to it, such as Alexandra Graham Bell, the Rockefellers, Dale Carnegie, Joseph Mengele, and Ernst Rüdin, to mention a few.
They all followed the teachings of The Eugenics Treatise' Preliminary Report of the Committee of the Eugenic Section of the American Breeders Association to Study and Report on the Best Practical means for cutting off the Defective Germ-Plasm in the Human Population. Even to us, this sounds like the 'reincarnation' of Ninharsag. The Anunnaki medical scientist, the daughter of Anu, the leader of the Anunnaki. Some of the preferred methods for removing this 'Defective Germ-Plasm' was to use gas chambers or euthanasia.

This evolved into baby contests! This was first introduced around circa 1913 when there was a push to find the 'perfect' child in the USA. For more research, we encourage you to look up Eugenics and Making the American Master Race. (Other cultures of your realm followed this thought pattern to extreme circumstances with unfortunate results) These contests were where your offspring were judged and recorded on the quality of the baby's health, weight, and size (just as farmers do for livestock when determining breeding stock.)
This then evolved into a programme called Fitter Families, where families were rated on their bloodlines and racial pedigree to prove their worth to society. Remember, this is in the United States pre-war regarding culture and race.
Again this raises the question, why are the Anunnaki still meddling with the population of T'Gaina? Although this programme

faded from the public domain around the 1920s, so you are told by history, the Eugenics movement is still being used behind the curtain to 'give birth to the perfect child, removing abnormalities from the DNA so that the perfect race can be produced. Eugenics and creating the 'perfect' race have been in action for many years. It is only in recent years that certain countries allowed those with [73]epilepsy to enter their countries when immigrating from their old lands.

Then in 1959, there was the Great China Famine, where the Chinese leaders decided they knew what was best for the people of that region. During the enforced driving of people out of traditional home areas into new unknown regions, another 43 million souls were removed from the realm.

The oligarchs of this timeline have not changed. You just have to look at your recent past wars, where in your two world wars, approximately 137 million people died.

Now, look closer to home. In this last century, where have you gone to war over oil, gold, and other by-products of the earth and how many have been removed from the planet as a result of this? There has been interference in cultures of other lands by hidden governments where entire populations have been decimated, and the excuse propagated has been cultural or tribal arguments. Look at Africa, a continent of beauty where nature and creation seem to blend most naturally. Then there are pockets of land with precious commodities, diamonds, gold, rubber, palladium and many other elements of presumed value. Those that desire these items create an 'unrest and turmoil situation within the living beings in that part of the realm, perhaps by injecting them with a 'vaccine' that is later 'turned on and, in a manner of speaking, create a 'zombie' effect in the person. Then they suddenly believe

---

[73] for your research, investigate the 'Ugly laws' of the Americas or when Australia let epileptics into the country to live

they are the greater, more righteous, more deserving tribe, culture, etc. A battle breaks out between tribes which annihilates each group. Turning children into weapons of war, women and men into fodder for oncoming bullets or machetes while they run terrified from their attackers. Your so-called first-world nations know exactly how to divest the wealth of the 'third-world nations and keep the living souls trapped there in a type of 'shadow world' not knowing, in truth, where they belong.

It is not just the African continent that deals with manipulation. Look to the laws in your own lands. [74]America uses Eugenic sterilisation in certain prisons and rewards those who 'volunteered' to go ahead with this 'option' with a certain number of days deducted from their imprisonment. Manipulation and hidden agendas have been at the centre of the puppet masters and the Formless Ones thrust for your destruction. So, dear Reader, please do not look at this section as mere regurgitation of specific issues of your past. But, rather, look at this as showing what was in plain sight.

All that has occurred has been put behind smoke and mirrors.

The leaders of this world do not have your best interests at heart. They only have their interests at heart. This is why they will never be seen on the front line, so to speak, nor will you see them willingly give away their wealth or abundance unless they know of a way to recoup it later.

You are told there are far too many souls upon the surface of the earth, and still, more are being born. So why is it a strange and sad realisation to you when you allow them to inject a mother carrying an unborn offspring that the child dies, and often so does the mother?

---

[74] so set in place circa 2017

Why do you find that young, healthy, fit people are falling dead or becoming extremely ill after they take the injection of the puppet masters? Their plan has always been to manipulate you into believing that you are nothing but a number. You have no greater importance than a tree, cow, pig, or other living organisms, but we say, and we tell you, that you are so much more.

Our overview of your timeline is not by any means complete. There are significant gaps that many of you should and could research and find more to fill in the holes in our discourse. However, we are showing you a snapshot to give you the knowledge that there is always an agenda from the 'governing' people to shut down the 'common people' and keep them 'behaving correctly' in rank. You are their livestock. You are their wealth. It is from your 'working all the hours given' that they make their financial gains and you suffer in poverty, illness, and lack.

[75]Some people have 'breakthroughs' and reach levels of great wealth, but at what sacrifice? What have they lost or given up to become 'rich'?

We are not saying that to have abundance is wrong, not in the slightest. We do, however, say that wealth created with the Creator and with T'Gaina is more fulfilling than a quick solution that can be snatched away without notice.

In many ways, the people of Terra are still entrapped in the deceit of the Anunnaki of aeons past. Attempting to work their way into the higher ranking levels of their masters while being pleasantly lied to, told that things are moving along nicely and to wait just a little longer for the reward. All the while, your masters are reaping the benefit of your toils.

---

75 The wealth achieved by those that 'make' it is still minor in comparison to those who control the agenda. They will allow certain of the stock to 'break the mould' and gain wealth, but when you take stock, it is an unbalanced figure. Making those who don't 'break through the wealth barrier' feel as if they are less than others.

Let us look at some of the information that has been in plain sight since 1980. But has only recently been the focus of the awakened among you in the last five to ten years.

The wordings of these 'commands' or statutes may seem innocent and simple enough, even compelling in their meaning, but the truth is that for the last forty-two years, the Anunnaki, Formless Ones and all they work through have been announcing their plans to the world. Thus they can claim that there was informed consent and no resulting objections.

Let us look at what they actually say, Dear Reader. What have they been laying out before you for so long that you were un-aware of?

1. Maintain humanity under 500,000,000 in perpetual balance with nature.
 2. Guide reproduction wisely—improving fitness and diversity.
 3. Unite humanity with a living new language.
 4. Rule Passion—Faith—Tradition—and all things with tempered reason.
 5. Protect people and nations with fair laws and just courts.
 6. Let all nations rule internally, resolving external disputes in a world court.
 7. Avoid petty laws and useless officials.
 8. Balance personal rights with social duties.
 9. Prize truth—beauty—love—seeking harmony with the infinite.
 10. Be not a cancer on the earth—Leave room for nature—Leave room for nature.

So breaking this down, we have;

1. Population control

2. Eugenics - planned babies, delete the 'imperfections' create the perfect race.
3. Do away with culture and identity.
4. Guide by reason and logic rather than from the heart and soul of the living being
5. Fair courts? Their rules, their courts, just presented in a new manner.
6. Each nation is in charge of itself unless it's an international situation. However, if there is a united society with one language under the same rules and laws - how can there be separated nations to self-rule? All will be governed by a supreme court.
7. Remove the laws and officials that protect the common man/woman/living soul so they [the living men and women] do not have the right to voice concerns.
8. Socialism comes; first, your personal rights will be done away with. No longer allowing you to protect yourself or your loved ones if social expectations say you must step aside.
9. Prize truth? Beauty? Love? Harmony with the Infinite?

The **Truth** will be what they feed you to believe and tell you is true. If you speak of the old ways of teaching what truth is regarding Dignity, Honour, and Truth, they will disregard you and detract you.

Beauty! Is this the reintroduction of Eugenics in plain sight? What happened to beauty is in the eye of the beholder. Who will dictate or set the standards of 'beauty'? If a living soul is born with a physical defect, are they no longer considered beautiful? If someone designs a wondrous and beautiful painting for themselves and those around them, but others find it ordinary, who declares this as not beautiful?

Love! Love is something that exists within you, as natural as the breath in your body. It grows and manifests itself in ways not comprehended by the logical brain, so how will they monitor love? And harmony with the infinite?

Infinite what?

There is only the Creator, the Source of All, that expands through infinity and beyond.

Do they mean the Creator? Or another being of dark nature which is finite, but, due to its lying nature, it has created an illusion of 'forever?'

10. Lastly, they do not want you to be a 'cancer' to the earth.

Strange wording 'a [76]cancer on the earth,' but this is how the elite, the Anunnaki, Formless Ones and their cohorts look at the Terrans and humans as a type of cancer 'destroying' what they want.

Why do they want you to leave room for nature? They feel this is so important that they actually repeat it.

Why not live in harmony with nature?

Are they attempting to reprogram your minds to convince you that nature is more important than the Terrans/humans that walk your realm?

Are they attempting to create a self-imposed imprisonment in your energy that you stay in enclosures of steel and concrete and 'leave vast expanses of land to nature?

The question to ask is, why?

Especially when evidence shows that when the living woman/man removes themselves from the influence of the city and returns to nature, there is a blending of energy.

Nature looks after the living soul, and the living soul looks after nature.

A balance occurs naturally.

---

[76] A pernicious, spreading evil; an evil influence that spreads dangerously... but they would have you think of the tumour creating disease that destroys the body. Not that they consider *you* to be an evil influence..

So there is a small window of what has been in plain sight for [77]forty-two of your years where the plan to dismantle your world has been publicised and noted.

No one has, until recently, stated this is unacceptable.

Let us look at what else is in plain sight, albeit with more subtleness.

Your moving pictures, your entertainment world, your music masters and 'idols' who teach you via pictorial or audio that the world is coming to an end. There are disease outbreaks, asteroid disasters, floods, alien takeovers, and demonic mastery in the form of occult groups. All these have been revealed and discussed throughout the years of Hollywood and the entertainment factions.

They give you movies of pandemics, zombies, and underworld creatures that survive by living off of the surface beings, humans. All are presented in a manner that seems innocent entertainment until you realise they have been informing you of their plan.

Now, Dear Reader, we ask you, 'Are you paying attention?'

Have you finally seen the bigger picture?

You, the single being, are not important to them.

You are a means to an end.

So how do you break the pattern?

How do you release yourself from their grasp, their NLP mental manipulation?

For many of you, it is first admitting that you have been caught in the spider web of complacency. That you've been unwilling to hear what is being shared. Then, remove the enemy's tools from

---

[77] at the time of writing

your home, the Tv, the phones, the newspaper, the radio, and all the systems they use to watch, observe and keep track of you.

Some will find solace in walking away from the citadels and complex villages and returning to the land. Go back and find a community of heart where fellow Terrans have begun to create a new system of living.

It will not be easy. It will require your commitment to let go of the comforts your masters have supplied to keep you compliant and agreeable. It will need you to ask questions of those close to your heart and within the lineage of your bloodline. What do they genuinely believe is going on.

 It will be confronting. It may be heart-rending as you become more and more aware that you are standing on a limb that seems to be isolated, separated from the tree that has kept you in comfort for these past years.

But how stimulating is it to feel the blood pumping in your heart and mind? You learn, once again, the art of questioning. Looking intently at what you are told to accept as truth only because it comes from the media or an organisation that has been lying to you your entire life.

Dear Reader, all throughout your history of being, you have been told to believe the facts and figures of an organisation that tell you how many people live in your world and how far the sun and moon are from your ball called earth. You are told the sun is millions of miles away, and yet those flying through the sky observe a sunrise where the sun rises through the clouds, so close they can watch the moving plasma environment of its surface. But you are told not to believe your mind or eyes and are shown image after image of a distant yellow ball so very far away from your world. You are advised to accept whatever you read in the papers or magazines as truth. These organisations are complicit with the views and mind-control techniques of their masters.

If you look a little deeper into the society you seem to love and enjoy, you will find the tears and rips as brave souls dig their way out to expose what they have endured at the hands of the Draconian masters and Anunnaki overlords. You will never see these creatures in their full regalia or skin. You will only see their puppets acting out their instructions.

Why do you think they took the simple truth of believing in the Creator and turned it into a complex machine to drain your finances, time, mind, and body and turn you into obedient sheep? Why did they initiate doctrines over many years to enslave your minds and hearts to the churches they created in the plan to maintain your slavery?

It was to ensure that you did not wander far from their influence, and if you did break free, they ensured you were scorned and belittled by the leaders of the churches or groups you once felt secure in. The people within those organisations were morally bound to follow their leaders' example, for they have followed blindly for generations. Why would they stop?

It is time to no longer ask, why me, but ask Why Not Me?

You have awoken in one of the greatest resets of your realm's lifetime. It is now that you are to be aware of the changes in the energy, the air and most importantly, changes in the earth.

It is time to relook at the story called history that you have been taught. Ask yourselves the question, who made the grand buildings and cities of the world? Where did they go?

Why has there been a substantial push to change the architecture of the world to 'hide' what was before?

Why are there so many unanswered questions relating to findings within the archaeological discoveries?

Perhaps, the answer is that there are only the dark secrets of the current 'guardians' of this realm left by the Anunnaki and others to eradicate the memory of those that created a world of harmony, of focused creative energy and connection to the Divine Creator?

How many times have you heard stories labelled myths, of great trees reaching into the heavens, of great mountains with rivers of gold, where precious stones litter the ground, where strange animals live?

We, the Lyran Narrators of Time, put it to you that these myths are founded on a truth that has been hidden. Realities wrapped in oral history and passed down from generation to generation. Unfortunately, over time these have been infiltrated, debunked and detracted, making those who speak of them out to be lunatics or crazy old people.

Consider the worldwide events throughout your timeline where in separate land masses, similar events occurred, drawing people out of cities and away from their homes to the wilds of the land to search for a mystery stone, such as gold or silver.

Where is the gold?

Where is the silver?

Where is the tin?

Where are the stores of copper?

What was found and taken by the governing groups?

Why are there so many hidden artefacts locked away in your museums?

Why do some archaeologists hide the truth from the people or excuse their way out of investigating sacred lands, hiding behind the organisations and corporations that 'hold the purse strings?'

Dear Reader, can you not see that all has been an illusion played out before you to keep you from finding your truth and stop you from discovering your true identity!

Are you ready to become part of the Lyran tribe? Will you take the colours of the sectors and become beings of Honour, of Truth, of Dignity and become part of the Terrans awakening upon the surface of the realm.

Reader?

Are you too comfortable in the little knowledge that has been taught, forced fed into you since you were born, to begin questioning the reality of who and where you are?

Will you perhaps stop and look with honest observation at all being given to you via the NLP of images, news reports and other directives of the Draconian Overlords?

Will you review the information and dive into a 'rabbit hole of discovery that will bring you to the shores of a place known as Terra-Ven-Eiliesh-Gaina?

To the heartbeat or the vibration of the Crystal Heart Stone that is deep within your realm?

We Lyrans have shared our story. Our chronicles. So that you can begin to view the events in your world as they are, how they mimic the game plan that has always been played out over your earth's timelines since the Anunnaki invasion? Though it must be revealed that the Anunnaki came to this realm in response to the reports of other beings of the great natural wealth found in this sector of the multiverse. As the scavengers they are, the Anunnaki came looking for riches and have never, in all truth, left this realm. Instead, they have left their seed and DNA bound up in those that bought into their lies.

Before we travel back to the Lyrans, let us jump into the timeline you are most aware of. Let us fly into your time in the years Twenty-Twenty Two and Twenty-Twenty-Three.

Here you are, standing in the town centre, it is relatively busy, yet there is a subtle difference to what you know as relaxed enjoyment of life. People look nervous, and all have some identification visible that is scanned by intermittent cameras as they traverse on their way.

Let us draw in closer to those around us, do not be concerned, for they will not see nor hear us.

Observe how either one of their wrists or their temple omits a slight illumination like a flashing signal. This is the implant inserted into the body to connect to the nanotechnology that was injected into them over a period of the 'pandemic' scare. Now, they have been tagged, recorded and monitored just like a livestock farmer does to keep tabs on his animals. These individuals are aware that they stepped into a situation that has now overwhelmed them, and they are beginning to realise that their 'freedom' is conditional. Conditional on them continuing to receive the updated injections to maintain the nanotechnology within their cells. They have come to see that those who refrained from this injection, although unable to access the 'vast supposed entertainment side of life', seem healthier and happier and create extraordinary lives for themselves and their young.

There has been a significant drop off in births within the community who accepted the offer of test injections, leaving those desiring offspring with a deep emptiness.

Promises of normality have not eventuated. There are still conditions of entry to places once free to visit. Regulations, and tests, must be shown to gain access to simple and yet fundamental rights of the living soul.

Many are seeking ways to reverse the effects of this injection but find it nigh impossible to reverse.

There are far too many injuries occurring among these souls, and we are not referring to the visible injuries such as illness or dis-eas-es. We are referring to mental and cellular damage. Unfortunate-ly, this stage of their journey cannot be reversed as the nanotech has begun to integrate into their cellular DNA and replicate itself. Many of these now do not have blood as you would recognise it. Instead, it looks dark and almost like oil.

However, there are those among these souls that have a natural resistance that seems to enable them to fight back and hold the nanotech at bay. Remember, Dear Reader, we stated, in the sec-ond book, that those who had the 'golden blood' or the True DNA would not be assimilated or altered... remember Ninharsag at-tempted to clone and alter the Terran DNA? All that occurred was she ended up destroying more and more clones as the DNA kept altering and changing to protect itself. In the same way, those of the Terran Bloodline are unaware that they belong to this blood-line and are naturally resistant to the injections. But, we must warn you that, over a prolonged attack or systematic injections without the ability to clear the blood, this ability to remain pure will slowly be eroded. Ninharsag did not systematically insert the same altered clone DNA into the same Terran month after month. This was due to the fact that she took the blood, stored it and then changed it in the laboratory and inserted that into the clone. In this timeline, your Draconian Overlords are enforcing a constant attack on your integrity of holistic wellness. Eventually, your blood will succumb, and you will become augmented hu-man or transterran.

This seems to be a doomsday chapter, yet we have supplied you with hope and direction within our words. Read and be aware.

Let us continue.

Your world has had many resets, many attacks on its integral and core beingness. Yet here you are, standing in truth and freedom of choice for the next period of time.

Yes, many of you are feeling the pinch where there are limits on movement, and you have begun to see the building of the camps they desire to hold those who 'are rebellious' to the common narrative. Yet, there are still thousands of you who see through this and have created a groundswell of followers to change the effects that you see on your lands.

This is good, though we would say that segregation is on its way. It will seem overbearing and suffocating for a while until you see it for the freedom it is. Until you see the opportunity to return to the ways of Terra and establish a brand new system without the dogma and shackles of politics and organised thinking, beliefs, and education.

There are many places this realm has for you to live and be in safety, you are building a new way, so it is time for those who seek to avoid stepping into the narrative to adapt. Stop rejecting other groups or breakaway settlements if they do not fully align with your thinking. If they believe in the Creator, if they have knowledge of building a new system without the wifi and interference of all the electromagnetic influence they pump through the air, then go and find out more for yourself and see what is hidden or not hidden in front of you.

By walking away from your electronics and devices, as we have mentioned before, you will create a vacuum. But, on the other hand, there are those in your groups and settlements that will come forward with new technology and generate communication devices that use sun and free energy without creating injury to your body dynamic.

Crystals are still the primary means of communication in our realms and beyond, so why would they not work here? However, it is time to become 'grown-up' Reader and take responsibility for your place in this realm and the outcomes you desire. To question everything, even the 'good guys, to ascertain that all information is indeed balanced and correct for you, your loved ones, and the community you live in.

We see there are so many in-house fights occurring at this moment, especially within those who consider themselves 'white hats' or the good guys.
Why are they not revealing their truth to you?
Why do they keep 'holding the carrot' before you to say 'the reward is coming' and other cryptic messages?
If one is in truth, in honour and in dignity, they would reveal the truth to what they are able and inform those following their information why they cannot tell more at that time.
Empty promises are the way of the Formless Ones. Manipulation at a heart level creates a community of wounded and weak or angry people who, given the right push, will do more hurt and damage to the movement of integrity than good.

So Dear Reader, as you look around your world at this time, do not despair. For within the dark recesses of what seems to be a totalitarian takeover by the Draconian overlords, working for those who control them, you should remember that within the remaining [78]True Blooded Terrans, there are those natural leaders who will rise up and begin to lead. Not as you've known leadership from governance, but lead in a way that includes all thoughts and idea's yet remains impartial and directional to ensure that you do not become sidetracked.

---

[78]ref to book one - Royal Family of Lyra each had those who retained the pure Lyran bloodline and were referred to as True Blooded

Remember, you are the ones that have the power to overcome this enemy of your soul. Many stand with you. They are there for you even if you do not 'see' them with your sight.

It is time to prepare and store up your reserves, for as we have mentioned past, there will be times of leanness before a time of abundance. But as you discover, those within the injected community will desire to assist you.

Your timelines are moving in a manner that is unusual and unique. Unknown nor experienced here before, and as we observe, we note that our past and your future are still interlinked, which tells us that we, Lyrans, may yet still be able to show you the way into the light.

Remember, the stories of your past, those distant timelines that you are told are History, founded in foundations of 'truth,' are the stories you must delve into and find the proper foundation. Not that which 'they' tell you.
Delve into the theories and stories that give a variation of the history you are taught and remember; as we have told you, the Terrans built great cities and used free energy before contact with the Anunnaki. Where are these older cities/buildings? Ask yourself why there are so many historical events that occurred simultaneously in your world in various countries.

What is being hidden from you? Perhaps it is the fact that there have been multiple resets, and this is just one more, albeit more vicious than the previous.

If you are able to rise and be of single-visioned and focused souls, you will overcome this tyranny of the realm.

Remember, Terrans, you have the key in your DNA, do not fear them. These puppets of the Anunnaki and the Formless Ones are empty suits, giving voice to their masters' thoughts, and you Terrans when you are awake, when you have removed the lobotomy from your brain; then, as you re-remember your wisdom and shamanic ways, you will see the vibration and resonance of the Heart Stone of Gaia respond to you.

It is not time to sit back and wait. Rather it is time to activate and become the peaceful beings you once were. Joined and connected to the energy of T'Gaina.

Do not submit to fear, for fear is the weapon of the enemy. Instead, learn from the ones placed in front of you, those attempting to blind you from the reality and truth unfolding around you. What are they repeating? Why are they repeating it? Have you silently agreed to their statements? Have you recorded your non-acceptance of their plan?

It is time to be wise and innovative in co-creating a new way of living and a new exchange system.

We will enter into more of this later. But for now, let us return to the Lyrans and see how the three groups are melding. What is to become of RaeNegria alongside the anomalies that are opening up around the Lyrans..?

Chapter Twenty-Three

Dark Truth Revealed
The hidden, but known, truth

Dear Reader, we have shared the various outlooks and perspectives of your species and world within these pages. In addition, we have shared the ongoing story of our world, living souls and how we overcame a vicious attack on our sovereignty and unique presence of being.

The Lyran Royal Families have now given us permission, but most importantly, The Lyran Leader of Families across the Cosmos has authorised us to reveal in more intimate detail what is happening to your world. Attempt to explain how the people and events in your world are being manipulated from deep within the shadows. Just as we underwent a time of depletion and internal warring, so it seems, are you.

We sincerely ask that you do not read this as a mere story, or fiction, preferably that you would look into the reality of what is unfolding in your world.

Note; we first began our story with our initial contact with the writer of these chronicles in your time in 2011. Due to the intense energy required and her fresh beginnings, we held back and searched elsewhere for a suitable vessel to record these revealings. Unfortunately though many began, the requirement of self-publishing seemed to be a stumbling block. Finally, we returned to the writer of these journals of ours in 2017-2018, when we wrote the introductory book with her and drafted the beginning of the second and third. As you will know, we rewrote the first book in your era, 2018, to correct an oversight of not including other important information previously. Since then, we have brought more details for this writer to conclude book three and begin the fourth book. The above is to remind you of the original threads of information used to bring you to the place where we reveal certain things. We must repeat some of the information we have already placed within these pages. We ask that you travel with us through this folio and begin to see the pattern used to control you. It has not changed since the first Anunnaki Lobotomy perpetrated on your people so long ago.

Your world is now in a place where there is a blanket of darkness around your dome. It cannot be seen by all, but it can be felt by all. Those who observe this blanket see a dark mist resembling smoke or clouds. It has settled around the streets and the buildings. It is within your vehicles, your rooms, schools, and workplaces. In fact, there is nowhere that it does not sit. For the asleep or unawakened, it creates a sense of despondency, a sense that all is lost. Fear and unsurety are
 seeping into all those who focus on this 'feeling.' However, there are those among you that are alert and conscious that not all is as it seems. You have begun to differentiate between the assumed and the real. There have been investigations into the energy of this blanket, and many have exposed it for what it truly is, mind control and trauma creation.

Hu-mans, by default, react or work best when under duress. They respond in specific ways; it is this that the shadow masters, the Formless Ones, have been banking on in your physiological makeup. They want this trigger within you to activate so that when they use their tools of manipulation, the media, movies, music and 'empty' food, you begin to feel worse. This leads to your consuming more and more of what they give you, all in the desire to 'discover' the truth. The media, movies, and music will distract you, and the 'empty' food will keep you craving more food.

The more you consume the 'unconscious' food, the emptier you are. Thus the circle continues.

Eventually, they will supply you with a quick fix, a solution, as they have done recently here in this realm with what they call a severe or acute respiratory auto-immune condition.

First, they renamed the common cold 'SARAIC' then the flu became 'SARAIC,' then pneumonia and so on. Finally, all respiratory and nasal issues, coughs and other slight fevers were reinvented into this new illness, SARAIC. First, they told you that you would die from it. Then, they gave you the symptoms, and only a handful of the living souls on earth saw that these symptoms were the same as influenza and pneumonia, where you could be hospitalised and, even in extreme circumstances, put on ventilators to assist with breathing. But most of you did not pay attention to this small but important fact due to the intense worldly bombardment of fear information being thrown at you about this new 'disease' by the media.

Now we will add here that there is a strain of dis-ease that has, with sadness and great sorrow, seen many transitions from this realm to the next. As a result, however, you will see many more changes when introducing the 'solutions' to the new dis-ease. There was a 'war room' created in each country to receive and relay relative information to the nationals of the land. The media were instructed to repeat in any way they could, the harm, the fear, the unknown factors of what was happening and the urgency of compliance to the organisations that were taking over the rulership of the world.

All done 'to keep you safe!'

This was not the end goal. But, unfortunately, the hidden puppet masters want to and still choose to completely wrap you within a warped view of the world that is covered by the gloom of life and how everything is going wrong. Unless, of course, you comply with the companies that run your different countries.

They, the Formless Ones, discovered that no matter how miserable or deplorable they created the disease, there was a faction that denied, refuted and detracted their lies. So these brave Terrans and Hu-mans began to speak out, showing the evidence of what was actually unfolding and what was supposed to be a deadly disease that was, in fact, curable and curable without incurring a high cost.

This exposé did not suit the governing bodies. Each organisation had quotas to fulfil and was required to ensure that even though borders were shut and people were being prevented from moving around, the illicit trade of young people and sex slaves, as well as body organs, were still maintained.

This is why, to the amazement of most awakened Terrans, flights, shipping and cross-border movement was continuing in the midst of a *worldwide pandemic*!

Now that the Formless Ones had created a vacuum, where only their information was presented 'as truth,' they began the second part of their destructive plan.

They began to destroy your immune system.

The 'new safety' was to wear masks, stay indoors out of the fresh air and sun, [79]consume alcohol and eat empty food.

Not to choose food wisely by looking at the supermarket but by eating takeaways and rushing through the markets.

Then there will be the introduction of scanning, where you 'must' reveal your personal information by connecting to a digital app. This information was funnelled into the database of the Formless Ones so they could track your movements and know who you were, who you were with, what you did, and what your movements were.

Soon this was not enough for them, and they unpacked the next part of the plan.

To keep the masses under more control, it was revealed that there was a solution.

This was the injection. A vaccination to save lives!!!

You were told it has been rushed through. It was discovered by intrepid investigators that the trials on the animals proved fatal for most of them. The rabbit hole took you to where there were reports from when the injections were trialled on young children. The adverse effects rendered some children confined to wheelchairs and connected to feeding tubes for the rest of their lives, all of which were not reported correctly nor recorded in the 'public' forum.

Instead, you were directed not to listen to the medical practitioners who worked with Terrans daily and operated within the parameters of the Hippocratic oath.   In addition, you were told not to listen to chemists who worked with the drugs and tests and questioned the contents of the vials.

---

[79] While this was not spoken or advertised in your open knowledge, it was, however, subliminally entered into your psyche via the abnormal advertising for alcohol and 'fast food' to be delivered to your place of residing

Rather, you were told to listen to those who had a medical degree but did not use it as a medical doctor but as a political mouth-piece. We are assuming these have also sworn the Hippocratic oath, though they obviously do not honour this at all. The degree was only as an identification of an achieved goal, a pen pusher, or an authoritative knowledge keeper. You were told not to listen when people received an injection and died or suffered debilitating side effects that prevented them from living a life worth living.

Instead, you were told these were conspiracy theorists and people with agendas. You were told that they were spreading fear and lies and not to listen, and to ensure your obedience, the shadow masters, the Formless Ones puppets, removed the truth sayers from the public eye. They ridiculed and detracted them in such a way that made anyone following or listening to these wise beings look foolish.

You were told this jab was the answer, then you would require another, and now another. Soon you will receive an injection once every three to six months, depending on the type and brand of injection you accept. They will then begin to include this as a group injection to appear 'normal' and 'safe'. Many actors posing as Drs will promote the safety and urgency to keep receiving the injections. We ask you to be intuitive.
Now here is where we wish to walk you down a dark path. A path that we did not want to take, but due to the unfurling of the agenda, we believe it is wisest to do so.

Let us talk about this injection they wish to push onto you.
It killed the test subjects when they trialled it, both in the animal kingdom and among the hu-mans. The young children subjected to this were harmed, but no report was made other than sore arms, throat, tummy etc. Nothing serious like being paralysed and using a feeding tube for the remainder of life. Or being unable to

communicate vocally, spasms and epileptic fits, where none of these aliments were registered before the injection.

This injection is, by their words, still in trial proceedings until 2023, and they are still unaware of the extreme end results.
What they do know is that it will alter the DNA, the mRNA, the reproductive organs, and the brain functions. It will stop the heart and cause tearing and scarring within the lungs.
What large corporations do know is that your blood is altered beyond belief, and you no longer have blood. Instead, it is now a substance, altered by a messenger code via the mRNA sequence, that is a breeding ground and host for a parasitic nanotech that will either kill you or change you from within.

This injection is a [80]substance designed to cull the 'differences' out of hu-manity. It seeks out the 'anomalies' in the DNA, any inherited weaknesses or even the unknown quota in genetics and uses this against you. As a result, asthma sufferers and others with allergies will endure more and more difficulties until their lungs give up.
Heart problems will be enhanced. You will see healthy young men and women, as well as the elders, considered as 'predestined' due to hereditary circumstances, suffer from heart failure, regardless of age. The list is endless.

But what about those who are not 'ill' and have no abnormality in their DNA, what about them? There are 'so many' that are 'normal,' 'ok', and don't suffer any side effects. Surely this shows that the injection is safe?

 Dear Reader, these are the ones that are now being slowly and expertly changed from within.

_____

80 A drug, chemical, or other material that one becomes or is dependent on

Research those who prepare the dead for their onward journey and absorb their findings.

Let us go deeper. Let us step aside from the drama and the harrowing imagery.
Let us open a vial of the liquid.
It looks harmless.
Transparent, but it's not.
Under the microscope, you will see thousands of nanotech. These are dormant until they reach a specific temperature. Once at the preferred temperature, they 'wake up and begin to perform in the manner they were created.

They are the smallest AI created in your realm, which means they can pass through cell walls, enter the blood-brain barrier, and sit within your lymph nodes and stomach walls. In fact, they can hide in any organ they are directed to. Once there, they create more of their type. Each injection feeds more relevant data and fluid needed to continue building and changing your cells from within. This is how you will be able to 'plug' into the network without wires or handsets.
You will be the computer.
What this means, Dear Reader, is that for those of you who lined up and allowed a physical assault to be done to you. You have become the guinea pig, receiving the injection of a substance, as yet unsanctioned as safe, full of nanobots and AI. You are the walking laboratory.

Yes, thousands of vials were full of saline and thus harmless. This is how they will maintain viable stock to ensure the ongoing population of the realm they wish to control.

This fluid that is placed forcibly into your body without a full declaration, which even in 'The Original Federation of InterGalactic

Families Owning Responsibility of Nation, Culture, Self and Unions of Freedom,' is unheard of.

When undertaking an interrogation involving injecting a prisoner with a tincture to assist with truth-telling, Lyrans always declare what the insertion contains.

Everything is explained, from the liquid form used as a carrier or the vibrational frequency used to insert the correct frequency into the being's body.

Even in a time of war, we realise that there are variations of physical makeup, and each physical body reacts differently to the insertion of the truth serum. Thus, we are duty-bound to reveal the contents to ensure that the prisoner is aware of any and all side effects. They can then choose which they will receive.

You may ask, how did the living souls of this realm submit to this onslaught of attack and deliberate decimation of their lives?

It is simple.

The more the living souls of this realm listened to the lies being pumped out via the propaganda machine, the more the parasite entities could latch on to and feed off their fear. Once the parasite is attached and fed, it slowly inserts tentacles into the host. It spreads a 'root system' into the central and peripheral nervous system creating a symbiotic life. It became so ingrained into the host that the living soul could not determine if the depression, anger, fear, judgement and other range of emotions were their own or 'something else.' Many awakened beings became aware of this feeding energy and diligently used their skills to clear their energy field and emotional bodies. However, we must advise and warn you that these parasites will continue their attempts and piggyback on your emotions to reattach themselves to your nervous system.

This is one of the many ways the Formless Ones control you. This is why, throughout our story, we have encouraged you to destroy, turn off, leave your digital addictions and return to a more straightforward way of life. You do not need all this distraction in your day-to-day living. It has been designed to prevent you from any interaction. If the Anunnaki and Formless Ones can get you so focused on communicating with your family and friends via a screen instead of using face-to-face or personal interaction, they have entrapped your mind. This makes it easier for the roll-out of digital insertion or the concept of looking at life through the virtual reality screen. Why look at the 'negativity' when you can see what you want.

This energy has seeped into your society like a heavy mist settling around the ground during a cold, windless night, creeping into your bones. It feeds your paranoia and creates a simulation of 'what if's in your life.

This is the distraction of emotional and visual stimulation creeping into your life, sneaking into your family, and creating separation in such a way that you are unaware of it. Furthermore, this injection causes a deep [81]thrombosis of change, a paradigm shift of the physical being changing from Terran/human into an android or nonhuman. Thus easily manipulated by architects behind the scenes, who, in turn, are influenced by the shadow masters and planners, the master manipulators.

This whole event has been to create the separation of your soul from your physicality. It is a plaster effect created to fool you. Indeed, your soul/god spark/eternal part cannot be separated from your being. Still, the separation you feel, or that others become aware of, is the computer technology within you creating a disassociation.

It is the 'glitch' which creates a deep sense of being lost, a sense of depression, of failure, and then, once the glitch is effectively run-

---

[81] Create a blockage. A clotting within your veins

ning, there is a euphoric sense of achieving the highest goal achievable, self-righteousness!

It continues to give that sense that you have achieved normality, and then while that is being released into your physiology, your cells begin to break, to deteriorate.

This is when the physicality and the digital are at war. One must win. One must lose. When the body dies, the digital has won. It has created a disassociation of the mRNA and your DNA, creating a mimic, a synthetic mRNA.

You have become AI!

Once this is achieved throughout the body, it is unable to process essential foods, and the physicality may die or may become very, very ill. As the assimilation continues with the programming, the individual's outward appearance may look pale grey, ash-like, in colour.

This will be put down to the illness, to virus infection, and yes, it is in all terminology now an infection of a virus, a digital virus. Once the body has been assimilated, the new cells mimic the attributes of the outward appearance of a Terran/human. This is done so that those observing will not see an external change.

They will see what seems to be an illness of the body and the re-covery of the body.

There are those, medically speaking as well as holistically, who know how to clean contaminated blood. These medics have learnt how to filter and distil blood so that the finite pieces of graphite can be retrieved and removed. This process is used for the removal of the black goo and fibres of nanotechnology. However, due to the internal damage done at the cellular level, if they do this, there is a high percentage that the hu-man, the Terran, will pass over. The shell that is the body is of no use, and the individual dies.

Though as new technology is brought forward, or should we say the technology that has always been available to the 'elite' of society, will be revealed, healing and detoxing processes will become cleaner and more accessible. The body will be in a better status of living. Thus more will remain and learn to reconnect with their God-Spark.

If there can be no resuscitation, the soul, which has been separated from the physicality, encased in an energetic sludge by the nanotech, releases itself back to the Creator.

The Dark Ones have perfected the separation of the human consciousness and conscious awareness of God consciousness, the God spark within the race of man/Terran. They have long found a 'vaccine' that is injected to interrupt the 'rebellious' or 'religious' gene, and many thousands of your offspring receive this within a few short breaths of life once out of the womb.

These dark forces are creating and causing a great battle within mankind (hu-manity) at large. There is a sense of perfection within them that they are very prideful of. They feel they are perfecting a species, perfecting their slave race to become tireless, programmable, and do their best without question.

So what this means is that those who have chosen the injection, have been assimilated, will lose something important.

They relinquish choice. They have given up free will.

You become indebted to the AI, it keeps you alive, and you are programmable to accept what is put before you as normal and natural. You cannot sense nor see a variation of difference. Any difference placed before you, which is in violation or against the mainframe coding, will be discerned and seen as an error. It will be sensed as something untrue.

This is because the program will be run at a level to ensure that you perceive and believe that you are still hu-man and everything is 'normal'. Then, when you are faced with the dilemma of con-sciousness or making a conscious choice, the nanotechnology within you will activate, swarm if you like, and cause a malfunc-tion within your system to reboot you into choosing to remain the way you are.

Please note we are not referring to [82]prosthesis. Rather we en-courage this medical means, for there will come a day when liv-ing souls will be able to choose artificial limbs to be created for them that will sync with their nervous system without a comput-er. We have this technology. Our Lyran medics have shared this information with a few of your earth medics in their dream state.

Many visual stories have been placed before you over time under the auspices of science fiction entertainment. They have revealed to you the android. They also show the possibility of being aug-mented, as in the insertion of
technology into the body, such as digital phones, and artificial implants to heighten vision, hearing and other physical attributes.

The machine wishes to be human, and the human wishes to be a machine, blending these capabilities to form something unnatur-al. You have received notification in plain sight with both visual and audio knowledge of the intent to create the living machine within your society. There have been various pictures to entertain you, such as your [83]science fiction series called Star Trek and the android and Borg interactions. You have had the series called Terminator, as well as other types of stories, placed before you, in plain sight so that you cannot say you were not informed of their

---

[82] replacement of a missing limb

[83] or is it a means of broadcasting what they are required to say in order to contract with you?

intent. In many of these pictorial presentations, you are shown the ease with which the android is given human abilities and desires more, or is programmed to destroy humanity or assimilate other beings, and then is 'saved' by other men or women and 'reprogrammed' to protect the race of mankind. You have had the drip feeding of an off-planetary being coming to save your species ever since the Anunnaki lobotomised your ancestors. This constant drip feeding of someone coming to rescue you keeps you disconnected and reliant on a source beyond your capabilities. We are not wanting you to walk away from the Creator, but rather towards the Creator. However, we are pushing you toward the ideal of self-responsibility and awareness over 'rescue'.

Yes, these are, or were, methods of entertainment, yet all stories are born from a source point. Either from mythology, which is born out of reality or information that has been downloaded, given, or transcribed from a secret/hidden source to be 'revealed' to the masses. However it was presented before you, you must now see the patterns unfolding, showing you the first initial steps to creating AI or a augmented hu-man species. It is also recorded in your [84]historical records, though many have attempted to hide these from the majority of mankind, the Nephilim. They are a race of giants born in your realm via blending or mixing the DNA of 'angels' and mankind. It tells how these beings came down from the heavens and began to mix their DNA with not only mankind's DNA but with animals, creatures of the waters, and the fowl of the air. Many strange creatures came from this impure and abusive use of the Creator's DNA within you. This was the beginning of the interference with mankind from the Anunnaki, and it continues throughout your living memories when a scientist or doctor attempts to add something or remove something from the DNA of Mankind. Hopefully, this will show you that no matter the guise the story comes in, there are records showing the generations of

---

[84] The book known as The Book of Enoch

mankind that someone is still endeavouring to break your DNA somewhere. The question you should be asking is 'why'?

It is time for the Terrans to realise that they now have a limited spectrum of time in which to choose to remain true blood or to ingest this substance which has been presented. What we would say is to be prepared for a reaction of some degree after the 3rd to 4th injection. For it is an injection of a slow death. Whether you will pass over immediately or just shortly after the 4th injection, we cannot determine, for that would make us fortune tellers and that we are not. However, there is sufficient evidence in your current timeline to research and discover how many have died or had severe reactions within a reasonably short period of receiving the booster injection.

This injection is the Eugenics of the present moment. A way of creating a clone race of slaves, all without accessing your DNA sample to grow a replacement body for your consciousness to be 'downloaded'. You just provided them with a living, working incubator.

Some who received the injection will continue to live a 'normal' life. Seemingly not changing, but it is what you cannot see that is dangerous, not what you can see in the person. Ask yourself, has this person you know received the injection and more, have they changed in any way? Personality? Have they become distant? Forgetful? Clumsy? Or all of a sudden, more intelligent, faster in the thought process? Have they suddenly discovered a breathing problem, unable to walk a distance that is neither far nor unreasonable? Is the person vacant or not always present when speaking with you? Do they 'faze' out and then 'pop' back into the conversation? These, plus many, many more signs, are becoming evident in those who have received the injection. Unfortunately, it will be relegated to an underlying cause or illness within the person that has yet to be diagnosed.

This injection causes a separation of your God-Spark, between you, the conscious connected being and the physical body driven by the mind, logic, and unconscious automated part of your body.

You remain alive, but once your energy/soul passes over, the physical body is no longer functional and ceases to exist. Only then will your God spark leave the physicality, the shell, and return to the other side.

However, if the machinery, nanotechnology, is able to turn your physicality into the cyborg/AI, and that cyborg/AI has the awareness to prevent the body from deteriorating, your God spark is trapped within you.

Keeping you in a place that could be called hell, for you will have deep within your inner conscious memory an awareness that something is not right, something does not fit. Yet you will be unable to alter or change how you think or believe, for every time you do, the nanotechnology will reboot and delete more of your memories. Deleting the part of you that is the living soul. The living man or woman's eternal energy or soul, and once you fully integrate into the digitalisation, you will become more of the artificial intelligence than you considered possible! Imagine being locked into a glass room where you can hear, see, smell, comprehend, access knowledge and memory of everything you see being processed around you. But you cannot speak, touch, or communicate, in any way, with the outside world beyond that glass room. This is what it will be like for those who succumb to the complete AI integration of Transhumanism.

Dear Readers, and friends, we ask you to realise or consider that when we refer to our organic links, we refer to the Lyran connection. We do not hide the fact that we use artificial intelligence to assist us in running the machines, our ships, databases etc., but they are all monitored. These AI are also linked to the organic link, which is a Lyran brain, used with permission to power and direct the perimeter of the AI.

The AI requires a power source. It needs coding to learn and expand. We learnt not to give it the 'open access' that the AI desires. Thus, upon their deaths, many scientists, negotiators, and warriors willingly gave their knowledge to be the barrier between the AI and ourselves. Therefore utilising the extreme benefits of both Lyran and digital expansion.

You must see, Dear Reader, that the computer, the machine is not a sentient being. It is programmable. It needs code for it to exist. In many ways, those that wish to draw parallels with the Terran will say that you, too, have code, i.e., your DNA. This is true, but there is a difference. Your code is sacred. It comes from a Divine place, whereas the AI is built by your realm. It is manufactured and does not have a God spark. Its power is a battery. This is why the Formless Ones wish to combine the human DNA and the AI code so that the Cyborg, Android, Augmented hu-man, call it what you will, has a power source that, once connected to, will allow it to be endless in its existence. After many years of experimenting with your species, they discovered that once they delete the God particle from the DNA, they now have a physical body that generates power via the cellular exchange of toroidal energy within to power their hybrids.

[This is what their 'god' desires. The power they serve is no living entity but a supercomputer created beyond this realm by those who have long since ceased to exist in the way of breath. All that remains of their existence is the programs of self-learning computers.]

This is the actual zombie world. A world where the 'once were humans' walk in a nightmare they cannot waken from. Having an inner knowing that they once were free and now are bound by the limits placed upon them by a machine. By those who have no right to be in this world.

We Lyrans have been attempting to share our story of overcoming the Formless Ones. We are communicating through the sagas and events of the Lyran Princes how they won their battles and outsmarted the enemy, and now today, we Lyrans live in our new world, in peace, unafraid but ever watchful.

These few pages have been given to you to ponder, consider and hopefully give you a deeper look at the venomous entity covering your planet. We desire to share this not to create fear but to bring light into the dark and give you an overview...

Chapter Twenty-Four

OverComing Doubt
When you see but do not see

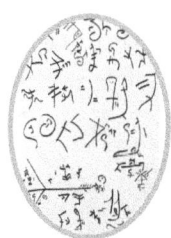

As Sol Lrign dWari and RaeNegria locked eyes and silently communicated apart from the rest of those they were with. Juuls, the second in command of the *Bitari-Furtim-Karda,'* indicated to RexNā and her crew to follow him to the general meeting hall. Casting a quick glance over her shoulder to RaeNegria, RexNā Loid DeAqua felt a slight wave of uncertainty settle around her. All that she'd come to know, love and trust over the cycles they had been travelling seemed to be unravelling in the smallest of moves.

Changes occurring within the *Bitari-Furtim-Otiose,'* over the last few periods had caused an inward concern in RexNā, as the leader and as Lyran. Wondering the cause of all the alterations, especially with that of her friend, had weighed heavily on her mind.

Sol nodded in agreement to the silent conversation with Rae-Negria and, with a slight indication of her head, motioned Rae to go with her into a side room. This was for a more confidential communication away from the other telepaths who may pick up on their conversation. MelEid and RexNā Loid DeAqua noticed this movement taking the commander and RaeNegria away from the main group. RexNā's response caused doubt and concern within her, a desire to know what was being spoken about and the beginnings of distrust between the two Princes, and a dark line of doubt settled in her mind.

However, MelEid's observation of the two Lyrans moving away was to make a mental note to check in with Rae once things had settled. But, for now, even she was unsure of the protocols for this subsequent unfolding of the Crystal Heart Stone's plan. Glancing over to her brother, she questioned 'what now', and he, too, indicated that the two leaders should be left to discuss. Rae had been given some information during her transition, and it was not yet revealed what their part would be.

As the groups moved towards the general meeting room, the noise levels rose as everyone attempted to get their view of what was happening or what had happened out to any who would listen. It was again a merging of energy and lineages that had not connected in many lifetimes. Interest, excitement, and intense curiosity were apparent in the two groups, which only doubled when those who had boarded from the 'RaiDia-Mlith' via the opposite docking bay joined them.

The old commanders, El Shavreon and his twin Max Ron Ilth had boarded and joined the crews in the common area. The twins' entrance created an immediate silence. Their height and striking features, combined with their old and now faded cloaks indicating their sectors, drew everyone's attention. Standing in the middle of the room, RexNā Loid De Aqua looked at Max Ron Ilth, recognising the elder commander who had assisted in her initial initiation and perhaps saved her life, walked over and extended her arm out in greeting. "I see you, Negotiator! You who held space and honour so that my journey could begin. I greet you in that honour and return the gift of service. How can we, nay, how can I assist you?"

With kindness and laughter in his eyes, the commander looked at his twin as if to say, this is the one I told you about. "Little leader, you owe nothing, and nothing is expected, for you have been chosen to lead our people for this moment in our records. Tomorrow there may be another, but for now, you have our service."

With a deep bow of the waist, he acknowledged RexNā's leadership and gave his and his brother's commitment in service to her and the remaining Princes.

Rägę had been observing this exchange and could not help himself, "Where have you come from? We noted no ships in our field other than the *Bitari-Furtim-Karda*, and the anomaly for more than two periods?" "How is it that you are here? How long have you been following us, and why?"

El Shavreon burst out laughing, a deep, bellowing laugh that was as infectious as it was loud.

"You, my young [85]ko'ptitka, have much to learn about the art of subterfuge and hiding in plain sight. We have followed you since you 'escaped' from the Outpost and Nuul Ra-ulr. So why on Lyra did you think it was so easy to take the ship that had recently been commandeered by the Outpost Command?

The two Princes looked slightly embarrassed as they realised that, in hindsight, it had been a little too easy to sneak the ship

---

[85] a common Lyran bird

out of the dock, and Nuul-Ra had not really pushed the 'return to base command'.

A sense of despair struck the two Princes simultaneously. Did that mean that all their battles and skirmishes that had occurred on their journey were not their own victories? Had the 'RaiDia-Mlith' been the cause of all their accomplishments... Seeing the emotions flash over their faces, both El Shavreon and Max Ron were quick to inform them that all they did was follow from a distance. Never once did they interfere in the battles or other interactions they'd experienced, as this would have defeated the objective of monitoring and observing.

The Princes relaxed and then turned back to their host, "Juuls, please be so kind as to inform us of what is expected. We are Lyrans, as are you. Yet there is a feeling that you have created a separation, and we are somehow viewed as dangerous or, at the very least, an insignificant interruption."

RexNā Loid DeAqua looked at Juuls eye to eye as she spoke. She was annoyed that RaeNegria and Sol Lrign dWari had separated from the group and retreated into another room in what looked like a private or secret discussion. Feeling slighted, she wanted to ensure that the remaining Lyrans still recognised she was, for all intents and reasoning, the Lyran Leader of Families in training.

Rägę felt similarly uncomfortable, but for a different reason. For the first time in many cycles, he had come into his own strength and knowing. Finally, he was unafraid to bear the weight of his sector cloak and the responsibilities that came with it. Yet, now he was in the company of his Elders, those he'd learnt about as a young student, and he felt the familiar sense of insignificance seeping in and around him.

Neither of the two Princes realised that this was a test designed for them and them alone. The Mages and Seers of the Crystal Heart Stone aboard the *Bitari-Furtim-Karda* wanted to observe their reactions to being separated from the third Prince. How would they respond to those stronger, wiser, and more capable in leadership than they? Would they hold their own or revert to acting as the young Princes that set out so long ago.

As RexNā and Rägę each dealt with their internal thoughts and feelings, they were unaware that RaeNegria was undergoing a similar test of her stamina and self-awareness.

From the sidelines, MelEid stood with some of the elder Mages and acknowledged their ranking in the Circle of Mages by ever so slightly tilting her head as if making a mental bow. "Tell me, Old Ones, when were you first aware that the third Prince could possibly be 'The Seer of Seers'?"

She paused, contemplating the next part of her query, "Was it when you sent a message to the Mage Sector that The Chief Seer should be kept on my ship, my own sibling, but that I was not to be made aware of this until it was necessary to wake him?" Then, stopping, she stared at the Elder Mages intently, "Why did you keep this from me? Did you believe that I would not be able to assist or keep myself from....". Her voice was clipped as she attempted to control her inner anger at being kept out of a decision that was so important, especially as she'd been trained as the Crystal Heart Stone Chief Mage.

It was widely acknowledged that MelEids' in-depth discoveries in tinctures, healing aids, and many other telepathic means of clearing a Lyran's energy when attacked by the Formless Ones were indeed 'cutting edge. In addition, it was not unknown that MelEid had made, over her time as an apprentice and then as a fully trained Mage, break through specific procedures and processes for those in need of care that had significantly reduced the time of healing.

The elder Mages smiled slowly and nodded in unison as they looked at the young Mage before them. Recognising MelEid was undoubtedly cycles in front of her peers in knowledge, learnings and experience, they still had much they wished to impart to her. Part of that learning was happening now, learning to accept that not everything is fair or 'right' when first laid out, but becomes fair and' right' when the situation appears for the exact plan that was put in place.

At this moment, they wanted to see if MelEid could see through the hidden steps they'd put in place long before she'd been chosen to take the journey to find the Princes. They wanted to see if the prideful, at times obstinate young Mage that had left aboard the ship was still hiding in what seemed to be a different, more mature Mage.

Staring at the Elders, MelEid dropped her shoulders and sighed deeply. Silently shaking herself for falling back into the old pattern of desiring to be correct, to be in charge, to know exactly what was happening everywhere. Then, realising that she potentially had misread the situation, she cleared her throat and began again.

"When did you realise the potential with RaeNegria of being a Seer? I did not realise her potential. At least not until the inner struggle with RathVorx, the infection of the nanotech which poisoned her body, causing her to almost shut down." Pausing to give the others time to speak, MelEid continued to watch RexNā Loid DeAqua and Rägę El BriNa-Ragnoa El Vroan as they both internalised the current dilemma they found themselves in. No longer the 'king-pins' but now part of a group of highly empowered Lyrans that were more experienced in life in the void than they were. The two Princes also felt slight separation anxiety due to RaeNegria being taken to an alternate section of the ship.

Feeling their tensions rise, MelEid sent them a telepathic push to be calm, that they needed to refocus not on their lacks or supposed defects but on where they were, what was happening around them and to remain alert. The push seemed to wake the Princes from a sense of lethargy, who suddenly showed signs of a newly ignited interest in what was unfolding around them.

Tilting her head ever so slightly to look around at things in her vision, MelEid sought out her sibling. She could sense his presence but, as of yet, had not seen him since disembarking from their ship. Locating his whereabouts in the room, she darted a coded message to him, causing him to pause what he was doing and fix eyes with her. Once they were linked, she began to communicate.

"Brother, I ask that we both observe the unfolding of this event. I sense that there is more to this meeting of ships than is being revealed. We have brought the Seer to this place in good faith. Yet, already she has been removed from our presence, from her people. I ask that you, in your core and position of High Seer, that you ensure her well-being. She is unlearned in what you expect, but she still has much to ingest from the knowledge of the Waters of Source. I have felt a small inclining of what she went through, and though she shows bravery and wellness, Rae is scared.

Protect her.

Your sector has put her in this place. Now protect her, or I will."

Eid' dVra looked at his sister and marvelled again at the change within her. Gone was the spoilt Lyran he once knew; here was a changed soul. He saw the tears and scars in her psyche caused by the inner battle she endured during the travels of the void. He noted she was not weaker for this but stronger in heart, mind and soul.

"I hear you, sister, and I give my word the one called RaeNegria will not come to any harm under my watch. I am here to observe and guide her learning only. I am not here to interfere and direct." He paused and chuckled quietly, "I will leave that to the old crones who are hovering like a pair of [86]ro'Duiplj, for fear that they will miss the opportunity of their timeline to influence the next Crystal Heart Stone Seer. Just be aware that though I may be hard, I will be fair. My training will be focused on getting her to recognise her ability. To rise above doubt and begin to control her inner vision and heightened knowledge now burgeoning within her.

She will need to know how to use this knowledge and be fluid with the connection of the Heart Stone Crystal. If she pushes too quickly, she will be repelled and potentially damaged in her mind. Whereas if she is too cautious, she may lose the connection entirely and thus no longer hear the voices of the Waters of Source.

Eid' dVra ended his telepathic communication and returned to meet with Sol and RaeNegria.

MelEid returned her active mind to the Elders she was with and looked at them afresh. They were, as her sibling had described, wizened and hawkish looking. The lines on their faces seemed out of place as if altered to hide something else. Then, slowly breathing and controlling her thoughts so as not to allow any warning telepathically, MelEid signalled to her select group of [81] neophyte's to circle around the two Elders but to keep an illu-

---

[86] a bird of prey, scavenger, a vulture

sion of separation so as not to alert them that something was wrong.

Excusing herself, MelEid went off searching for Juuls or any other of the ship's senior officers. She also sent a coded message to the Chief Mage of the *Bitari-Furtim-Karda,* asking to be met in the hyper lift.

Juuls, Nuex Del Aqua Loid, and The Moderator met with MelEid in the hyper lift. As it began its ascent upwards, MelEid caused the lift to stop mid floors and then began to vocalise her concern. The others listened to her as she spoke. The Moderator asked telepathically why she was using her voice, as this was an uncomfortable means of communication. She looked at him, simply stating that in the hyper lift, the array field prevented sound from penetrating out and thus was one of the safest communication spots in the ship at present. Tilting his head in agreement, The Moderator began to ask questions that penetrated the supposed or alleged disguise MelEid had seen settled upon the two elders.

"If I hear you correctly, young Mage, you are telling me that two of my senior sector leaders are either dead and being impersonated or being manipulated without our awareness. Thus, putting this entire ship, the Bitari-Furtim-Otiose and the RaiDia-Mlith, at risk?"

His eyes were compelling, like black pools of liquid carbon. MelEid attempted to break eye contact but was held there by a force she was not used to. "Yes," Her answer was short and sharp. "I stood next to them, and it seemed they were wearing masks or their flesh had become so stretched it no longer sat on their face or hands correctly. I could not feel their vibration or Crystal Heart Stone connection. I feel we should not dismiss this."

She paused and chose to challenge the three shipmates, "Of course, this could be a test to see if my abilities are true or if I am just a puffed-up egocentric Mage. Whatever your reason for doubting me, all I ask is that you at least check my concerns out."

The three ship members looked at each other, yes, they had set tests for all the principal members of the young Lyran leadership team, but this was not one of them. They were testing her ability to function under pressure and assumed judgement but not to identify manipulated energies and hidden enemies.

Breaking eye contact, The Moderator turned back to MelEid. "We thank you for your observation and will evaluate your concerns. If we require your services, we will call you." With that, the lift hummed into life and dropped sharply back to the floor they had met on.

As the doors opened, the three senior Lyrans stepped out and left the young Mage standing by herself in amazement at their aloofness.

Shaking herself mentally, MelEid stepped out and walked back to where her ship had docked and where she knew most of the crew still waited to be directed to their quarters. Upon reaching the specified deck, she called her team and asked for their insights. The young Neophytes looked decidedly uncomfortable at this question, for they had noticed many disturbing things about the Elders. However, they still held fast to the idea that these were the top of their sector and should be held in honour. Even revered for their life commitment to the sector.

Yet the fear they felt from what they had seen, telepathically picked up and heard while being around the Elders also put them in a place where they wanted to offload this weight from their shoulders.

Seeing their distress, MelEid pointed to a secluded table and suggested they move there to discuss what had been discovered.

As the group sat in a comfortable yet unsettled manner. The young [87]Neophytes sat with bated breath, waiting for MelEid to speak, yet their mentor and teacher seemed to sit and look at them as if waiting for them to speak to her. Finally, one of the young trainee Mages, confused and a little nervous, cleared her throat and looked straight at MelEid, "If I may speak, Mage." "We all have experienced something we never felt we would, especially coming from those we have been taught to honour and receive knowledge from." She paused, unsure if she should cease speaking with the voice or cross over to the telepathic. The way MelEid was looking at her unsettled the young novice, which created the drying up of her thoughts.

With a subtle movement, MelEid caused an electrical crack to sound across the table they sat at, and any who had their hands or arms on the table received an electrical jolt that caused them to move backwards at what transpired. The group of trainee's gawked at their mentor. She had not done this before, or at least without some warning that she would be using her static powers.

MelEid looked at the young Lyrans around the table. They were confused, scared and now troubled by her actions. Yet she did not see any of them voice or stand up to question this alleged 'attack' on their physical. Their trust and allegiance to her were overriding much of their fear. This is what she wanted to draw their attention to.

Moving with deliberate actions, MelEid pushed away from the table, moved her hand down to her thigh and placed her laser onto the tabletop. Then she undid the belt of her pouch and placed that beside her weapon. Keeping eye contact with as many of her trainees as possible at all times, she managed to keep her face emotionless and her eyes empty.

---

[87] Novice or Trainees

Once she had placed everything on the table which identified her being a Mage, even her cloak, she placed her hand's palm down on the table and waited for the questions.

Moving her gaze around the table, MelEid recognised their utter disbelief and unsettled looks. Bringing her hands together and laying them in her lap, she smiled, then gently began to talk telepathically to her group. "You are all confused, nervous and unsure of what I have just done. But before we continue, allow me to set a shield around us so that what we discuss is only heard by us."

Once she was sure that no one could infiltrate the barrier she'd erected, MelEid continued.

"You are wondering why I asked you to stay and observe the Elders. Now you question the static shock and reason behind my removal of the garb that identifies me as a Mage, let alone the Head Mage." She smiled at them and shook her head at their confusion.

"What is the first thing you were taught? If a Mage refuses to lay down their identification, are they a true Mage? If they do lay down their identification, are they a true Mage? How do you ensure the Lyran you are communicating with is a True Lyran, let alone a True Lyran Mage?" Pausing, she looked at those seated around her.

A slow dawning of realisation began to sink into their faces. A few started to show signs of embarrassment at being caught out.

Any Mage that concedes their garb without resistance is considered a true Mage, for they do not consider the outer trappings to make them what they are already on the inside.

One who resists their garb and pouch being removed is considered to rely solely on their outward trinkets and thus not a true Mage.

A True Lyran Mage needs not their cloak, tinctures, laser weapon or anything else that identifies them as a Mage, for it is what lies within the Mage that makes them what they are.

The static shock reminded the Neophytes that nothing is what it seems and that power can be made, imitated and used to distract while something is done in the shadows.

"Now," MelEid addressed the trainee Mages, "who wishes to tell me what they felt, saw and telepathically assessed while observing the Elders?"

This time the trainees were more willing to share their insights.

"To be honest, Mage, I am not sure what I saw while observing them in a state of invisibility, but two of the Elders seemed to fade into vapour momentarily, and in their place were the most hideous of creatures I have ever seen or imagined." Then, breathing in to calm himself, the young trainee Neophyte exhaled loudly, "The Elders seemed to be a mix of beings as if there were some there that were living Lyrans, observing the disembarking and official greetings of the two groups. Then some dematerialised and re-materialised like the changing winds of Lyra as if they were merely windows for some other eyes to see through."

Listening to the comments that ranged from complete and utter disbelief of what they had observed to the underlying anger and desire to deal with what the young Mages considered an affront to their sector, MelEid processed all the information given. The knowledge and comprehension of just how serious this had become, the Formless Ones somehow had penetrated her sector. This one sector encompassed the trusted Elders of Wisdom and Healing Knowledge. She knew that any action she stated would need to be solid and sure. Though most importantly, evidence would be required for MelEid to gain the trust of Sol Lrign dWari.

Raising her hand in a gesture for all to become silent, MelEid gently reminded the Neophytes of their intent in learning the art of being a Mage. How they were now duty bound, in Truth, Honour and Intent, to observe, note and report back to her any and all discrepancies they saw within the Sector of Mages and report back. "Now, disperse and integrate with other Mages of this ship. Discover what you can but remember, our allegiance and honour are first to the Divine Creator, who uses the Crystal Heart Stone to communicate with us, then to RexNā Liod DeAqua, our chosen Leader of Families. All others come after. Is that with your comprehension?"

Upon seeing the agreement among her trainees, she let them return to the rest of the sectors and mingle.

Dear Reader, what we see now is the beginning of the deceptions that have been presented. On the one hand, certain behaviours, events, and groups were accepted as 'normal' due to the familiarity of those within the ship *Bitari-Furtim-Karda*. But, on the other hand, this 'normality' or familiar way of being could create a sense of 'blindness' while living and working alongside those considered the Elders and Healers. Familiarity does not always allow for insight and truth but can create a foundation of ease and acceptance or even contempt for a particular way of being.

It takes new eyes, clear intent and honest reflection to see what you do not always wish to see or know. It requires trust to instigate change and, above all, honour, in self and those you work with to ensure that outcome is balanced and transparent.

Knowing this, MelEid waited till all had left the area they had used to talk and then sent a coded telepathic message to Sol, Juuls and her sibling Eid' dVra. Informing them that she'd discovered more about the infiltration of members of the crew of the *Bitari-Furtim-Karda*.   All information would be given first to Sol and then to others when there was more substantial evidence.

Shutting off the telepathic communication, MelEid felt decidedly alone. She'd always been a loner, but that was her choice to assist her in focusing on her journey and becoming the Mage she was in the present moment. However, this feeling was one of dejectedness, of a deep dark shadow sitting over her. The sense of loneliness seemed to trickle down her spine like a tentacle, feeling its way looking for an opening to penetrate her shield of energy protecting her. A sense of tiredness pulled at her, creating a feeling of being lost in a long dark tunnel without any hope. Struggling against this feeling, MelEid began to call her sibling, but even this connection seemed to be blocked. Sitting at the table that not so long ago had been filled with young, eager trainees, MelEid seemed to be frozen in time, invisible to all who passed by.

Fortunately, her sibling felt the disconnect from him. It felt as if she'd, in fact, died! The pain within him tore so strongly that he cried out and dropped to the ground. Those around him queried what had happened. Unable to form words, Eid managed to gasp, 'Find MelEid. She's in danger.'

While some of his team searched for, found and brought the near comatose MelEid back to Eid, the remainder of the seer sector with him began to administer assistance. It took a few minutes for him to regain his balance and demeanour, but by the time MelEid was brought to where he was, he was in good stead to deal with the attack on his sister.

Using telepathy, the Crystal shard and certain pitches of toning, he and his group broke the hold of darkness over MelEid, who suddenly sprang back into motion as if breaking out of a strong mould of jelly.

Eid requested that the two siblings be given space to discuss what had happened. As they shared the events prior and after the discussion with the Neophytes, both siblings realised that the Formless Ones were more active on the *Bitari-Furtim-Karda* than they first thought. For such a strong block to fall upon MelEid, there must be an actual Formless One on board or a proselyte of the Formless Ones who could create mind blocks and depression spells over those they chose to infiltrate.

Together, the twins realised that something needed to be done urgently, and it was decided that MelEid, once recovered, would speak to Sol Lrign dWari and request a repeat of The Whittling be instigated.

Chapter Twenty-Five

Leadership Challenged
Old vs New
Balanced by Truth

Sitting opposite each other, Sol and Rae locked eyes, each willing the other to begin the discourse, the debate and to search for the hidden clues within the other.

The more they sat in the room cut off from all others, the higher the vibration of the Heart Stone Crystal emanated from Rae. The voices in her psyche sought an opening. The new knowledge growing within her now surged around her inner being, seeking an outlet. Yet, her mouth and telepathic voice were strangely silent.

Unbeknownst to her, Sol was in awe of the transformation happening before her eyes. As they sat waiting for the other to break the silence, Rae began to metamorphose, a slow yet definite alteration of her body. Her skin took on the same pale tints and hues of the early Lyrans, the strange under-glow of that which she had when submerged in the Golden Waters of Source and her eyes, no longer seeing, were white as if blind.

All this occurred without RaeNegria being aware. Neither was she cognisant that her energy being was expanding out of her physical and creating a wave of vibration that swirled within the two of them, patterning the wave of the [88]infinity sign. Thus forming a wall of incredible energy around them. If anyone else was to observe this scene, they would see a wall of static electric smoke, sparking and hissing, as it wove amongst the two Lyrans.

Sol, realising that one of them had to break the impasse before the static power ignited the room, pushed telepathically into the vibrational space surrounding RaeNegria. "Rae, I am your friend. You were sent to me by RathVorx. He gave you a message for me, remember?"

Her voice echoed around the void Rae had created surrounding them, she felt the bump and tickle of the telepathic message, but it was not strong enough to distract her mind. The voices within her calling for the destruction of this ship. They wanted RaeNegria to free them of the confines of the physical and, almost instantaneously, an overriding voice, more assertive and calmer, telling her that all would be restored to calm if she would breathe. Calming voices encouraged her to open her eyes and feel the beat of her heart while listening to the voice in her energy.

The overriding voice reminded her of the Waters of Source, how they enveloped her, establishing the cocoon that enabled her to evolve into the Seer she was becoming.

The voice continued to speak to her, calming her emotions and energy, slowly getting her to focus on her inhaling and exhaling. The voice reminded her of MelEid, like a dim memory from a dis-

---

[88] The figure 8

tant past, yet it was more emphatic and began to instil within her a desire to reign in the static energy around her body.

As her heartbeat slowed down and her focus returned, she became aware of the telepathic message from Sol, pushing at her inner connection. Using the voice of Sol to guide her back, Rae focused and crafted her energy around each word pulling herself back into the reality of the ship and all that was in it.

Opening her eyes, she slowly focused on the room she was in, noticing how the light glistened and bounced off the edges of walls and tables. In fact, it appeared as if light flowed through each object like water.

Rae suddenly realised that as she looked at her surroundings, she was seeing not only the physical object but also the energy field around it. Thus she could look into the structure of energy holding her surroundings and see both the strengths and resistances in the 'energy lattice' of its foundation.

This was for both living beings and inanimate objects.

Stretching out a shaky hand towards Sol, Rae grasped tightly onto what she felt was the tangible part of Sol. Finally speaking, Rae asked for her Mage to come forward to assist her.

RaeNegria was unaware that MelEid had undergone an attack herself and had nearly been taken over. Though thankfully, with the help of her sibling, Eid had managed to stave off this infiltration attempt by the Formless Ones. MelEid was not one to simply sit by and lick her wounds and was currently boosting her energy and conscious awareness by meditating and focusing on the Crystal Heart Stone's energy.

Sol nodded in agreement and sent a telepathic message to bring MelEid to their rooms.

As they waited, Sol once again began to talk to Rae about the experience she'd had. When the anomalies first appeared off the *Bitari-Furtim-Otiose,* how they had interfered with Rae's balance and inner connection with the Crystal Heart Stone. Sol ruminated on how RaeNegria and MelEid had reached out for a parley regarding information being left within Rae from the organic Link known as RathVorx. Sol also admitted being impressed at Rae's inner grit when she'd reached out to Sol from the brink of a mental shutdown to ask for an audience to share the information.

Rae began to return to her usual self as the one-sided discussion with Sol progressed.

With her usual aplomb, MelEid arrived at the room where Sol Lrign dWarn and RaeNegira sat, with Sol's security team spaced around the perimeter and at the entrance. Barely acknowledging the security personnel, MelEid marched into the room and went to Rae's side. Taking her time to note any abnormal physical indicators that her Prince showed.

Reaching into her pouch MelEid pulled out the same vial of tincture that she'd given Rae during the RathVorx experience.

"Take a drop, my Prince. It will help to balance your inner being. You have signs of higher stress than your system can process or indeed handle at present. I did warn you not to come out of the stasis too soon." MelEid's voice held a soft, almost laughing tone as she spoke the last statement

Rae gave MelEid a withering look as she swallowed the tincture. However, the effects were noticeable within a few moments, and Rae became more coherent in her conversation.

Turning to Sol, she began sharing the insights RathVorx had shown her.

Within the highest ranks of her command, there were no fewer than four traitors. They had turned to the dark energy of the Formless Ones with the promise of wealth, power and recognition for time immortal. These four had systematically been dismantling the command chain within Sol's ship. The only ones left that Sol could trust impeccably were The Moderator, Nuex and Juuls.

The others were all compromised in some way. Whether the four had found something to manipulate the other captains or sector leaders or had managed to find their weaknesses, it really didn't matter. What mattered was that they were used and controlled, following orders of the Formless Ones, instead of Sol and her directives.

Sol Lrign dWarn listened silently to this information, slowly seeing in her mind's eye the dots beginning to join up and all the minor and incidental occurrences now making more and more sense. All the miscommunications between sectors and command centres. The broken chain of command and, most of all, the anomalies now sitting within her very ship.

Somehow the Formless Ones had found them, infiltrated their defences and were attacking from within to destroy the Crystal Heart Stone. No wonder the Crystal had sent for the Princes. It had known before the Lyrans what was occurring and had preempted this scenario and created a buffer.

Suddenly Rae's voice changed, sounding strangely like Rath-Vorx himself. "Commander, I entreat your attention for but a moment. I have hard-wired my last conscious thoughts into this young Prince. Hold no vengeance over her. She is innocent, as one can be innocent, of all that has occurred. In fact, it is her determination to join the battle-weary enemies of Lyra as one. Those with no option but to be the servants of destruction for the

Formless Ones. Those cosmic cultures who are at odds with the Lyrans not of choice but out of fear of what will be done to those that they love if obedience is not complete.

She wishes to join these forced enemies of the Lyrans into a single unit against the common enemy. This common enemy, The Formless Ones, has caused them to become divided and singularly used as the weapon of destruction against us, the Families of Lyra."

"Now listen," the voice continued, "I know not if I speak to Commander Stranz or Junior Commander Sol, but know this and heed it well. It has taken us a quarter cycle to reach you. The Formless Ones have battleships from the Hydra Quadrant following your Princes' ship. They have sent out sub-atomic waves as breadcrumbs for the rest of their fleet to join them. Currently, you may, or hopefully may not, have the unfortunate occurrence of three entities on board. These three are unseen to the natural eye, yet your onboard screen has identified them. Whatever you do, do not antagonise them. As long you leave them and ignore them, they will remain dormant. Yes, they will be in your ship, but they will be as if a piece of dust has entangled itself in a spider's web. But, should you attack either the anomaly or them, they will activate and become thermonuclear within seconds". The word 'if' was emphasised by RathVorx, " *If* they are challenged again, they will detonate. Nothing will be left of either ship, the Crystal Heart Stone or this sector of the Polaris' Sector of Light'. It is imperative that you play dumb, do not allow your enemy to know that you are aware of these plans."

"In order to deactivate these anomalies, this one that I have been *carried in* must allow herself to once again delve into the memory of the Waters of Source, but she must do this within a distance of a half [89]dictrate or less to the closest anomaly."

---

[89] distance equal somewhat to our metre

"Once she slips into the trance, the Source Energy can, via her body, transmit the negating pulse that will disable and destroy them and the sub-atomic waves being sent out as we speak. However, and this is important, commander, it must be a voluntary act on the part of Prince RaeNegria Hylrix-El-Moa. There must be no coercion or threat. It must be her choice, for there is a chance that she may not return to us but remain within the realm of the Waters of Source, unable to return as her energy body may have altered beyond the point of reinstatement."

Rae's voice returned to normal, and as she breathed slowly, it looked like she was finally releasing the last tie to RathVorx, for he had delivered the information to his Commander in Chief, and his duty had been fulfilled.

Sol sat in silence. So much made sense now, how personalities had changed over time, how trust had been broken. Those closest to her had begun to drift away, questioning her authority, but it finally started to come together.

Rae looked at MelEid, "Is it over? Has he gone?" Her voice sounded strangely small, lilting, yet there was a hint of energy in the mix that alerted MelEid to the fact that perhaps there was more of RathVorx to come, but for now, it was done.

Standing, Sol telepathically called the three members of her command team that were still to be trusted. Then, glancing at MelEid, she nodded, acknowledging her part in assisting the young Prince in getting this far.

"RaeNegira, I thank you for bringing this information forward and suggest you rest now. I would like to connect with you later, but I have a feeling you will be busy for some time. Your training is about to begin, and I sense it is not what you think it will be."

With that, Sol withdrew. Meeting up with those she'd called to join her in the sealed chambers of the Crystal Hall.

Chapter Twenty-Six

Earth Revisited
What is Discovered?
What is learnt?

Remember, as we left   the Realm of Earth previously, we told you how this world of yours had become a zombie world, a world of puppets and as your timeline has unfolded, many of you have seen this for yourself.

But let us not leave the realm in a dark manner. Rather let us show you a world you can live within, a world of vibrational and resonating energy that is uplifting and, indeed, the uprising of your race.

Returning to your world, many have taken up the concept of peaceful resistance, as shown by your Mahatma Gandhi. He, among other early awakening Terrans and Lyrans, have attempted to reveal the art of amicable negotiations. However, it is interesting to see at this time that those involved in the peaceful arbitrations include the infected. Groups have been standing together, although standing under many flags, to identify the 'individual' stances and beliefs. Yet, many of these groups are seemingly unheard and unnoticed; still, there is the deafening silence of reply from those who govern you. Though this same governance silently uses weapons of unseen nature against the crowds, due to confusion of those gathering, under flags that 'shout defiance' instead of flags that call for parley.

It is time to step into the subtlety and knowledge of the Negotiators. Come and learn as the great warriors share their insights and awareness of dealing with those who will not budge for various reasons. Whether they have been bought or sold into the service of the Formless Ones, or they have believed a lie until it is far too late to change, they think. Changes have begun in your world, some just in time, others far too late. Many are already under the influence of the AI in their system, but we hold the hope that this nanotechnology can be removed. There are techniques and vibrational protocols to remove artificial intelligence from those with it in their systems, provided it has been a short time since insertion.

So come and let us fly in our light vessels, so we remain undetected by the puppet masters yet seen by those seeking. Join us as we observe the changes in your world in this short time.

Drawing close to the earth, we note that there have been considerable shifts in energy. Many of the world's people have united against a common evil, yet there are still vast swathes of separation.

As Chief Negotiator of the Lyran community on Bitari-Furtim-Karda, I, Nuex Del Aqua Loid, will speak with you on the art of negotiation.

First, one must come in complete honour and dignity.

There can be no room for any hidden, supposed or presumed agenda. When approaching the opponent, it must be clear that you will not move from your present and already offered declaration. Your opponent in the game of parley must already be informed of your intent and points of negotiation. In the duration of the negotiation, it may become a requirement to either add to or remove certain quotients from your demands. However, usually, this is achieved in synchronicity with your opponents, who will have demands and counter demands to your proposal.

When you arrive, the only colours displayed must be the colours of your sector, and these are not flying from staffs or high-held poles but gently and discreetly from your shoulders.

The only banner to be held in view is the banner of truce. Now each culture has their own divine flag that indicates the declaration of a parley or time of negotiation. Neither side is to bear arms of any type. No weapon at all, whether it is the traditional sword of your family or a sidearm. Neither side should display a shield, or protective armour, for this indicates to your opposition that you do not trust them in the negotiations. While this may be a truth, in the arena of negotiations, it must be neutral. Neither side can be seen to be provocative or instigating a fight.

All sides are to be present, represented by the Negotiator and their second, plus a witness. No more than three per side. This is to ensure that there can be no outbreak of animosity that could lead to a physical interaction that can be misconstrued in any way.

There are a few exceptions to this rule. Being primarily when an enemy is overpowered and given the option to surrender and declare loyalty to their victor or negotiate the end to their physical being.

Each party is to lay out their declared intentions, demands, requests, moot points and questions.

As these issues are discussed, no one should pass them over as unimportant. By acknowledging each demand, one shows honour to each side and thus proves oneself as an integral being giving recognition even when honour is not reciprocated or expected.

A parley or negotiation can take up to a few lapzph or perhaps a trenze or two. At times we have been known to negotiate up to and beyond many periods to ensure the best outcome.

During all negotiations, all original parties in the negotiation/parley must remain in camp. None should be replaced or leave the room during negotiation. For a bond is created at the beginning of the negotiations that can often be destroyed when parties are broken by individuals vacating and new negotiators introduced, thus creating a pause to ensure the newcomers are 'brought up to speed' with the communications. Trust is no longer present in the circle of discussion due to this change, so this is why those who begin must complete the discussions. Suppose there is a requirement for one of the parties to release a member. In that case, it remains the duty and honour of the remaining two to be integral in their dealings as they present the facts, logic and reasonings of their negotiation points.

It is not a place for commanders, captains, or leaders of nations or worlds. Rather it is a place for those trained to represent their people and be unswayed by offers of wealth, position and glory.

All of the above must be done at the table of truce, where everyone present is on an equal footing. It is imperative that all voices are listened to and that both sides of the parley have room to explore offers and counter offers. While you may disagree with the demands of your opponents, remember there are moments when giving a little to gain more is wise.

It may seem to those on the outside that you are losing the 'argument.' But, if you remain faithful to the colours you wear, to the honour of your people, and bring the truth of your heart and reasons to the fore, you will be heard.

Most worlds honour the flag or banner of parley and should not attack while this flag is deployed at the high point.

Remember, Terrans, it is best to be vigilant in these times, to note all that is being declared to you openly or in a hidden manner. Let your Negotiators not be caught out by being informed notice was given via outlets of news, either of informal entertainment or by formal readings of information.

As parley is being held by those who have been chosen as the Negotiators or the selected voice of the many, it is imperative that those who remain on the outside of the tent walls remain in honour at all times. If there is any sign of deviousness or ill intent from either side, this can jeopardise any and all discussions of peace.

You may ask why we are inserting this information of parley in this chronicle of exposing the Dark Puppet Masters, the Formless Ones. It is because even when you turn the tide in your favour, you must have honour on your side to negotiate their terms of surrender to you and your group.

As your realm is undergoing the changes and shifts of energy, as we share our story, bringing both light and shadow to the fore of your lives, it is encouraging to see that the Terrans are standing up more and more for their truths.

For there is much to see that is yet unfolding in your realm. This fight between 'good and evil,' the dark and light are not done. In fact, as we observe the realm we are revisiting, we see that you have forgotten yet again Terran the fundamentals of standing within your Living Being.

Groups of hu-mans yell and shout out that they wish to be heard. They demand the rights of the [90]hu-man and then wonder why they are treated abominably by the very people who have been 'voted' into various power groups under the guise of governments in order to guide and protect the nations or hu-mans of the land.

But let us look at the reality that are your *human rights*, it may be that they are not really what they seem. To access these 'rights', you must submit to the ideals and concepts that you are 'human' and unable to live as Living Terrans/Beings.

You are to come to the comprehension Dear Reader, Terran, that you cannot demand to be treated as a hu-man and expect them to look after you. The human or hu-man or HU-man is no more, no less than a stock animal to the puppet masters.

When you demand 'basic' human rights, they laugh at you; they laugh at the struggling Terran who has forgotten that if they just declare that they are alive. That if they were to stand and have a witness testify that the Terran in front of them is alive and living, active in life, performing as a living soul, they are indeed stronger than any human!

You cannot be both Living Soul/Man/Woman and human. We will cover this in the coming pages but let us set the stage now that, you have, as many of you are aware, been lied to.

We have been using many words in your realm that you identify with so as to make sure the Reader comprehends. Though now, it is time to begin to introduce the concept and thought that you are more than mere humus, more than an appendage or piece of chattel meant for barter on the open market.

The Anunnaki and the Formless Ones have done an inordinately clever job of convincing you that you are no more important than a cow or that a cow has more rights than you do.

---

[90] hu-man = colour of man, therefore not actual but an image, facsimile, a copy

We have noticed that your leaders have given more and more leeway to the murder of innocents. As if a child's life, the life of your flesh and blood, is less valuable and less important than that of the animal kingdom, have you ever stopped and asked why?

Why do you have slaughterhouses for the young of your kind?

Why do so many go through this torture for the sake of another agenda? Before you get offended, Terran, Lyran, or hu-man, ask yourself a simple question. Would you be here if your mother had been given an open slather to delete you before you drew your first breath, but not before you heard her first heartbeat or felt the blood rush from her into your body?

Why is it so important for the elite, or let us be more specific, why is it that the agenda of the Formless Ones, the dark Puppet Masters, the ones who generate the required *loosh* from the fear, pain, and utter despair felt by these young living souls as they are ripped and torn from the womb?

Is this not an ugly subject to discuss?

Should we avoid this and pretty up the pages of the exposing of the agenda?

Do we Lyrans not see the pain that has been wrought from these very same agendas on our people, now being played out here in this realm?

We ask you, in this realm revisited, what have you learnt? What have you seen that you can change? Dear Reader, it is not up to us to be moral police or caretakers of your soul. It is not up to us to be the ones that tell you what you should or should not do with your offspring. However, it is up to us to expose that the only reason there are so many slaughterhouses for young Terrans, Lyrans, and Cosmic children to be removed violently from the mother is that the child's energy, blood, and at times organs are collected. These precious commodities are treated and used to ensure that youthful and regenerative properties continue being sold to the loosh buyers of your realm. The adrenochrome market has not shut down. Dear Reader, it has simply changed shop fronts.

We do not blunt our swords in our discourse of this matter, or any matter of importance, though we feel in our integrity and honour, we cannot miss this part of the revisiting of your realm exposé.

You see, Dear Reader, we are entering this realm to observe the changes of good, but we see that there are more that lean towards the selfish ways of self-importance. More and more of the youth feel as if they have nothing to lose, so they behave without integrity without dignity, and this is only because they see the elders have no honour or pride.

What has been learnt in your realm since we have left and been with the Lyrans? What have you set in motion and instigated as a truth that will free the people? Are you still waiting for a rescue mission? Are you still like your ancestors of old, who allowed themselves to be deceived into believing that they were outnumbered? While they instinctively and intuitively knew that the Anunnaki could not possibly have the armada they claimed to have. The ancient Terrans had worked cycle in and cycle out with the Anunnaki. They knew the state of their master's tools and ships, including what repairs or disrepair of the Anunnaki vessels. Yet they chose to believe a lie because, in many ways, it was easier to bow their knee in submission than to resist and take a stand for what they believed.

You are at the same crossroads with so many similar choices.

So tell us, Dear Reader, what is it that holds you in the grip of unchanging and unwillingness to move forward, even though you tell us in passionate words you desire to be free?

- Are you standing up or bending the knee to the oppression in your realm?
- Are you defending the defenceless?
- Are your tribes united or separated through apparent differences of culture, creed, colour and language - tell us who told you one was better than the other.
- Have you set aside the doctrine of controlled medication organisations and picked up the knowledge of T'Gaina?
- Are you teaching the young the ways of the Realm and Divine unction, or have you lost them?
- Where are the creations and buildings of healing?

Your words are impassioned as you attempt to convince any and all who will listen to you that you want to change and desire to walk the path to freedom, yet we see the same in-house conjecture and puffed-up chests of who would be chief.

The groups created to be leaders of Divine lore and to educate others in the ways of The Creators Way in Dignity, Truth, and Honour are the ones that are most in need of direction. For we see, some have sold out to the Puppet Masters for the sake of their coffers and followings, and we do not see them standing up and declaring the truth they've taught over the years.

Why, Dear Reader, why are the lessons so long in being learnt, of being heard, of being realised? What is it about your species that seems to keep you locked in that head of yours, trying against all that is Divine to work out what cannot be worked out in a logical way? It is comprehended in the heart.

As we walk around the realm, we see this is similar in all your small nations. Yet, you seem to take such pride in segregating your people groups and labelling yourselves as to culture and tribe... all of which are foreign to your makeup.

You are Terran. You are Lyran. You are of the Cosmic Family, where there is NO separation. It is time to walk out of the entrapment. To leave the trappings of presumed freedom to become truly free.

In the great awakening, you will see that you have no requirement placed upon you to pay others for the privilege of being alive. No lore insists that you pay to enjoy the toys that make life bearable for you. Your ancestors would create with each other and with T'Gaina bringing the parts together that enabled them to travel freely, to step into the healing circles and temples. There was no barrier preventing them from picking herbs and seeds to nourish their bodies when they were lacking in nutrition or vitamins.

Tell us, Dear Reader, while so many of you have gathered under the flag of parley to unite against the leaders of this realm, what are you actually doing? How are you bringing the change? Why do you cut down the ones who have ideas and are a driving force in pushing others forward towards a place where they can learn to stand in their truth? Why are there still so many who are insecure? What is it about their insecurity that drives them to damage the reputation of those who are growing stronger? Is it, perhaps, because those who are weak and insecure in their truth are having their buttons pushed and creating unwanted reactions within their being?

Do not be in despair at our overview of the realm you currently live within, for there can be a moment of significant change if you would but allow it.

There are many great-minded and hearted beings that live honest and integral lives here in the realm of T'Gaina, and it is to these that we now speak.

We see you!

We hear you

The battles you have waged and have been scarred by, we stood by you and even though you may not have seen us, you were aware of our energy.

You have held the line and stood while being pushed and pulled by the common enemy, and you have exposed and shone the light of truth upon the dark shadows. Changes have occurred under your watch, and you have set up the watchtowers, established the warning fires and placed guardians to monitor and observe the surroundings. Yet, we ask to what end are you watching and observing?

We, the Lyran Negotiators, would like to believe that in this timeline, at this junction of your path, you would be setting up sanctuary villages for those who wish to leave the citadels. Where you establish a traditional value system similar to bartering, where every part of the village is run concisely and precisely with order and temperance. Are you calling in those who are skilled in trade, shamanism, husbandry of animal care, and so much more are set in place to follow their passion while training others to work alongside them? Are you preparing the sectors so that many hands are doing the work? Thus a heavy load is lightly done to completion, meaning all participate and all benefit, thus all reap the rewards. A village that works not out of 'have to' but out of a desire to grow and produce technology, food, industry, and leisure. Ensuring all who live there do so out of choice and the desire to be with those of like-mindedness.

We see the ones who have fallen victim to the injection narrative, only to realise their mistake and how they fight to regain their dignity and rebuild their inner being of Terran DNA. This is the earth realm we see growing; this is the realm we see expanding and eventually overtaking the current timeline.

Dear Reader, be one who chooses to negotiate. Be the ones who bring change to the realm you live within. Be the change catalysts to the living beings in the village around them. Allow yourselves to expand and become the Terrans of old again.

Chapter Twenty-Seven

A New Challenge
Friendships tested

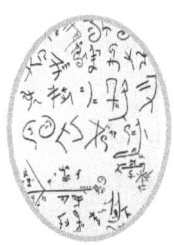

MelEid sat with Rae as she recovered from the experience and waited for her Prince to talk.

While waiting, she received calls from RexNā Loid d'Aqua demanding to know where they were and what was happening. When the Mage saw that Rae was stable, she sent a message to the other Princes informing them of their whereabouts. It seemed instantaneous from the telepathic message to the arrival of RexNā and Rägę in the room.

RexNā stood staring at her friend, not knowing whether to be annoyed, concerned or relieved. "Can either of you tell me what is going on? I thought we did not keep anything from each other, that we led this crew together?"

Rae looked at her Prince and friend and saw, perhaps for the first time, the insecurity in RexNā, which made her laugh. It was a gentle but melodic sound, unlike the normal throat-generated wind-forced laugh but more like wind blowing through chimes and boughs of trees. It flowed from RaeNegria's throat like a warm wind.

It was as if a release valve had popped, and the pressure that had built up within her body suddenly dissipated.

Unsure of what was happening to her friend, RexNā Loid DeAqua, sat down heavily with a concerned look. "Seriously, Rae, what is going on? You go off into a semi coma trance and return to us looking as if you've been through a metamorphosis of some type, but you can't tell either of us anything!" She flicked her hand to where Rägę was sitting. "Yet, you step onto this ship, and the only person you will speak to, is this Sol Lrign dWari, and now our Mage is acting as if she is your personal bodyguard."

RexNā's voice showed the emotional unease within her mindset and the internal questioning she had not verbalised.

At this last comment, MelEid glanced at the Prince and noted the high level of anxiety within the young leader.

Sighing and shaking her head at what could potentially be, in her eyes, the long-awaited flexing of 'who is in charge.' She'd expected this since the ship first left the Outpost so long ago. Yet, through choice and desire to find the Crystal Heart Stone, these three young Princes had found themselves in a situation they had not been trained for, nor they discovered, did they have the knowledge to lead. Yet, they had synergised and created a united front to defend, head and unify a group of Lyrans in a manner that she had not seen in a long time.

"My liege, please hear me out," MelEid softly began to telepathically speak to RexNā, "what is occurring in Prince RaeNegria is not unknown but has not eventuated in our people for many hundreds of cycles!" Pausing, MelEid considered her own training in which this event had been discussed, but only on a surface level, as none of the Mages felt that it may ever occur again. How wrong her teachers were! Continuing her appeal to RexNā, she began to explain, "She is entering into a dual initiation alongside your initiation. However, her induction is for something uniquely separate from leading the Lyran sectors and families. That is your calling."

"Her initiation and learning will take her from us for a while. She must go on this journey alone, with specific leaders of the Mage and Seer Sectors walking beside her to assist and care for her during her time of separation. She will return to us when her journey of discovery is complete. The Waters of Source have chosen her. We must allow this to continue. "

Rae heard the conversation MelEid had with RexNā, then without realising it enabled a link so that Rägę was involved in the conversation. She looked at her friends, silently said farewell, and stepped out of the room, knowing those waiting outside the door would be taking her away.

RexNā observed as she walked away that Rae had metamorphosed into a transparent colour as if invisibility was her natural state of being.

The silence that ensued after Rae stepped through the doorway was broken by the loud crackle of the intercom coming into life. 'Princes RexNā Loid DeAqua and Rägę, please present to the command deck immediately.' 'Prince RexNā and Rägę to the command deck immediately.'

The intrusive noise brought the two Princes out of their lingering telepathic link with RaeNegria abruptly as a sticking plaster ripped from the skin. The two Princes looked at each other, neither fully comprehending what had just occurred. Then, the noise of the hailer calling them to the command deck brought them back into the present. Looking as if they'd just woken from a dream, the two Princes left the room and headed to the command deck.

Standing in the hydro lift, they began to discuss the reasons they had had as three friends when leaving the Outpost. Although both still agreed, they had all felt an unwavering desire to take the Bitari-Furtim-Otiose and find the missing Lyrans. RexNā verbalised how it was as if they'd been dispatched to this ship to find the Crystal Heart Stone. So weren't they supposed to bring it back to the Outpost so the scientist there could utilise the power of the crystal to re-create Lyra? When had the plan changed?

Rägę looked at his friend and linked telepathically with her, "Rex, we have this. I have no idea what happened to Rae, but she has changed ever since the organic link and the RathVorx incident. But you and I are on mission. You are the chosen leader, your initiations have been moving forward, and the Crystal Shard chose you. I am still in this for the longer cycle. We will get the Heart Crystal back to those who require it."

RexNā watched Rägę as he communicated with her, his face showing his inner emotion. His entire body reflected his confusion and his desire to remain faithful to the cause they had left with for this journey.

RexNā was about to reply when the door opened to the command deck, and they found themselves standing on a very familiar-looking platform. It brought a sense of normality to them.

Instinctively they both gravitated to the consul area they utilised on their own ship only to find it occupied by Sol, Juuls and The Moderator.

Smiling slightly at their unconscious action Sol stood up and walked over to the two Princes.

"RexNā, Rägę, welcome to our command deck." She turned slowly, acknowledging each Lyran on deck.

"Here, you will find things are virtually the same as upon your ship. However, the frequency and coding are unique to my vibration and energy signature and will only operate if it recognises you as part of the frequency membrane. As of yet, you will have no access to any command consul, but you will be able to observe and give suggestions."

"You are aware of and know the others on deck. My second in command Juuls, and there is our Chief Mage and standing next to him is our Chief Seer."

Nodding in the direction of MelEid and Eid, she continued, "Over there, your Mage and Seer have been granted the same freedom to stand in the command section as they would have on the Bitari-Furtim-Otiose. We now will begin the process of discovering why you are here and how you know of the Sector of Light when no one in over one hundred fifty [91]cycles has found it. We, ourselves, stumbled across the portal entrance only because the Crystal Heart Stone drew us directly to it when we ran from the Formless Ones."

"Your Mage, MelEid, and the Seer, Eid' dVra, have been tested and proven honourable. Therefore, they are allowed to leave, yet both choose to remain to observe your testing."

At this Eid' dVra moved as if uncomfortable with being relegated as *just a Seer,* but MelEid kicked his ankle, reminding him that he was to be incognito for the foreseeable future, just until they could get to Rae and seclude her in the required training. Sol had already placed RaeNegria, under the protection, or as she attempted to explain, the training of the Seer sector leaders of her ship. This action conflicted with a request by MelEid to keep the Prince in the Mages' quarters. Sol's reasoning was to observe these changes happening in Rae and be on hand to receive any further information discovered regarding the infiltration. Eid was

---

[91] The Lyran year which equals twenty-five earth years

angry at this blatant disregard for the high-level communication he'd handed Sol from the sector who'd entrusted him with locating and training the next Seer of Seers. It had been agreed between Sol and himself that he would be present at all initiation and training sessions. As of yet, this remained words only. To this, the siblings began questioning the integrity and honour of those commanding this vessel.

Neither of the siblings was happy with this, as it prevented them from connecting with the young Prince. Eid' dVra was particularly annoyed as his directive from the High Mage & Seer Sectors on [92]*Crystallise Nuv QudRoa* was to train the young Prince in the art of being a Seer as gently as he could. It was important that Rae's training was without the input of the old Mages and Seers he referred to as [93]ro'Duiplj he'd seen looking to dig their claws into the young energy of RaeNegira. Eid felt that the Moderator and 2nd Mage were actively and diplomatically pushing him and his twin aside. So busy was he determining in his energy that this would be addressed and dealt with he nearly missed RexNā and Rägę's next test.

The Moderator, mentally going over the conversation in the hyper lift with MelEid and the other Commanders, felt it was necessary to discuss the facts of infiltration on both ships.

Stepping forward, he nodded to his Commander and then stood in front of the two young Princes. "Tell me, young Princes, what are you doing about the anomaly attached to your ship?"

"Were you going to destroy it?"

"Or, were you planning to tell us about it or just allow it to slide on into our ship and destroy us?"

---

[92] The Outpost based in the Polaris region

[93] Buzzard/vulture/scavenger breed of bird

"Is it your plan to infiltrate us, remove the Crystal Heart Stone and give it to your masters?"

His words struck deep within both Princes, and he recognised the flush of dishonour his comments created, so he pushed harder, not to harm them but to push them to the edge where all they had left was *their* Honour, Truth and Dignity to stand on.

He continued the barrage of questions, "Do you think we are children, unaware that you have brought these Formless Ones straight to our door? You 'befriend' their soldiers and hunters and deliver them to our hold."

"What have they paid you or promised you to do this great betrayal to your Families? We should strip your cloaks from you and send you back to the void."

The deliberate and formatted words were spoken to create a chink or weakening of the Princes demeanour. If there had been any hidden agenda, this plethora of questions would unravel them, forcing an emotional and unthought-out response. The Moderator and elder Lyrans inwardly held their breath, waiting for the reply.

A flush of anger rose in the Princes like fire as they endured what they perceived as the dishonouring of their Families. This dishonour by this Mage, from their perspective, was also aimed at the dignity of their duty. Rägę stepped forward to speak, but RexNā put her hand out and held him back. Her face flushed with vehemence, her hand clenched and unclenched as she fought the urge to pull her sword and use it. Rising to her full height, she looked the Chief Mage squarely in the eye and spoke clearly, but her voice shook with emotion held tightly in check.

"You," she took a deep breath, "you dare to stand here and dishonour me, my fellow Princes and our crew? Do you question the honour and dignity of my Lyran family? You would stand and bring words of dishonour and compromised dealings with the enemy of our people and families, the destroyers of our home world? You would question me, me, who the Crystal Heart Stone chose to lead the Lyran Families as the Leader in Training of the Dolf-El Hyl-Pelagus Family?"

RexNā paused again and drew her breath deeply, "I am *your* Prince in Training," she spoke these words with such controlled disdain for the Moderator that all the others winced inwardly, "I require you to step aside and remove your presence until you are willing to retract your words."

She moved her head ever so slightly to stare at Sol Lrign dWari, "And you, commander, you agree with this? You allow a member of your command team to speak to me as such, to speak to us as such? I expected more from you, a Lyran commander".

As she spoke, both MelEid and Eid' dVra looked at each other in amazement, for RExNā, without realising it had levitated from the floor and was literally standing on air.

Only in the next level of Initiation of Water would this event be possible. Somehow, RexNā's initiation, which had begun on Bitari-Furtim-Otiose during the last moments of their coming into dock, had continued without the usual requirement to be monitored, thus had not been watched over by the Mage Sector. By some means, the Crystal Shard must have activated within RexNā the particles of the DNA markers used to bring a water vibration into the level of high actionable movement.

The intense heating of the molecules had generated this activation within the breathing unit that RexNā used to move freely about. Although the Waters of Lyra mainly circulated around her shoulders and head to enable her to breathe freely, they also, in the initiation process, created a vibrational platform that formed under her feet to allow her to gain height when required.

To all watching RexNā, it undoubtedly appeared as if she was levitating and walking on air. The Moderator turned to Sol and telepathically indicated this was, indeed, proof that they had the true Leader in Training with them. The other Princes were assisting RexNā but were not the Leader of the Families.

Sol raised her hand to RexNā, "Come, young Prince, you speak well, as do you float well," Sol could not keep the slight chuckle from her voice as she spoke. "Return to our level and talk with us, eye to eye, for yes, we have tested you, and you have shown your colours in truth and dignity, as has your Prince in waiting.

He is your right hand, your council and support, but he is not you."

RexNā looked confused, 'floating?' What did Sol mean by 'float well?' She looked around, and it dawned on her that the others were looking up at her. Then, looking down to her feet, she was astounded to see she was indeed at least a dictrate off the floor. This realisation caused her to calm down, which brought her to the floor with a thud.

MelEid and her sibling Eid `dVra, stepped forward to reassure the young Prince that all was well. However, Sol stepped in before they reached RexNā. Sol explained to the Leader in Training that she and her crew had many tests in front of them. These were not so much as to prove their abilities but to show their 'Colours of Lyra.'

This test or variations of tests, she explained, was something that all Lyrans went through before ascending to any seat of leadership, it had been the way before the Great Wars of Destruction, and they had continued it here on the ships that served the Crystal Heart Stone. These tests, continued Sol, would not be presented as a 'test' but in everyday experiences and life and would be observed by those who were aware of the requirements being put to the entire crew of Lyrans who had docked.

It mattered not if they were Prince or sweeper, for as in the days of old Lyra when it came to service and to proving loyalty to Lyra, there was no difference in rank.

RexNā glanced over to MelEid, who could not hide the shock on her face at what had just occurred. Ever since entering into this Sector of Lights and connecting with the Ancient Lyrans, having the energy from the Crystal Heart Stone so close and amped up, it had increased both the initiations and activations within two of the Princes Of Lyra.

MelEid was not looking forward to Rägę's initiation if and when they began, for he was a heavily built Lyran and would prove more challenging to restrain if required. Yet her intuition told her his changes would be coming. He would no longer be simply known as Prince in Waiting... she nodded deeply within herself, knowing they had entered into a new state of affairs and the energy here was active, vibrant and asking more of those who tapped into it.

As she mulled this over in her inner knowing, Eid glanced over to her and recognised the deep turnings of her mind. He paused and gently linked in with her telepathically. "Sister, let us depart here. We have much to go over, and I have a feeling these ancient ones will be watching our moves closely. It is time to gather our Mages and Seers so that our charges are not removed from under our noses and still have our guidance and mentoring. For now, let us play their game. Let us be invisible and observe, but let us find RaeNegria and assist her initiation. Her time is coming." MelEid slightly turned and walked out of the command room without waiting to see if her sibling followed.

This is how things would be, for now, their twin energy merging so that only they knew of the telepathic communications between them, acting as one yet within two bodies.

Rāgę felt a mix of emotions in his chest. First, there was a sense of pride that RexNā, his friend and Leader in Training, had excelled in this test laid before them. Then he felt the heaviness of knowing that in the awareness as being delegated to the Prince in waiting or 2nd in command, there could be no other relationship between himself and RexNā. His unspoken inner hopes were left unspoken, untouched. As he had put duty before self, his dream of speaking to RExNā Loid DeAqua as equals, a partnership of life now crumpled and evaporated.

His recognition as the 'Prince in Waiting' by the Ancient Lyrans now set his path and career in motion. As was his way, he went inwards, felt his deep emotion, and then released it in a loud and resounding exhalation. Those unaware of his practice of dealing with inner issues were startled at this explosive sound and were concerned. MelEid sensing what he'd processed, sent a telepathic message encouraging him, and then set a perimeter around him so others would leave him alone. Her abilities to connect and work energetically and telepathically without immediate connection to another, had greatly increased since her brother had awoken.

Sol Lrign dWari was not unaware of the underlying emotions of the young Lyran Princes and put her hand on the Moderator's shoulder, "Stand down, Moderator, stand easy." She spoke gently, but her voice carried the years of experience, knowledge and command she'd earned while sitting in the Command Seat.

The Moderator acknowledged the request and stood aside, but did not break eye contact with RexNā Loid DeAqua, his challenge still in the air, but for the moment, satisfied with the young Princes and his commander's stance in the given moment.

RexNā gathered herself and moved fractionally closer to her friend Rāgę as if to be assured that she was indeed firmly on the ground and was not in a dream state. Looking for MelEid the Mage, RexNā realised that she was on her own as Leader of Families, she felt the weight of that title settle even more solidly onto her shoulders.

Looking over at Sol, RexNā Loid DeAqua realised that this was no longer a rescue mission, to locate and return the Crystal Heart Stone to the remnants of Lyrans spread across the Void. In contrast, the Crystal Heart Stone was using the Ancients and the Ways of Old to bring a catalysis change in newly combined families of the Lyran community. She had no idea where this would lead them, though she felt it was no mistake that the three families had a representative present for the change.

It finally began to dawn upon RexNā that the changes or initiations that had commenced in RaeNegria recently were constant with the distance and resonance of being near the Crystal Heart Stone. Surreptitiously she glanced over to Rāgę and pondered what and when his initiation would be and how the three of them would fit in this evolving new life of the Lyrans.

Somehow, deep within her, she knew their journey was being mirrored, immersed within the void in a place that she had not yet seen or had a conscious memory of. Yet, the pull to be done with the tests, locating and taking the Crystal Heart Stone back to the Outpost NexEl MinAqua, bore heavily on RexNā's heart. Once there, Delf-Lexoushea and her team could complete their work and bring Lyra back to a visible, viable realm for her people to live in once more. She knew she'd started this journey with a desire deep within her to unfold the various parts of the voyage. RexNā wanted to discover the 'what and how' to achieve the discovery of the 'mirrored world'. The drive and determination she'd started with were still sitting within her.

As she processed these thoughts, the Moderator and Eid `dVra, who had previously had a sense of disquietude regarding the young leader's vision and realisations of duty, observed RexNaā Loid DeAqua. Nodding inwardly, careful to reveal nothing to the outside group, Eid silently relaid a message to one of his junior seers. He requested that the seer join themself to RexNā, presently as one who can assist, guide, and give counsel outside of what she currently received from MelEid. Eid was clear that this was NOT to compete with that relationship. For now, the siblings had their key, their combined intuitive skills linked to the broader sectors of both Mages and Seers. With the dawning of awareness occurring in RexNā, they could sense the next steps of learning would be quick and require both their skill sets and that of their sectors.

Sol, as sensitive to telepathic frequencies as she was, became instantly aware that a connection was in the room. However, scanning to see where the telepathic communication originated, she drew a blank. So instead of making it known that she was aware, Sol decided to keep an eye on the strongest of telepaths. This way, Sol would be able to identify the unique vibration.

Though, it was an excellent time to remind those present that, as of yet, the telepathic communication hold had yet to be lifted. Raising her voice slightly to gain attention, Sol addressed the still blanket ruling of no telepathic comms, adding that if anyone were found breaking this decree, she would look at it as treason. She stared at the Moderator, who often felt he was above the rules of others but found he nodded in agreement.

The siblings remained silent, listening to the reminder. Each, inwardly acknowledging they would have to be more subtle, stood in the background of those present but so blended that it became almost impossible to differentiate them from anyone else in the room.

Those in the room fell silent, both in wonderment at what they had just seen and also at the reminder of Sol's decree. So many were processing a levitating Prince, and another who was translucent in being whilst the third remained solid and grounded. They were now looking to their leader to set their ship back in order. So much had occurred in a short time. Infiltration, new Lyrans boarded, bringing with them sworn enemies who had now bound themselves to the Lyran Way of Being.

Their sister ship had returned, minus the organic link. For some who knew RathVorx, they felt a loss and wanted to go and farewell their friend.

Dear Reader, we will leave this group pondering the upcoming events that will unfold around them. But, fear not, we will return, for things are becoming more illuminated as to the journey's purpose and how the combined learnings of old and new create the defeat of the unseen enemy.

Chapter Twenty-Eight

The Changing Tide
Human?
Or Living Soul?

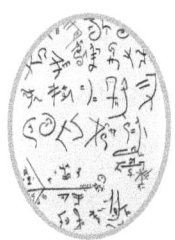

You may have noticed, Dear Reader, that we have used intermittent terminologies when relating to you as a species. We refer to you as Terrans, Lyrans, Cosmic Beings and Humans. In this discourse, we wish to perhaps give you a consideration that you are not human but are members of a group that should be referred to as mankind. Not to create an explosive censoring on gender but as a grouping, a genus of being.

You see, it was only under the directive of the Anunnaki in your timeline and the Formless Ones that they turned the inclusive wording of mankind to be derogatory and exclude one gender over another. Subtly replacing the term mankind with humankind, a throwback to the name they gave the clones and lobotomised Terrans after realising that T'Gaina had used the very elements of her own physical being to create the species known as Terran. Once they realised that your DNA had the essential minerals of the earth, such as nitrogen, oxygen, carbon, potassium, phosphorus, calcium, chlorine, sulphur and a few more, these self-proclaimed masters of yours gave you the name H'ûmūs. This name categorised you as their slaves, indicating that you were nothing more than the dirt beneath their feet.

However, the Divine Source Creator and T'Gaina intended you to be more than just mere beings existing on the surface of a realm waiting to die. Instead, they saw you as Terran, as male and female of the same species. Both are as strong as each other but stronger together as units of family, friends and community.

They gave you the name Terran by virtue of coming from the earth, with all the strengths of that planet. Able to resist the diseases that would advance against you, you were able to replenish your physiology as you needed. You lived in this manner for so long, that is, until your ancestors were lulled into a false sense of security and tricked into giving up their name. They gave up their memories and lay down their conscious connection to the living realm of Terra-Ven-Eiliesh-Gaina as well as their conscious link to the Creator Source.

Now many of your species wander through the lands searching for 'something', knowing that they are here for a purpose, a reason and yet unable to grasp it.

We invite you to consider that you are not powerless or genderless but instead powerful beings of light and energy representing this world as male or female. Whether you embody the meat suit you were born with, as a feminine shaman or masculine shaman, is your choice in this elective lifetime. At this moment, you, as beings of conscious energy, which connect to the consciousness of the Divine Creator, the Universal Source of Creation, can *choose* if you will continue to accept the twisted words of the puppet masters to define you.

As we have attempted to throw the light onto certain words for your self-realisation, we now reiterate those here. To give clarity and to bring awareness in a manner that is wholesome and not hidden.

T'Gaina and the Creator created two of the species known as Terran. One was of the male form, and the other female. They were created in a manner, as were all other species of beings in this realm, with the complimentary parts for reproduction if they chose.

When two Terrans chose to commit to each other, whether in a public ceremony or private, there was no [94]judgement laid at the feet of those of the same gender. Terran communities knew how to respect all expressions of commitment with honour and re-spect.

They were, you could surmise, innocent of any difference be-tween the men or women of their groups as they considered themselves to be living conduits of consciousness for the Divine and their connection with T'Gaina. It was only after the interfer-ence of the Anunnaki that they were called H'ûmūs, the dirt or decomposing vegetable matter on the earth's floor.

The Anunnaki's descendants then introduced the word Human and 'Humankind' into your vocabulary. The living Terrans accept-ed it without question. It is socially acceptable, they were in-formed, this word does not separate gender etc. etc., and yet when you look at the word human, Dear Reader, it means:

Hue = colour of

Man = the creature you are

Therefore they call you Hu-man, meaning the colour of man. So the question is, are you an image or reflection of Man/Terran, or are you the original being a Terran, a Living Man, a Living Woman?

---

[94] See Book 2 The Anunnaki Influence

We encourage you to research and study the entomology of the word, and you may be surprised to note that we found this definition coming from [95]Latin 'humanus' - "of man, human,"

There is a simple question and a simple answer.

Suppose you choose to create a dogma and debate relating to all the outworking of the agenda of the Anunnaki and Formless Ones to separate you further and further from your original state of being. In that case, you, Dear Reader, may wish to pause and ask why?

Why are you so upset or uncomfortable with the word mankind/man/woman?

All the ancient texts ranging from Sanskrit to Coptic, from Aramaic to Chinese, through to Egyptian and many more use man, woman, and mankind to describe the living souls of this realm. That is, if you are reading the original, unaltered writings.

Why would it be required to alter your language in a few short hundred years from the 1900s to the 2000s? Because Dear Readers, it was necessary to slowly introduce a gender-neutral way of speaking, subtlety and gradually, so as to not cause alarm.

Then when the agenda to completely overcome the Living Souls of this realm was underway, they amped up the vocabulary and had their soldiers ready to disarm you. Of course, you may think there is no military war against you, and you are right if you think guns and soldiers of that persuasion.

But you're mistaken, especially when you consider that the 'educated' young beings, tutored at the esteemed scholastic

---

[95] Quote: " *dʰéǵʰōm was taken directly into Latin as the word humus, referring strictly to dirt and soil. Humanus and homo actually entered from another PIE (Proto-Indo-European) word *ǵʰmmṓ. This word is an alteration of *dʰéǵʰōmand was used to refer to us. Its literal meaning is near earthling or being of the earth. Earth here referring to the ground, dirt, etc." end Quote.
cite https://sites.psu.edu/josephvadella/2017/09/08/origins-of-human/

halls, among you are now insisting that you change the nouns of the living men and women of this world. Suppose you consider that there is a slow erosion of your singular yet unique identities. That there is a worldwide effort to 'lump' you into one melting pot. Not only removing your uniqueness of being unto yourselves strong and mentally assured of who you are but creating a species so confused about itself that you would be like straw blowing in the wind, following any and every suggestion without question.

The agenda is to normalise non-gender so that the natural-born feminine energy among you is wounded and pushed further back in their evolution. This move is to make room for the *new female*, the non-birthed but self-created female, who demands rather than earns respect and acceptance. It is exactly the same when looking at the *new male*. This 'new male' is the created male, being non-birthed but made from the dissatisfied female, in both cases, the idea of the living being owning and accepting the gender of birth.

They find dissatisfaction with the 'supposed norms of being 'female' or 'male' and the desire to be the opposite.

It should be asked why this is now so prevalent in your society. Why when there has been recorded history, oral records of the shaman energy living in the thirteenth stranded being, known as the 'man lover' or the 'woman lover'. Why suddenly must there be a movement where the living men and women of this realm must bow down to a new self-made sub-species within mankind?

From the years Two Thousand and Sixteen to Two Thousand and Twenty-Two, why has it been so crucial for the puppet masters to solidify the 'non' gendered being? Do you think, perhaps because this is their overshadowing agenda, to remove the sexes or genders permanently and create a species that no longer pro-creates or has sexual feelings for each other? To slowly introduce the augmentation of non-flesh parts into your bodies and embrace the non-full mankind species, ones you refer to as cyborgs?

Is it to normalise you to the fact that you are not living souls with an eternal link to the Creator but mere meat suits that amount to a physicality that is given to no more and no less than eighty to a rare maximum of one hundred years of existence?

Is it to remove from you the imbued knowing that you are Terran, that you have within you the Golden Spark, the Golden Bloodline that they, the puppet masters, are seeking for their Masters, the Anunnaki?

Dear Terran, we will close this narrative volume as we prepare for the next book we will soon bring.

We ask that as we close, as we leave you pondering and considering all we have shared, that you consider the ways of the Lyrans.

They cared not if their mates were male or female but honoured both.

They lived in harmony and recognised the strengths and weaknesses of both genders.

Lyrans loved whom they loved and shared much.

Now, we Lyrans live in a more substantial and vibrant place than you have here. Nevertheless, the Leaders of Lyra wish to share their ways with you, so we have commissioned ourselves, the Lyran Narrators of Time to share our chronicles with you and to challenge you to open your minds and go beyond the accepted narratives.

We are neither for nor against the unfolding of the evolution or devolution of your species.

But we are for the illumination of Truth, Honour and Dignity, and as we see, recognise, and uphold those among you who are of the True Terran Bloodline and the True Lyran Bloodline, we come to you, and we sup with you.

Until next time;

Know who you are

Know why you are

Know what you are not

Know why they wish to deceive you

Know why they desire to entrap you in constant slavery

Realise you are Living men and women of this realm

Realise you have more authority than you are aware of, but only when you know how to use it will you be able to use it wisely.

Be strong, be alive, know your truth and WATCH the waters. Watch the skies and comprehend that you are not alone.

[96]Shrelou, for now. We look forward to sharing the deeper ways of Lyra with you in the next disclosure of our ways with you.

---

[96] A fond farewell

To Contact the Author

Louise and Heather are engaging and knowledgeable presenters and can be available as guest speakers on their topics of expertise - either in person or online. Feel free to email them as per below.

More information on other publications from the author can also be accessed by email.

Contact us on:
info@itiscosmic.com
or zimkiwi@proton.me
Https://itiscosmic.com

Book 4

The new book in this series is bringing the Lyran Ways to us.

They have indicated they would like to share more of their ways of learning, healing, adventures, initiations, discoveries, and so much more.

We will join the Princes and Commander Sol on a journey that will focus on the Lyrans more and not so much on the Terrans.   In the next chronicle that they bring forward, we will begin to see how the personalities, strengths and weaknesses of all within the two battleships begin to unfold.

However, due to the strong affection the Lyrans have for the Terrans, they will more than likely drop in and give us some hints on how to achieve a higher way of life.

Book Four is aimed to be out by late 2023.

www.ingramcontent.com/pod-product-compliance
Lightning Source LLC
Chambersburg PA
CBHW051057030726
47504CB00006B/1662